THE WAR BROUGHT THEM TOGETHER!

Startled, Leanna glanced at him. She felt an odd breathlessness and forced her eyes away. "I thought I recalled something about your having a fiancée, Major." She glanced back to him for his reaction, startled to see how darkly handsome he was. How surprisingly gentle . . . How tantalizingly dangerous!

She collapsed in his arms, with a final, choking sob, bathing his uniform in tears, moaning her grief against his chest. Leanna knew no rational thought. She felt him lift her in his arms and made no protest, only turned her face to meet his in a kiss.

THEN THE WAR TORE THEM APART!

A REBEL'S HONOR

JESSICA ST. CLAIRE

PINNACLE BOOKS NEW YORK

A REBEL'S HONOR

An original Pinnacle Books edition, published for the first time anywhere.

First printing, October 1983

ISBN: 0-523-42082-X

CANADIAN ISBN: 0-523-43037-X

Cover illustration by Dan Gonzalez

Printed in the United States of America

PINNACLE BOOKS, INC.
1430 Broadway
New York, New York 10018

A JOAN HITZIG McDONELL BOOK

9 8 7 6 5 4 3 2 1

BLYTHESWOOD

Chapter One

It was 1863 and autumn in the Shenandoah. It was a war year, as the past two had been and the next two would be as well. The colors of the Eastern United States were the Blue and Gray of bloody Civil War, but the slopes of the Virginia Blue Ridge Mountains were burning today with softer colors too—bright golds and salmons marked sugar maples; darker reds and rusts showed chestnut, oak, and hickory; there appeared the occasional emerald of an evergreen. Along the base of Massanutten Mountain, the Shenandoah River curled like a satin ribbon, silver beneath the deepening blue of a sunset sky. Leanna Leighton shivered slightly in the growing coolness, watching the long, dark-blue column of Yankee cavalry winding over closer to the stone pillars that marked the entrance to Blytheswood. They stopped at the distant gate and slowly turned, starting down the long, graveled drive toward the white col- umned house. Huge chestnuts lining the way twined their top branches overhead, forming a living archway of entrance. In their shade, the dark blue of the Federal uniforms turned nearly to black—a grim and ominous contrast to the brilliant colors of the autumn mountains behind them.

The breeze gusted again, cold enough to remind her of winter's approach, and Leanna shivered once more, reaching to touch the handle of the loaded dueling pistol she had concealed beneath her linen shawl. There were two balls in the chambers. If the Yankees were coming to loot the house, or burn it, or force themselves on the handful of women here, they would do so over her dead body. Blytheswood belonged to her, the only Penley left to hold it. Four generations, long dead, would be watching her now. And she would defend it to her death.

"You got dat look in yer eye, chile." A black woman took a waddling half step in front of the slender girl. Her eyes gleamed intently. "Not even Jeb Stuart'd be taking Yankees on with the kinda odds you looking at."

Leanna only shrugged for reply, stepping around Jewel to cross the white painted veranda. A board was warped loose, the paint was beginning to flake in spots, but it made the place no less precious to her. Everything had suffered a bit from the war. Like battle scars, the old plantation house bore the war marks proudly. She walked to the very center of the wide stairway that dropped from the porch to the drive, and there she stopped, planting herself, raising her chin in a mixture of anger and unadmitted fear. Damn the Yankees anyway! Riding so coolly into the Valley, into her very home. After the Confederate defeat at Gettysburg this summer, they were bold as wolves. And Stonewall Jackson, who had chased them willy-nilly out of the Valley a year and a half ago, now was dead. General Lee and his Army of Northern Virginia were east of the Blue Ridge defending the Confederate capital of Richmond. The war had gone badly farther to the west. Who was left to defend the Shenandoah Valley? Anyone?

The Federal column halted before the stairs. Momentary chaos erupted as men farther back failed to hear the shouted order to halt, and horses collided beneath the arched chestnut trees. An officer turned in his saddle only a dozen steps from Leanna, gesturing angrily and shouting for the rest of the troopers to file around him, pointing toward the blackened stone of the main barn before turning back to her.

Leanna reached beneath her shawl to take a better grip on the pistol. She swallowed against the sudden dryness of her throat, the sudden thundering of her heart.

"Mrs. Leighton?"

The officer swung down from his horse. He tossed the reins of the animal to another Yankee and frowned

2

down at a paper in his hand. Then he stepped around his horse and started toward her. "Are you Mrs. Leighton?"

Leanna's hand tightened on the pistol as the Yankee started up the stairs. Her heart was pounding so loudly she could hardly hear his words. A Yankee. A goddamn Yankee. On Penley land, Penley steps. Without conscious decision, she began to draw the revolver out of her skirt band, her thumb fumbling for the cold metal of the flintlock.

"Yes, she's Miz Leighton." Jewel stepped closer to the younger woman. She'd seen the hint of movement beneath the linen shawl and reached to take Leanna's arm in a quick grip. "Appears the cat got her tongue just now . . . which may be all the best for you. She don't cotton much to Yankees."

The officer didn't change expression. He only stopped where he was on the stairs, his brown eyes flickering quickly from the black woman's face to Leanna's. From down the step, his eyes were at perfect level with hers. For a moment, he met them directly. Leanna's breath caught in her throat, strange dizziness swept her from head to toe. Maybe it was only the shock of staring so closely into Yankee eyes—the first Yankee she'd seen this close since the war had started. Maybe it was a trick of shadows from the sun falling behind the western mountains. She tried to hold his gaze, tried to radiate her hatred of him and all his kind. But she had the sudden sensation of falling into the dark amber eyes that returned her stare, a sensation of the world receding. She turned her head with sudden near desperation to break that gaze. Her hands trembled beneath the linen of the shawl and for a moment, the pistol was forgotten.

"So kind of you to come out and welcome us in person, Mrs. Leighton." The Yankee major studied her, noting the faint flush of color rising on her ashen face. For some reason, he'd expected an older woman, middle-aged, portly—homely, to be frank. But the one standing before him was exquisitely beautiful, slender, very

3

young. If she were more than twenty years old, he'd be surprised. Strange, that feeling when their eyes had first met.

"I don't welcome Yankees to Virginia let alone to my home." Leanna managed to raise her chin and confront him again. "If I could beg the reason for your intrusion onto my grounds . . . ?"

He held her defiant violet eyes for a second, almost curiously, but nothing seemed strange anymore. Only another pair of Confederate eyes, blazing hate. "Very simple. My troops and I are under orders to occupy this position for the winter."

"The *winter?*" A faint, mocking grimace touched Leanna's mouth. "The *entire* winter? Major Mosby's Rangers will chase your Yankee hides down the Valley before the *week* is out."

"You speak as if you have Mosby's personal promise, Mrs. Leighton. Do you?"

Leanna flushed at the sarcasm, her arrogance shaken. "Perhaps I do. Anyway, I know what he does to Yankees."

"Well then, the next time you see him, perhaps, you'll be kind enough to relay a message for me. Tell Major Mosby that if he's looking for a fight, we'll be happy to oblige him. Granted, of course, that he can tear himself away from midnight raids on General Meade's wagon trains, on the other side of the mountains. From what I understand, he's content enough with that sort of thing just now."

Leanna flushed again, hating the sarcasm and, more, the unruffled confidence of the Yankee officer's voice. What he said was true enough to sting her pride and she turned on one heel to conceal tears of frustration. She walked for the doors of the house, speaking over her shoulder without looking back. "Let me know when these Yankees have departed, Jewel. I'll be staying in my own rooms upstairs until then." She heard Jewel's murmured assent, heard relief in the black woman's voice, and fresh anger surged through her. Damn Jewel, too, then. More like a mother to her than her own

4

mother barely remembered. Jewel would still welcome the damn Yankees promising freedom for her people. She heard Jewel speaking to the officer behind her as she opened the door. She slammed it shut in the midst of his reply. 'Major Courtland, Eighth Pennsylvania Cavalry . . . a Federal order signed by Secretary Stanton authorizing military occupation of the Virginia Valley plantation known as Blytheswood . . . no harm to come to civilians nor to civilian property as long as no resistance was offered the Federal troops, etc., etc. . . .' No harm indeed, she mocked his words bitterly as she started up the wide, curved staircase that dominated the graciously elegant old foyer. No harm to anybody but the Yankees, pray God. Mosby—or someone—would surely ride thundering in to chase the Yankees back North. They always had in the past—chased them all the way back to Washington, D.C. It never occurred to her they wouldn't—or couldn't—this time as well.

It was equally beautiful in Philadelphia that October 29th. The same sunshine that bathed the Valley of Virginia and silvered the Shenandoah River shone on William Penn's city and the Delaware River. Joshua Courtland closed his office at the banking house early and went for a carriage ride on cobblestoned streets near Penn's Landing. It wasn't just a question of winter approaching that made him decide to enjoy the fine autumn day. It was also the matter of his age. It was his birthday today. He was fifty-nine. And this past month, he had suffered the first of the chest pains that had begun his own father's illness and heralded his eventual death. So time was running out. He accepted that. Days like this were numbered as they had never been before. And there was still so much to do—and a question of how little time was left to do it. Three years ago, it wouldn't have mattered so much. The family banking house, with its tradition of a Courtland at the helm, had seemed secure in its future. The family itself in good shape, a fortune waiting, children grown to man or womanhood. And then the war—and Josh, Jr., the oldest son, trained to inherit, dead at Bloody Shiloh in '62. Elinor, his only daughter, living in England, more a stranger now than ever. Chase, the youngest, so much his mother's son, so damn stubborn, so determined to finish out the war in the Federal cavalry despite his brother's death, despite his father's need—somewhere in the Shenandoah Valley now, doing God knew what.

Pray God, when the war ended, Chase would be alive still. And prepared to assume his dead brother's place at the bank. A Courtland would be sorely needed then, for war debts and Southern deposits frozen at the outbreak of hostilities remained dangerously unsettled. With every passing day, board members and stockholders got bolder—speaking nobly of the 'Best For The Union,' reparations of damage to the North, etc. —thinking secretly how best to grab a piece of the Southern money pie that lay temptingly undefended in the bank's vaults. If Joshua died before his son got back, or if Chase too should be killed in the war, only his daughter, Elinor, would be left to see whether the bank's tradition of honorable dealing could survive this terrible war. And Elinor was an enigma that plagued him unmercifully.

Funny. Almost funny, at least. Joshua sat in the sunshine of the carriage, looking out over the broad gray waters of the Delaware River. Funny how the war boiled down to such an essentially personal issue. Yankee or Confederate, all rhetoric aside, people were just trying to live the lives they'd been taught to live, trying to keep their world from falling apart, trying to keep things going as they had for generations before. Trying not to lose ground gained by people now long dead, wondering how and why they'd been the ones trapped in the middle. Why me? Why now? Three years ago, he'd had two sons, and plenty of time, and he hadn't needed either. Now he had no sons, no time, and a desperate need for both.

He knew it was bad for him, but he lit a cigar anyway and leaned far back in the carriage seat. He could pull political strings in Washington and land a danger-free desk job for the remainder of Chase's enlistment. Plenty of other men in his position had. But could he sacrifice another man's son to spare his own? And even if he tried, Chase wouldn't tolerate it anyway. God would work things out, he told himself. God would have to, he decided, or the Southern depositors could sue Him for their money. We mere mortals can only be expected to do so much.

"I ain't taking no Yankee part." Jewel had followed the girl upstairs as soon as she could. "Far as I'm concerned, I only got one cause in this war. That be the Penley family—or what's left of 'em. But you make it terrible hard for a body to help you when—"

"I don't want your help! I want those damn Yankees away from Blytheswood!"

"Well, I ain't no witch woman, chile! I can't snap my fingers and make two hundred men disappear! Them Yankees gonna be here awhile, plain and simple!" But Jewel's tone softened at the ashen pallor of the girl's face, the glistening unshed tears in her violet eyes. She was so young yet. Only a child, really. A willful one. And a beautiful one. Lord, she'd been born both. Now twenty, she was enough to melt stone with her black hair and wide-set, black lashed eyes. Even the defiant set of her mouth, trembling ever so slightly at the edges, only added to her loveliness. Even before the war, she'd been a willful girl. Now, 'Rebel' was an apt description for her in more ways than one. "It could be worse now, honey," Jewel took a coaxing route. "That Yankee major ain't the devil. Quartered his men in the barn and the wagon sheds. His officers in them house-slave cabins out the back door. Only the major hisself even be staying here in the main house. Maybe if you was to try more honey, less vinegar—"

"Here in the house?" Leanna's head had snapped up, her eyes flashing. "How dare he! Intrude right into my—very home?"

"He could have 'intruded' you right out into the chicken house! Be thankful for what you got!"

7

"Never!" Her voice was whisper-soft, but her hands were clenched hard at her sides. "Blytheswood is a Confederate house! The Penleys are a Confederate family! Never will I treat with those Yankees, Jewel! You suit yourself—you will anyway. But we haven't lost this war yet, not by a long shot! The only part of these Yankees I care to see are their backs—when they're galloping north again!"

Jewel snorted in worried exasperation as she turned her rotund bulk toward the door. "You stay here and have yer way then, Miz Confederate Penley. I got dinner to start cooking."

"They're planning to eat here as well?"

"You think they's planning to starve theyselves all winter? Course they planning to eat here! Dinner gonna be late tonight. Mebbe seven."

"You may send my food up on a tray then. I won't share a table with them."

The black woman only grumbled and shrugged, pulling the door closed behind her.

Leanna kept her show of unshaken confidence intact until the creak of floorboards from out in the hall signaled the black woman's retreat, but then her anger broke loose. It wasn't fair! The South was right—the cause was just. The Constitution had promised a government to serve the people, Southerners included, not to dictate policy to anyone. Not to send hundreds of thousands of Yankee invaders into the South and to burn and bully and kill and shove further injustices down Southern throats. Gettysburg this summer. The humiliation of retreat there. And Vicksburg falling. New Orleans occupied. Now Yankees in the Valley. The Granary of Virginia and the all-important route to the north, the protection for Lee's army to the east. What if the Valley too should fall to the Yankees?

Leanna lay down on the soft goose-down bed, determined not to pursue those thoughts. On her nightstand was her husband's picture, framed in silver filigree. She looked at it now and found it offered no distraction. It was only another reminder—Stewart dressed for war.

8

As he had been in Richmond in the spring of 1861 when she'd met him, and after a whirlwind courtship of less than a week, had married him. The morning immediately after, he'd ridden off to join Jeb Stuart's Confederate Cavalry command. Now he seemed but a handsome stranger who'd been home only twice in the past two and a half years. Once in that glorious spring of 1862, when he'd been assigned to Ashby's cavalry, serving under Stonewall Jackson for the Valley Campaign where 16,000 Confederates had defeated combined Union forces of nearly three times their number. That had been a wonderful year. Proud and full of hope. Really the last one. Stewart had come home once again early this past summer, just before the Southern army had begun their Northern march to Pennsylvania and bloody defeat at Gettysburg. But he'd been different then. Distant. Cold. Preoccupied and weary, and aged beyond his twenty-eight years. Sharper too, even with her, and rarely smiling.

Leanna returned the photograph's unfocused stare, reaching to pick it up in one hand. Perhaps war did that to me. Perhaps nothing or no one would ever be quite the same again. Perhaps it would change even proud Blytheswood, cringing for the first time beneath Yankee boot heels. Would these dark years shadow all the future ones to come? Or would the war, when finally gone, vanish in memory as quickly as the carefree, earlier days had seemed to at its approach?

She sighed and set the photograph back on the nightstand almost impatiently. She had not aided the Confederate cause today. She had allowed Yankees into Blytheswood without even a token resistance. Not that she knew what else she could have done. There was only the vague disturbing certainty she'd somehow failed.

"Miz Leighton?"

Jewel had retreated to strained formality. Leanna sat up and pushed tear-wet wisps of raven hair away from her face as she turned. "Yes, Jewel, what is it?"

"Dinner's gonna be served." The woman opened the door slowly, her black eyes growing compassionate at the sight of the ashen-faced girl, her tear-bright eyes. "Oh Lordy, chile, no sense carrying on so. You'll be sick. That won't do nobody no good." She stopped, frowning and sighing, then coaxing with a forced smile. "It's a wondrous meal. Come on down. Honest-to-God sugar and real coffee. Smells like heaven in the kitchen. Them Yankees turned their supplies over to me for the price of my cooking 'em."

Leanna only shook her head, turning her face away. She could smell the aroma of the coffee even from up here, coming in the open door behind Jewel. It took an effort, but she shook her head resolutely and kept her seat on the bed.

For a moment more, Jewel waited by the door, thinking the girl might yet see the sense of the situation and change her mind. But except for a single tear trickling down her cheek, Leanna was motionless. Seeing the proud and stubborn set of her chin, Jewel turned back through the doorway in resignation. At the top of the stairs, she shivered and muttered a superstitious prayer against the foreboding that lingered after it. Two hundred Yankee soldiers all around them—not Southern gentlemen, well bred and bound by rigid rules and a thousand courtesies, nor black men, broken by a lifetime of slavery and submission—but *Yankee* men. Come from a world alien to all the South, a world Leanna Penley Leighton neither understood nor had any rightful place in. Now this damnation war had broken out, maybe there wouldn't be no more left of the Penleys' world once it was finally over. There wasn't none left at Blytheswood at least, not after today. It was her fault, maybe, for not thinking of this, Jewel accused herself. For not thinking the girl might ever need to be taught how to bend before the wind of an unkind fate, or practice a gracious sort of surrender, or swallow any of that terrible high Penley pride. If there was trouble ahead, the blame was partly hers for raising the girl as she had. And with Yankees bent on staying at Blytheswood and Leanna just as terrible bent on having them go—she could hardly see no way there wasn't gonna *be* trouble sooner or later. The only question was what kind it would be—and when it was going to come. And what she could do to try to ease it.

As Jewel reached the bottom of Blytheswood's grand staircase, the front door swung open with an authoritative click. The chill air of the October night flowed in along with a dozen rough Yankee officers. Despite herself, she froze in place, unconsciously assuming a stance of protection, blocking the stairs and setting her huge bulk between the entering soldiers and the girl upstairs.

Most of the soldiers didn't seem to notice. They strode by without a second glance, looking ominous indeed with the dark, dull blue of their uniforms, the polished jet of high boots, and jangling spurs on several belts, sabers swung in perfect rhythm. Only one of the younger men, one whose face was less grim than most, thought to offer a smile. That was the doctor, Jewel recollected. Lacey, she thought. Last in was the Yankee major who commanded the battalion that had seized Leanna's precious Blytheswood. He noticed her stance and checked his step, catching the black woman's eye with a silent question.

Leanna, upstairs, must have heard the sound of the Yankee boot heels, at first loud on the polished wood, then muffled on the fine Brussels carpet of the dining room. She chose that moment to slam her bedroom door in angry reaction. In the foyer below, the sound exploded like a gunshot, and Jewel flinched as its echoes lingered in the air. The Yankee major frowned, lifting his head to stare in the direction of the invisible, but hardly inaudible, door. Weariness had been on his face when he'd walked in. Now anger lay there as well. Cold foreboding gripped Jewel's heart in a breathless vise, but she didn't move. Didn't dare to. She caught the Yankee's dark eyes and held them with a silent plea.

For a moment, he did nothing, didn't even move. Then he merely sighed softly, and glanced back from the black woman's face toward the hallway upstairs. Mrs. Leighton was determined to be a problem, then. Damn the Confederates—their women were as fanatic

11

as their men. Well, he could pass her absence at the table off tonight with a smile, perhaps, but if a few days didn't show some marked change in her disposition, then he'd have to meet the problem head on. How exactly, he couldn't say, especially when he could not help but feel some sympathy for her. War was one thing when only other soldiers were involved in the fighting—he took the same risk as any other man in uniform, and he was prepared to take the same as he gave out. But it was something else again when women— and children—were caught in the middle.

"Come on, Major! We got chicken fricassee waiting like I haven't seen since I joined this damn army!"

He smiled faintly and nodded and followed his officers in toward the table. Mrs. Leighton could wait. After the day he'd had, hot chicken fricassee couldn't.

"Are you going back?"

"To do what?" Lieutenant Colonel Stewart Leighton shrugged restlessly, frowning at the courier's back as the young man sat at the fireside eating. He'd picked a good night for dinner anyway. One of the troopers had shot a deer while on scouting patrol. The men would eat fresh meat tonight—the first for over a week. "I don't like the idea of Yankees at my place any better than you would, but there isn't much I can do by myself to get them to leave."

"What if you requested a furlough?"

"Waltz back to Blytheswood and be made a prisoner?" Stewart lifted the brim of his battered black felt hat and pushed a stray lock of blonde hair out of his blue eyes. "Thanks, Captain, but I find that unappealing."

Stewart's young captain glanced at his superior oddly but shrugged, saying nothing else. He guessed he understood the lieutenant colonel's feelings. In absolutely practical terms, he was right. But if it had been *his* home, *his* wife, surrounded by Yankees, he would have felt obliged, to at least try.

"Good evening, Colonel Leighton, Captain Bryant."

The young captain stood hastily, saluting and gesturing

his commander to take his seat. General Jeb Stuart nodded his thanks and sighed wearily as he sat on the vacated tree stump.

"Sure smells good here. What is it?"

Stewart managed a half smile, shrugging. "Deer meat. You're welcome to share a bit."

The Confederate cavalry general declined with a shake of his head, patting his stomach. "Ate already, thanks. Though not that well, I'm afraid." He glanced at his officer sharply, stretching one high booted leg out in front of him. "I gather you've heard what I came over to tell you . We've got Yankees in the Valley."

Stewart nodded. "At Blytheswood, actually. Yes, the courier came by here, too."

"Sorry to hear that."

"Me, too. Fortunes of war, I guess."

"From what I hear, they aren't misbehaving too badly. At least not yet."

Stewart's smile was bitter. "I'm sure they'll get around to it. They usually do. I hope my wife had the good sense to bury the silver someplace and keep the pistol I left her well hidden."

"From what the Jenkins boy said, she's doing a brave job." Jeb Stuart frowned, shaking his head slowly. For a moment, he was silent, then he sighed again reflectively. "You know, for all of this," he gestured around the crude camp, dark with night shadows, cold except within a few feet of the crackling dinner fires, "I'm glad I'm a man, Colonel. Rather be here in the Army than waiting it out at home like the women do. Maybe they're more comfortable there not dodging bullets, but it must be frustrating as hell for them. Your wife, for example. What's she supposed to do with a battalion of Yankee cavalry knocking at her door? Let 'em in whether she likes it or not, I suppose."

Stewart shrugged, his blue eyes unreadable as he glanced toward the Blue Ridge Mountains, a distant darkness separating the Shenandoah Valley from Lee's army here by the banks of the Rapidan River. Between the CSA and the mountains, the campfires of Meade's

Union Army glowed in the darkness miles away. A thousand of them at least. Where in the hell did all the Yankees keep coming from?

"What are you going to do, Leighton?"

He started at the sound of Jeb Stuart's question, and shrugged his indecision. "I've been wondering myself."

"Afraid your wife needs you?"

"Afraid she might," he admitted. "But maybe the Army needs me more. Right where I'm at. If officers begin to take off for home when the Yankees arrive, what are the enlisted men going to do?"

The Confederate general shrugged beneath the gray cloak of his overcoat. "Very true." There was a long pause. "Just between you and me, I'd like you to stay, Colonel. Things are going to stay hot and critical. General Lee's planning the last push before winter closes in, up toward Bristol Station. I'm going to need every man I've got—especially my veteran officers. God knows this last campaign was brutal for reducing them."

'This last campaign.' Jeb Stuart rarely mentioned Gettysburg by name; the memory was too painful. Largely because of his mistakes, Lee had blundered into the Federal troops unwarned. By the time the cavalry arrived at all, it was too late—only exhausted troopers trying desperately to ride a hole through the Yankee cavalry and attack Meade's rear. Trying and failing. Gettysburg—a disaster that grew more tragic as the Confederacy grew ever weaker. The men lost there could not be replaced. There had always been a shortage of adequate weapons—of guns, revolvers, artillery, ammunition. A shortage of clothing, of supplies, of horses. Of transportation. Of industry. Now there was a shortage of manpower, too. Dear God, how much less could the South have and still continue to fight?

"May I assume you'll be staying, Colonel Leighton?"

Stuart's deep baritone was a whisper among the night sounds, but Leighton heard him and took a last deep breath, reaching inside for a decision. Before the war, choices had always seemed clearer. You knew where honor and duty lay. Life ran according to rules a century old. But now—what to do now? Stay with the army? Or ride home, perhaps unnecessarily, to aid a single woman at Blytheswood?

He pushed to his feet, aching all over as he usually did by this time of night. He took one step toward the west, looking to the black hills beyond the campfires of the Army of the Potomac. His eyes were grim but he nodded once, unconsciously straightening his shoulders. "Yes, I'll be staying, General. The greater portion of my responsibility lies here, I believe. I'll be staying."

Leanna's days settled begrudgingly back into their usual routine. As time passed, it became painfully apparent that Confederate cavalry were not racing down Blytheswood's graveled drive to chase the Federal intruders back north, and sulking—besides being alien to her disposition—was a luxury she simply couldn't afford. There was too much to do at Blytheswood to spend all her days in her room. Even before the war, running a plantation had been hard work. With the outbreak of hostilities, Stewart had sold the few remaining slaves or shipped them farther south, and only a couple of youngsters from neighboring farms had been available to take their place. Anyway, even in her rooms, she couldn't ignore the fact of the Yankees' occupation—every glance out every window showed dark blue uniforms by the score. One of the hired servant girls, Hilda, flirted outrageously with the soldiers, rousing Leanna's temper every time she caught her. Stewart's letter, smuggled in to her by another of the girls (one of two stolidly CSA sisters, Rosie Jenkins), held news of a weak Confederate offensive around the Bristol Station area, north of the Rapidan River. Her husband and brother both were fighting there, Stewart commanding one of General Jeb Stuart's cavalry regiments. He could not be spared to come home to her at Blytheswood, and, Leanna read between the lines, he did not see much chance he could for months yet. So if she was determined to stay at Blytheswood, she must stay alone, without his company. He sent his affection, as usual, and there was concern

15

amid the anger he expressed. If the Yankees grew discourteous or offensive in the slightest regard, she must leave the plantation and travel south to Staunton or beyond—wherever the Confederacy's hold seemed stronger.

But abandoning Blytheswood was unthinkable. It was more than her home, it was her secret heart, a part of her very soul. It had been ever since that first summer when, as a three-year-old, she'd stepped off the chugging, smoking steam train, and gazing across the silver Shenandoah River, saw it in all its green and gold, elegant and aged beauty. Here Great-grandfather Penley had cleared the huge virgin chestnuts for fields, almost a century ago. Her own father had been born here. And here, she and her brother had played during the long hot Virginia summers—a blissful childhood of lightning bugs and tree frogs, barbeques and sugar cookies stolen from the kitchen. Before the storm clouds of war had begun to gather along the Mason-Dixon line, here she and her brother, Jonathon had ridden balky ponies and searched for Indian arrowheads along the riverbank and fished in their secret place by Crooked Run Creek, where the old willow leaned out to darken the muddy water and the fish, like the children, had liked to hide in its shade.

Leanna sighed and pushed her memories away, unconscious of the accompanying frown. Such happy days were long past, her father dead this past year of consumption, her brother Jonathon serving a commission in the Confederate cavalry. And Yankee troopers fished in their place for a bass or a croppie to vary their rations of salt pork or cured beef. Still, she would never abandon Blytheswood to the enemy. Never, never, never.

"Miz Lea, you're frowning again." Jewel glanced up from the kneading bowl to scold gently. "You gonna age yourself doing that."

"What is there to smile about, Jewel?" Leanna gave the last pinch to what would be dinner rolls for the evening meal. Going to feed Yankees. "We're both up before daybreak. Getting food supplies parceled. Knead-

16

ing what seems like dough for a hundred loaves, making rolls and muffins, scalding breakfast dishes until almost noon. The house to keep clean, cloth to make, patterns to cut, butter to churn, eggs to collect."

"It could be worse," Jewel countered softly. "You could be starvin' like half Virginia is. Could *be* no dough to fix, no chickens to lay."

"And never any free time any more. Leanna continued ignoring Jewel's efforts to pacify her. "No time for the piano, no one to play backgammon, no visiting, no company, no parties. I can't even ride Jasmin like I used to."

"Mrs. Leighton?" A bearded young Yankee captain knocked at the door frame to interrupt her and Leanna turned with a frown, her eyes instantly cold. The man met her gaze for a moment, then shifted uneasily, the muscles of his jaw twitching in tension.

"You like oatmeal cookies, Captin?" Jewel ignored the exchange, stepping around Leanna. "Got a plate full, fresh and hot."

Leanna frowned at Jewel, but she seemed not to notice. The black woman had adapted easily to the Yankee occupation. Too easily. She acted like they were house guests rather than enemy soldiers. Leanna still took her meals in her room and made a point of avoiding the soldiers whenever possible. "I'll be in my room, Jewel." She gathered her skirt angrily and started out the other way. "Call me when the kitchen's *unoccupied* again."

"Wait," the captain swallowed the cookie hastily, taking a step forward. "Mrs. Leighton, the major asked me to fetch you. There's people coming up the road. Somebody named Angus and a lady and—"

"Whitney!" Leanna forgot her anger instantly and started running toward the front door. Oh, thank God. Maybe she had brought a message. "Jewel, Whitney's come to see us!"

The black woman tried to hide her own pleasure beneath a snort of outward exasperation, mumbling to herself as she hurried in Leanna's wake. "Jes' two more

17

mouths to feed fer all yer complaining 'bout work, chile. Jes' two more bodies making mess . . ."

"I thought they might have burned it or something," the young woman murmured softly to Leanna, her gray eyes scanning the grounds of the farm swiftly. "Good Lord, Leanna, the place looks better than ever. That new section of fence, and a whole new barn . . ."

"For their horses," Leanna explained curtly. "They plan to winter here."

Whitney gave her sister-in-law a sidelong glance, falling silent. It was obvious that, whatever else the Federal troops had accomplished in their ten-day stay, they had not yet achieved a truce with Leanna Penley Leighton. No wonder Jonathon had worried so over how things were going. "They've been quite nice with Miranda." She nodded her chestnut head toward the two-year-old child, happily ignorant of political implications and enjoying the second half of the young captain's oatmeal cookie. "Why Major Courtland—"

"Don't be a fool, Whitney," Leanna snapped and colored instantly, murmuring an apology. "Whitney, forgive me. I'm in a terrible temper all the time now. I don't mean to bite your head off. But it doesn't matter what they do. I don't care if they build a hundred barns—they'll probably only burn them all anyway when they leave—the house, too, most likely. They're still Yankees. I won't be happy 'till the last one is off Blytheswood land. I hate them!"

"But Jonathon is worried to death over you, Leanna. If you're so miserable here, why not come back with us?"

"And abandon Blytheswood altogether to them? You should know better than that."

"Aunt Leenee!" The child spied Leanna suddenly and tore away from the Yankee officer at a dead run, chubby arms outstretched, a jubilant joy lighting her small, round, curl-framed face.

Leanna turned to catch her up in her arms, returning the child's joy with a soft, gentle laugh. For a moment,

18

with the child in her arms, she almost forgot the Yankees. "Oh Mandy, my most special little girl!" Leanna felt tears of joy spring to her eyes as she nuzzled the soft silk of the girl's raven hair, squeezing her hard in a sudden, almost desperate surge of emotion. "Oh, Mandy—thank you for coming to visit. I've missed you so!"

Across the drive, Major Courtland passed them on his way to the stable. He was frowning faintly, deep in thought. Angus, the old man driving the carriage, would have to be searched, of course, and questioned. Actually, he guessed he should have refused them admittance to Blytheswood, but that had seemed unnecessarily harsh. War was grim enough, even tempered with such occasional laxity. Laughter sounded suddenly from across the way and he checked his step and half turned toward it, startled. It was Mrs. Leighton. She was holding the little girl—her brother's child from what he understood. Joy radiated from her, and she was transformed. Perhaps because of how closely she'd guarded her heart, he found the demonstration of its warmth deeply moving.

Leanna glanced up suddenly and saw the Yankee watching her, noticing only the intensity of his gaze and not its expression. Probably suspicious of the child, she thought with a surge of instant hatred. Probably wondering if this was another 'Secesh' plot against his precious Union. Her gaze, warmed by Mandy's delight, cooled immediately to ice and she whirled on her heel, carrying the little girl inside and away from prying Yankee eyes. "Come on inside, Whitney—Jewel will bring some tea in. We'd best tell Angus to put your things in the guest cottage, that Yankee's in the house suite. Besides, Mandy will have more room there to play." She stopped just inside the door, safe within the sanctuary of the house, and reached to take Whitney's hand in silent thankfulness. She wasn't alone after all. How good it felt to know that again. "Bless you Whitney for daring to come. I can't tell you how grateful I am to see someone other than Yankee soldiers. I've had a bellyful of *them*, I freely admit!"

Whitney squeezed her hand back as they started up the stairs and laughed softly. "That's what family is all about, isn't it? Those Yankees haven't cowed the Virginia Penleys. If they don't know that by now, I think they ought to learn."

"And they will," Leanna vowed softly. "They will."

Whitney glanced at her sidelong, thinking how much that sounded like something her husband would say—Jonathon Penley, Leanna's borther, and much like the woman who walked beside her. So proud. So strong. So fiercely Southern. They never doubted their superiority to the bullying Yanks for a minute, nor questioned their ability to defend Virginia's sacred soil. She wished she shared that same boundless confidence. The way the war had been going lately, though, the first fearful whispers of doubt had begun to chill her heart.

"Have you brought a message from Jonathon?" Leanna murmured gently. "Is our cavalry coming to make a fight of it?"

Whitney glanced sideways in surprise at the question her sister-in-law had asked in such a careful undertone. Despite herself, she looked around, nervous it might have been overheard. "No, Lea." She regretted the disappointment that instantly flashed on Leanna's face. "No, I'm sorry. Jon only asked me to find out how bad the situation was. He said nothing about troops coming."

For a moment only, Leanna was silent with the pain of dashed hope. Then she shrugged it off, raising her chin again, and the set of her mouth indicated still unshaken confidence. "Well, they'll come eventually, I know they will. We can't afford to lose the Valley to the Yankees. General Lee knows that."

Whitney nodded once, keeping her doubts unvoiced. As they finished the stairs, she only reached for Leanna's hand to squeeze it, and managed a smile.

Turning abruptly, Leanna gestured curtly at the first door of the hall. "That's where *he*'s staying. Right in the house. Can you imagine such gall?" She started on for her own room further down, and Whitney followed without comment. "Let me freshen up and take this apron off. Then we'll get you settled and I can visit with Mandy awhile. "She smiled at that thought and the softness that Major Courtland had been so struck by shone once more in her violet eyes. "Good lord, how she's grown. And talking like a little magpie. You're a lucky woman, Whit. Bless your heart for daring to bring her—for daring to come at all. We'll take good care of you both, I promise, and I'll make those Yankees behave themselves. At least in the guest cottage, you'll be shut off from them. They never go near the place."

"We shall have a lovely visit, then."

"Yes, Yankees and all, we shall."

Whitney said nothing, but the steely tone of Leanna's voice had not gone unnoticed. Cow the Penleys, indeed! The Yankees were a far cry from doing that.

Chapter Two

"Fire!"

Leanna struggled up out of sleep, trying to place the cry within the context of the dream it had interrupted. She'd been exhausted tonight. Doing all the usual work of mistress of such a large household, up too late last night talking with Whitney, then playing the afternoon away with Mandy by the shallows of cold Crooked Run Creek.

"Fire!"

A door slammed down the hall and woke her completely. Fire? Dear God. Where? What? The barns? The sheds? The house itself?

She dressed as she ran, instantly and coldly awake, pulling a day gown over her head as she dashed for the door, and buttoning up as she took the steps with dangerous haste. The house was black as pitch inside, slate gray where the front door stood wide open. She ran through it without pausing to wonder why, nor did she feel the shock of the cold November night air as she burst out into it.

"Hurry up with those buckets!" An officer, half dressed, went running by her, more men stumbled sleepily out into the night to place the disturbance. "Pierson, Wendell, Kelley—!" The man ran back, gesturing, a black silhouette dancing against a charcoal sky. He brushed against Leanna but never paused, not even noticing perhaps, though she stumbled off balance and almost fell.

"Where?" she demanded, searching the black buildings with a rising sense of panic. Where was it? The main barn was dark. The new one, too. The sheds? Oh, my God! Across the drive and quite apart from the

22

other buildings, a dull glow lit the night. Now she could smell it. The night breeze had shifted this way. Her breath caught in her throat, her heart hammered a rhythm of rising horror. Oh, no, dear God, no, she prayed as she ran, not feeling the driveway stones beneath the thin kid slippers she wore. Please God, not the guest house—anything but the guest house. Whitney and Mandy were in there. Somehow the Yankees must have set fire to it.

"Damn it! Use some creek water then! Who's working the well, anyway?"

"The fire's spreading! What the hell else can we do?"

"Over here! More water over here! Fast!"

"Start wetting down this side of the barn! If that wind shifts back it's all over."

It was a nightmare, but Leanna gradually realized she wasn't dreaming. The cold air burned her lungs as she ran, sobbing now for breath. Her hair was undone from sleep and its waist-length curls whipped her face in the wind and tangled in front of her eyes. She stumbled over rocks and roots unseen in the darkness, pushed her way through milling throngs of sleep-confused soldiers, heard water sloshing in buckets passed hand to hand, felt wetness spilled beneath her feet as she grew closer to the cottage. It was ringed by a crowd of Yankees three or four deep and she had to push and pommell her way through them, stopping with a gasp of horror as she finally reached the inner edge of the circle. The front door stood wide. Flames licked at the frame of it. More flames devoured the small parlor inside, climbing the wooden steps toward the loft. "Mandy!" She screamed without knowing it, starting forward toward the blazing doorway. "Whitney!"

"Whoa, lady. You can't go in there!"

Leanna jerked her arm free of the soldier's grip, suddenly acutely aware of the fire's blistering heat warming her ice cold skin, the thick smell of it, the grotesque shadows cast on surrounding faces by the flames' orange light. She started forward again. "Whitney!" A tall dark shape blocked her path toward the door and she ran

23

into it, trying to push it aside. It turned instead, reaching one hand out to grasp her and pull her backwards.

"Trooper! Hold on to this woman!" Major Courtland thrust the girl roughly into the arms of a nearby soldier, turning again even as he spoke. "Heinrich! Heinrich, where the hell are you?" A huge, bearded blond giant shoved forward into the circle, a water bucket dangling from one massive hand. The wind gusted and yellow sparks lifted toward the now bare treetops. A rising roar of fire almost obscured their voices.

"Can you stand with my weight on your shoulders?"

"Ja, if I must." The giant nodded, moving forward. Leanna tried to follow, pulling at the trooper's hand on her arm. "Let go of me! I've got to find my sister-in-law! Please!" Leanna was sobbing as she cried, tears streaming unheeded down her cheeks. The Yankee soldier held on to her grimly, trying to pull her back from the worsening blaze.

"You can't go in there, ma'am. I'm sorry." He shouted to be heard above the confusion of voices and the crackling sound of timbers breaking. He forced Leanna another yard away from the house, doggedly shaking his head. "We tried already—a couple times. We got the lady out, but the stairs was already burning. No way anybody can get up them."

"Oh God, no! The baby was upstairs. The baby's still up there! Mandy!"

"Let me through. Let me through, please."

A quiet voice touched Leanna's ears, not intruding on her agony.

"Let me through, please." .

"I've got to do something," Leanna begged the soldier in a desperate voice, starting to pull again. "My little niece is still in there . . . my brother's baby."

"Doc, you got any brandy? This lady could use some."

The officer with the quiet voice paused only momentarily, glancing at Leanna's face as he passed. He shook his head. "In a minute, Adams. I want to see to the other woman first. Then I'll be back."

He stepped through the crowd and Leanna followed

him with her eyes, trying to go after him. A doctor. Surely a doctor would be willing to try to get the child out if only she could get to him, beg him to help. "Whitney!"

Like something from the Bible, soldiers had melted before the doctor's quiet order, clearing a path for him. Leanna could see him kneeling, a small space clearing around the form of a woman lying deathlike on someone's cloak. With a cry, she surged toward her, pulling the soldier along. "Whitney! Oh my God, Whitney don't die!"

"Easy, ma'am, she's only fainted. She was trying to go in after her little girl when she realized she weren't out too, but the troopers couldn't even make it to the stairs."

Leanna cried aloud, a wordless sound of utter despair that drowned out the rest of his words. Oh, Whitney, forced to watch her baby being burned to death, everyone helpless to save her. There must be something she could do. If she could only get this damn Yankee to let her go.

The window of the parlor exploded suddenly from the terrible heat. Bursting splinters of glass showered the ground for a dozen yards all around. Leanna screamed instinctively at the sound of it, throwing her arm up in front of her eyes as she whirled back to face it. Suddenly she froze, staring at the cottage. Someone was standing . . . no, two men, one on the other's shoulders. . . .

Water from a bucket flew past her face to hiss against the cottage wall, but she ignored it, struggling forward to try to see. In an instant, she understood and her heart soared with breathless, mindless prayer. One of the Yankees was trying to reach the small, one-sided roof of the loft's single window. Brass buttons gleamed in the firelight from an unfastened jacket; she glimpsed a metallic gleam of shoulder straps. The Yankee major stood on the shoulders of the biggest man she'd ever seen, a blond bearded man who stood grimly still, ignoring the sparks that flew all around him, singeing his beard, blackening his bare chest with flying ash.

"Damn! It's too high!" Major Courtland's voice was a frustrated curse as he swayed, grabbing for the ancient drain pipe that edged the roof and ran down the side of the ivied stone cottage. "Can you grab my boots—push me up?"

Leanna watched mesmerized as the man below obeyed, reaching to grasp the heels of the officer's black boots.

"You say when."

He fought for his balance on the man's shoulders. Then suddenly, he flexed his knees and spoke the order. Heinrich pushed, Major Courtland jumped, his hands just grasping the edge of the high, steep roof, sliding down, finally maintaining a tenuous hold on the very edge. The blond giant reached up, trying to push again against the major's boots. But sudden flames poured out of the window where he was standing and drove him back. He cried a last warning to the officer above and leapt away toward the circle of other soldiers.

Leanna smothered an involuntary cry, raising her hand to her mouth, biting on the knuckle of her finger. The major hung motionless from the roof's edge for a seemingly endless moment, a black shape against the fire's orange light. Slowly, he began to raise himself, chinning his body's weight against the edge, then freeing one hand for a desperate grab at a higher handhold, pulling again. For Leanna, he was suddenly the only person in the world, his struggle to gain the roof her only focus. If he fell now, there would be no second chance. The confusion of running soldiers, the shouting, the slosh of water buckets, the hiss of fire meeting water, the crackle of flame all receded. Her heart hammered a desperate sympathy. Her body trembled watching the terrible effort of lifting that weight up and up against the narrow roof.

He raised a knee to the edge, missed and tried again, clenching his jaw against the trembling weariness of overtaxed muscles. This time, he felt the rough shakes of the smoldering cedar roof snagging the broadcloth of his trousers. He paused for a last deep breath, then pushed once more, scrambling toward the tiny loft window. One kick of his boot heel shattered the glass. He raised one arm over his face and plunged inside.

Leanna couldn't take her eyes off the black hole of that shattered window. A passing soldier buffeted her, blocking her view and she cried a frantic protest, pushing him aside. A tiny wisp of smoke began to curl out of the window frame, the fire within rising eagerly to the source of new air. Another window exploded by the door, the roof above the parlor began to hiss when water hit it, and steam rose in gray clouds to mask the flames. And still, no one moved out of that loft.

"All right there, Major! Over here!"

"Throw down the child. We'll catch her."

The soldiers saw him before she did. Their eyes were more practiced at discerning night's shadows. She heard a sudden odd stillness as if everyone had suddenly paused to watch as she did. It startled her and she glanced around. Such intensity on the men's faces as they stared at the high roof—the Yankee officer half sliding, half crawling toward the edge, the motionless child slung over one shoulder, held by one arm. Damn them! Leanna thought suddenly, furious tears pricking her eyes. How dare they look so concerned! What had they thought when they'd set fire to the cottage to begin with? Hadn't they thought then of the little girl sleeping upstairs?

The soldier's grip on her arm had loosened as he watched and Leanna tore away with a sudden jerk, running toward the side of the cottage where a dozen hands reached up into the night to grab for the falling child. She pushed at the backs of the curious, heard the Yankee major coughing, half choking as he swung down over the roof edge into flame, then jumped for safety. But she no longer spared him any thought. Mandy was her only concern. Where was the baby? Was there any chance she could be living still?

Doc Lacey crouched low over the little girl, waving angrily at the circle of soldiers that contracted ever closer around them. "Move back! Move back all of you. Give me some room, some air down here."

Leanna was caught in the crush as the soldiers in front tried to obey, backing into their fellows a half step behind. The press tightened a moment before giving way one reluctant backward step. Someone stepped into the crowd ahead of her, an officer, shoving through the throng, and Leanna tried to follow as the soldiers let him through. She managed a step or two, then lost him as the ranks closed tight behind his passage. She sobbed her frustration, beating dark blue backs until a way opened toward the front.

"—smoke in her lungs . . . no burns that I see, but . . ."

Leanna pushed into the open space with a sobbing cry, standing motionless a moment as she stared down at the ground. The Federal doctor was bent low over Mandy's tiny body, leaning over to breathe in her open mouth, pressing her whole chest with just the palm of his larger hand. Major Courtland knelt on one knee, nodding at something the doctor had said, starting to speak in return and coughing instead, raising one hand to his ash-smeared face.

Leanna leapt forward in sudden, ungovernable grief, throwing herself down between him and the tiny, too motionless child. Something terrible burst inside and she turned on the Yankee with a sob of insane fury, raising her hand to strike at his face with all her might, then scrambling to put herself between him and the tiny girl as he jerked backwards in startled reaction.

"Get your hands off her! Get your damn bluebelly hands off her! Haven't you done enough!" Leanna reached to strike again, missing as he raised his hand to deflect hers. She writhed and clawed at him as he tried to grab her arm. "Don't you touch me, you Yankee filth!" She was choking on her tears, trembling in hysterical rage and she fought his grip on her with the ferocity of a wild bobcat. "Is this how you Yankees make war? Burning helpless women and children? I wish you'd died yourself in that house! I wish you'd—all died."

Jewel's face suddenly appeared between Leanna's and

the major's. For a moment, his startled brown eyes were close, then distant as the black woman dragged the girl backward. For a long time, Leanna continued to struggle. Then she surrendered with a last sobbing wail and allowed Jewel to pull her away from the milling soldiers, her tear-chilled face buried in her hands. "Oh God, Jewel, I wish I'd shot him that first day on the porch! I wish I'd tried to shoot all of them, every last murdering Yankee in creation."

"Hush you mouth, chile. I think you's gone plumb outta your head!" Jewel shook her head, her black eyes glittering faintly in the gleam of the still raging fire. "You hittin' that poor man after what he done!"

"It was the Yankees that caused it all! Yankees that started that fire in the first place! If not for them . . ." Her voice trailed off in bitter hysteria.

"If not for them, Miz Leighton, *both* Miz Whitney and little Miz Mandy be dead right now! That's fact, whether it suits you or not! And it weren't the Yankees what started the burning neither. It was a couple of no good's from the hills used to be some of Captain Stump's raiders 'til he wouldn't stand them no more. The Yankee pickets caught 'em going out and shot the pair and more's the riddance!" Jewel dropped Leanna's arm and stared at her a moment in silence, her eyes cold with contempt and sorrow. "You gots such a deep down hate of them Yankees it shames me, chile. I mostly raised you. I thought I taught you better. 'Pears I didn't."

Leanna felt a cold shiver settle at the base of her spine and she trembled with it, staring at the black woman in silence. "Not the Yankees?" She couldn't believe it. She'd expected something just like this of them since the moment they'd set foot in Blytheswood. "But . . . I was sure . . ." She shook her head slowly, feeling a terrible weight begin to settle on her heart. "But it must have been them," she whispered in denial. "Why would any of our side do something like that to their own?"

"Maybe they thought Yankees was living there. Maybe they done it out of sheer spite 'cause the Yankees is in

29

Blytheswood. I plainly don't know." Jewel's voice had softened, but her eyes were still cold as she reached for Leanna's arm, pulling the girl toward the house. " 'Pears to me you might have asked, though, before you waded in slappin' and screamin'."

And maybe they'd done it on purpose, Leanna's mind whispered in incredulous horror. Maybe they'd known Whitney and the baby were sleeping there and had chosen the cottage deliberately, thinking it was one of the officer's families, wintering here—or maybe not caring. Maybe figuring that it didn't matter as long as the Yankees got blamed for it, as they were sure to do here in the Confederate Valley. Thinking it would only serve to make the Yankee intruders more hated, more unwelcome than ever—the people more eager to volunteer for any mission to attack such animals. "No, I don't believe it," she whispered aloud in denial. "Not using women and children like that. I don't believe it." She jerked suddenly to a stop, pulling her arm from Jewel's and beginning to turn.

"Where you think you're going now?" Jewel's grip on her arm was nearly painful.

"I have to go back." Leanna shook her head hard as sudden tears began coursing down her cheeks. "I must apologize, Jewel. I have to. Even if he didn't save her, at least he tried."

"Saved who? Chile, you're talking crazy again. Now come along here with me."

"*Mandy*, Jewel. The Yankee major tried to save her. I saw him climb the roof. But I thought then that he knew his own men had started the fire."

"You ain't going nowhere else tonight, least of all near any more Yankees. I thank the dear Lord you didn't have no gun or you'd been shootin' them 'stead of hittin' 'em."

Suddenly, Leanna whirled to face Jewel, her eyes widening, her breath catching with dizzying hope. "What did you mean about Mandy? When I said the major tried to save her and . . .?"

"The child gonna be all right. Doc Lacey's probably got her up to the house already—her mammy, too."

Leanna stood stricken. "She's not dead?"

Jewel crossed herself, frowning, and shook her head once more.

"Jewel, oh, thank God! Don't you understand, I thought she was dead!" Leanna raised the skirts of her long dress with a sudden grab and began to run toward the house, crying and laughing both. Soldiers were still passing her, going in the opposite direction, still shouting to one another and carrying water buckets. Behind her, had she looked, she would have seen the last flames being quenched in the guest cottage, orange embers and black ash floating skyward in a slowing spiral. Most of the front was completely gutted, the windows blown out, the roof still smoldering. But the old gray stone walls remained and a good portion of the rest.

Leanna was not thinking of the cottage as she ran, but of the tiny girl so precious to her, thought lost and now, miraculously, refound; thinking of her brother and that portion of him that lay in Mandy and added so greatly to her love for the child. She'd been to terribly still— and hadn't the doctor said something about not being able to help her?

She stopped short on the last block of the front walk, freezing. Two officers stood speaking on the porch above, and in her confusion she'd forgotten the Yankees would be here, too. Then she forced herself toward the house again, one slow, painful step at a time. At the last stair, she stopped awkwardly, silent in the shadowed darkness, and tried to gather the courage to walk between them.

"I'm fine, I tell you. I want to see how the child is."

"Fine, are you, Chase?" The shorter of the two men glanced up with a wan smile, closing the zipper of the small black bag he carried. "You say you're fine, but I'm the doctor, and—"

"I've got things to attend to," Chase interrupted him.

Leanna gasped as the doctor suddenly swung his left hand, hitting the Yankee major squarely in the belly. He bent over in surprise, choking, and began to cough

31

again a dry, rasping, convulsive sound. The doctor offered an arm for support.

"You're not fine when you're still coughing smoke, my friend. Six more laps around the courtyard. Deep breaths, please. Out with the bad air, etc." He gestured almost cheerfully and Leanna thought she heard him chuckle. "When you can control that coughing, then come inside and get to bed. I'll be up to give you any reports you want."

Major Courtland shrugged and turned, starting down the step. He stopped in surprise to find himself face to face with the girl as she forced herself the last agonizing step forward. Her cheeks were deathly pale, her hands trembling, but she had forced her eyes up to meet the Yankee's.

"Major, I—about this evening—earlier tonight, I mean—"

He cut her off. "Not just now, Mrs. Leighton." His brown eyes were cold as they touched hers briefly and then lifted.

For a moment, Leanna had the impression of standing uncomfortably close to him. He was a big man, she realized, near six feet if not more. Broad shouldered. He smelled of smoke and his face was streaked with ash, his dark brown hair tousled from wind and maybe from sleep. Obviously, the cry of "fire" had roused him from bed also. His trousers were beltless, his dark blue jacket only half buttoned. Where his bare chest showed, there was a shadow of hair, and streaks of what looked like dried blood.

Leanna's hand drifted instinctively up toward them, but he shouldered past her in the next instant and disappeared into the blackness of the driveway. She watched him go, flushing deep color in the darkness. It had been difficult enough to try to apologize to a Yankee without having him rebuff her so harshly.

"Mrs. Leighton?"

Leanna started in surprise and quickly turned. "Oh—Doctor Lacey, is it?"

"Yes, Doc Lacey." The man's eyes studied her face a

moment in the darkness. Leanna had the impression of deep and genuine compassion flowing from him, but an unsettling, almost intimate, feeling too, as if he were reading her mind. Uneasy, she only nodded and quickly began to turn for the house.

"Mrs. Leighton, are you feeling better, or would you like me to give you something to calm your nerves?"

She felt her face blush with hot color but she managed to reply coolly. "No, I'm fine now, thank you."

"You mustn't be miffed all over again at us just because Major Courtland was curt with you just now. He's had a trying evening, to say the least."

She took one more step, then slowly came to a stop and turned. "And I was not the least of his trials," Leanna admitted with a stiff nod. She was angry at herself but she found herself unable to meet the man's eyes. "I should apologize to you, too, I suppose, doctor. I was beside myself."

"Human, that's all. Maybe a trifle feminine as well."

Leanna glanced at him sharply, beginning to frown at the amusement she thought she could detect in his soft voice.

"I mean no disrespect, Mrs. Leighton. Humor is my only weapon in this war—the only thing that keeps me sane. We all need something, you know. Something to use for balance."

She risked another sidelong glance, confused but at the same time understanding. For balance. Yes. That's what she'd lost when the Yankees had invaded Blytheswood. The sense of the world turning in its natural order. "Is my niece going to be all right?"

"Yes, she'll be quite all right, I'm sure. Probably feel far better in the morning than either her mother or you, who were old enough to understand what was happening."

There was a long pause and Leanna stood uneasily. One part of her was anxious to walk away, into the sanctuary of the house, to close the door on this dreadful night. But another part was compelled to know the truth. "My housekeeper told me it was Confederate raiders who started the fire." Her statement sounded like a question and she blushed at it, irritated. Like a small child, she thought, not wanting to believe her heroes had feet of clay.

"Confederates?" Doc Lacey had a slow way of speaking. He replied just as Leanna began to wonder if he'd heard her. "I'm not sure of that. They wore no uniforms. And they were both beyond my skills before I reached them."

Leanna nodded, pausing to be sure he was finished speaking. She appreciated the carefulness of his answer, the tact deliberately shown. But there was one more thing that she needed to say, and she took a deep breath. "It's important to me that you, that someone, should know why I reacted as I did earlier. I thought Mandy was dead. And I thought the Yankees—I mean the Federal troops—were responsible."

"I understand," the doctor smiled briefly. "Remember, I overheard your speech to Major Courtland."

Leanna fell silent a moment, startled. For a moment, she merely looked at him, feeling the night winds chilling her face, hearing the night cries from the cottage area finally fading. Doc Lacey met her gaze levelly, but without condemnation. Slowly, she felt a lump forming in her throat. "I . . . ah . . ." she cleared her throat softly, blinking at tears that threatened to form. Yankee or not, his sympathy struck a chord within her. "I wanted to tell him, to apologize to Major Courtland also."

"I'll extend your apologies, Mrs. Leighton. Perhaps in the morning, though." He turned for the house, offering Leanna his arm. For a moment she hesitated, then blushed at her hesitation and accepted his arm with murmured thanks. After what had happened tonight, she was in their debt. She must try to offer them greater courtesy.

"He risked his life to save my niece. I confess, I don't understand that. It's hardly what I expected from a Yankee officer."

"Good men wear both blue and gray in this accursed war, I'm afraid. Maybe they do in all wars, I don't know. Chase Courtland is a good man, Mrs. Leighton. You don't know how lucky you are to have him in command here. Troops follow their officers' lead—in more than battle charges. Had you, by the luck of the draw, gotten another man in command, I can assure you you would feel the difference. Doc Lacey dropped Leanna's arm to open the door for her. He shrugged and smiled again, almost coaxingly. "We miss your presence around the plantation, Mrs. Leighton, especially at dinner. Men grow tired of other men. They miss the softness, the uniqueness of a woman's point of view on things. Especially in wartime."

Leanna gave a quick sidelong glance at the sudden shift of the conversation, as she let go his arm. She had the sudden suspicion she was being manuevered.

"Perhaps, Mrs. Leighton, if this evening has proved we are not all merciless villains, you might consider joining us for dinner one of these nights. It would be an excellent way of showing some appreciation to those officers who worked so hard on your behalf tonight."

There was a sudden silence at his words and Leanna drew a step farther from him. Rising anger began to dispel the earlier softness she'd felt for the Yankee doctor. For a moment she did not speak, merely stood motionless, staring at him, framed in the soft darkness of the Virginia moonlight graying the white painted carved-wood pillars of the doorway. When she did finally speak, her voice was cold once more. "I do believe I just heard you invite me to my own supper table. Have you Yankees no end of gall?"

The doctor answered first with silence, his smile fading. "You have been conspicuous there only by your absence, Mrs. Leighton. 'Your' table has been graced only by Federal blue uniforms. And I have heard even lawyers aver that possession is nine-tenths of the law."

Leanna faced him squarely, trembling in growing anger. "No," she murmured with icy calm. "Not here." She reminded herself that the Yankee major *had* saved Miranda's life tonight—and for that she was in their debt. But it didn't really stem her anger. Regardless of who had actually lit the blaze, the Yankees presence here had caused it. "Blytheswood *does not*—nor will it *ever*—belong to Yankees. Blytheswood is *mine*, Captain. It has belonged to Penleys for nearly a hundred years. And I will die before I relinquish it to you or anyone else."

There was a strange, almost satisfied gleam in Doc Lacey's eyes as he met her icy stare. He smiled faintly and raised one brow. "Then I suggest you place your ownership in greater visibility, Mrs. Leighton. Perhaps I shall expect to see you tomorrow evening or so, at the table."

"Perhaps you shall." She turned without further courtesy, still trembling as she started up the wide, shadowed stairs. It made her no less angry to realize that one way or another, the Yankee doctor had acheived his purpose. But if it was a 'woman's softness' he was expecting to be rewarded by, he would find himself sorely mistaken. The fight for Blytheswood, apparently, had only just begun.

"Susan! What a delightful surprise!" Joshua Courtland rose from his leather desk chair, extending a hand in greeting. "What brings you into this part of the city?"

"I'm here to catch a train, actually. I just stopped to say good-bye." A young woman with soft brown hair and a sweet smile blushed faintly, as if embarrassed by the exuberance of the older man's greeting. The hand with which she reached out to squeeze his had a diamond sparkling on her third finger, and Joshua felt it in his grip and smiled wider. It was tangible hope of a future for the Courtland family.

"Planning to run up to New York for some shopping?"

"No, to Washington, actually." The girl offered an almost apologetic smile and a shrug. "Chase didn't tell you?"

"Tell me? Tell me what?" Joshua held her hand with a tighter grip, unaware of the pressure he exerted. Had Chase finally given in? Decided to marry the girl before the war ended? God, he hoped so. It would make everything so much easier for both families.

"I've volunteered as a nurse." She blushed as she spoke, embarrassed by the question she read in Joshua's eyes. Too often, she saw the same one there in her own parents' eyes. "I hope you aren't angry. Father thought it was all right. I hope you agree."

"Oh. A nurse." His voice betrayed disappointment and he sighed softly before he could stop himself. "That's *marvelous*, Susan," he exclaimed with obviously forced enthusiasm. "Don't apologize. No reason the women can't contribute something to this war effort, too. Don't listen to those old fuddy-duddies that disapprove."

"That's the way I felt." She smiled faintly, beginning to withdraw her hand. "I just thought I'd stop to see if you'd heard from Chase lately. Since he reached the Valley, I haven't heard a wor.." She turned as she spoke, almost ashamed to have asked, and hoping it had not sounded too much like a complaint. But Chase so rarely wrote. She tried to believe it was from lack of time rather than lack of inclination, but these past few months she'd begun to wonder. Begun, for the first time in her life, to question whether she even knew the real Chase Courtland. Or whether the image she had formed growing up practically in his shadow—he'd been her older brother Benjamin's closest friend and almost a god to an adoring little sister—was not more myth than actuality. Not that it changed anything either way. She wore Chase's ring on her finger. As far as she was concerned, that meant she would become his wife.

"I wouldn't worry, dear. You know Chase by now, or you ought to. I'm sure he's fine, but he's not much for writing—even to me."

"Oh." Susan turned back, and managed another smile. "Yes, of course, you're right. He's busy, too, I'm sure." She reached for her gloves. "Well, I'd best be off then. I don't want to miss my train."

"Yes. Washington, you said?"

"Yes. I thought I'd be closer there if Chase gets some

leave granted this winter. Perhaps I can coax him up for a visit."

Joshua smiled and nodded, not sure what else to say. It was a pity. A damn shame. Susan Stratford was a fine young lady. She'd make an excellent wife. But Chase wasn't in love with her. He was finally beginning to realize his son had never been, beginning to fear he never would be. As well as he usually understood Chase, he could not say he understood this. The sudden engagement at the war's start had pleased him, but startled him. He had not pressed the match on the boy. Chase had done it of his own free will—then ridden off to war and years of leaving the girl to wait.

"Well, I'll send your love when I write—or if I see him." Susan was smiling once more, gathering her long dark-blue skirt in one hand to leave. "You take care of yourself now, too, Mr. Courtland. I'll write if I hear any news worth passing on."

Joshua nodded and held the door as she went out. Susan Courtland. It didn't have the right ring to it. It didn't sound like it was meant to be. Still, it *would* be someday. He must write a protest to Chase—find out exactly what the boy thought he was doing. Such commitments were not taken lightly in the social circles both families moved in. Engagements were nearly as final as marriage. It would become a scandal soon the way Chase was delaying the actual ceremony. Susan had been too young, perhaps, at seventeen in 1861. But not any longer. And even if Chase wasn't head over heels in love with the girl, love was not the only consideration to base a marriage on. Even if they lacked the one, they had the others in abundance. So it was time Chase fulfilled his responsibility to Susan and to his own family and placed a wedding ring on her finger.

He shook his head with a deep sigh and glanced back at the work that lay piled high on his desk. Among those papers was an invitation that had arrived today—a most peculiar invitation. A supper meeting of a dozen of Philadelphia's richest and most powerful men. Men Joshua Courtland knew, but neither liked nor trusted. Men who had used the war as an opportunity for huge profits and personal fortunes that ran to the millions. Men like Rockefeller, Mellon, Wanamaker, Jay Gould, and others. Profiteers, some called them. Jackals, he thought. Fattening themselves on human blood and misery. It didn't bode well for the world that such men should be gathering together. If they were planning something, whatever it was would stink to high heaven. He'd decided not to go when Henry Walters had first extended the invitation. Now, on second thought, he'd changed his mind. Forewarned is forearmed, Joshua reminded himself. He thought maybe he'd make plans to be at that intimate supper meeting a month from tonight. If evil was to be organized, at least one Courtland would be there to try to stem its success.

Chapter Three

"I wish you'd stay longer." Leanna didn't usually give in to tears, but she was hard pressed today to keep from letting some fall. She hugged a squirming Miranda for the tenth time. "At least promise me another visit, Whitney."

"Well, I . . ." Whitney blushed, and glanced around the carriage quickly. No one else was within earshot. But it was early to announce anything. Even Jonathon didn't know yet.

"I'm going to feel more alone now with these Yankees than ever," Leanna lifted Mandy up to the carriage seat beside her mother. The horse moved restlessly and Angus checked the animal with a growl. But Leanna knew it was time for them to go. The trip to New Market took nearly five hours. She didn't want them delayed and forced to travel in the dark. After the attack on the guest cottage the other night, it was unthinkable to travel after nightfall.

"I wish you'd change your mind still and come home with us. That's what Jonathon was hoping for. Come back to Cool Spring."

"Let's not start that argument again," Leanna shook her head. "I won't run away and abandon Blytheswood to the Yankees."

"But what good do you think you can do Blytheswood by staying? Leanna, for heaven's sake, there are two hundred soldiers here. You can't stop them from doing anything they want to do. And if you *do* try to defy them, it will only suffice to place you and Blytheswood both in greater danger."

"I won't leave."

Whitney recognized the expression that hardened her

sister-in-law's violet eyes and she sighed. But she made one last try. "It's that Yankee doctor, isn't it? What he said about keeping your ownership of Blytheswood visible. It's simply nonsense, and you're taking it far too seriously."

"No, it isn't just that. But he was right, Whitney. If it were Cool Spring you'd feel the same way."

Whitney didn't argue but privately, she doubted that. Her attachment to her home was nothing like Leanna's attachment to Blytheswood. Always strong, it was practically obsessive now with the Yankees' threat of taking it away from her. She sat silent a moment, then sighed. "At least promise me you'll be as polite as possible, then, to them. And stay close to the main house where Jewel or their officers are. I was a little bit reassured, I admit, after sharing dinner with them last night. Most of the officers, at least, seem prepared to be gentlemen. I confess I almost enjoyed it once I finally stopped shaking in fright! Jewel's good cooking and men at the table. It almost seemed like the days before the war."

"You only enjoyed it because that Captain Grier doted on your every word." Leanna spoke arrogantly, but couldn't quite keep from smiling. "God preserve me from Yankees in love! I thought his heart was going to break right there in Jewel's deep-dish apple pie when you announced you were leaving today."

Whitney smiled back, but shook her head in gentle remonstrance. "Now don't be cruel, Leanna. That's unlike you. Yankee or not—he's a good man, and we mustn't mock him."

Leanna smiled but nodded, curbing her mirth. Whitney was right—about him at least. Yankees in general, though, were another story. "Promise you'll come back for another visit before winter," she coaxed once more, reaching for Whitney's hand. "Please."

"Well, I . . ." She colored again and finally laughed softly. "Well, I don't really think I can, Lea. Not that I wouldn't like to. The coffee alone is worth the trip! But I . . . well, you know, Jonathon was home for a few days in September—"

41

Leanna frowned and immediately caught herself, forcing her annoyance away. It seemed her brother got home fairly often while Stewart—

"Anyway, I think I may be with child again. At least I hope so. Jonathon would love a son."

"Whitney!" Leanna reached for her sister-in-law's hand. "Oh, I'm thrilled for you! Truly I am! Does Jonathon know?"

"No, not yet. I wanted to be certain. But I wrote to him last night. Rosie Jenkins said she'd get the letter to him through her brother."

Leanna swallowed against the thickening in her throat. Her brother would be deeply pleased. He adored Whitney and Miranda so. He wanted a large family. Suddenly she ached a little and her own happiness dimmed. Jonathon and Whitney were so very, very close. Sometimes, comparing them with herself and Stewart, she could not help but wonder whether some essential intimacy wasn't missing from her marriage.

"So, that's why I hesitate to travel more, Leanna," Whitney finished apologetically. "The Valley Turnpike is in awful condition now."

"Yes, I know. Oh, of course you mustn't take any chances," Leanna agreed hastily. "Perhaps you might send Miranda up sometime, though. Especially if you begin to feel poorly at all."

"That much I'll do," Whitney promised and leaned over the carriage side to kiss Leanna an affectionate farewell. Not related by blood, they had still become closer than sisters. "Now you take care—and watch your temper, Lea. Maybe they aren't our own, but at least a few of the Yankees are decent men. I believe they'll treat you and Blytheswood kindly enough if you'll let them."

Leanna nodded, leaning in for a last kiss to Mandy. Then she forced herself away, waving Angus on. As the carriage started up, a detail of Yankee troopers swung into their saddles. They would escort the carriage as far as Strasburg where the main pike started. And Leanna admitted some small gratitude for Major Courtland's

42

extraordinary thoughtfulness in ordering it done. The Valley was no longer the peaceful place it once had been. And not all the troublemakers wore Yankee blue.

Captain Grier stood at one side of the drive. He waved as the carriage rolled by, calling what was obviously a farewell of false cheer. Leanna watched him for a moment, surprised to feel compassion for the Yankee. Then, from down the drive, she heard Major Courtland's deep baritone. He was starting up toward the house where she stood. Without meaning to, she found herself studying him, comparing him to Stewart. He was taller. And he was more solidly built. Dark, of course, where Stewart was fair. Handsome like her husband, but with a difference. Something in his eyes, perhaps. Or— Leanna! She caught herself in horrified shock, blushing furiously and more than a trifle angry at herself. She turned quickly and retreated into the house before anyone could guess her thoughts.

"Oh, Major!" Whitney touched Angus's arm to stop the carriage. She leaned over, reaching one gloved hand down toward the Yankee commander. "I'm so glad I caught you before I left. You weren't at dinner last night."

"Riding a patrol." He glanced up as if surprised, but shrugged pleasantly, halting his step.

"Yes. So your captain said." Whitney's eyes shone with sudden intensity. "I wanted to thank you for what you did the other night, at the risk of your own life."

"Thank God, instead." He smiled faintly. "I think He kept me on that roof."

Whitney shook her head, not allowing him to treat the matter lightly. "God helps those who help themselves. Anyway, thank you, Major. From my husband and me both."

He nodded once, glancing toward the house. Leanna was just disappearing inside. "Your sister-in-law isn't going back to New Market with you, I gather."

"No. Leanna is deeply attached to Blytheswood. She refuses to leave." There was a strained silence. Whitney managed a final smile. "Actually, I'm somewhat reas-

43

sured about her decision to remain. Men who save children are not generally . . ."

"Mrs. Penley," he interrupted, glancing past her toward Miranda. For the instant he looked at the child, Whitney noticed an unexpected gentleness in his eyes. He looked back at her and the softness was gone. "On behalf of your little girl, let me offer a few words of advice. If you'll listen to a Yankee, pack up yourself and the girl and move farther south come spring. Below Lexington at least. I believe you'll be safer there."

Whitney blinked in surprise. A Yankee offensive in the Valley? Was that what he was trying to warn her of? She remembered the last one. Jonathon had been on Ashby's staff then. She remembered the charming little house in Winchester where General Jackson and his officers had spent the winter of '62. Roses on cream-colored carpet. Delicately carved wooden trim decorating the side porch. 'Gingerbread,' Jonathon had called it. Violets had grown by the stepping-stone walk beneath the shadows of a few tall pines. Jackson had cut the Yankee offensive that spring to ribbons. But Jackson was dead now. Shot accidentally by his own troops in the dark—just after the victory at Chancellorsville. They'd amputated his arm, but he'd died anyway a few days later of pneumonia. Yankees would be in Stonewall Jackson's Winchester house now. And recalling Jonathon's last letter—the lack of food, of men, of horses, of weapons; no ammunition for half the guns they did have—she wondered what would stop the Yankees this time if they drove up the Valley in force? "Thank you, Major," she managed to reply softly, and without fear. "Perhaps I'll do that."

He nodded once, faintly smiling, and tipped his hat as she signaled Angus to move the carriage on.

But dinner that night was far more strained. Half the officers were out on an extended patrol. The gathering missed Whitney's gentle tact and Captain Grier was trying, and failing, to mask his melancholy at Whitney's absence. He retired early and his lieutenants went with him. Before Leanna had quite finished her dessert, there was suddenly only Major Courtland and Doc Lacey still sharing the table with her. She glanced uneasily toward both of them and hurried her own eating. The major was finished, but Doctor Lacey was only half through his pie. It would be unspeakably rude for her to leave before he was done, and she began to wish she hadn't come down again tonight. She hurried another mouthful and glanced warily up again—this time to find Major Courtland's eyes studying her.

"Mrs. Leighton." His voice was quite soft, but it startled her nevertheless. She almost dropped the fork. "What have I done to deserve your unrelenting enmity?"

Leanna felt her face flame scarlet. For a moment, she said nothing, hoping Doc Lacey or Jewel might interrupt and save her from answering. But each second passed like an eternity and still there was only an expectant silence around her. "It isn't you, Major . . . I mean you personally." There was another silence. She felt Major Courtland's eyes still on her, and she was careful to avoid his gaze.

"You mean it's simply the uniform? Simply because I'm a Federal officer?"

"Major, please. I cannot see where a conversation of this sort can lead us."

"What can it hurt, Mrs. Leighton?" he returned. "We've got a long winter coming up. I'd just as soon know the reason for your hostility. Perhaps I can do something to alleviate it and things would be more pleasant all around."

"Nothing will 'alleviate' it." Leanna raised her eyes at last, their violet depths flashing with resentment. "Nothing less than packing up your entire battalion and going away!"

"Any place in particular?"

"I can think of *one*, but I'm too much a lady to name it!"

Doc Lacey cleared his throat and concentrated intently on finishing his pie. Leanna glanced at him in irritation, wondering if there was a trace of amusement there on his face.

"You are, I believe, the most stubbornly Confederate person I've ever met. Your sister-in-law wasn't as fierce a partisan."

Leanna's eyes flashed again and she slammed her fork down against the plate. "Damn you Yankees!"

"As referee of this debate, I must raise my first objection." Lacey interrupted with a smile he no longer bothered to hide. "Name calling shall be a penalty. Mrs. Leighton, the major was courteous enough to refer to you as a Confederate, rather than a 'Johnny Reb' or 'Secesh' or 'Rebel.' You should, at least, respond in kind. 'Damn you Federals,' for example."

Leanna stared at him speechless for a moment, then finally nodded once, very stiffly. "I thought I was coming to dinner, not to a debate. As for your being a referee—"

"I didn't ask for the position," Doc Lacey shrugged and gestured around the room. "It seems mine by default. As a doctor, my only interest lies in keeping both of you from attacking each other with your pie forks."

Leanna stared at him a moment, frowning. He returned her gaze levelly, with obvious amusement, and more maddeningly, a challenge lying in his eyes.

"Mrs. Leighton, please." Major Courtland moved restlessly at the end of the table opposite Leanna. He pushed his dishes away and leaned forward to rest his folded forearms on the table. "I don't mean to upset you any further. I just thought we could somehow come to an understanding." He paused and frowned. "Why are you such an ardent Confederate? Have you lost brothers or cousins, maybe? Have you been mistreated by other Union officers?"

"No, Major, thank God. I am a Confederate by conscience."

"You mean you're pro-slavery?"

"I mean I'm a Secessionist, Major." Leanna blushed faintly at his question. Slavery was a delicate issue. She'd argued once with Stewart over it, the last time he had been home. He'd objected to Jewel's status in

Leanna's affections and had tried to convince her of the Negroes' basic inability to accept freedom.

"I have the feeling you're making a distinction of some kind," Major Courtland spoke slowly, his eyes still on Leanna's face. "As if there are two issues here."

"I told you I was a Secessionist, Major. And—"

"But when you say you're a Secessionist, does that mean you're anti-slavery? Are you an abolitionist then?"

"Hardly," Leanna's eyes flashed again and Major Courtland frowned, leaning back in his chair. "That damn Emancipation Proclamation was the dumbest thing your Mr. Lincoln has yet done!"

"You believe in the validity, then, of slavery?"

"I believe it's ridiculous to free forty percent of the South's population, Major, without regard to the fact that most of those people can't read or write, have never been even remotely responsible for their own existence—haven't made their own clothes, found their own food, nursed their own sick." She spoke in a rush, her face flaming, forgetting she was a woman who was expected, as such, to have no depth of thought. "Not to mention the financial loss incurred by the owners! And no thought given to replacing the labor force the South is losing! You might as well have freed every two-year-old in the South, Major! That would have made as much sense!"

Chase Courtland watched her lovely face growing scarlet as she spoke. He was surprised at her reply, but careful to hide that reaction, realizing it would be insulting to reveal he hadn't guessed her capable of such eloquence, or of such intelligence. He was finding Leanna Leighton more complicated than the average woman—certainly far more than the average Southern belle—and with it, he admitted to a certain fascination with her. Fiery, strong, beautiful. Soft when he least expected it. Stewart Leighton, he decided slowly, was on the wrong side of the war, but other than that, he was beginning to consider him a lucky man.

"I was in hopes, before the war, of some saner program to accomplish the same ends." Leanna spoke more calmly now, relieved at the Yankee's lack of argument, the absence of the usual moralizing. "But it's too late now. And it has the whole South twice as fiercely united. It did accomplish that much. Everyone is scared to death, quite simply, of what is going to happen now if the Yankees do win. Scared to death at the thought of all those thousands of slaves roaming wild, stealing for food and clothes, perhaps forming into bands that will attack white farms and such, scared of murder and rape and pillage on a mass scale. We remember Nat Turner's rebellion, and the massacres that accompanied that."

He only raised one brow thoughtfully and took a slow breath, forcing his mind back to the conversation he'd begun. That had *not* occurred to him. The fear. The fact that perhaps part of the Southern perpetration of slavery was rooted in a deep terror of the consequences of ending it. "I see your point."

Leanna blinked and stared at him. "You do?"

"Am I an idiot, Mrs. Leighton? Unable to understand the spoken word?" He frowned at her down the length of the table, irritated at her surprise. He'd gone out of his way since arriving here to offer kindness and courtesy. In return, she continued to act as though he had horns on his head and a forked tail. "Do I look like another Reverend Brown, arming slaves with steel-tipped lances and inciting wholesale massacres?"

Leanna flushed and the anger returned to her eyes. "Do I look like a Simon Legree, Major Courtland? Yet don't all your Yankees out in my barn think part of being a 'Rebel' is our love of whipping black women and children?"

"Foul," Doc Lacey injected firmly, raising his hand. "On both of you."

Leanna fell silent, startled by his interruption.

"Haven't you anything else to do, Doctor?" Major Courtland asked pointedly. "Any patients to see to?"

Leanna hid a smile at his irritation and perversely exerted herself to be charming. "Please stay, Doctor." She met the Major's dark gaze tauntingly. "See how reasonable we rebels can be? I'm willing to trust the impartiality of one of your own men."

There was another moment's silence, this time broken by the major's sigh. "Somehow, I am the one who's beginning to feel outnumbered."

Doc Lacey glanced at him with an odd smile. "Paranoia now, Chase?" he questioned softly. "You doubt my impartiality?"

Leanna looked on quizzically, half frowning. The two men exchanged wordless looks. She had the feeling suddenly that this exchange was wholly unrelated to her. Something else was being discussed now wordlessly.

Major Courtland stood up suddenly, gesturing toward Leanna. "Perhaps we can continue our discussion another time, Mrs. Leighton. I have enjoyed it."

Leanna was too startled to return the courtesy. She followed him out of the room with her eyes, instead. Enjoyed this discussion? Was he being sarcastic? If he'd enjoyed it, why had he so abruptly terminated it?

"Sorry, Mrs. Leighton, I'm afraid I've interrupted your conversation." He too was watching his commander's departure and Leanna's frown grew more quizzical. He had an almost worried look on his face. His 'doctor look,' Jewel called it.

"I'm afraid I don't understand," she murmured finally, shaking her head.

Doc Lacey seemed to draw his attention back to Leanna with an effort, offering a distracted smile. "What? Oh, it was nothing you said. He is moody sometimes. The more so lately."

She had the feeling that was all the explanation she was going to get, the feeling of a door being closed on her—firmly, however gently, the feeling of ranks being closed. "I see," she said, not meaning it. "I believe I'll retire, then, Doctor." She nodded politely as she rose, beginning to turn toward the door.

"Mrs. Leighton, did you find our discussion offensive to you?"

The question, startling her, caught her at the door and she turned. "Offensive?" She considered it a moment, wondering. "No." Her answer was vaguely surprising to her and she shook her head with a shrug. "No, although it probably should have been."

"No," he assured her almost fervently, rising to his feet and shaking his head. "No, I'm sure Chase didn't mean it to be. I think he was quite sincere about wanting to know your feelings."

She half frowned again, looking at him strangely. "Chase?"

"Yes, the Major's first name. Short for Chesleigh, actually, though he'd not like that fact to get out I think."

Leanna managed a faint smile.

"We doctors have more leeway than most officers. I usually remember his rank, but now and again, when I'm dealing on a more personal level—" He broke off. "Anyway, that's probably irrelevant."

Leanna only shrugged. She was having a hard time disliking this particular Yankee.

"You will come back again for dinner tomorrow night, then? You aren't angry at us?"

Leanna considered, then nodded. "Yes, I'll come back, Doctor."

He smiled at that, looking strangely pleased. "Personally, I enjoyed it. I think Chase did, too. Well, good night then. See you tomorrow."

She was in her room before she thought of something else, something equally surprising. Major Courtland had spoken to her as an equal during their discussion. He'd been genuinely anxious to hear her thoughts, conceding a point when she earned one, not astounded that her brain was capable of deeper thought than whether to bake light or dark muffins for breakfast. Whereas Southern men, Stewart at least, would have listened with a condescending smile. They would never have reacted with anger. They would never have taken her seriously enough to argue back. And then, so suddenly, he'd simply walked out. It never occurred to her that part of her uneasiness at that moment might have stemmed from a concern for the man inside the uniform. She did not think of him yet as a man. Only as a Yankee. She shook her head wearily as she dressed for bed, summing the whole evening up in a single word. Puzzling. The whole thing, from beginning to end, had not clarified any of the problems at Blytheswood. On the contrary, it had confused them even further. The last thing that caught her eye as she extinguished the bedside lamp was dust on the night stand. And she reminded herself she must speak to Hilda tomorrow. The girl was paying no attention to her work. Enigmatic Yankees or not, she had a house to keep running and that came first.

Hilda giggled and pressed closer to the Yankee trooper, stealing another swift glance toward the main house just visible through the trees. "Gosh, I'd better get going." She sighed and ran her hand up the side of his dark blue jacket, pressing her hips a little closer to his. "You know she'll be lookin' for me. I can hear her now. 'Hilda, did you dust that night table?' She mimicked Leanna's patrician tone. " 'Now scrub up that walk, Hilda, it needs it badly.' "

"Stay a bit longer." His voice was husky, his hands bolder as he pulled the girl closer and nuzzled her hair. One sun-tanned, lean hand slid up her belly to cup her breast beneath the stiff homespun fabric.

Hilda smiled and relaxed against him. A surge of excitement tingled in her loins. His hand tightened familiarly on her breast, his thumb teasing the tender flesh of the nipple as his mouth touched her neck. She closed her eyes and stood still for a moment letting him do as he willed. She always allowed them just this much—and no more. Five of them, she was working on. Five narrowed down from a hundred. Lordy, she thought to herself, smiling as she felt the trembling in the hard male body pressed behind hers, surely one of them would give in soon! Offer the wedding ring she was holding out for.

He groaned against her ear, turning her around to face him. As he kissed her, Hilda could taste the sweetness of the hard cider he'd shared with her a moment ago. Some of the men had made it from apples left on the ground in the orchard up the hill, then let it ferment well hidden from officers' eyes. She'd been hoping when he showed it to her that it would loosen his tongue enough to pop a proposition of marriage. She gasped suddenly, startled to feel his hand sliding down her belly to seek the woman part of her. She began to pull away. Then his hand found her and it felt good, teasing the desire of her own young body. She debated a moment, her eyes still closed, her mouth still pressed to his. She felt his tongue at her teeth and opened her mouth farther to let it in. The cider taste was strong on it and she kissed him back eagerly. His fingers were working busily on her below and it started a throbbing in her loins she'd never felt before. This was more than she'd ever let any of them do to her before, and for a moment, she was a little scared, thinking maybe she should make him stop. But a full two weeks had passed since she'd decided her ambition and she was getting a little impatient to have it realized. She was tired of being a servant girl, tired of fetching and carrying and working at Leanna Leighton's whim by day, and at her father's when she got home. She wanted her own house. Her own place to live in. And the only way to get that was to get a man first. Preferably a Yankee since it was pretty plain they'd be winning the war. Practicality was Hilda's long suit.

"I wish we was married, Georgie. Then we could do it all." She prompted him breathlessly, unconsciously arching her back to offer herself easier to the trooper's strong hand.

He only moaned for answer, burying his face against the side of her neck.

Hilda smiled, encouraged. At least he hadn't said no. She dared another swift glance over her shoulder toward Blytheswood's main house. Mrs. Leighton would be missing her soon and come looking. Time was running out. She hated to accept another day of failure, so she decided on a gamble. If it didn't work, there was always four more Yankees. "Oh, Georgie, that feels so good." It wasn't a lie. His hand bunched her skirt up by now and he was touching her through only her light linen bloomers. She felt a strange wetness spreading on the fabric as the throbbing grew more intense. Maybe if she were a touch bolder, it would overcome his last resistance. He would beg her to marry him so he could have his way with her. It was an easy course to take by now. It fit well with what she wanted to do. But, she reminded herself through a growing haziness of thought, she couldn't actually give him what he wanted 'til she got that ring on her finger. It might ruin everything.

Hilda let her hand wander down the dark blue jacket to the brass 'U.S.' of his belt buckle. It hesitated there a minute, touching the smooth leather of his wide black belt, then slipped an inch lower—to the first button of his trousers. He was so swollen she could feel him even there, hard and warm beneath the light blue of his pants. She fingered him curiously. It was the first time she'd ever touched that part of a man, and she was surprised at the size of it. He groaned again and shuddered at the stroke of her fingers, tightening his grip around the girl. Hilda gasped as his hand suddenly pulled at her bloomers, tearing them and freeing her to his touch. She started to pull away, but his fingers found her first, rubbing at her and then suddenly plunging inside the wet heat of her young body, his palm hard against the throbbing flesh as he half lifted her off the ground in his eagerness. Hilda struggled against that pressure with sudden fear, only succeeding in driving his fingers deeper into her. With the suddenness of thunder cracking in a storm, a burst of ecstasy exploded in her loins, shaking her to her very soul. For a moment, she hung there helpless on his strength, her hot juices running down to bathe his hand. An instant later, she felt the cold ground beneath her back as he clambered over her, his hand desperate at the buttons of his trousers. Hilda cried out in fear, struggling helplessly beneath the soldier's weight.

"No, Georgie—no, no, no!" She gasped and choked on her words. The hard tip of him was already probing her wet flesh, pressing against the soft skin of her inner thigh, then withdrawing to search again. She felt the tickle of him amongst her pale, tightly curling hair and cried a last frantic denial, struggling all the harder. He entered her like a battering ram, hot and swollen, as hard as stone. He met the resistance of her maidenhead and groaned in desperation, holding the girl tighter as he pulled himself out for a harder thrust. Hilda was sobbing and trying to hit at him, but choking on tears that coursed down her face. Her struggles seemed only to incite him further, the writhing of her hips beneath his only firing more frantic greed to bury himself in her. He found the entrance to her again and rammed at it with brutal force, hitting the maidenhead again and not retreating this time, forcing the spear of his body through it. Hilda screamed in pain, her body arching instincively against it. Her movement only allowed him deeper access to her and he plunged fully inside her, grunting with the ecstasy of it. Five times more he repeated the process. Each time Hilda felt his withdrawal, she cried in relief. Each time he forced himself in her again, her body cried protest; the hugeness of him seemed too great for her tender flesh to accommodate; each time it gave way before him she felt it must this time rip asunder. At last he moved convulsively within her, forcing a last cry of pain from the girl as he speared her to her very core, filling her so tight and full of him she dared not move for fear of further agony.

He lay panting and spent above her, dripping sweat, and Hilda pushed him from her, off onto the ground, as she scrambled to her feet and began to run toward the main house. Half blinded by tears, she stumbled more than once, feeling the agony burning still between her thighs, the wetness of his leavings and her own blood running down her legs as she ran. Jewel was standing in the door with a last tray of bread to be cooked in the outside bake oven, and Hilda collapsed against her with a cry. The loaves fell unheeded to the mossy step. One look at the girl's ashen face and the blood staining her skirt was all Jewel needed. She pulled the sobbing girl inside and got her onto the bed of Jewel's own quarters by the kitchen. Then, her black face grim, she went to call Leanna.

It was hours later when a very sober Georgie Barnes stepped through the doorway into the black woman's quarters. Major Courtland followed hard on his heels, mad as hell at the young trooper, but a little sympathetic too. He glanced questioningly at the doctor as he entered, gesturing the soldier to stand to one side.

"She's fine, Chase. Just a—"

"How dare you bring that man in here?" Leanna rose to her feet, sputtering with fury. "How dare you parade that scum right into my house?"

The trooper flinched guiltily, but the Yankee major turned with a frown, glancing over one shoulder to meet her eyes.

Jewel saw a warning in that dark gaze and reached to pull Leanna's arm hard enough to make her sit. "Hush up, now. Let the man speak."

"Thank you, Jewel. It's nice to deal with a reasonable woman for a change. There seem precious few of them left in this part of the Valley." He turned to look at Hilda. She colored under his gaze and stared at her clasped hands, renewed tears springing to her eyes. It had been a shock seeing Georgie come in and she felt an anger toward him that was mixed with concern. She was not entirely unaware of her own guilt in the matter.

"Trooper Barnes and I have discussed this unhappy situation at some length already," Major Courtland said finally. He turned back to Leanna, frowning and raising one hand to brush some dark hair back under his felt hat. "He's offered to marry the girl, and it's my opinion that might be best."

"*Marry* her?" Leanna jerked to her feet again. "That's rewarding him, Major, not punishing him! If that isn't a typical Yankee trick! Your soldier rapes the poor child and all she gets for compensation is the priceless opportunity to marry the louse so he can do it again!"

"Well, what's your suggestion then? Hang him, maybe? Or call out a firing squad? Would they suit you better?"

"You Yankees are showing your true colors now!

Every filthy story I've ever heard about you is proving true!"

"And what shall we say about Virginian women, Mrs. Leighton? That they play the dirtiest game on earth and then complain when the cards fall against them?"

"Are you implying that this is somehow Hilda's fault?"

"I'm not implying a goddamn thing! I'm saying straight out that I know the whole story and the blame is not entirely one-sided! I warned the girl myself not three days ago."

Flushing with fury, Leanna instinctively glanced at the Union doctor for support.

"Don't look at me, Mrs. Leighton." Doc Lacey shrugged and offered a faint smile. "I volunteered to referee between you two once before—only because you had pie forks that looked to me momentarily dangerous. Neither of you have a weapon now, so rant on at one another. Yell to your hearts' content."

Jewel grunted something suspiciously like agreement and Leanna felt tears stinging her eyes. "I'm only trying to look out for Hilda's best interests!" Her voice broke but she kept her head high. "The rest of you apparently don't care!"

"That isn't true!" Major Courtland protested grimly. "I regret the incident deeply! I did everything I could to prevent its happening in the first place."

"I suppose you think we should feel honored then, Major, that a *Yankee* should offer to marry a Virginian girl merely because he brutally assaulted her." Leanna's voice dripped sarcasm.

"They's gonna start up all over again," Jewel grumbled disgustedly.

Doc Lacey sighed and shrugged. Hilda gave a cautious glance over to where Trooper Barnes stood dejectedly by the doorway, his face as pale as the whitewashed wall behind him.

Hasn't it crossed anybody's mind that Hilda would want to see justice?" Leanna raged.

"Justice!" Jewel interrupted with a glare at Leanna's

56

flushed face. "You talking on and on, you two, 'bout what you wants done! In the name of justice! Ain't nobody goin' to ask the girl what she thinks 'bout all this?"

"Please, everyone, let's try to be as reasonable as we can," Doc Lacey spoke into the pause. "Jewel has a good point. What do you want done, Hilda? You want to see a Yankee hang or would you agree to some less gruesome solution?"

There was a short silence while the girl considered, staring down at her hands. She could feel everyone watching her and she reddened under their stares. "Well," she spoke softly at last with a small shrug, "Doc Lacey told me it only hurts real bad like that the first time. He said after that, it don't no more." There was absolute silence in the room as she considered her alternatives. The way she saw it, having the Yankee hanged wouldn't help. That wouldn't make her a virgin again. Worse, after what had happened, none of the other soldiers would dare come within twenty feet of her. So she'd likely never get married and out of working here and her Pa would give her a whipping for sure. "I guess I'll marry him, then."

"Good. Get over there, Barnes," Major Courtland gestured impatiently, taking a black-bound book out of his frock-coat pocket. "Mrs. Leighton and Doc Lacey can be witnesses." He began reading an abbreviated version of what Leanna guessed was some sort of civil marriage ceremony. It was over in moments, and she got up to leave, stiffly silent as she scribbled her signature on a paper handed to her. Then, without a backward glance, she began to walk on into the kitchen.

"And you, Barnes, will be spending your wedding night walking the drive with your carbine at dress position. In fact, you will be spending every night for a week doing that and every morning you may expect to undergo dress inspection. Is that clear?"

"Yes, sir."

"And after that, I'd better hear only glowing reports

concerning your behavior as a husband. Is that also clear?"

"Yes, sir, that's also clear."

"All right." Leanna could hear the major's angry sigh as he turned to leave. "You're dismissed."

Leanna heard bootsteps a moment later signaling the Federal officer's entrance onto the brick-floored kitchen and she took her stand grimly by the working table. Maybe they thought this confrontation was over, but they'd find out differently.

"—try to get out and find that foraging detail, but it . . ."

"Major Courtland," Leanna interrupted. She stepped forward for them to see her. "I have a few questions."

"They will have to wait for another time, Mrs. Leighton. I have things to do."

"Don't you always, Major? Where were you anyway for the past two hours? While this catastrophe was coming down on our heads?"

"One of our foraging parties isn't back, Mrs. Leighton," Doc Lacey interrupted with a conciliatory tone. "We are naturally concerned about the six men missing."

"I don't care if you've mislaid your whole battalion, gentlemen! They aren't my concern—Blytheswood is! And I doubt very much whether you even have the legal sanction to perform a marriage as you just did! Was that some Yankee trick to pull the wool over our benighted southern eyes?"

"Captains of ships do it. Guides on wagon trains. If it bothers you that much, I'll check with General Sigel's adjutants, Mrs. Leighton. How much does it matter? They think they're married so they'll behave that way. I think what's really bothering you is that the whole thing ended a little too easily. No blood and guts. No Yankees strung from a tree." His eyes flashed grim fire as he turned to face her. "Is that it? Got your bloodlust up and now there's no way to satisfy it?"

"That's a disgusting thing to accuse me of!" Leanna went rigid with fury. "I demand an honorable solution and you—"

"Honorable? God damn it, honorable?"

Despite her fury, Leanna took a half step backward, cowed by the danger she could see suddenly flashing in his eyes.

"What's honorable about this whole damn thing? Is it honorable for a girl to lead on a half-dozen different men looking for a marriage proposal? Honorable for one of those men to finally rape her? What the hell does it matter if the solution's honorable when none of the rest of it is?"

"Naturally, you'll go to any length to excuse your men."

"I'm not excusing anyone or anything! Damn it, don't your ears work right, Mrs. Leighton? I'm sorry it happened. I regret the incident deeply. That doesn't undo it! Hanging the boy wouldn't undo it either! Now whether that satisfies you or not, I've no time to continue this discussion. I've got a half-dozen men out in enemy territory and no idea where, why, or how." He turned on one heel, not bothering to touch his hat this time in farewell. "Now good-bye, damn it!"

He brushed past her so angrily that Leanna flinched, staring after him as he disappeared through the dining room and out into the main hall. The front door slammed a moment later. Only then did she realize she'd been holding her breath and she forced it out in a shaky sigh.

For a moment, she found herself dangerously close to tears, but couldn't begin to find a reason to feel so stricken. She would have been shocked to be told that she cared for Major Courtland's good opinion of her. Doubly shocked to learn how deeply she'd come to depend on him—his air of quiet authority, his distant kindnesses, the order out of chaos he'd brought with him to Blytheswood. The events of the day had shaken her badly. His leaving just now had seemed a desertion of some kind, abandoning her to face it alone.

"You touched a sore point, I'm afraid, Mrs. Leighton."

Leanna started, flushing and turning her head to find Doc Lacey standing almost lazily by the sideboard. "Excuse me? I'm sorry, I didn't hear—?"

"A sore point," he repeated with a shrug. "With the major."

Leanna followed his gesture toward the fading echoes of the slammed front door. She frowned, feeling suddenly weak in the knees. She sat down with a murmured sound of weariness. God, she was exhausted. She felt like something had run over her. Recently.

"Some brandy?"

Leanna shook her head, not reacting to the nonchalance with which he served himself. What a terrible day. Dealing with such atrocious matters. Stewart should have come home. Stewart should be dealing with this, not her.

"Drink this, Mrs. Leighton. Doctor's orders."

She accepted the glass he pressed into her hand numbly, unable to argue anymore. Outside, the last of the sunlight had begun to fail. Long shadows grew in the disordered kitchen. Horses' hooves scattered gravel as the Yankee patrol galloped past to begin their search for the missing men.

"Chase truly does regret the incident deeply, Mrs. Leighton." He pulled out a chair and seated himself at the table with her, pushing a dough-stuck bowl away. "That's why he reacted so angrily to you. That and the detail that's overdue. He's got those men on his mind, too."

Leanna only shrugged and drew a deep breath, sipping her brandy. Its liquid fire burned her throat as she swallowed it, but it felt somehow reassuring—a physical thing easily controlled. In control to the confusion of the day, it was a comfort.

"I couldn't believe Hilda decided to marry him. I just couldn't believe she'd do that. She has no sense of honor at all."

Doc Lacey hid a small smile as he glanced compassionately at Leanna, watching her a moment before answering. Her beautiful face was shadowed in the failing sun, and there was much of the child showing in it just now, vulnerable, chastised, a trifle forlorn. Usually it was formidably strong, coldly arrogant. He smiled gently. "You and Major Courtland are much alike in some ways. If you would both just recognize that fact, you might get along better."

Leanna frowned, beginning to draw back in her chair. Doc Lacey pretended not to notice, continuing in a soft, almost absentminded tone. "This obsession with honor, for example. You both have it. It's what got him so riled at you just now—what got him into the war to begin with. He was in England, visiting his sister and her husband when it started. Did you know that?"

He glanced at Leanna as if expecting an answer. It startled her and she only shook her head, unable to think of anything to say.

"When the news of Fort Sumter arrived, he came home immediately. He thought it over for a few weeks and volunteered for a cavalry assignment. That was in July of 1861. Honor, Mrs. Leighton." He smiled faintly, bitterly. "The war was honorable then. And honorable men enlisted in it. Pity so much of that honorableness is dead now, isn't it? Dead and buried six feet under the cold earth."

Leanna gave him a strange look, wanting to excuse herself but unsure how to do it. She wasn't sure he remembered she was still there. He sounded as if he were thinking out loud, talking to himself, of strange and chilling things.

"To win the war with honor. That was it in the beginning, wasn't it? And then the battles came and men died and honor began to get pushed in the background just a bit. It's hard for a man to choose honor over life, you know. Some of them did, of course. They were usually the first to die. And then honor itself began to get a little harder to define, a little less clear. What was the most honorable way to kill people? What was the most honorable thing for a commander to do—honor his responsibility to his own troops' survival or honor some archaic rules of chivalric war? Are the enemy due honorable treatment or are they mad dogs to be shot at any opportunity? You can see how it happened, Mrs. Leighton. An age-old question actually. If the final end is honorable, does that justify less than honorable ways of achieving that end?" He frowned for a moment thoughtfully and then suddenly turned his head to look at Leanna. "What do you think, Mrs. Leighton? How would you answer that question?"

Leanna was taken aback. "Well, why, I—"

"You'll have to answer that question sometime during this war, you know. We all will before it's done."

Leanna spread her hands in an uneasy gesture, silent.

"Honor isn't important to me."

That flat statement startled her into staring at him. She'd have thought him the last of all the men in the Yankee battalion to say such a thing.

"That shocks you, doesn't it?" He smiled faintly, meeting her eyes briefly. "Because you like me. Oh, don't deny it, Mrs. Leighton, I know you do. We doctors achieve a sort of perspective on people. Maybe because we see so much of people's private selves, their personal hells—we learn to step a little farther back and from there we can see things clearer than the people directly involved. I know you like me and I like you as well. That's why I'm saying these things. I want you to understand. Honor doesn't mean a damn thing to me. Life does. I'd take the sneakiest, most awful solution available if it could end this monstrous war, end the killing and the maiming. Never think twice."

Leanna frowned, wary of such a statement. It sounded far too simplistic to be true. "I can't believe you mean that, Doctor. I can't believe you or any other decent man could so totally disregard honor."

Doc Lacey startled her again by laughing softly as he shrugged. "Inconceivable I should not care about honor."

"Yes," she agreed. "To me."

"Oh, you are like Chase, Mrs. Leighton. My sympathies to both of you."

She frowned, puzzled.

"Honor is a terrible cross to bear, dear. Look at Chase out there right now—leading a patrol for those missing men of his. He's tired as hell, but for some crazy sense of honor, he thinks he's got to lead the

62

patrol himself. He's upset over this—incident—because one of his men did a dishonorable thing. And by now, he's mad at himself for yelling at you, because that's not an honorable way to treat a lady like yourself. All for honor. And liable to get himself killed out there to boot."

Doc Lacey frowned suddenly, staring down into the single remaining swallow of his brandy. "Though I sometimes begin to wonder if that isn't what he's looking for by now; an honorable way out." He shook his head as if at the thought he'd spoken so softly aloud, obviously to himself. He rose to his feet suddenly, draining the last of the brandy, then looking down to catch and hold Leanna's eyes, smiling faintly as he reached for his hat to leave. "Think about it, Mrs. Leighton. What I said. Start working on an answer. In case you haven't noticed, the war has come to Blytheswood."

Chapter Four

As if fate had overheard Doc Lacey's warning to her, Rosie Jenkins slipped two letters into Leanna's hand only a day later. She didn't look at them right away—Yankees were nearby, and she was busy picking the last of the year's herbs and tying them in small bundles, tacking them upside down to the kitchen beams to dry and keep for winter seasonings. The autumn had been long and mild, but it was past mid-November now. The bitter edge to the night's cold heralded the coming of winter. The women of Blytheswood worked long days in preparation—putting up the last of the year's fruits from the orchard, giving the house a last thorough cleaning, airing linens and curtains and beating rugs that would not be aired again until spring broke in March. The Yankees were equally busy. They refit barn and shed doors against winter's wind blasts, repaired chinks of mortar from between chestnut timber walls, laid up a veritable mountain of firewood, cut and stored the last high meadow grass for winter hay, and doubled the number of hunting parties to lay up game. Blytheswood's domestic stock alone could not support the two hundred plus men who would winter there.

It was late afternoon before Leanna retired to her rooms alone. There she took the letters from their hiding place in her skirt pocket. One was from Stewart. She recognized his handwriting instantly. But the other . . . she frowned at it, curious enough to open it first.

Major John Singleton Mosby. She stared aghast at the signature of the short note. Rosie Jenkins had taken a risk forwarding this one. There was bad blood between the guerilla band and the Yankee cavalry. Plus, the threat of Mosby's daring rangers at the Yankee backs—on the other side of the Blue Ridge Mountains, but near enough to strike at the northern end of the Valley—through Ashby's or Manassas Gap. A well-timed strike by Mosby's men could cut the battalion at Blytheswood off from the troops stationed at Winchester, and from the home base, too, of Harper's Ferry, where she knew the main portion of a Yankee army was wintering. Not cut them off for long, maybe. Not with tens of thousands of troops between Winchester and Harper's Ferry. But it would shake Yankee command to lose this battalion at Blytheswood. It was their southern-most outpost in the Valley, their skirmish line to test the waters for a more aggressive move southward come spring. Maybe it would shake them enough to pull their troops from the Valley altogether, figuring the Valley was still too diligently held by the Confederates to make such an invasion reasonable.

All those possibilities occurred to her as she hastily unfolded the note and read it. She read it once, then carefully reread it a second time. Then she rose to feed it to the flame of the oil lamp on her bedstand, and her hands trembled as she lit a match to the cotton wick. Major Mosby wanted her help. A map of the Yankee's military objectives in the Valley for one thing. Plus—more importantly—the Yankee code book. Good God, she found herself thinking. The map would probably be possible. She herself could practically draw one out of common sense. But the code book! To translate the coded telegraph messages sent from the battalion here near Front Royal back to Winchester and Harper's Ferry, the code book never yet gotten hold of by any Con-federate, anywhere; the answer to a puzzle the CSA could not seem to crack! Only one person here could have such a desperately concealed document, Leanna realized with a sinking feeling. Only one person. Major Chase Courtland. And of all the men sent here to spend the winter, watching and riding and on their guard, he was the last person she would have chosen to play such a dangerous game with. God alone only knew what he'd do if he caught her. She could refuse to risk it, of course. Lie, and say she'd tried and failed. But her husband was willing to risk his life—her brother, too. Could she in all conscience do less than they did? The answer was 'no' and it came swiftly, but she found no joy in the prospect of what lay ahead of her because of it.

Lieutenant Colonel Stewart Leighton raised one hand to his horse's neck, apprehensive lest a low whinny gave an untimely alarm. It was Thursday, November 26th. The first national Thanksgiving Day holiday. The Yankees were clustered unconcerned by their campfires, enjoying the day's superior rations. He and his own troopers had dined on four ounces each of fat bacon, a half-cup of corn mush, and a handful of parched rye that took the place of coffee. The officers had shared a half-dozen apples contributed by a local woman. But they would dine better yet before the day was out, he told himself grimly. The Yankee supply wagons were crammed full of salt beef and pork barrels and weevily hard-tack. Disdained by Federal troops. A treasure for the starving CSA.

"When?" Major Jonathon Penley rode quietly to his elbow and whispered.

Stewart glanced sideways at Penley's face, shadowed in the starlight of a cloudless, bitter cold night. A small puff of vapor marked his voice more than sound. Stewart managed a faint smile and a thumbs-up sign of encouragement, thinking of Leanna as he always did when seeing Jonathon's clean cut, darkly handsome features—the similarity in the expressions, those same startling violet colored eyes. There was a sudden ache in his loins for her. He hadn't been home since . . . when was it? Last spring sometime. A lifetime ago, at least. "A few more minutes." He smiled bitterly as he added. "Let them get our dinner cooked for us first."

Jonathon didn't smile. He frowned instead and shrugged. Stewart noticed, but said nothing. Jonathon didn't like this kind of warfare. Well, hell. Who did? Sneaking in the woods like common thieves. Surprise almost the only weapon left to the nearly prostrate South. And there sat the damned Yanks—well-clothed, well-armed. Men, horses, ammunition all to spare. Why shouldn't they share generously with their Rebel brothers? Didn't they keep insisting the whole point of the war was that they were all still *one* country? *One* people? Whether the Southerners liked it or not?

Stewart raised his hand slowly, holding it high so all the men could see it. He kept it there a moment, feeling the strange mixture of dread and excitement that always came before a fight. His heart beat faster. His breath came shorter. His body fairly quivered with energy ready to explode. He smiled suddenly and dropped his hand, swinging down low over the horse's neck as they plunged forward under low-hung tree boughs. The first crack of a revolver sounded and he drew his own Le Mat, aiming at a Yankee's head not sixteen feet away from him. Chaos exploded in the Yankee camp and Stewart joined his men in screaming the wild Rebel yell, drawing his saber as his Le Mat ran out of bullets, ducking as a Yankee fired a desperate round at the charging Confederates. The fight was over, he sensed intuitively. And victory was sweet. Only the mopping-up action remained.

It was over in minutes. Yankees on foot went crashing through underbrush. Confederate cavalry rode on to capture the abandoned wagon train. Haste was imperative. Stewart only had a single battalion with him—and soon Yankee soldiers would recover from their shock and come storming back. He led the wagons southeast through the woods at a reckless gait, and they were safely back inside Confederate lines before an hour had fully passed. Stewart grinned a weary triumph to General Stuart's staff before halting his lathered horse and swinging down. "We got them. Happy Thanksgiving, General."

"Colonel Leighton?" Captain Bryant appeared suddenly at Stewart's side, saluting as he interrupted. "Captain Carlson just asked after Major Penley. Have you seen him, sir? He isn't with his men."

Coldness gripped the pit of Stewart's belly. His grin

faded as he turned around, startled. "Penley? No, not since before we started in anyway. He's not with the wagons either?"

Bryant shook his blond head grimly. "Captain Carlson said he checked there already."

Stewart looked anxiously over one shoulder in the direction they'd come from. It was too late now anyway, if Jonathon had fallen there in the Yankee camp. "Ask around, Captain. See if any of the men saw anything." He had to do that at least for Leanna. She would want to know.

"Lost your major, Colonel?" Jeb Stuart clapped the famous long plumed hat on his head as he ducked under a tent flap, then stood and straightened, looking at the long line of wagons with obvious approval. "That's a shame. Still, not a bad price to pay for these supplies. I hope to hell there's some ammunition in one of them. We're awfully low."

Stewart nodded, walking up to stand with his commander. The comment didn't seem callous to him. He'd been in this long enough to know lives lost were simply one side of a mathematical equation of war. It might as easily have been *his* absence Jonathon Penley worried about.

"No sign of the major, sir," Captain Bryant reined in his horse and leaned down to speak. "One of the men said they thought they saw him get hit as we were coming in, but in the confusion . . ." His voice trailed off. The young captain shrugged, his mouth grim. It wasn't good news. Why the hell, if someone saw him hit, hadn't they made an effort to grab for him? To get him back to his own lines? He would have if he had seen it.

"Fine, Captain." Stewart accepted the information calmly. He had expected it as soon as he'd had to ask. Damn. It was a damn shame. Penley was one hell of a good officer. One the CSA could ill afford to have lost. Damn those Yankees. "Thanks, Captain. Better go see to those rations' distribution now. The men are getting hungry." Stewart spared a single last glance toward the

Yankee camps to the northwest and stood a moment after his general turned to gesture him inside the head-quarters tent. Damn, he thought again with a deep sigh. Leanna was going to be devastated.

Leanna opened her eyes and rolled over restlessly in the darkness. Thanksgiving night, November 26th, and nearly a week since she had received Mosby's urgent plea for aid. And she had nothing so far to show for the passing of those days. Any qualms she'd originally had about playing spy had been quelled by Stewart's last letter. Confederate soldiers were getting paid eleven dollars a month. But in Richmond, flour was two hundred dollars a barrel, coffee eighteen dollars a pound, butter four d llars a pound, eggs three dollars a dozen, bacon eight dollars a pound; clothing, fresh meat, pins, paper, and sugar nearly unobtainable. President Jefferson Davis's wife was passing out recipes for rat meat. The Federal blockade had tightened along the coast. Vicksburg had followed New Orleans's fall this summer, and the Yankees held the whole Mississippi River now. Overtaxed rail lines were breaking down. Inadequate ironworks could not manufacture ammunitions and loco-motives both. Even the promise of bumper harvests in the Valley and the lower South wouldn't help if there was no way to get those supplies up North where Richmond and the Army of Northern Virginia were starving. The CSA was in trouble. It needed a dramatic turnaround.

It wasn't that she hadn't tried. But, no sooner had Major Courtland returned with his lost detail than he had set out again, leading half the battalion across the river along the Manassas Gap Railroad lines to Front Royal, and then a long, sweeping look at the country around it. They hadn't returned until this evening—interrupting a Thanksgiving Day feast Jewel had worked all day long on. Irritated by that, and even more, Leanna admitted candidly to herself, by Jewel's exhuberant plea-sure to see the Yankee major there to enjoy the fine meal, she had lost her temper and said several spiteful things. Hostility had flared once more down the length of the gleaming mahogany table. And she was not an inch closer to getting the information Mosby wanted so desperately. If anything, she was probably farther. Major Courtland had looked grim indeed by the end of the tense meal. Even Doc Lacey had caught her eye, raising a brow in gentle remonstrance after a particularly nasty exchange. And he was usually careful to avoid taking sides.

A sound from down the hall drew her attention and she sat up slowly in bed, cocking her head to hear better. Major Courtland? Still up at this late hour? It had to be. Everyone else in the house was long asleep. She heard the carpet-muffled step of boots and then the soft click of the library door just down the hall. It was a combination sitting room and upstairs retreat, actually. Her father had used it in years past as his office. It was a comfortable room that Leanna remembered well from childhood—a masculine room, wood paneled, with a large, leather-covered sofa and a well-used, massive oak table marked by men's boot heels and the ash of burning cigars.

For only a minute, she hesitated, debating the wisdom of what she contemplated. Then she rose quickly from her bed to draw on a dressing gown and a soft-soled pair of slippers. Dressed like this, she could pretend she didn't know he was there. Simply walk into the room as if indulging the whim of a restless night. It was improper, of course, but that might be the very thing to prove her story. Apologize for her behavior this month past, and offer . . . what? Her future cordiality in return for his code book? Hardly. What then? Perhaps a comment, all in innocence, that she might make amends for previous unpleasantness by drawing him a map of the nearby Valley for his patrols. That might work better. It ought, at least, to help her find out if he already had one—maybe even where it was kept, or who had it.

The door was open. Soft moonlight illuminated the small room from the central window, and Leanna paused a moment, wondering at the lack of a light inside. Finally, she caught the pale golden glow of a lamp trimmed down nearly to extinction. Major Courtland sat silently on the dark leather sofa beside it, his boots resting heel down on the table, his head back and one hand pressed wearily to his eyes. Leanna stood a moment in awkward stillness, suddenly hating to intrude. Obviously, he had not heard her approach. He was either asleep or deep in thought. The soft light of the oil lamp barely touched his face, but Leanna could see weariness etched deeply upon it. He looked surprisingly human as he sat there . . . and dangerously handsome. Soft light showed the fine, patrician cut of high cheek bones, a straight nose, the square lines of a strong jaw. Thick waves of dark brown hair softened what could have been an over-harsh face. That and a surprisingly gentle looking mouth, usually hard and grimly drawn, but now relaxed, and only parted slightly in thought or sleep. It occurred to her almost as a shock that he was a Yankee, yes, but he was also, very undeniably, a man. And they were very much alone, and the rest of the house was sleeping. Damn Mosby, she thought suddenly. It was dark and she was half undressed. Let him get his own codebook!

She reached to gather her long skirt to return to her room, and then she saw it. A book of some kind, black-bound, lying open on his lap. She felt a surge of nearly physical desire. If he were asleep and she could somehow get to it without waking him—

"Oh, Mrs. Leighton."

She had taken only a half-dozen steps before he dropped his hand from his eyes and looked around. Leanna felt her heart drop and she fought to keep disappointment from showing on her face. "Oh, Major Courtland." She was careful to feign startlement, drawing to an immediate stop. "I'm sorry to intrude. I didn't know you were here."

"No problem. I'm sorry I startled you." He managed a brief, apologetic smile, beginning to rise to his feet, taking up the book in one hand and closing it as he moved. Even that single swift glance in the near darkness had sufficed to show she was dressed for bed, her hair undone, her slender body draped by a high-necked, flannel gown that somehow managed to show the youthful curves of her figure better than the hooped skirts and laced waists of her daytime attire. He had felt an instinctive warming in his belly and was careful not to look again too closely as he spoke.

Leanna thought only of the book, watching it as he laid it down on the table before him. No title. No words at all on its black leather crown. Only 'U.S.' stamped in gilt. No ordinary volume from the library shelf then. What the CSA could do with that. She gestured casually toward it and managed a smile. "Not much light for reading by, Major."

"I'm not reading so much as thinking." He returned her smile with a shrug, but his expression was not unkind. "I think better in the dark, I guess."

She took a few steps toward the table, stopping at the far end of the long sofa. Leanna dared one glance more at the book, fighting an urge to lunge and snatch at it. Instead, she stood motionless while her brain moved. The major simply stood silently, watching her. Obviously, he was waiting for her either to excuse herself or to speak again. She spoke before the silence could become too obviously awkward, not daring another look at the book lying just out of reach. "I—as long as I've run into you here, Major, let me take advantage of the opportunity to apologize for my behavior earlier, at dinner. I certainly hope you will forgive me."

"No apology necessary, Mrs. Leighton. My own behavior was far from exemplary in return." He cocked his head in the near darkness, hesitating before he continued. "Actually, I spent some time this past week thinking of the way I spoke to you that night of . . . well, the unfortunate incident regarding your girl."

"Hilda."

"Yes Hilda." Her eyes touched his momentarily and he quickly turned away. "I had made up my mind most resolutely I wouldn't let that happen again, argue with you that way. Yet, tonight at dinner, I caught myself several times doing just that." He paused again and Leanna heard the sound of a soft sigh. "How is the girl, by the way? Adjusting to married life all right?"

Leanna flushed at his question, tensing in remembered anger. Hilda's smug insolence, informing her that, as a married woman, she would no longer be working as anyone's 'step and fetch it' servant. "She quit, actually, the next day."

He lifted one dark brow in surprise, his gaze sharpening at the expression on Leanna's face. "Mmm. Well, I guess Barnes will be well punished anyway then for what he did. Imagine being tied to that for the rest of your life."

Despite her anger, Leanna felt a small vengeful smile touch her mouth. "Personally, I hope after the war, he'll take her to Minnesota or some such place to live, where she'll be buried up to her neck in snow every winter."

His dark eyes gleamed, a wider smile curved his mouth. "Barnes, I believe, is actually from New Hampshire. And from what I've heard of their climate, you might very well get your wish."

Leanna laughed softly, forgetting Mosby long enough to allow her eyes to briefly catch his in shared satisfaction. It startled her how good it felt—that sense of partnership with a man. Even a Yankee. But the silence began again as amusement faded and Leanna took another single step longingly toward the book. She couldn't just walk up and take the thing with him standing there. He'd never let her do that if it was what she hoped it was.

"Mrs. Leighton, can I make an observation without offending you? This is the first conversation we've had where we weren't at one another's throats by now. I, for one, find this far more pleasant." He offered a tentative smile, a gesture of conciliation. "Shall we make a midnight pact to try to end our quarreling?"

Leanna glanced at him sharply, startled. It would be to her advantage, she realized instantly. It would make it far easier to get information. Wasn't that how Belle

73

Boyd had done it so successfully last year in Front Royal? "Well, Major . . ." she stalled for a moment, thinking quickly. If she agreed too readily after the hostilities that had lain between them. . . .

"A simple truce. You watch your temper and I'll watch mine. It can only be to both our benefits."

"Well, I must admit you Yankees have behaved better than I first thought you would." That much was true. "Blytheswood isn't suffering under your hand as I originally feared."

"Nor have you poisoned our pudding."

A reluctant smile touched Leanna's mouth and she nodded. His sense of humor surprised her and she found herself thinking how those rare smiles softened the grim strength of his face. She allowed another smile and nodded once more. "Done, Major. A truce." Too late she realized she'd effectively terminated the discussion that excused her staying. Major Courtland had begun to turn back to his seat. "I'm surprised to find you up so late, Major. I thought after your patrol you would be tired tonight."

"There were things to be done."

"Oh? Something I could help with?"

A smile flickered across his mouth, his eyes gleamed wry amusement as he shook his head. "Military matters, I'm afraid."

"Oh." Leanna feigned careless acceptance. The map? The code? What the devil was in that book lying by his right knee? "I wondered while you were gone, Major, how you found your way on your patrols. How do you know where you're going? Surely, you can't stop and ask the locals for directions." She played coquettishly with the lace of the dressing gown's sleeve, not daring to meet his eyes. She felt a sudden intensity in his gaze, a sense of quick wariness. Then he shrugged.

"We manage."

Damn, she thought angrily, that told her nothing. Have you a map, Major? If so, where do you keep it? May I have a copy please? He was silent. Standing by the sofa, his dark eyes were studying her curiously by

74

now. She knew he must be wondering why she didn't leave. There was only one more chance. And she knew well what she was risking to even try it.

"When I was a child, I used to come into this room often. My father used it. And sometimes when he was tired, I'd stand behind him on the sofa and rub his neck. He said it made him feel better." She gave him an innocent, disarming smile that would have made proud the best actress. "Sit down, Major, and I'll do the same for you. As a gesture of our new truce."

He hesitated a long minute and Leanna felt her heart beating faster while she walked to her place at the sofa's back. He was going to refuse. He was going to ask her what in the world she thought she was doing. She found her place and patted coaxingly on the pillow, managing another of those artless smiles. He stood another moment, half frowning, a tall, black shape against the silver gray of the window behind him. Finally, he shrugged as if at a question he'd asked himself, and obeyed her gesture, drawing his long legs up again to rest on the table, one boot heel dead center atop the book. Leanna released one thankful prayer and made a new one. It used to put her father to sleep when she did this. Pray God the Yankee would do the same. God knew he had to be exhausted, riding all day, up half the night already.

"That's good, Major. Just relax." She lifted one hand from the wood frame roseate of the Victorian sofa, dropping it to lie on one broad shoulder. The warmth of him surprised her—that and the shock of touching him at all. She tried to ignore it, rambling on in a soft voice of childhood memories . . . her father, her brother, herself . . . what little she could remember of her mother. It had to bore him. If she'd dared, she'd have sung him a lullaby. Her fingers began to cramp and she ignored that, too, encouraged to feel some of the tension of the sinewy muscles beneath her hands begin to relax. He'd closed his eyes as well, leaning his dark head back against the edge. The softly curling edges of his hair tickled her hands as she worked. The stiff, stand up

75

collar of his blue uniform was hard to press through, but the cloth was finely woven, she noted, as her fingers moved over it. No standard issue jacket—even for the Yankees with all their luxuries. Like Stewart then, or Jonathon, Yankee officers of substantial private means must get their uniforms done by their civilian tailors. One dandy in Jonathon's VMI class had had his imported from Paris, back when French ships were still entering Southern ports frequently.

She frowned suddenly, realizing she'd stopped talking. Now she was afraid to begin again lest she startle him. The absolute stillness of the sleeping house seemed suddenly overwhelming, the feel of a man's muscled shoulders beneath her hands awkwardly intimate. He wore no padding to broaden his shoulders, she noted, blushing faintly at the thought. And the power of his body seemed both frightening and compelling to her. But her fingers had begun to ache badly. Go to sleep, she commanded silently. Damn you, Yankee, go to sleep.

"Mrs. Leighton, what is the point of this?" He spoke without moving, only opened his eyes with a half frown as Leanna froze behind him. "I've been sitting here trying to figure it out, and I can't. What do you want from me?"

She snatched her hands from his shoulders and whirled on one heel, not feigning the anger that sparked in her eyes.

"Wait, Mrs. Leighton, I didn't mean to—"

He'd rounded the end of the sofa quickly enough to bar her retreat and Leanna glared up at him as she tried to push by. "Get out of my way! You may insult me some other time."

"I meant no insult."

"Get out of my way!"

"Not until you tell me where this sudden urgent friendship comes from."

He moved a step to keep between Leanna and the door, raising one hand to grip her arm. "You want to go visiting friends somewhere in the Valley? You want to have someone here? You want a new barn or an old one whitewashed? Pins? Cloth? Sugar? Just tell me what."

"I don't want anything from you!" She hissed it in genuine fury, all the more furious because she knew, even in the midst of her anger, that she dared not reveal what she'd really been after. And the things he suggested were demeaning in their triviality.

"I didn't mean I would be adverse to granting any of those requests I named, Mrs. Leighton," he continued firmly. "Only that I'm no mind reader. I don't know what you want unless you ask. I kept waiting for you to do that, but finally I thought I'd save us both time and energy to simply ask."

Leanna stared up at him in sudden deep shock. Her fury faded and her body began to tremble in its passing. He had not been malicious then. He had not meant to taunt her. There was a strange gentleness in his dark gaze that conveyed that more clearly than words.

"Don't you think I realize how hard it is, what you're doing here? Trying to run this place by yourself, trying to deal with a whole battalion of enemy soldiers that have suddenly appeared all around you? My first duty is to my men and my cause, but you're a woman, not a soldier, and I'll help if I can ."

She trembled harder, seeing his face through the blur of tears that began to mist her eyes. God, how good that sounded—some help. She was tired of trying so hard, tired of being so strong, knowing she could not, *dared* not, admit the slightest weakness to herself for fear she'd stop right there, fall down in her tracks and never have the courage to get back up. Overseeing all the myriad facets of Blytheswood—making sure the fields yielded grain and stock for the army, the looms yielded cloth, the carcasses leather, and the bake-oven bread— now playing spy for Mosby. What else could anyone ask of her? What more could she give?

She jerked away from his grip with a wracking sob, trying to run for the door. Somehow he stepped in front of her again and his arms closed around her, holding her while tears washed her face and choked the breath in her throat. Helplessly, she pressed her face against the hollow of his shoulder, her black hair tangling over the brass buttons that lined his chest, sobbing and choking and utterly unable to move. This was what she needed so desperately—the strength of a man to aid her. Southern women were raised to depend on men—their fathers, their brothers, their husbands. Then they had all abandoned them, riding off to war. And she, who had been pampered and shielded from birth, was left behind desperately trying to find the strength in herself to do what she'd never considered doing before—living without them.

Chase held her while she shook and sobbed in near hysterics, finally lifting one hand to disentangle strands of her hair from the buttons they caught in, bending his head to murmur comfort against her ear. At last, her tears subsided and he stroked wet wisps of hair back from her ashen face. Her body pressed to his was covered only with a light bed gown, a dressing robe over that, and he could feel her trembling from head to foot. The soft, feminine scent of lavender drifted up from her hair, her slender body was warm and soft against his. Moonlight shadowed her face, but even the darkness could not hide Leanna's loveliness. He lifted one sun-bronzed hand to her cheek to wipe it dry and she raised her head at the touch, her beautiful, violet eyes meeting his. For an instant, he stood motionless, then slowly lowered his mouth to hers. Warmth and softness and the wet taste of salt met his lips. He felt her shudder slightly in his arms as he drew her closer against him, his mouth taking hers in a sudden, blinding burst of hunger.

The world ceased to exist for that moment. Leanna clung helplessly to his greater strength, feeling his arms tighten to hold her, responding to him with a sudden deep longing. Her breasts throbbed against the hardness of his chest, her hips accepted the pressure of his. His mouth over hers was gentle one moment, demanding the next, and she yielded helplessly, parting her lips for his deeper possession, her senses exploding in breathless

78

ecstasy as he took what she offered, her soft lips crushed joyfully beneath the all-consuming passion of that kiss. She felt his hand on her breast, cupping its soft fullness in his palm, his fingers tightening to search for the nipple, feeling it rising even as he found it, caressing its taut peak through the thin layers of her nightclothes. Pleasure akin to pain exploded at that touch, shivering down into the pit of her belly, the depth of her loins, and she moaned, nearly senseless in his arms. Never at Stewart's touch had her body reacted like this, never had her husband awakened this ungovernable, bursting, wanton craving.

"No!" She gasped her denial with her last remaining shred of control. Stewart. Her husband. She must stop. Chase's arms loosened slightly at her cry and she tore away from him in a single, breathless lunge for the door. She heard him start after her, felt the touch on her arm of his outstretched hand and fled from it, stumbling blindly down the hall to her room. She half ran, half fell into its darkness and slammed the door behind her, leaning back and covering her face with her hands. Boot steps sounded outside, walking slowly. They came part way to her door, then stopped, silent a minute, then started again in the opposite direction. She shook her head at a deep desire to follow them, to offer all of what Chase Courtland had only begun to possess of her. And though she forced herself to deny that wish, her body flared at its mere thought, aching, throbbing, and demanding in ways she'd never known before. Stewart. She made herself think his name, forced it over and over until its echoes began to cool her inflamed senses. He stood there watching her from the photograph near her bed—a silent accusation in his eyes. She moved toward it, trying to meet that tintype gaze with her own, trying to excuse herself for what had happened just now. She was lonely. She was tired. It was the weakness of a single moment. It was the book she had wanted—the one Mosby had told her to get. But through it all with soft insistence spoke another voice. You are falling in love with him, it whispered to her. Falling in love with that Yankee . . . no matter how angry he sometimes makes you, no matter how deeply you hate the uniform he wears, there is a man beneath it and you are falling in love with him. And nothing she could think of to say in rebuttal served to stop that soft, insistent whisper.

Chapter Five

Jonathon Penley had never known such pain. It seethed in his stomach, spread fire through his limbs. The Yankees were moving their lines back from along Mine Run, farther away from Chancellorsville and Robert E. Lee's still dangerous Army of Northern Virginia. The ambulance wagon bounced in mud-rutted roads, its springs old and stiff with December cold. Whitney's gentle face flashed into his mind, her agony as he'd stood beside her while she'd given birth to their little daughter, Miranda. He'd been sweating, almost sharing the pain he saw on her face. He wanted Whitney with him desperately now. He wanted her holding him while he died.

"Major Penley?" An impersonal voice intruded on his thoughts and his efforts to keep sane despite this tearing fire in his gut. Someone crouched over him in the wagon. "Swallow this."

Something liquid and faintly sweet dribbled into his mouth. He swallowed to keep from choking, and found it left a bitter taste on his tongue. The wagon's front wheel bit deep in a soft spot and shook violently pulling free. The agony exploded through his body in redoubled intensity, and he lost consciousness to it and laudanum together.

At one edge of the bench where the Federal assistant surgeon rode with these most critically wounded, an orderly belched and scratched at the lice in his beard. "Stubborn, them Rebs. That one should have been dead days ago."

The doctor only shrugged, not bothering any longer to preach compassion for the wounded, Blue or Gray. It had been too long a war for that. "Well don't give up, Wolmer. We've a long ride yet to Culpepper."

The orderly grunted and shoved an unconscious man's mangled leg aside to stretch his muddy boots out. It stunk in here, he thought disgustedly. The wagon jolted again, shaking sideways before settling down, and the groans of the conscious men rose like a Banshee's wail. But on the other hand, he told himself, it beat hell out of walking the whole bloody way with the infantry. By nightfall, some of 'em would be dead anyhow. There would be more room in the wagon tomorrow.

"This is very beautiful country."

He startled Leanna as she was standing still for a moment's rest, staring wistfully off at the mountain across the river. It was a gorgeous day, the first of December, a gift of a generous God. A day to be out and enjoying that beauty—not beating a dusty rug. She recovered herself to stammer a reply, careful to avoid his eyes. "Yes, but there seems always so much to do, these days . . ."

"I was thinking of playing truant this afternoon, myself." He smiled faintly and stepped closer, reaching for the wicker rug beater in her hand.

She watched him warily as he slapped at the rug draped over the low bough, noting the play of powerful muscles beneath the dark-blue broadcloth uniform, remembering the feel of them beneath her hands with uneasy acuteness. There was something in him that pulled at her. And something about the power of that pull that frightened her.

"You've been avoiding me, Mrs. Leighton."

She blushed darkly; her throat began to feel dry.

"I thought we'd agreed on a truce the other night," he continued evenly, watching the rug instead of Leanna's face. "I hope you haven't changed your mind."

She said nothing, only watched the dust flying from the deep burgundy pile of the Oriental rug as he whacked it.

"I considered apologizing to you for what happened

that night." He spoke in a low voice, barely audible even to Leanna only a few feet away. "But I decided it would be hyprocritical of me. I'd do it again if I had the chance."

"Please, Major, I can't listen to such things. I'm a married—" Leanna began to turn shakily, raising her long skirts in one hand.

"I know you're married." He turned after her, reaching to grasp her arm. "As much as I'm beginning to regret that."

Startled, Leanna glanced at him. His eyes were dark meeting hers, unexpectedly serious. She felt an odd breathlessness and forced her eyes away. "And I thought I recalled something about your having a fiancée, Major." She glanced back to him for his reaction, startled to see only a faint frown touch his face, a flash of some sort of puzzled irritation flicker in his eyes.

"Oh, yes, my fiancée . . ."

She half frowned, waiting. But he offered no further explanation.

"What I came over here for anyway, Mrs. Leighton, was not to make you this much more uncomfortable with me. Nor to beat your rugs for you." He half turned and reached out to give her the stick. "I was thinking of going riding today—a pleasure ride. And it occurred to me you might enjoy one also. I'd like your company. And I could use a guide."

Leanna shook her head. "I'm afraid that's impossible, Major. It would be most improper."

"I'll have some of my men accompany us."

Leanna glanced again at him. How darkly handsome he was. How surprisingly gentle the eyes in that strong face. How dangerous it might be to agree. But could it do any real harm? They would be chaperoned well enough, she needn't risk a repeat of what had flared once before between them. "All right, Major." She prayed she was not merely making excuses to justify a sudden, yearning impulse to go. She loved the woods this time of year. She hoped it was only that. "All right, Major, I'll trust you."

He nodded as he turned, then glanced over one shoulder to call back to her. His eyes touched hers and dark fires were burning there. "Don't trust me too far, Mrs. Leighton," he said with a smile of wry amusement. "That's the last warning I intend to give you."

Leanna blinked, beginning to frown. Then she thought of Mosby and what she planned to do to aid him. She shrugged, returning his warning with a cryptic one of her own. "Yes, I quite understand. All's fair, we'll say then, Major—in love, or war."

He had chosen well for a way to try to disarm her enmity, Leanna admitted to herself. Peace and serenity had always been here in the mountain woodlands. It was here still, untouched by the war that raged elsewhere in the Valley. As Leanna led the way through huge and silent bare-boughed groves, she found it hard to remember it was an enemy who rode beside her. Great gray granite fists of rock thrust up through the leaf-covered forest floor. Here and there, their surface was silvered by water seeping from between black cracks. In the spring, wild violets would grow there. The forest and meadows would be sprinkled with rose azalea, redbud, lavender, wisteria, jack-in-the-pulpit, lady slipper orchids, trilliums, wild bloodroot, gold marsh marigolds, blue iris, yellow trout lily—later mountain laurel and dogwoods and rhododendron. God's hand had dealt lavishly with this land. The Indians had saluted this when they'd named it Shenandoah, Daughter of the Stars.

The growl of a wild mountain cat sounded once in the distance and Major Courtland had reined his horse closer to hers, drawing his carbine. Later they'd glimpsed a black bear ambling through the meadows, in search of a last meal before winter's long sleep. Deer abounded. Elk were more rare, but they saw tracks of one by a small, crystal-clear stream lined by spongy low banks. They rode in lazy inattention to direction, slowly working their way up the mountain's northern ridge. Finally, they rode out of the cover of great boughed branches, out onto a huge granite promontory that guarded the river. Blytheswood's distant buildings lay below and beyond where they stood.

Leanna drew rein and looked down at the small plantation. It had been a long time since she had been here. Living on top of it she hadn't realized. But from this distance, she could see that Blytheswood looked better than it had since the war had begun. Fences were straight and even again, the roofs all repaired; tree lines edging pasture and field were cut back and contained. Major Courtland reined in beside her, following her gaze before turning toward her.

"Blytheswood looks fine, Major," Leanna spoke softly. "I hadn't realized how busy you must have been."

Leanna turned her head finally and realized that all the while she'd been looking at Blytheswood, he had been looking at her. She blushed faintly, uneasy at the sudden hammering of her heart. He was strikingly handsome sitting there so casually astride his restive horse, dark hair blowing in the gentle breeze—handsome and powerful and very male. His knee brushed hers as her mare sidestepped a cloud's shadow, and a shiver trembled up her body at the contact. It was a startling feeling suddenly—as if only he and she existed at this moment in time. Only he and she, resting atop the world, looking down on the land they held together. Uneasy. Exciting. A frighteningly intimate sensation. His eyes still held hers in a magnetic, compelling gaze, and she felt a sweet softness spreading inside her, a wish blooming as slowly as a flower, that she might shed her separateness and be one with him. They could hold Blytheswood together. He was what the land had needed. Blytheswood and she, both.

" 'Scuse me, Major. Jewel packed a supper if you care to share some with us."

The trooper startled her. Leanna felt the spell break— the outside world reclaimed her instantly. She dared a single quick glance at him and saw a frown gather and pass in the space of a single breath. Had he been caught in its power, too?

"Some supper?"

His deep voice betrayed nothing and Leanna studied him another second before she nodded. If it had, he was showing no sign of it. Still, she busied herself deliberately with napkins and dishes. And reminded herself more firmly than ever that given who she was and given who he was, there was no possible future for them together. Even disregarding the fact of her marriage to another man, Confederates and Yankees stood on opposite sides of a terrible line. Far from being the man to hold Blytheswood with her, he was the one man who could take it away.

They'd dawdled riding up. Now, going home, they hurried the horses as dusk shadows lengthened in the woods. The December air grew cold without sunshine to warm it, and Leanna shivered crossing the railroad tracks, shivered harder splashing down into the icy Shenandoah River. Blytheswood's main house was a dim white blur through the bare poplars that crowded the low bank, and Leanna rode silently. How could it be that she found herself liking so many of these men who wore such a hated uniform? Doc Lacey for one. Whitney's Captain Grier. Major Courtland himself. And yet, she could continue to plot their ruin by remaining dedicated to her plans to steal their military information and pass it on to Major Mosby. And Mosby might well use it to kill these very men who lately had shared her life in a pleasant way. Strange, she was thinking. Sad, what war could do to the pleasant rhythms of ordinary life. In another time, they might have been friends.

Leanna's horse trusted a rock she shouldn't have. The little mare scrambled for balance and failed, went down into the dark river water with a suddenness that caught Leanna by surprise. Ice cold water closed around her. Her long riding skirt sucked thirstily at it, caught in its current, and began to pull at her. She scrambled to regain her footing in the shallows of the ford, more desperately as she felt it giving way to deeper water as the current moved her downriver. The long veil of her riding hat wrapped around her face, blinding her, her boots filled with water, and she felt an icy numbness seeping through her limbs. Strong arms were suddenly helping, pulling her up, and Leanna gasped for breath, choking on the river water she'd begun to swallow.

"Up you go, Mrs. Leighton."

There was concern in the deep voice at her ear. She began to turn toward it and found herself hoisted high in the air instead, landing with a soggy plop on a Federal cavalry saddle. A saber jangled under her left leg as she instinctively gripped the saddle astride; the bulge of a Spencer repeating carbine lay under her right. A moment later, Major Courtland mounted behind her.

"I expected you would know how to swim or I'd have ridden closer. You're all right?"

Leanna nodded, shivering violently in the gentle breeze that felt now like invisible ice. "I do know how to swim, but with all these damn skirts and all these damn veils—" She flushed as she realized she'd been swearing and murmured a hasty apology. Stewart would be horrified. Ladies didn't talk like that.

"Sorry for what? Falling in the river or cursing about it?" He flashed a rare grin, tightening an arm around her waist as he started the horse forward. "If it was for cursing, you needn't bother. You've done it before. Personally, I'm relieved not to be the object of it this time." A small smile answered him, and Leanna raised one hand to push at her much askew, river-soaked hat. "I'm beginning to wonder about your family, though— how you ever survived without me. It looks as if saving various Penleys could be a full time job."

Leanna could not withhold a rueful laugh, even while she mourned the loss of her little mare as she shivered harder. "That's not very gallant, Major."

"I didn't say I didn't enjoy it—this time especially." His voice was serious and Leanna looked up with a wordless glance. His strong, fit body was pressed close to hers on the saddle, her hips rested on his lap, and the hard muscles of his thighs pressed hers. She shivered again, not entirely from cold, and closed her

87

eyes in a silent prayer for strength. Remember Stewart, she told herself. Remember Mosby and the map and the Confederacy.

"Cold?"

"I'm freezing," she answered truthfully.

He nodded as his horse scrambled up the low bank of the ford, then tightened his arm around her as he urged the animal into a canter. "We'll be home in a minute. Lean closer against me—it'll keep the wind off you anyway."

Jewel was standing on the porch as they finished the ride at a near gallop. Leanna opened her mouth to explain what had happened, but the black woman spoke first, her voice breaking with emotion. "It's Mister Jonathon, Miz Lea. Thanksgiving night. He's missing in action."

Without thinking twice, Leanna turned to the man behind her with a desolate cry. Somber brown eyes returned her distress and he nodded once, briefly tightening his arm around the shivering girl before he lowered her from the saddle. "Of course, I will. I'll find out whatever I can," he answered her wordless entreaty. "Now for God's sake, go on inside. You'll catch your death of cold out here and that won't help anyone." He frowned as he spoke, and thoughtlessly, Leanna turned in obedience. She was already in her room before she remembered his earlier words and the prophecy, which at the time, had seemed only a jest. Saving Penleys indeed. But this time, it might be beyond his reach.

December in Philadelphia is a gray month mostly. It was gray today, and a cold drizzle fell on the cobblestoned streets of the elegant old square. Joshua Courtland didn't particularly care. He was inside the Rittenhouse Club by a bright fire, sipping on good brandy and lighting a fine cigar as he settled himself in a Chippendale leather wing chair. Built only a few years ago, the club nevertheless radiated the sort of mellow air usually associated with old English establishments, an aura created by unobtrusive servants, the smell of fine Havana leaf, comfortable armchairs, rich oak and mohogany woodwork, luxurious Oriental rugs, chess sets left out on tables, yellowing newspapers, and an excellent library. It was, of course, exclusively male, as were all the better clubs. Ladies might, on occasion, be allowed in one of the marble and crystal dining rooms downstairs, but nowhere else. Certainly not up here in the second floor library.

A large, gilt-framed portrait of Abraham Lincoln stared sightlessly from one wood-paneled wall, but Joshua didn't stare back. A letter from his daughter, Elinor, had arrived today from England and he was busy reading it. Her viscount husband's crest was rather overlargely done at the top, gold stamped on vellum, and he folded the paper over to conceal it from curious eyes. Pompous ass, he thought blandly to himself, considering his son-in-law. Bitch, he decided of his daughter as he finished the letter. 'I' . . . 'I' . . . 'I'. Had no one ever taught the girl another word? How had it happened? Her mother had been one of the sweetest, most self-effacing women on earth, God rest her soul. Maybe he'd done it, then. He toyed cautiously with the thought. Maybe as the only girl and such a perfectly beautiful child, he had spoiled her. If so, he regretted it. But he didn't quite know what to do about it now. Maybe it was too late to do anything. Maybe she'd remain this way until she died.

What a depressing thought. He refolded the letter to send on to Chase, knowing his son knew his sister well and would probably think much the same of it as he had. But never admit it. Neither one ever did to the other. It was one of those unspoken family agreements to pretend everybody liked everybody else. Absurd maybe, but it was habit by now and hard to change. Thank God Elinor had married her viscount and ended up in England. It was easier for everyone that way.

"Scowling, Joshua? That isn't like you."

"Was I?"

"Like a thunderstorm."

"Oh." He managed a cordial smile, shoving the letter

in the inside pocket of his silk-lined coat. "News of the war, Henry?"

"Nothing major. The usual dribble. Propaganda for the masses mostly. General Meade sniffed a bit at 'Marse Robert's' army and got his toes stepped on, so he's back wintering at Culpepper now. Our good, cautious generals." He grunted an exasperated sound as he took a chair near Joshua's. "Better news from the western theater. Sherman and Thomas beat the Rebels at Chattanooga."

"That's good." Joshua was ardently pro-Union, though unemotionally so. Most of the club members were the same. Several were war contractors. Wealthy older men fighting the war in their own way with economics. And with industry. Less bloody—no less devastating. Some of them had sons in the field, like Chase. But a few had kept them home in the accounting room. The Mellons, Rockefellers, and others like them had proven that it could be a very profitable war. And there was Elinor in England, complaining because cotton was finally running short overseas and she was having to make do with silk for undergarments instead of the fine combed cotton she preferred in the winter.

"Are you going to marry the Widow Bowles?"

Joshua snorted and tamped his cigar ash. "The Widow Bowles hopes so."

Henry Walters chuckled. "Watch out, Joshua. She can be devilishly persistent." He shrugged, eyeing his friend. "Not a bad-looking woman, though."

"What's Wall Street look like this week?" Joshua decided to change the subject. "The Chattanooga victory ought to pump things up a bit, but Meade quitting for the winter with nothing to show for himself—"

"Mr. Courtland, sir?" A servant interrupted smoothly, offering an envelope on a silver tray. "Telegram for you."

Joshua paled and tried not to show it as he reached for the thing. One such missive in April of 1862 had told him his oldest son was dead at Shiloh. He wondered if he would ever be able to open another without remembering, without wondering, this time, if it were

Chase. "It's from my son," he exhaled in a sigh of relief, sending up the usual prayer of thanks. "He's stationed in the Shenandoah. Been pretty quiet so far."

Henry nodded. He knew Courtland was talking just to cover up the silence of his relief. He knew the young man was in the Virginia Valley. More would be, he thought, before it was all over.

"Unusual . . ." Joshua frowned curiously as he read it. "A request for me to gather information—about a Confederate major, maybe captured by our troops."

"Stanton could help you."

"Yes, though I hate to trouble him. Still, I doubt Chase would ask if it weren't important to him." It would have to be Stanton, he decided, the Secretary of War. Seward, the Secretary of State, he considered an ass. What he would have liked to have in Washington were a dozen Abraham Lincolns. Chase, however, with his military outlook, had disagreed the last time he'd been home on leave. 'With a dozen Lincolns,' he'd muttered, 'no general would get to command his own shoe-shine boy without interference from Washington.'

Granted, Joshua thought in retrospect. Both Lincoln and his Confederate counterpart, Jefferson Davis, interfered too much in military matters. Forty thousand troops guarding Washington, D.C., for instance. An absurd number. Men who could be better used elsewhere. Still, Lincoln was a good man, an honest one, and most astounding of all, a man who genuinely cared for his country. Chase was too young to realize how rare an attribute that was in a president, but he would understand it some day. When he had as many gray hairs as his father had. . . . God willing he'd live that long.

Henry murmured something and wandered off. Joshua laid his head back on the chair and closed his eyes. The telegram lay forgotten in his lap. His mind was back on his daughter, Elinor, retracing early memories and wondering still how he and his wife could have gone so far astray with the child. He fell asleep that way and never woke up until evening.

Chapter Six

The elegant, white brick townhouse overlooking London's most fashionable St. James Square was softly lit by twin lamps at the carriage entrance and a single Louis XIV crystal and gilt chandelier in the parlor. Parisian hand-painted wallpaper lined the inside room, ornately worked peacock-blue silk damask shrouded the windows from an outsider's eyes. Twin settees, also Louis XIV and covered in shimmering white silk, completed one corner of the room where the Viscount of Whittenshire and his wife were talking. Lady Elinor Courtland Bennington was staring at her husband aghast. "You did what?"

The Viscount of Whittenshire turned at the sharpness of her tone, frowning. At twenty-nine, Elinor was still a spectacular woman—her face impossible to fault, topped with high-piled golden curls; her bustline high and firm beneath décolleté brocade; her waist still barely larger than his handspan. She had never conceived, let alone borne, a child. She looked still like the girl of twenty he had married. And men still looked at her as they had then. But these past years, her tongue had grown sharper if her features hadn't. "I just told you, Elinor, I sold the Scottish estates—both of them."

"But—but why?"

"For money, my dear. It's what one usually sells things for."

"You never consulted me!"

"I saw no reason to."

"No reason—?"

"Elinor, I told you some months ago our financial position was weakening."

"Every spring you tell me it's weakening. It's never been true before."

"Something always came up before to pull it out. This time nothing did."

Elinor's eyes narrowed as she stared at her elegantly dressed husband. Being wealthy was not a privilege as she saw it, but a right. She'd been raised with lots of money. The idea of its absence was absolutely inconceivable to her. "You had plenty when I married you. At least you said you did."

"You have a rare ability to spend it," he retorted drily. Danger signals flashed in her green eyes and he hastened to soothe her temper. Elinor, crossed, could be most unpleasant. "It's the war in America. I never expected it to last this long. No one did. Textile mills need Southern cotton to be profitable. Unfortunately, we've about run out."

Elinor flushed slightly under his level gaze, not realizing how much more desirable she looked to him that way—not, at the moment, particularly caring. "You needn't look at me as if I've anything to do with that, Hadley. *I* didn't make the war."

"Your family is hardly opposed to it, though."

"Is that my fault? God, I thought they'd have the good sense to quit being so noble when Josh Jr. was killed."

Hadley only shrugged. He'd long since given up expecting his wife to express normal emotion. She was what she was. Sexually, she was incredibly enthralling. That was enough for him. "Anyway, my dear, the war is—"

"Boring! The war is simply boring!" Elinor was cross now; her rose-tinted mouth pouted. "And it isn't just the war, Hadley. It's those clipper ships you insisted on buying! I told you to buy steam ones instead, but you wouldn't. Now those precious sailboats are sitting rotting at the docks!"

"They were bought to freight cotton."

"Cotton, cotton! Well, if it's all going to be about cotton, then go get some. Take your damn boats and get some cotton. I don't intend to be poor."

Hadley began to frown and turn away. Suddenly, he stopped, smiling and looking at his wife strangely. Go get some. . . . He fingered his waxed blond mustache as he considered. Maybe, just maybe. . . . It was Elinor's idea. Perhaps she should go, too. He smiled slowly and crossed the room to bend and nuzzle her hair slowly. "London is so gray this time of year, my love. Perhaps what we should do is plan a trip."

Elinor looked up warily, met the gleam in her husband's eyes, and smiled, raising her face to offer her lips in sultry invitation of more. The discussion was effectively terminated for the time being, but the idea, once planted, lingered on.

Whitney's pains started at noon. The bleeding began shortly afterward. Angus was at Blytheswood by three o'clock, his bay gelding standing steaming in the gray December cold. Rosie Jenkins ran for Jewel, Jewel for Leanna. Leanna grabbed her heavy, hooded cloak and started out the door, fighting a sense of panic. First the news of Jonathon. Now, not three days later, this. Angus stood outside in the drive. A pair of Yankee soldiers stood flanking him. She stopped at the sight of the dark blue with a start of remembrance. She was not free to leave Blytheswood. Not without permission. Thank God Major Courtland was here today, not out on patrol as he so frequently was. Only he had the authority to let her go. She fumbled shakily with the gilt catch of her cloak as she ran back through the house, around the kitchen table where she'd been working, through Jewel's quarters and out the back door. The Yankees were closeted in a staff meeting in Captain Grier's cabin. She ran toward it, bursting through the door. The black book she wanted so desperately lay on the table only inches away from her hand, but she never noticed it. "It's Whitney—Whitney's having labor pains," she burst out breathlessly.

A dozen officers jerked around, startled, gaping. Major Courtland made a quick gesture to Grier and stepped around the table toward her. Behind him, whatever had been laid out on the table was hastily being refolded.

Leanna noticed the stares suddenly, and glanced around. "Oh . . . I'm sorry. . . . Excuse me," she muttered awkwardly. She'd thought only of Whitney, she realized. Barged right in on some secret planning session apparently.

"Let's go outside." Major Courtland's hand fastened firmly on her arm, turning her. Leanna was flushing deep scarlet, embarrassment adding to her fears for Jonathon's unborn baby. She murmured another apology, lost in the sound of Major Courtland's deep voice calling orders over one shoulder as he urged her forward.

"Watch the step, now," he frowned, as he guided her to the door, seeming unconcerned by his officers' reactions. "Is Whitney here?"

"No, she's at home. She sent Angus up." Leanna stumbled on the uneven stone of the walk, then reached up to try to wipe the mist from her eyes. Tears only reformed faster. They startled her. She hadn't realized she was crying.

"When did the pains start? Is there any bleeding?" Doc Lacey had materialized out of nowhere to walk at her other side. His eyes were dark with concern. "I didn't even realize she was expecting. She can't be close to term."

"Not until May."

Doc Lacey frowned over her head at Chase's glance of inquiry and shook his head. Five months premature? Not a chance. Not a single, bloody chance.

"I ordered the carriage around." Chase frowned as he said it, handing Leanna up the doorstep into the back part of the kitchen. "Though it might be more sensible for her to come here, rather than you to go there. At least Doc Lacey's here."

"Travel over that Turnpike as rutted as it is?" Doc Lacey shook his head. "Liable to kill Mrs. Penley. I'll go there instead."

Leanna turned to him with a startled look, but he had turned toward Major Courtland.

"That is, if my commanding officer will let me."

Leanna was aware of a sudden, long silence.

"It's against orders. We're specifically ordered to stay north of Strasburg—even on patrols."

"That's military oriented, though," Doc Lacey argued in a low, quiet voice. The two men stood in a long, uneasy silence, meeting each other's eyes. Leanna watched helplessly, ashamed of the selfishness of her own desperate hope.

Chase shrugged finally, frowning. "No. The order's clear enough. But I could say that's how I understood it anyway. Go ahead. I'll send—"

"No, don't send a troop or two with us. It would likely do more harm than good. I'll be in the closed carriage with Mrs. Leighton. Even if someone spots my uniform, we doctors are better tolerated than you strictly soldier types."

Chase frowned still as he turned away, his mouth unusually grim. "I'll see how ready the carriage is."

"I'll get my bag."

Leanna murmured thanks that neither man responded to if they heard at all. She understood what each of them was risking. Doc Lacey, death or imprisonment. With the South starving, Yankee prisoners were faring poorly. Major Courtland was in for a severe censure and loss of rank, if not a court martial. All this for a Confederate woman carrying a Confederate child. It shamed her now, recalling how hatefully she'd treated the Yankees when they'd first arrived at Blytheswood. Doc Lacey had been right telling her good men wore both colors in this war. She'd been the one who'd been wrong.

Chase was waiting by the mounting step to help her into the carriage. The day was cold, the sun low already, and he shivered as he stood, his eyes dark, his face grim. Leanna paused, stealing a precious minute to thank him, letting her eyes say more than she dared put into words.

"Do you need me to come?"

His soft-spoken question caught her halfway inside

the carriage and Leanna glanced back, startled. New
tears stung her eyes and she shook her head, only
reaching back to touch his hand before he closed the
door. Inside, she buried her face in her hands to cry.
She said nothing, letting Doc Lacey assume it was
Whitney she cried for. But it wasn't. At least not entirely.
Chase Courtland would have come with her. Would
have risked everything, if she had asked, if she had
needed him that much. There was not much question
any longer whether the Yankee had fallen in love with
her. Nor much question that she returned the feeling.
Nor that it was something that should never, in a thousand lifetimes, have been allowed to happen. What could
lie ahead for either of them but anguish?

Even pushing the horses at a desperate pace, it was
fully dark long before they reached Whitney's Cool
Spring Manor home. Lights gleaming from a day room
window downstairs showed the way, and Doc Lacey
spared no explanation to the servants who stood gawk-
ing at this stranger wearing a Yankee cavalry captain's
uniform. Leanna didn't wait either—only saw the immediate hostility on faces, hate blazing in narrowed eyes,
and felt sick with shame, wondering if she had looked
like that, too, when the Yankees first entered Blytheswood. Angus came in last and he explained. Gradually,
the servants melted away. Neither Doc Lacey nor Leanna
cared. They were busy with Whitney in the manor's
back room.

Whitney managed a smile at Leanna's entrance, but
at Doc Lacey's, she gasped and stared in surprise. The
midwife standing by the bed glared, no more cordial to
the woman who walked with the Yankee than the Yankee himself.

"It's all right, Mrs. Georgas," Whitney gestured weakly
toward the pair. "They're friends."

"I ain't working with no Yankee."

"Than go," Lacey replied curtly, nodding at the
doorway. "Mrs. Leighton can help me."

Leanna paled at that assumption. It was her one true
weakness, one aspect of her femininity she'd been unable

to change. The sight of blood made her nearly faint. But the midwife was already leaving with an ugly backward look, and for a moment, Leanna forgot Whitney and felt a surge of apprehension. Coming down here, of course, no one had known there was a Yankee in that carriage, but the news would have spread like wildfire before they started for home.

"Have you heard any news of Jonathon?"

Leanna glanced down at her sister-in-law quickly, shaking her head. "No, I haven't heard anymore," she lied. A letter from Stewart had arrived two days before. Her brother had been shot that night, badly enough that he'd been unable to keep his seat. Jonathon, who could ride bareback like an Indian—and had as a child, tearing up hills and over fences that way while Jewel had ranted and raved in frightened anger. Only a mortal wound would have taken him from his horse. She wouldn't tell Whitney that. Not now.

"Give me those pillows." Doc Lacey startled her, moving Leanna aside to grab for them himself. "Good lord, what do those damn midwives do for brains?" He snatched the pillows from behind Whitney's head, placed them instead beneath her feet. Leanna watched, frowning, trying to help, and getting in the way.

Whitney cried out suddenly, putting her hand over her stomach, and Leanna paled.

"Pains still?"

"They come and go."

"And the bleeding?"

"Yes, it's a little heavier."

"Damn it."

Leanna turned her head to hide tears. The look on the Yankee doctor's face was wordless testimony to his thoughts. Why the baby, God?, she asked bitterly. First Jonathon, and now his child.

Whitney reached suddenly for the doctor's hand, grim determination in her usually gentle eyes. "Doc Lacey, I want this baby. It may be all I'll ever have now of my husband. Help me keep it."

"You'd do anything?"

"Anything," she agreed without hesitation, though her face paled slightly.

"Good." Doc Lacey took a moment to smile. "One thing modern medicine has never found a replacement for—the patient's own will power. I'll do what I can, Mrs. Penley. It's why I came all the way down here." He turned his head. "Mrs. Leighton, go find some wood for me, firewood if that's all there is—varying widths, please."

"Firewood?"

"I want to raise the bed—head down, feet up. That's the first step—an essential one."

Leanna nodded and hurried out of the room. Even as she was leaving, she heard him murmuring a question to Whitney, heard her agreement and saw a dark scarlet blush spreading on her sister-in-law's face. He wanted to examine her, she guessed, and Whitney had given permission. Scandalous it would have seemed a few months ago—her own brother's wife, no less. Now that seemed trivial. "Honor," she had told Doc Lacey. "Life," he had replied. Maybe he'd been right all along—the only sane one of all of them.

He'd finished by the time she returned with the wood, and he only shrugged at her wordless glance of inquiry. "I don't know," he muttered softly. "I don't like the position of the uterus, for one thing. It's too low. Tell me, her labor for the little girl, was it unusually long or hard? Any bleeding after delivery?"

Leanna blushed and looked away. "We Southern ladies don't generally discuss things of an intimate nature."

He fixed her with a shrewd eye, impatient. "But you and she did, didn't you?"

Leanna flushed darker, but managed to nod admission. She and Whitney were so very, very close. She'd asked her because she'd wondered, without her own mother to ask what it had been like. "It was difficult, I guess. I'm hardly an expert."

"How long?"

"About a day and a half."

He frowned, shaking his head. "Some day, we'll have

a better way, Mrs. Leighton. I swear to you." He drew a deep breath and reached to put something back in his bag. Then he seemed to change his mind, turning back to Leanna and showing her the bottle. "Lime chloride, Mrs. Leighton. If you or anyone close to you should need a doctor after we Yankees have gone our merry way, this is an antiseptic. Make sure it's used. In Europe, they're calling this treatment asepses. Here they call it hogwash. But I've used it in the field for two years now. I believe in it. I don't know why it works, but it reduces infection."

Leanna managed a nod, trying to conceal the sudden pain his words had caused. The Yankees leave, Chase leaving. . . .

"Now about your sister-in-law." The frown returned. "The next few hours are critical. If the pains continue, if she goes into full labor, we haven't got a chance. You'd better know that now—get used to the idea. If it happens, you'll need to be in shape to help her through it, not dealing with your own grief."

Leanna nodded, forcing her chin up. "I'll be all right."

"Good." For a moment, he smiled, his eyes searching and kind. "Say, one more thing. Do twins run in your family?"

"Twins?" Leanna gasped. "Twins? Why, no."

"It's far too early to be sure. There's still a good chance this pregnancy's lost, anyway, but the uterus is large for so early along."

Leanna shook her head, forcing the shock away. "You think she has a chance to keep the baby? How good a chance?"

"Right now, maybe one in ten. But even if she makes it this time, Mrs. Leighton, I have to warn you—it's not likely she'll carry that baby to term. When was she due exactly?"

"Late May."

"Not a chance. Not with trouble this early. Especially if it *is* twins. Maybe early May, at the very best. We may still be at Blytheswood, but if we aren't, don't let her be here with a midwife. You'll lose the baby or her, maybe both."

"But what am I to do?"

"She needs a hospital, a good one. Richmond, maybe."

"They're short on beds there, Doctor." Leanna avoided his gaze, conscious of a painful sense of failure. "And short on medicine, food . . ."

"Not Richmond, then. Washington D.C. Better yet, Philadelphia or New York. One of the teaching hospitals."

"But that's in Yankee territory."

"I don't care if it's in Hades, Mrs. Leighton," he burst out, suddenly angry. "Now you listen to me! I risked my life to come down here tonight. Chase Courtland risked his command. Don't you dare repay that with Confederate bigotry!"

Tears sprang to Leanna's eyes and her voice broke as she replied. "That's not what I meant! I only meant—" Her voice failed momentarily, her lip quivering. She struggled to continue. "How do you expect me to get her there, Captain? Just waltz up to the border and beg a pass from the Yankee pickets?"

He shrugged apologetically, frowning. "I hadn't considered that."

Leanna wiped her tears away angrily, desperate and suddenly twice as forlorn. Oh God, now with Jonathon gone, maybe dead, Whitney was her responsibility, too. It felt as if the whole world were her responsibility. It was, she realized in shock. She might be the only Penley left now. It was up to her to see the family survived.

"Chase might help you, Mrs. Leighton," Doc Lacey offered after the long silence.

"Major Courtland?" She smiled, or made an attempt to anyway. "He said once already in jest that the care of my family seemed to be a full-time job. And that was before I had to ask after Jonathon."

"Do you really think he minds?"

It wasn't his words, but his tone of voice that startled Leanna, made her look up at him so quickly. His eyes met hers and immediately she knew he knew. She looked away, shaking her head. "No," she said haltingly, "as I

101

come to know him better, I would guess he doesn't. You told me once he was a good man. I gave you an argument at the time, if I recall. Now I think you understated the case."

There was another silence before he spoke a last time before turning back to check on his patient. "Damn shame you're married," he sighed softly.

Leanna turned to follow him, trying not to let herself agree to that statement. But there was a heaviness on her heart that came with his words, and it lingered for hours while they kept vigil by Whitney's bedside.

The dawn sun was grayed by winter clouds as it rose over the Blue Ridge. Leanna shivered in its cold half-light as she climbed into the carriage. "Are you sure it's safe to leave her?"

Doc Lacey managed a smile, a weary one for the night had been long. Midnight before Whitney's bleeding had begun to stop, almost daybreak before he'd dared draw a deep sigh of relief. Leanna hadn't slept either. Her eyes were ringed with shadows by now, her breath made tiny puffs of vapor in the dawn morning cold. "Safe as it will be until she actually has that baby or babies, as the case may be. She's sleeping now and I left strict instructions for the next few days."

"But she won't be able to do what you told her. There's too much here for her to do just to keep Cool Spring going."

"Then she may have to make a choice between Cool Spring and that child she's carrying. Stacking firewood like she did yesterday will cause trouble again—maybe not something so easily controlled next time."

Leanna sighed and nodded, closing her eyes. She knew he was right. She'd been thoroughly impressed with the Yankee doctor tonight—this time as a doctor, not just as a man. He'd saved Whitney's baby this time. But next time, if there were a next time, even if he were still stationed at Blytheswood, there probably wouldn't be another miracle.

She woke with a start, blinking in the dimness of the

carriage interior, sitting up straighter under the heavy woolen carriage blanket someone had pulled over her. She didn't remember falling asleep and she had no idea what had awakened her. But the heated bricks of the foot warmer were cold beneath her feet. Hours had passed then. Strasburg must be near, Blytheswood only a few miles beyond.

The carriage bounced as a wheel hit a wide crack in the Turnpike macadam. Leanna frowned, raising the curtain to peer outside. The gray gloom of winter drizzle greeted her. Then a shout sounded from the woods to one side and Leanna dropped the curtain to turn for the Yankee doctor. That's what had awakened her. Someone had challenged the carriage and Angus had put the horses into a gallop to outrun pursuit.

Doc Lacey was awake already, kicking free of the blanket and leaning forward in the seat. "Lie down, Mrs. Leighton. If there should be shooting—"

"Hold on inside."

Angus's voice shouted above a sudden explosion of sound—men yelling, horses hooves pounding the road. The carriage bounced and leaped like a mad thing, and Leanna grabbed for the velvet hand strap in panic. The Yankee leaned over her, calling out the window to Angus. "Slow down!"

"Not unless Mrs. Leighton tells me to," came the reply. "I ain't giving you up without a fight!"

"Tell him to slow down," Doc Lacey ordered Leanna. "He's liable to kill us all."

"Do you have a gun?"

"A gun? No, I'm a doctor not a gunslinger."

"I'm not telling Angus to slow down then," Leanna gasped as the carriage careened wildly on two wheels for a moment before dropping back down. "We'll be at Strasburg soon and in the main part of town."

Bugle calls clamored suddenly in front of them and Leanna stopped speaking, grabbing for the curtain again to try to see. A half-dozen roughly dressed men were wheeling their horses away from the side of the carriage, galloping back toward the woods. The sound of more horses galloping was getting louder. An instant later, dark blue uniforms burst into sight and the carriage slowed to a jolting halt.

"Mrs. Leighton, are you all right?" Captain Grier was breathing hard from his recent gallop and Leanna smiled as he wrenched open the carriage door to lean anxiously inside.

"Quite all right, thank you." The smile played on her lips and suddenly burst into a reluctant laugh. "Lord, I never thought I'd be so happy to see Yankees coming!"

"Captain Grier." The doctor smiled too, and tipped his hat. "Somewhat south of Strasburg, aren't you?"

"Hard to say," he shrugged. "Not much sun today to judge by." He smiled faintly and shrugged again. "How did your night go?"

"Sleeplessly . . . but successfully, I'm happy to say."

For a moment only, a kind of bittersweet pleasure flashed on Captain Grier's cold-reddened face. Then he nodded. "Well, that's wonderful news. Mrs. Penley's all right, then?"

"For the time being, anyway."

Leanna reached to touch the young captain's hand, nodding toward the south. "Shouldn't we get going?"

"I've twenty men with me. I doubt we need fear."

"S'long as you got an escort, maybe I should head back to Cool Spring." Angus's grizzled head poked into the doorway. "Borrow a horse?"

"Yes. And make sure Mrs. Penley follows the instructions I left for her," Doc Lacey agreed quickly, all business again. "And watch out yourself."

"Those men won't trouble me none. I ain't wearing the right color," Angus grunted. "Though as soon as I hear who it was pestering us, I'll hang them upside down in a pig trough. I sent my boys out earlier on to spread the word you was only a doctor come to help Mrs. Penley. Nobody shoulda bothered you."

Leanna was not the only one who gave the old man a sharp look. But before she could speak, he continued, almost apologetically. "Them fellas weren't no regular boys, I promise you. Only riff-raff of some sort. Don't think too bad of the Valley boys, Doc. None of them would have made trouble knowing what they knowed."

"You take good care of Whitney, Angus," Leanna hurried to speak before the Yankees could, fearing the old man had said too much already to them. Practically telling them he could provide a list of which men were regular partisan rangers, and which weren't. "You keep her on that slanted bed for three days and watch after her like a hawk."

"I'll do that without needing telling," he grunted, already moving away. "I'll be in touch, too, which'll be yer next question."

Leanna nodded, holding her breath and not daring to look at either of the Yankee captains until Angus trotted out of sight. A cold drizzle was still falling and Captain Grier finally seemed to become aware of it as Angus and the temptation of his knowledge receded into the midst.

"Next stop, Blytheswood." He managed a smile finally and nodded as he shut the carriage door, remounting his horse to lead the way. Leanna said nothing, closing her eyes again to pretend sleep, for she could feel a question burning in Doc Lacey's eyes as they studied her. A question she prayed he wouldn't ask. One she had no idea any longer how to answer. She'd recognized two of the men that had been chasing the carriage, yes. But did she owe it to the Yankees to turn them in? Turn them in to be shot? Or hanged? Or sent to a Yankee prison for the rest of the war?

The carriage rolled to a stop finally at the marble mounting block by Blytheswood's front walk. Doc Lacey leaned forward to reach for the door, but it opened before he touched it. As Leanna opened her eyes at the sound, she saw Doc Lacey bending down to go through the low carriage door, weariness on his face, his doctor's bag in one lean hand. She wasn't very surprised when the next thing she saw was Major Courtland, reaching in to lift her down. And when she stumbled on the step with fatigue, she made no protest as he turned and lifted her in his arms to carry her the rest of the way to her room.

Chapter Seven

Army hospitals in 1863 were as dangerous a place for soldiers as a battlefield—maybe more so. Stethoscopes were a rarity, thermometers, too. The idea of sterilization was a radical one adhered to by only a handful of doctors, though the aroma of vinegar and chlorine did occasionally mingle with less sanitary odors in the huge wards lined with bed after bed of wounded or diseased men. Water dripped from small bags onto freshly dressed wounds, keeping the bandages well moist. This encouraged the formation of 'laudable pus,' which everyone agreed was necessary for healing. Maggots were less kindly regarded, but they too usually made an appearance at some stage of recovery from open wounds wounds, and occasionally, their larger cousins, the black-headed worms, joined them. Doctors who saw them usually tossed some chloroform into the wiggling mess to kill the worms. Usually that worked. If it didn't, no one worried too greatly. Maggots didn't seem to cause half the complications gangrene, lockjaw, dystentery, or pneumonia did. And they were equally omnipresent.

CSA Major Jonathon Penley opened his eyes to that nightmare only once, soon after he'd arrived—moved from the front lines in a mule-drawn ambulance over rutted roads, then loaded onto a hospital ship for passage to a permanent, land-built facility. There he was put in the Confederate prisoner ward and compassionate Washington women volunteers bathed his unconscious face with water and spooned broth into his mouth while he lay senseless. He'd regained consciousness once when the doctor in charge of the ward had torn blood-caked bandages away from the gory hole in his stomach. The agony had woken him from the nothingness of the long torture of days of living like that. But one look had been all the doctor had needed. He'd shaken his head and merely left the wounded Rebel to die at his own speed, not even bothering to redress the wound with lard and wax ointment, nor to rebandage it with less filthy rags. It was a waste as he saw it. He marked the young man's card under his name and rank: 'Minimal care, laudanum as needed. Wound definitely mortal.' And left Jonathon Penley slowly, agonizingly, dying.

The rain had turned to sleet as the night wore on. Stewart pulled his black slouch hat lower on his head and raised the rain-soaked cape of his greatcoat higher around his face. Neither seemed to offer much warmth, but they interrupted the interminable waiting at least, gave him a few seconds of something to do besides sit freezing on his equally frozen horse, wondering if the feeling would ever come back in his hands, wishing he were back in the cabin with the other officers of his regiment.

It was a complete nightmare. All of it. The whole war. The cold, the hunger, the lack of supplies—the lack of victories. Stewart had never thought, as some had, that it would be a one-week war. He'd been to school in the North. He knew the resources the South was challenging. But it would be three years this spring and he was tired. It wasn't glorious anymore. It wasn't exciting. What had gone wrong? How had he ended up here in a night grove of woods in freezing rain, waiting for a load of black-market guns that were *supposed* to have arrived hours ago?

"Colonel!" His young captain pointed to brush moving on the forest's fringe. "I hope that's them and not some Yankee patrol."

Stewart nodded, catching a glimpse of a shadowed face and spurring forward. "Major Mosby. I'd about given up hope."

"Sorry for the wait. We ran into a supply train and couldn't resist the opportunity. Two wagons of bought guns, four wagons of Yankee ones."

"Good. The Yankee ones always work better. Two out of three of the others are usually junk pieces."

"Anything new here?" Mosby's bright blue eyes gleamed even in this pale light, and Stewart shrugged for answer, wishing he had better news for the fervent partisan.

"Nothing. Everybody's set up for winter around here. Have you any news of the Valley?"

"Quiet there. The Yanks are being careful to stay north of Strasburg and Front Royal."

"They should be. Both of those towns are militarily indefensible. They learned that in '62." Stewart shrugged. Wagons were rolling by and he watched them, half his mind on them instead of on the conversation. Black-market rifles and ammunition. From Yankees willing to sell out their own people. Disgusting. But necessary to deal with. Enormous risks, of course. Equally enormous profits. They'd probably made six hundred to eight hundred percent profit on this single shipment. How thin the line of the South's survival. Compromising the very honor they'd thought to fight for in the beginning. Worse—what were they going to do when the money ran out? Black-market profiteers didn't accept the weakening Confederate dollar. And CSA gold was running low. General Lee would have to make some stunning victories this spring when the campaign began anew. Desperate measures were needed if the South were to survive.

"Colonel Leighton?"

Stewart forced his attention back to Mosby, murmuring an apology. "Sorry. My thoughts were wandering. What was that you said?"

"Wondering if you were related by any chance to a young woman in the Valley, same name."

"Blytheswood?"

"Yes, that's the place. Occupied for the winter by the Yanks."

"She's my wife. Any problems?"

"Quite the contrary." Major Mosby gave Stewart a strange, measuring glance before he continued. "Did you know I asked her help in obtaining some military information from the Yanks there?"

Stewart looked startled and Mosby gestured in quick apology. "I didn't mean to spring that on you."

"Don't give it a second thought," Stewart said stiffly. He frowned, trying to think quickly without betraying the first, gut-deep anger he'd felt at the news. Leanna hadn't mentioned it, fearing, perhaps, that her letter might be intercepted.

"It didn't seem all that risky to me," Mosby continued quickly. "Look at what Belle Boyd got away with during the Valley Campaign. A man they'd hang or shoot. But even if she got caught . . ."

"Has it come to that, then?" Stewart interrupted in a low voice, faintly angry. He didn't look at Mosby, but at the shadows beneath black bare trees, thinking out loud. Had the Old South died already with the war not even lost yet? That a Leighton woman must sneak and spy?

"I beg your pardon?"

"What?" Stewart glanced back at Mosby with a frown. "Oh, just thinking aloud, I guess."

"You're not pleased, I gather." Mosby shrugged, turning his intense blue gaze back on the CSA officer. "I don't like it either, but desperate situations require desperate solutions. I don't think it hurts a woman or child to die any more than it hurts a man. And without desperate measures, the CSA is going to go down."

"Spare me, Major." Stewart saluted in curt dismissal, reining his horse around. "I appreciate your notifying me of what you've asked my wife to do. But don't expect my blessings. If I'd wanted her involved in this war, I'd have brought her with me into the army." He nodded only once and rode away, following the already retreating wagons.

Damn! Anger surged and slowly began to fade as the wagons creaked and sleet-soaked men rode a cold, dark trail back to camp. Had he been unfair with Mosby, he asked himself finally? What if Leanna could get information that provided enough advantage for a Confederate victory in the Valley? Desperate situations and desperate solutions. In the old days, it would have been inconceivable to involve the women—any woman, let alone his wife. How badly do you want to win this war? a small voice asked softly. Badly enough to risk Leanna? What if you lose? it continued. What if you cling to all the old rules about what's fair and what's right and you lose the war because of it? Then what? Will you be content with your honor if you've lost everything else? Lost the plantations, the slaves, the ships, the privileges . . . ah, the privileges—growing up among the elite in an elitist society, being envied, being served, being on top. What would it be like to be poor? To be just a common person grubbing in the rocky fields for a crop?

Fear that never rose in battle rose at that thought and he began to sweat beneath the sleet frozen overcoat. They couldn't lose, he told himself. But logic argued. They could. They would the way things were going. The CSA could simply lose. The merchant Yankees of no breeding and no graces could win. And if that happened, the South would lose everything—everything it had once stood for, everything it had tried to fight for.

Honor be damned then, he decided in a rush of fearful anger. Do whatever needs doing to win. Worry about restoring the tarnished virtues later. If the South was worth dying for, it was worth sinning for as well. Wasn't it? "Hurry those wagons," he called suddenly, spurring his tired horse to the front of the line. "Our boys will have something better than an old musket to shoot Yankees with tomorrow."

"Where's Mrs. Leighton, Jewel?"

The black woman turned at the sound of the deep voice behind her. Major Courtland back from a four-day patrol around Front Royal to Manassas Gap. Looking for the CSA army? Or flaunting its absence to the Valley residents? Jewel didn't care, so she began to smile, genuinely happy to see him. He was the man of the place now in her eyes. She felt better when he was

110

here. "What's wrong, Major?" Her smile died. Fear took its place. There was a message in his tired eyes. "You got bad news?"

"It's Leanna's brother." Chase didn't realize his use of her given name—he didn't think of her any more by her married name, but he made an effort still to use it. Partially to remind himself. "My father made some inquiries for me about him."

Jewel began to tremble but she kept her head up, even managed to nod once. "My boy ain't comin' back, is he?"

It wasn't spoken as a question but as a statement, and the Yankee officer sighed softly and shrugged. "Jewel, I . . ."

"You gonna say you'se sorry, ain't you? But it wasn't you killed him. It's this damnation war." Her voice broke as she finished and she turned away to hide her grief. Her fine young Jon . . . never gonna see her fine boy again, so handsome, so good. "You go on and tell Miz Lea for me if you will. It'd break my heart to have to be the one to say it."

Chase stood silent for a minute, motionless. It was times like these he caught himself wondering whether Doc was right, the rest of them wrong. Even after two and a half years, the grief still touched him, tore at him, wounded him in some nonphysical place. Was anything worth this? And there was this terrible, awkward sense of helplessness that always accompanied it. This feeling of wanting to apologize for something. The sense of somehow having failed. "Jewel, I—"

"I know, son." She made an awkward little gesture with one massive black hand, as if waving to him backward. "You done what we asked you. You found out what we was wanting to know. Don't come as no surprise, entirely." She shook her head slowly, trying to walk toward the kitchen where she could mourn in private. She felt old suddenly. Old and slow and defeated. "Miz Leighton's in the guest house, tidying it for Miz Whitney and Miranda if they was to come for Christmas. But I reckon—" Suddenly she couldn't talk any more, and she merely waddled faster, an odd rolling gait, soundless except for petticoats rustling.

Chase stood watching her, not saying anything else. Not knowing what he could say. Jewel disappeared into the dining room. As he began to turn, he heard a single, soft wracking wail of grief. He took a deep breath and raised the collar of his dark-blue greatcoat as he went back outside, forcing himself each step forward. God, he didn't want to tell Leanna. Maybe he should have lied. Maybe he should have pretended he had no news.

"Jewel?" Leanna heard a soft step on the rag rug, the click of the door closing down below. "I'm up here in the loft. You know those Yankees even made a new bureau to replace the old one that got so charred? And found some glass, too, heaven knows where."

"Mrs. Leighton?"

She turned, startled, then quickly blushed and began to stammer an apology. Major Courtland stood at the bottom of the stairs—not Jewel. "Oh, Major, I didn't mean 'Yankee' as any offense."

"That's all right." One of his rare, soft smiles flickered on his face. He looked up from the stairs below her. "By the time I leave Blytheswood, I'll answer to Yankee like a given name, I think."

It was said without rancor and Leanna returned his smile, reaching up to tuck a few stray wisps of black hair back into place. "You look tired," she decided aloud, her eyes gentle as she studied the man standing below. "And wet. Did you just get back?"

Chase shrugged, taking his coat off and carefully avoiding her eyes. The softness of her tone touched him, made him feel better in one way, worse in another. I love you, Leanna, he thought silently. Damn rotten shame, isn't it? "A few minutes ago." He nodded and started up the steps.

Leanna half frowned, stepping back. It was highly improper, not to mention, after what had happened between them Thanksgiving, a little dangerous. "Major, perhaps I should come down."

"With all respect to propriety, I think what I have to

say to you is better said in private. I telegrammed my father about your brother, and there was an answer waiting for me yesterday when I arrived at Front Royal." He stopped at the top of the stairs and met her eyes for the first time. He saw them open wider, the fear begin to show in their beautiful violet depths. "He was mortally wounded, Thanksgiving night. Taken to a Washington hospital, but beyond saving."

"Mortally wounded?" She said it softly, wondering why it should shock her so when all along, after Stewart's letter, she'd feared the worst.

"The telegram was dated the fifth—nearly a week ago. I'm afraid . . ."

"No!" It wasn't a denial so much as a protest, and Leanna's lip began to tremble with the cry. "No, not Jon!"

"Jewel's at the main house. She asked me to tell you."

"But there might be some mistake," she said jerkily. She half turned, closing her eyes as she struggled to draw a normal breath. One part of her was trying to not believe Chase's words. Another was trying to accept them. Inconceivable, she told herself. Jonathon couldn't be dead. Other men might die in the war, plenty already had, but they hadn't been *her* brother—Whitney's husband, Mandy's daddy. They hadn't been Jonathon of the thousand memories, of childhood squabbles and secret pacts. No one who had occupied that huge a space in her life could simply cease to be.

"Leanna, I'm sorry."

"Sorry?" In her grief, she turned on him. "Why should you be sorry? Isn't that what you're here for? To kill Rebels? You should be celebrating." It was anger that said it, hurt that demanded to be revenged, and it came out along with a single, deep sob. But it was true, too, wasn't it? It *was* a Yankee bullet that had killed Jonathon. She'd begun to shiver as if from a chill, and she found herself unable to stop.

A muscle tensed white in Chase's jaw as he looked away. "I hope to God you know better than that."

"Do I? What's the difference between you and the

Yankee that shot him?" Tears were spilling now and Leanna was helpless to stop them. Her voice broke badly, but her eyes accused him without mercy. "All for your Union, aren't you? You as much as any of them? Sacrifice anyone or anything that stands in your way."

"Stop it, Leanna. I'm not the one who shot him! Even if I were, I couldn't apologize. This is a war, damn it. People get killed every day. Your brother was a soldier. He knew what he was risking."

"I hate you! I hate all you damn bluebellies, all your guns and your—"

"No!" Pain flashed on his weather-browned face as he grabbed for her arm. "Leanna, for God's sake!"

His touch on her arm was like a match to powder and she wailed in a choking sob, blinded by tears, raising her hand to slap at him with all her might. "Damn you! Damn you!"

Chase jerked back as her clenched hand hit his face, instinctively raising his arm to deflect the next blow. Then he reached to pull her against him, wrapping his arms tightly around her struggling body. "Leanna, I'm sorry, God I'm sorry. What more can I say? I can't give him back to you. I can't undo this awful thing."

She groaned in anguish, helpless to do any more.

He buried his face in her hair, tears starting to his own eyes at her cry. "I'm sorry, Leanna. Honest to God, I'm sorry."

She collapsed in his arms with a final, choking sob, bathing his uniform with tears, moaning her grief against his chest. Chase held her tightly, kissing the raven curls that strayed from her chignon, apologizing for something he'd never done. His heart ached more for her sorrow than it had for his own when his brother had died at Shiloh. He closed his eyes hard against the pain of it, wishing he could take more to spare her its awful weight. Why her, God? Of all the Confederates fighting that last, damn, useless week before winter, why did it have to be her brother killed?

Leanna knew no rational thought. The pain of her

grief was too overwhelming. It buffeted her like a tempest, and she clung blindly to the Yankee major for support, not caring any longer who he was or why she shouldn't. She only knew he offered some comfort in this agony and she clung to that desperately, trying to hide from the pain in the warmth of his arms. She felt his lips on her hair and cried all the harder against him, holding him tighter. When it changed from comfort to passion, she never knew afterward, turbulent emotions surged and merged in ungovernable confusion. She felt him lift her in his arms and made no protest, only turned her face to meet his kiss. His mouth was gentle on hers, sweet beyond words, his arms strong and safe as he carried her to the soft down bed. The sun was sinking over the western mountains and shadows were dark in the tiny room. She opened her eyes only once as he laid her down, meeting amber brown eyes as gentle and loving as spring sunshine meeting winter's last snow. It was comfort he offered at first, in the only way he truly knew how to give it. Words seemed banal; worse—insincere. He had never been the type of man that womanly words came easily to. Now, sharing Leanna's desperate grief, aching for her and with her, they were farther from him than ever.

Leanna was beyond realizing that. Beyond realizing how dangerous the comfort he offered could be. The physical strength of his arms was comfort, the gentle, wordless murmurs against her ear, the strong steady beat of his heart thudding against her breast, the warmth of his breath, the mute protection of his body pressed to hers, shielding her physically, or trying to, from something that was beyond his power to shield her from. She knew that he shared her pain. Knew too, that he shared it only for her sake and not his own, and that made it somehow more precious to her. Time moved unnoticed in the agony within her, and the sun sank fully over the western ridge of the Alleghenies, and only the faint half-light of dusk remained in the room. And still she clung to him, to his strength and his offered love that eased the grief, refusing to let him go, refusing to acknowledge the outside world again with its taboos and its many agonies and injustices.

It was a moment of supreme selfishness, she would think later. A moment born of anguish that would give birth to many more such. She felt him stir in her arms, as if to move away from her, and she refused to release him, refused to open her arms for him to go. He raised his head and met her eyes for a moment in the shadowed dimness of the tiny room. And beneath her, Leanna was suddenly acutely conscious of the softness of the down bed cradling her body, the chill of the air and the warmth of his body touching hers.

Then his dark head began to lower over hers and she raised her hand to touch his face. How handsome he was in this half-light, she thought dazedly as she closed her eyes. The strength of that hard, square jaw, the unexpectedly tender gleam of his black-lashed eyes. His mouth touched hers almost tentatively, soft as a whispered word, brushed hers once and then settled more surely, covering hers with sudden fire. She felt his hand at her throat, slipping the tiny buttons of her high-necked blouse, opening the bodice to his lips. Leanna moaned as he dropped his head to her breast, nuzzling it first as a child might, then finding the dark nipple with his mouth and covering it, teasing its peak with his tongue as surging pleasure swept her body. She tangled her fingers deep in his dark, thick sweet-smelling hair, kissing him in sudden desperation. Tears gathered at the corners of her eyes, born of a joy soul-deep, but she was unaware of them, lost in the rapture of his touch. He murmured her name softly—once, and then again in a soft half sigh, lifting his lips from her breast to seek her mouth again, no longer gently. Leanna could only yield to him, pressed deep in the soft mattress as he suddenly moved on top of her. His weight startled her. She gasped at the sensations of her breasts, bared now, crushed beneath the unyielding hardness of his chest, throbbing against him and aching with a wanton need. One hand reached to cover her breast, kneading it and teasing it, demanding and giving. The nipple rose so

116

taut that pleasure nearly merged with pain as he bent his head again to it, his hand holding it still against the nipping hardness of his teeth, the soft wet heat of his lips. She lay helpless beneath him, wracked by hunger she'd never known before. He showed no mercy as he reached to pull her head toward his again, taking her mouth beneath his and parting her lips with his tongue to plunge within her. Her whole body trembled and she moaned as she opened her mouth wider to him. His hands worked to loosen the band of her skirt, unfastening it to slip it down her legs as he lifted his hips from hers for that moment. Leanna followed him mindlessly with her body, arching her back to lift herself toward him. His hands were on her suddenly, exploring her through the light linen of her undergarments, and she cried out in a wordless sound, pressing herself upward. Chase dropped his head to lie against her neck, nuzzling and kissing her bare skin as he unbuttoned his own clothes, shedding them to lie with hers on the wood floor.

Leanna reached mindlessly for him, missing his weight on her and the hard, lean heat of his body. Her hands found the warmth of bare skin as she encircled his back with her arms and pulled his close again. One knee pressed at her thigh and she obeyed its urging with another moan, allowing him back against her. She could feel him now, swollen and pressing against her through only the fabric of her underclothes, now moving and teasing her unbearably as he kissed her again, his hands on her breast, his breath mingling with hers as he explored her mouth with his tongue. He slid one hand down her body in lazy, powerful possession, sliding the last of her clothing free. Leanna's hands reached for his hips, pulling him down to her, arching her back to receive him. She felt his probing heat touch against her and cried her need, opening herself wider to him, suddenly limp in the power of her passion. She laid her head back on the pillow with a helpless moan, turning it restlessly back and forth until his lips found hers and claimed possession.

Thought was impossible now. Her body only begged him to fulfill the craving he had created. She could no longer demand it of him, only ask, raising her hips to him as he slid one muscled arm beneath her to draw her higher. He played her as a master a precious instrument, sensing her surrender to his will, to his power, to his masculinity. He breathed once of his love for her and accepted her gift, pressing her deeper into the bed as he raised himself over her and dropped slowly inside her. Leanna felt the pressure of him and gasped her ecstasy, arching to meet him and pulling his hips down on hers with renewed frenzy. He slid into the dark wet heat of her with a trembling moan, forcing his body deeper as her tight flesh gave way before him. Leanna writhed in ecstasy as he filled her full of him, withdrew and plunged again, harder this time, and harder still each next thrust as her body accustomed itself to that sweet intrusion and reached to seek it. Fires never known before swept her up in ungovernable passion. The world outside ceased to exist and there was only him, this man who was so sweetly, so fiercely loving her. She moved with him as one, the pleasure building to frenzied need, and then suddenly she cried aloud. Ecstasy burst from deep within her, and something like fear rose as the terrifying, unknown force of it washed over her. She cried out again and clung to him. Chase held her closer, lying motionless within her, his mouth on her throat, his lips whispering loving reassurance. This was not something to fear but to rejoice in. The ultimate gift of a man and a woman to each other. She surrendered to it joyfully then, feeling his deep shudder against her and understanding, holding him tightly as his head dropped heavily against her neck, a soft half moan escaping his lips.

Something was over, but something remained. There was a deep, sweet softness enveloping her, something that bound her irrevocably to the man in her arms. Leanna smiled gently as she felt his lips brush hers and she opened her eyes to meet his. The tenderness she saw there banished the last shred of fear at what he had offered, what he had taken. There was only peace and a deep, quiet sort of contentment. She lifted her lips to his to tell him that without words. He took them gently now, the fury of the passion past, then lifted his lips from hers to touch her eyes, her cheeks, the love-damp wisps of black curls that framed her lovely face. Leanna lay content beneath him, only holding him still. She began to feel a strange fullness deep within where he lay in her still, and moved to him as a faint, sweet throbbing began to grow once more. She felt his heart beating against her bare breast in a stronger rhythm, his breath growing shorter again as he bent his head to take her mouth. This time she knew no fear and went joyfully with him into that strange world.

Darkness greeted him as Chase opened his eyes, and he glanced down to where Leanna lay sleeping on his bare shoulder, her black hair undone and waving in disarray, her lips parted slightly and curved by a faint smile. 'Well done, Chase,' he thought bitterly, closing his eyes in a long silent sigh. 'Onward with honor,' indeed. He slipped gently from beneath Leanna's arm, allowing himself only a single final whisper-soft brush of his lips on her hair. Did it matter that he hadn't planned it this way? Wasn't the result still the same? He'd dishonored them both, allowed something to happen that could not bring either of them anything but greater pain—Leanna especially, married to another man. The shame of this, the guilt . . . but he was not any the less in love with her for it. Possessing her physically only heightened his need to possess her completely, to claim her as his entirely. And now what? Now it would only be twice as hard. She might hate him when she woke. Could he bear it if she did?

The plantation grounds looked deserted as he dressed and stared broodingly out the high, narrow window. The sleet had stopped. Light shone from the dining room of the big house some distance away. It would be dinner time then. Jewel and the other officers would notice his absence, and Leanna's, too. There would be soft snickers and snide glances. Roger, at least, would know what had happened in that uncanny way he had. And the others?

He turned back to the bed, wrapping the sleeping girl carefully in the thick rag quilt. He wasn't leaving her here alone like some twopenny whore, at least. If he could get her back to her own room, himself make an appearance at dinner, it might leave the issue of her absence in some question.

Leanna stirred only once, as he laid her on her own bed and drew the covers high over top her. She murmured something with a faint smile and reached to take his hand. He smiled then, but briefly, watching her and wondering whether he would, in his lifetime, ever know such sweetness again. Then he gently withdrew his hand and turned to lay her clothes neatly on a chair back, taking the quilt with him to return later to the cottage. No one had seen him carry her in, at least. For that, anyway, God had been kind.

He walked into dinner midway through, offering little in the way of explanation and relieved to note Jewel's absence. "I'm leaving first thing in the morning for Harper's Ferry, Doc," he commented at last. "I'll be four or five days there at least. Are you coming or staying?"

Doc Lacey raised a single brow at the bluntness of the question, wondering at his friend's expression. Penley's death, he told himself unconvinced. Perhaps Mrs. Leighton had taken it hard. "Staying," he decided quickly. "Though I'm sending another request for transfer with you."

"Hospital duty, still?"

"Yes. It's where I can do the most good and you know it, Chase."

"We'll miss you. We may yet have some work for you to do right here with us, especially come spring."

Doc Lacey smiled faintly, watching the last of the other officers leave before he turned back to fix his friend with a searching eye. Chase frowned and looked away, his handsome face grim and dark and tightly closed. "Not you, Chase," he sighed finally, shaking his head. "I know you too damn well, you know. You won't need a surgeon this spring—not the way you're going. You'll need a hearse. And I don't want to be around to try to scrape up the—"

"Excuse me, Doctor. I have work—"

"Chase, for God's sakes, how do I get you to listen to me? It isn't worth it!" He jerked to his feet to catch at Chase's arm as he started out. "Get out if you need to. Desert, for God's sakes! Live in a cave or change your name! But don't—"

"Good night, Doc."

Chase pulled away hard enough to break Doc Lacey's grip and his friend watched helplessly as he started toward the stairs. "If you don't care about yourself for God's sake, what about your father? Your fiancée, Susan? What about—?" He gave up with an angry sigh, shaking his head. It was no use. Chase would never listen. He never had, he never would. Sparing himself pain or death just wasn't in his nature—not when it ran counter to his sense of honor, that damn, obsessive demon. "Good night, Major," he said finally, softly, turning back to finish his meal. "And good-bye."

Chapter Eight

"Assassinate the President?" Joshua Courtland felt his hands beginning to tremble and he moved them carefully to his lap beneath the table edge to conceal it. Good God, this was monstrous!

"Oh, that was just a hypothetical question, wasn't it, Henry?"

"Of course. If the President's proving detrimental to the society he'd been elected to govern—"

"The old 'ends justifying the means,' Joshua. Hardly a new debate. Lincoln's stand that the South is still part of our country, that we're all brothers, is ridiculous at this point. It will be three years of war this spring. The South isn't an ally, for God's sakes, it's an enemy. When this war is finally done, I see no reason to reward those very people who—"

"We're getting farther off track, gentlemen." Roland Hodges waved a massive, diamond-studded hand impatiently. "The point of our meeting tonight is twofold, neither of which we have adequately yet addressed. First, do we wish to form a coalition to act on mutual interests in this next year or so? Second, who do we support for the Presidential election this coming year?"

"Vallandingham," one man grunted assertively.

"God, no. He's for ending the war!" There was chuckling around the dinner table at the speaker's expression of exaggerated horror.

"Kill the goose that's laying us golden eggs?"

"Bite your tongue, Springer. I just got a governmental contract for ten thousand repeating carbines—regulation equipment come spring. I make ten dollars on every twenty."

Joshua felt sick. His heart ached as though it was

being physically squeezed. God, no, he prayed. Not now. Not another attack. I must stay and know what godawful things are in the making.

"You're looking pale, Joshua," Henry Walters was genuinely concerned. He reached to pass the brandy. "You're all right?"

"Fine," Joshua managed a faint smile, nodding. "It was just Roland's comment about the rifles. My son is still serving in the cavalry."

"Oh, that's right. Well, he'll be pleased to hear the news then, Courtland. Seven-shot Spencers—"

"He's got one already. He bought it this fall, privately."

"It will make the cavalry a real fighting force, they tell me. No more escort service and general's guards . . ."

"As they say in Washington, 'who ever saw a dead cavalryman?' "

Joshua paled further amid the laughter. I have, he thought. My oldest son. "Chase is concerned about the carbine's accuracy over a couple hundred yards."

"Tell him to get riflery lessons then," Hodges snorted with a snide grin. Several men laughed.

"That's unfair," Henry Walters defended his silent friend uneasily. He'd wondered whether to give Courtland's name at all when Hodges had approached him about this meeting. He wondered even more now as the evening progressed and Joshua grew even paler. "I've been hunting with the boy myself. He's a dead shot and a quick one. If he says the carbine's unreliable, it's unreliable."

"Oh, don't get so ruffled, Henry. It was just a little joke. You know Washington anyway. If they want the Spencer, the field troops will get the damn thing even if it shoots backward."

"Which has happened on occasion," someone chuckled.

"That was that machine rifle, I think."

Joshua drank another brandy and ignored the squeezing feeling around his heart. Two hours already of this and it looked like more to come. Horror after horror. To think any man could be so unabashedly greedy, so inhumanly callous. They spoke of the war as they might

123

a chess game. A diversion. Luckily, a profitable one. The only question they pursued was how to prolong it, how to eke out the maximum time to reap the contracts' benefits, and still have plenty of good opportunities lying in the defeated South. If the war went on too long, it would devastate the Southern states too greatly— too greatly to be to their eventual benefit. Timing, as Roland Hodges called it. The trick lay in timing. Oh God. . . .

"Are you in, Courtland, or out?"

Joshua was startled by the sudden question. His thoughts had been drifting. He hadn't realized the vote was being taken. That, too, happened more often as the days passed, another signal of an imminent end. One second he had to decide. All he'd ever stood for, lived for, worked for, taught his sons to believe in—all lay in the balance. Say no and keep his honor uncompromised, his name forever unbesmirched, and leave these jackals free to weave God-knew-what plots in the year to come. Say yes and lose everything but a single, remote chance—if he could survive long enough—of somehow thwarting this unholy coalition from the inside. "In," he said, smiling as he spoke, nodding once for emphasis. The word was spoken firmly, none of his thoughts showing on his face. Next to him, Henry Walters breathed a barely audible sigh of relief, and Joshua turned his head to smile at him, passing the brandy decanter back. "A toast, I think, gentlemen. Peace and prosperity—but not, necessarily, in that order."

Frost had touched the bare limbs of the trees, silvering them, and laying crystal splinters on the lawn of Blytheswood. The sun had come out again, finally, sparkling colors in the melting ice, but it was still bitter cold and no one was doing work outside. Leanna was cutting patterns out of homespun linsey woolsey, spread out over the dining room table that had once known only Irish lace and English porcelain. It no longer even occurred to her how much her life had changed since the war began. Now this was normal. Doc Lacey had volunteered to help her and that was luxury enough in these days, having an extra pair of hands.

"I'm still not sure," Leanna argued softly, shaking her head. "I know you're worried about what the shock of it might do to her—to the baby really—but Jonathon was Whitney's husband, after all. I don't feel right not telling her."

"Why endanger the baby for no reason? Whitney will need that child more than ever when she does finally have to know. And, on that point, have you done anything yet about making arrangements to move her? To a hospital, I mean? Remember, I told—"

"I remember," Leanna interrupted with a frown. "But you don't understand how desperately overcrowded Virginia hospitals and doctoring staffs are just now."

"They'll have to make room."

"Maybe they could in Savannah or Columbia—farther south. But here, military needs are overwhelming. They have top priority and civilian problems just go by the boards."

"Washington, then, perhaps. Would you consider that? If I get the transfer I've requested, I could perhaps pull strings there. The Northern hospitals aren't so overworked. Mrs. Leighton, that woman needs professional care, and right now, or you can start unraveling those baby buntings you've been knitting."

"Hello."

Leanna had missed the soft click of the front door closing, but she heard the soft knock against the dining room door frame, the deep sound of that baritone voice. Her breath caught in her throat as she looked up.

"Pleasant trip, Chase?"

"Uneventful." He shrugged and stepped forward with a smile, gesturing to the cut cloth. "Domestic little scene."

Lacey grinned, holding up the shears and waving them gaily. "Staying in practice for my chosen profession."

Chase grimaced and half turned, glancing toward Leanna. Their eyes met for a fraction of a second. Her heart skipped a beat and a blush began to rise on her cheeks. How handsome he looked standing there against the white painted woodwork, despite travel-muddied boots, the damn Yankee blue of his coat. A portion of her was uneasy at his return. It had been four days, and the last time she'd seen him she had been in his arms, shame and guilt thrown to the winds. But the greater portion of her simply rejoiced to see him again. Her heart lifted and sang for all she tried to silence it.

"You look . . . well."

He walked toward her and his hand touched her shoulder gently, tentatively, lingering a moment more than it should have. Leanna glanced up again with a strained smile, nodding more to the expression in his soft, dark eyes than to his words. "I'm fine, thank you."

He smiled then faintly, nodding once, his eyes holding hers for another instant in a wordless question. Do you hate me, Leanna? Can you forgive me for loving you so?

"And what's the verdict from our beloved commander?" Doc Lacey didn't glance up from the pattern he was cutting, but he was neither unaware of nor altogether surprised at the undercurrents of emotion passing between the other two. And it was another reason he'd requested transfer. The sort of pain that lay in store for them was beyond his province of healing. "Goeth we forward? Backward? In circles?"

"None of the above." Chase turned with a forced smile, walking toward him. "We winter right where we're at." He avoided looking at Leanna as he spoke, wondering whether that news would please or displease her. Bittersweet, maybe. It had struck him that way. "Or I should say, most of us. You're transferred to your Washington hospital, Doctor. Effective the fifteenth."

"Day after tomorrow."

"That's right."

"Who's my replacement?"

"We don't get one—at least not right now. I guess they figure we'll stay healthy even this far south in the Valley."

Doc Lacey frowned, turning to Leanna. "That makes what I was just telling you doubly imperative, Mrs.

126

Leighton. Your sister-in-law can't remain at New Market without a doctor within fifty miles." He glanced back at Chase, half smiling. "You pulled some strings to get me moved so fast."

"Did I?"

"Oh, you had your father do it. He has Stanton's ear obviously."

"Are you complaining?"

"Not at all. I just wish you'd take as good care of your own happiness as you do of mine."

Chase shrugged and turned away. He didn't want to get into another discussion of that, especially with Leanna present. "I've a report to finish. I'll be down for dinner."

Leanna dared a last glance at him as he walked out toward the stairway, wondering what exactly that was all about. It echoed something Doc Lacey had said once before at an early dinner, something she hadn't understood then, either. Inexplicably, she felt a soft rush of fear rising and she shrugged it away, forcing her mind to other things. Would it help Mosby to know the Federals were wintering here? And if so, could she tell him? Could she risk her Yankee major for the sake of the CSA? She wasn't sure any longer.

"There, all done. Now what?"

Leanna forced all other thoughts away and went to show him.

They remained at the dinner table after the others had left. Like a family, Leanna thought wryly—the mother, the father, the eldest son, the younger children sent off to bed while the grown ups had brandy and a fine-leaf cigar.

"I'll just stay in the house then for one more night. It seems senseless to move again," Doc Lacey was saying. "Though with you back, I doubt the ladies would need my protection."

Leanna blinked to hide the surprise of a sudden realization. Far from imposing on her at the beginning, Chase had taken a room in the main house to offer protection. After all, there were two hundred men stationed here, many of them uncouth, maybe even dangerous. That hadn't occurred to her until now.

"Suit yourself," Chase shrugged agreeably. "I think I may move Captain Grier in when you go. Since we're to be here longer, and I'll be gone now and again—"

"Major Courtland?"

A young lieutenant appeared in the doorway, looking anxious. "Pickets on the west are reporting light musket fire."

"All right. Order a patrol saddled. And draw the other picket lines in to defensive positions." Chase managed a weary smile and nodded to Doc Lacey and Leanna as he stood up. "Apparently duty calls. Enjoy your brandy and your port without me."

"Be careful," Leanna urged softly, trying not to let her fear show. "Keep your head down, as they say."

"That's in trenches, not on horseback," Doc Lacey only chuckled, looking unconcerned.

"Well, whatever—just take care." Leanna was flustered and trying to hide it. Chase had gone when she looked up again and fear renewed its relentless gnawing. Now she must worry for two men, she found herself thinking. The man she'd married and the man she loved. Two men on opposite sides of a tragic, deadly war.

"Not worrying over some damnyankee, Mrs. Leighton? You needn't. Chase can take care of himself."

The words were soft and kindly said, but she only shrugged, little comforted. "I thought my brother Jonathon could have, too." Leanna did not know her brother clung yet, however precariously, to life in a Washington military hospital. She thought of him dead and buried. And the idea of Chase following him there was not something she could easily shrug off.

Doc Lacey watched her a moment with a serious eye, his smile fading. "I meant well, you know, when I challenged you that night of the fire to come out of your rooms and confront us. The North is going to win the war. There's going to be Yankees around Blytheswood for some time yet. More rather than less. I thought it best you should adjust yourself to that harsh reality and learn to live with us while someone like Chase Courtland was in command and liable to forgive the worst of your defiance." He sighed slowly as he shook his head, and looked thoughtfully back down into his brandy glass. "Now I'm not at all sure I did you or Chase any favor that night."

"I've still got Blytheswood, at least."

"Yes, you do." He managed a faint smile, remembering how many dinners had passed where Leanna had carefully remarked over a wall that needed shoring up, or a line of fence not quite straight. Inevitably, the next day or so, he would find a detail of soldiers attending to the thing. Yes, she had very definitely retained possession of Blytheswood. "I only wonder now what price you've paid to do that."

Leanna glanced at him sidelong, considering. "I believe you tricked me, Doctor, into doing what you wanted. I suppose I should be angry at you for that."

"Angry? I hope not. I warned you, if you remember. I told you my only allegiance in this war is to the preservation of life. On either side. I warned you I would use any means available, honorable or not."

"Yes, I recall that now. We had quite a discussion on that point."

He smiled, faintly. "As important as Blytheswood is to you, you may be quite content with how my little game played out. But Chase, on the other hand—I'm more concerned about now than ever."

"Why?" Despite herself, Leanna's face paled, and her eyes searched the Yankee doctor's anxiously. "You just told me yourself that he could take care of—"

"As far as the fighting goes, yes," he hastened to assure her. "He's an excellent soldier, Mrs. Leighton. You haven't seen that side of him, but he's one of the best officers I've seen wearing a uniform. It's not bullets I'm worried about. Not his ability to avoid them if he chooses, anyway. But Gettysburg changed something in this war. Changed something in its basic nature. It used to be army versus army, a gentlemen's duel on a grander scale. There used to be honor in it—or an attempt at honor, anyway. Gettysburg changed that, I'm afraid. All those slaughtered thousands, Pickett's men alone stacked up like human firewood around the bottom of that stupid hill he was trying to capture. More than just men died there. Honor did, too. All the chips are on the table now, neither side can afford to risk allowing 'honor' to weaken their hand. It's like two bull terriers, now, with their teeth in each other's throats, Mrs. Leighton. It's the death struggle."

Leanna said nothing, but she watched his face as he spoke. An anguish almost personal lay etched upon it, and she felt a deep, cold stirring of fear. What was he trying to tell her?

"Chase is an intelligent man. He's not insensible to the changes I've been describing. He knows that when the war reopens this spring it will be a different kind of war than we've been fighting up to now. It's going to turn desperate—and ugly. But Chase is a gentleman. To the very core. He won't abandon his principles, and that's going to put him at a severe disadvantage. Not only with the enemy, either, but with his own side." He paused and glanced up at her sharply, gesturing in the air above his glass. "Have you ever seen an eagle in a storm, Mrs. Leighton? Flying against the wind? Exhausting himself and gaining no ground for all his efforts? That will be Chase Courtland this spring."

"You can't expect me to express disapproval of that, Doctor. I quite understand his commitment to honor. And not every man is going to abandon his sense of fair play, either, regardless of what you say. General Lee, for example, will never fight that kind of a war."

"Then he will lose. He may, if he holds as true as you seem to think, lose with honor, but he will still lose. That's inevitable. I've tried to convince Chase of the insanity of subjecting himself to it. His father is a very powerful man in Washington. He could easily arrange a safe desk job for his son that would eliminate the double dangers he'll face in the field, but Chase is too damn stubborn to take that course."

Leanna smiled faintly, a bittersweet smile. She could understand. Doc Lacey had once noted how much alike she and Chase were. Even while she ached for it, she understood what he was doing. "Why tell me about this, Captain Lacey? You can't expect me to agree with you?"

"I was hoping, quite frankly, that you would see the sense of what I'm saying and use your own influence on Chase to urge him to get out of a situation that is liable to kill him. We both know he's in love with you. You're in love with him, also. I had hoped deeply enough to place his survival above some archaic code of honor. Was I wrong?"

Leanna had blanched white at his words, praying no one else had heard them, feeling half sick even to hear such a guilty admission spoken aloud. "Please, Doctor. You forget I'm a married woman. A Confederate one, as well. I have no say in Major Courtland's choices."

"Yes, you do. For God's sake, can't we for once be honest?"

"I simply cannot listen to any further discussion of this, Doctor Lacey, I'm sorry." Leanna rose shakily to her feet. "You must excuse me now."

"For God's sake, won't either of you listen to me?"

His words caught Leanna at the doorway. She didn't look around, but the genuine desperation in his voice checked her exit for a moment. She closed her eyes helplessly, reaching for the door frame for support.

"Don't kill him, Mrs. Leighton, that's all I'm asking you. Don't add more weight to a burden he's already going to be struggling under. At least convince him not to throw his life away to gain nothing."

There was only another silence for answer and Leanna waited, half sick, half stunned.

"I'll be expecting to see your sister-in-law at the hospital in Washington at any time." He sounded tired suddenly, his voice soft, as if defeated. "Chase should be able to arrange safe transportation for her. I'll try to arrange it so she can live with one of the women nurses there."

There was another silence and Leanna nodded finally, starting toward the stairs. "Thank you, Doctor. I'll try to talk her into it." Behind her, she heard him sigh, heard the scrape of his chair as he sat back down to finish the last of his brandy. For an evening that had started out so pleasantly, it hadn't ended well at all, she found herself thinking. Not well at all.

"You're still awake?"

She managed a smile and spread her hands in an awkward little gesture, almost regretting the impulse that had made her open her door as she'd heard his returning bootsteps in the hall. "Yes, I—well, I was concerned about you."

"You needn't have been," Chase offered a one-sided smile and a shrug. "It was only a couple of youngsters with a squirrel gun. We spanked their bottoms with the stock of the gun and sent them home."

"One day it won't be youngsters."

"Yes, I know." The smile faded and he glanced away. Silence followed, heavy in the air. Finally, he raised his eyes to hers again, speaking softly. "Anyway, I'm glad you're up. And alone. I wanted to talk to you about—"

"Please, no, Chase." Leanna spoke in a rush. "Please, let's just accept it as something that happened and try to forget it. I have to. I'm married, and nothing can change that."

He nodded once, aware of the strangeness that lay heavily between them, aware of how carefully they were keeping several yards away from each other in the shadowed hallway. At least she didn't blame him for what had happened. At least she didn't hate him for it. Her eyes said that clearer than words ever could. They had that afternoon when he'd first gotten back. "I bought something for you while I was in Harper's Ferry. I hope you'll accept it. There wasn't time earlier this evening to give it to you."

Leanna was startled to see him reach in his coat pocket as he spoke, oddly touched that he should have carried it there rather than packing it in his saddlebag or

132

trunk. Gold gleamed in the faint light as he handed it to her, shrugging his uneasiness. "I'm sorry. I suppose I should have thought to have it wrapped or something."

She managed a smile, rather than cry, as she took it. Crying had been disasterous in the past. The metal was still cold from the December night, but it warmed quickly in her hand as she turned it over. "It's lovely." It was a locket, plainly, but beautifully, made. The inside of it was empty, but she could feel engraving on the underside and turned it to the light. 'For a Rebel's Honor,' the inscription read.

"I thought a lot about what happened, Leanna, between us." Chase stayed a step away from her, speaking in a low murmur. "I wanted to . . . to give you something to try to tell you that . . . well, that, there was honor and not shame involved, I guess. Sometimes, a thing may appear dishonorable on the surface, but when you look deeper, it has its own, private kind of integrity."

Leanna nodded, knowing better than to try to speak when her throat felt this way and her lip had begun to tremble.

"Anyway, I wanted you to have that as a reminder to balance against any memories that might—some day—upset you."

Leanna felt tears blurring her eyes, so she only nodded again. He smiled once, briefly, as if it were an effort, then forced himself to move, turning toward his own room. "Good night then. Sleep well."

She barely had time to murmur a farewell before he was gone, the door closing softly behind him. Another door closed downstairs and startled her. Doc Lacey, she realized instantly. Probably also waiting up to see the soldiers safely home. She closed her fingers around the locket as she turned for her own room. It was not until she was in bed that she remembered Doc Lacey's earlier pleas regarding the Yankee major. What would he have thought if he could have witnessed the scene just now in the hallway, she wondered. Approved or disapproved? Could he possibly be right in what he'd said about Chase earlier? Could honor ever prove the desperate

133

disadvantage he'd said it would be? And if so, where did her responsibilities lie? To her own honor? To her own cause of the Confederacy? Or to the Yankee she had no right to love: She had no answer, but the locket remained in her hand when she finally fell asleep.

The assignment to the Confederate prisoner ward was not unexpected, Doc Lacey mused silently as he followed the older man into it. Lowest in rank and seniority of the staff here, he would be given what no one else wanted, which was all right with him. Life was life as he saw it. He didn't care what color uniform it wore.

"Amputation of the right leg to the knee—gangrene developed in the field hospital, so we cut to the hip joint.

Lacey followed Surgeon Colonel Peterson down the long row of narrow cots, nodding to brief explanations gestured at some of the beds, never breaking stride. Peterson was a nice enough fellow. Decidedly pleased to be unloading this inglorious position. Old school type. He had a habit of running his hands through his hair and then examining an open wound, and his fingernails showed dirt beneath them. He would do well for himself, Lacey decided drily. Rock no boats and rise predictably to a fine career.

He stopped suddenly behind Peterson, frowning at a nameless young man lying unconscious in a bed. A strange, semifamiliarity struck him, and he stared at the man thoughtfully. Fredricksburg? Chancellorsville? Gettysburg? Maybe he'd dressed some minor wound for him once.

"Oh, don't worry too much about him," Colonel Peterson shrugged with a frown. "Stomach wound—bad one. We've been expecting him to go any time."

Doc Lacey stepped carefully to the side of the cot, practically wedging himself between the tiny space between one cot and the next. Peterson flipped through a handful of cards as he followed. "Here it is. Admitted on the fifth of December."

134

"Anything done for him?" Lacey reached for the card as he questioned.

"No sense in it. He's on morphine now for pain, but he hasn't been conscious for days."

Doc Lacey glanced down at the card and froze, staring at the name carefully written at the top. 'Penley, Major, CSA.' Dear God, Leanna's brother! He shoved the card back at Peterson and leaned over to rip the sheet back from the bed, trembling with a strange mixture of anger and hope. His heart dropped as he saw a thick wad of bandages bound to the young man's stomach— filthy, and dark brown with dried blood. Damn this war. Damn it. He pulled at the mess in mingled care and haste, ignoring Peterson's curious mumblings to call for more light.

"Really, Captain Lacey, you're not even required to start duty until tomorrow."

Lacey shrugged dismissal and gestured a young woman holding a lamp to come closer. He saw her rather pretty face pale as she glanced down, but she stood stoically, making no protest. He smiled grimly. "Ever work in surgery?"

Susan Stratford, Chase Courtland's fiancée, shook her head, trying to force an apologetic smile. She was new at this. She'd only begun work a month ago.

"Good. I won't have to untrain you than of sloppy habits." He paused a moment, waiting for her startled glance. He got it and smiled again, holding her eyes. "Would you do it? Help me, I mean? Would you be willing to learn?"

She blinked in momentary indecision, cringing inside, but equally determined to do it. It could be Chase lying there. Or her brother, if he hadn't died at Chancellorsville. "Yes," her voice was not as firm as she tried to make it, so she nodded for emphasis, "yes, I'll try."

Doc Lacey smiled, gently and thankfully, and Susan began to blush as he bent back to his examination. It wasn't as bad as it could have been, he was thinking. Penley was lucky that they'd given up so easily. They hadn't dug clumsily around in his guts for the Minnie ball. Hadn't stuck dirty forceps into the wound. It was ugly and it was dark red, but it wasn't infected. And if he had lived this long with the damn thing, maybe, just maybe. . . . "How much lime chloride have you on hand, Colonel?"

Peterson blinked, totally confused. "Lime what?"

Doc Lacey smiled and sighed softly as he straightened up. It was a good feeling really, the sudden realization of being where he belonged, where he would be staying for the rest of the war. Penley was first, but there would be others—hundreds of them. Young lives to wrestle away from the war's ugly grip. "Lime chloride, Colonel. I'll need it by the gallon. Chlorine, too, and Dakin's solution. You just got a break, sir, the rest of the day off. I'll be on duty beginning right now."

Chapter Nine

Jewel looked tired today. She'd aged with the news of Jonathon's death, and it occurred to Leanna with a shock that the woman was no longer young. More gray than black now hid beneath the red scarf she wore on her head. And these cold mornings, her fingers were too stiff to knead the dough like she used to. She smiled gently and reached to touch Jewel's massive hand. "Take a rest, Jewel. I'll do whatever needs doing."

"Can't be, chile." Jewel shook her head. "I got to tidy the major's room. It ain't proper for you to be doin' it!"

"Proper," Leanna forced a half laugh, avoiding Jewel's eyes. If she only knew how improper she'd already been. "Who's going to know the difference?"

"I am," Jewel grunted, her black eyes gleaming stubbornness. "War or no war, I ain't raised you to be playin' maid servant to no stranger."

"Major Courtland's hardly a stranger any more. Good Lord, he lives right here in the house with us."

"You knows what I mean."

"I'll leave the bed then." Leanna smiled wryly at Jewel's look of shock at her bluntness. "And do the rest." She turned to avoid more argument, starting up the stairs. Jewel muttered behind her but she ignored her, only stopping to pick up a dusting cloth. She should have noticed how worn out Jewel was before, she scolded herself.

How old was the woman, anyway? She'd been too deeply engrossed in her own problems—Jonathon, Whitney's struggle to keep that last precious child, Stewart, and Chase, Blytheswood's demands, this endless, damnable war. She stopped short as she began to dust the carved oak desk by the window. A single letter lay there, written in an obviously feminine hand. Chase's sister. Or his fiancée? A wave of jealousy surged through her at the thought, then anger at herself for a sudden desire to open that letter and read its contents. Her hand jerked with reaction and the edge of the cloth flipped the closed inkstand off the desk top. Damn it. She dropped the cloth and crawled beneath the desk, groping for the ink stand. If the fall had knocked the lid open, it would be a real mess. Ink on the carpet, likely on the bottom of the draperies as well.

She froze suddenly, frowning, closing her fingers around something and drawing it slowly out. A book. *The* book, she corrected herself with a half-sick, half-stunned feeling. It lay black and ominous as she put it in her lap and stared down at it. Oh, God . . . why did she have to find the cursed thing now?

Footsteps sounded suddenly in the hallway outside the door. Jewel, she figured. Coming to finish. In unthinking reaction, she pushed the book down into her apron and scrambled to her feet, grabbing one handed for the dust cloth. Chase Courtland opened the door, looking as startled to see her there as she was to see him. The book suddenly felt cold and shameful where it pressed against her belly and Leanna paled, turning her head to avoid his eyes. Oh, God, now what? Now she'd already taken the damn thing.

"Leanna, are you all right?" He smiled faintly, cocking his dark head to one side. She was pale as death. "Did you need me for something?"

Leanna flung him a startled glance. "What? Oh . . . oh, no. I was cleaning. You just startled me."

He began to frown. "Cleaning in here?"

"Well, Jewel usually does it, but she's not as young as she used to be."

"You have enough to do without this, for God's sake." He looked faintly angry as he walked forward. "You needn't turn yourslf into a servant girl."

"Well, someone has to do these things and the day girls didn't come today because of the storm." Leave me

138

be, Chase, she begged him silently. Turn around and go out again so I can decide what I should do.

"Leanna, I mean it. I don't want you cleaning up after me like a damn maid. Give me the cloth, I'll do it myself."

He snatched the thing from her hand and Leanna blinked in surprise, shaking her head and grabbing it back. "Southern men don't dust."

"I'm not Southern, remember?"

"I don't believe Yankee men dust either."

"Well, this one does apparently, if it's a choice between you doing it or me."

"But it hardly needs doing!"

Chase raised one brow. "Well, then why are you so determined to do it?"

There was no answer to that. None she could give him anyway. Fate, Leanna began thinking. This was the hand of fate. Her finding the book when she did . . . him coming in just then . . . now refusing to leave and let her decide. Her heart began to thud sickly. She just didn't want to do what she knew she ought to do.

He smiled quizzically, his brown eyes gentle as he looked down at her. "Leanna, are you sure you're all right? You're not yourself."

"I'm fine, Chase, really I am." It sounded false even to her ears and she wasn't surprised he questioned it.

"You don't seem it. What's the matter?"

She had to turn away from the softness of his gaze, struggling for a feasible answer. "Well . . . I'm just . . . well, I wanted to go riding this afternoon. And there's so much to do."

"Riding in the snow?"

"Well, the snow stopped this morning. The sun's out now."

"It's still cold."

"I like riding in this weather. It's one of my favorite times, actually." If she could get off by herself a few minutes . . . to think this thing over. . . . What if she decided to put it back? How could she? What if Chase discovered the book missing in the meantime? Dear

God, couldn't he see the damned thing under her apron? It felt huge—terribly, terribly visible. She had to make a choice and fate was giving her no time to consider.

"Well, I'll go riding with you, then." He smiled faintly and turned his back to reach for something. As soon as he had turned, Leanna started for the door.

"No, that's not necessary, really."

"I must insist." He smiled, but his voice was firm, his eyes still shadowed by puzzlement as he watched her retreating. "It's not safe, Leanna, for you to go alone. You know that."

Leanna stood staring at him, feeling the trap jaws close on her. Here, Chase, she wanted so desperately to say. Here's your book. I found it by accident. I don't want to give it to men who might use it to hurt you, to kill you. Why didn't you keep it out of my way?

"Especially after that guerrilla raid on the last supply train. It was only two days ago."

She stared at him a moment longer, feeling tears start to her eyes, feeling her heart aching as though it would break. She would never have gone looking for the book—not any longer, not since she realized she loved this man who should have been her enemy. But it had fallen in her lap, practically. To do nothing with it now, to throw away such a priceless, desperately needed advantage to the South—to break the Yankee code, maybe change the whole tide of the war. She had no choice, she realized suddenly. Fate had made it for her. "All right, I'll get changed."

There was an odd, despairing note in her voice and Chase frowned again, more puzzled than ever, opening his mouth to ask her once more what was the matter. But he changed his mind before he spoke. Jewel, maybe, he thought. She's concerned about Jewel. "I'll get the horses saddled."

Leanna nodded without turning back. Tears were spilling to stain her apron and the black leather of the book was showing through the wet spots.

* * *

It was now or never. The Jenkins farm was just over the hill. From there, she could get the book to Mosby. The thought echoed like a death knell and Leanna closed her eyes in a silent prayer for strength. You've got to, Leanna, she told herself. It was important enough for your brother to die for, important enough for your husband to risk dying for—your husband, Leanna, remember him? The one you've already betrayed once with the Yankees. Now's the time to balance the scales. Chase was riding only a half-dozen yards from her, silent as he had been for most of the ride, as if respecting her strange mood. She could not resist a last glance at his handsome face, dark against the blinding white of the slushy, half melted snow that covered the ground and left mud in the horses' tracks. Good-bye, she thought to him. Chase, I'm sorry. . . .

She set heels to her mare in that instant, and the horse leapt forward, glad to stretch her legs on such a briskly cold day. She saw Chase rein in his horse in startlement. Heard him call to her in anxious question. Leanna bent lower over the mare's neck, urging her to greater speed, raising her riding whip. The sudden pounding of Chase's horse following sounded behind her and she whipped the mare, turning her toward a split-rail fence. Jasmin would take the jump easily. She was used to such sport. Pray God, the Yankee animal would be unable to follow.

The mare's ears went up, Leanna felt the tension of her body as she gathered herself for the jump, and she gave the horse her head. They started up into the air, and suddenly Leanna was grabbing desperately for a handful of mane to save her seat on the sidesaddle. One of the horse's hind legs had slipped in the slushy snow. The rail came flying to meet them with a sickening, splintering sound, and Leanna went off in a somersault as the mare went down into the fence. She was dimly aware of Chase calling to her as the ground came up and then, for a moment, she was aware of nothing but a black explosion of pain.

"Leanna! Jesus God, you scared me half to death!"

141

She opened her eyes to find Chase bent over her, raising her against his chest with one arm, his face ashen testimony to the sincerity of his words.

"What in the world were you thinking of, trying to take a jump in this footing? You're lucky you didn't break your fool neck!"

She couldn't speak for tears, only laid her face closer to his shoulder and closed her eyes. It hadn't worked then. She had tried and failed. At least she'd tried. But she was honest enough to admit that the tears that burned so hotly on her snow-chilled cheeks weren't tears of despair, but of relief.

"Are you hurt? Here, maybe I'd better take you back to the house." Chase started to reach beneath her. Leanna felt the book suddenly, loosened from her fall, beginning to slip as Chase tightened his grip.

"No, Chase, no. I'm all right." She tried to twist out of his arms to make a one-handed grab behind her for the book. But he was already reaching an arm under her knees, beginning to lift her. Leanna felt it falling and made a last desperate, futile effort. She missed. The book slid out of her riding skirt waistband, hit his arm, and fell from under her cloak to land in the snow with a soft plop.

"*What?*"

She didn't bother to look down. She kept her eyes on Chase's face as he began to frown, releasing her slowly to reach beneath her. "Chase, it isn't what you think." She spoke it urgently, reaching to grip his shoulder. "It's not that I wanted to hurt—"

"So now I understand your sudden passion for riding in the snow." Chase stared down at the book, turning it over slowly to brush the snow off it. "Your sudden passion for a lot of things, maybe."

Leanna paled as if he'd struck her. There was a silence. Then color flooded back into her face with a scarlet rush. "You can't mean that you think—"

"Major! You all right?"

Mounted sentries galloped up, rearing to a sliding stop. Chase slid the book into an inside pocket as he stood. Leanna reached for his arm, trying to hold him, but he jerked away, his face dark and frighteningly grim.

"I'm fine. She might not be."

Leanna watched his face beseechingly, afraid to say anything with the others so close. Chase didn't look at her. He turned away on one heel to grab for the reins of his horse.

"I'll run down the mare." He spoke over one shoulder and mounted without a backward glance.

Leanna scrambled to her feet as she saw him begin to turn his horse, desperation overwhelming caution. "Chase, for God's sake!" she cried out in a sob, reaching after him as he turned. "Chase, listen to me!"

He spurred the horse away from beneath her hand, not looking back. She stumbled off balance as the horse's passage buffeted her. Pain shot up her leg from the ankle. She took another futile step after him, then halted with a sob, tears running down her face to drop in the snow at her feet.

Behind her, the troopers exchanged long looks and a silent shrug. It was a matter of some interesting discussion among the enlisted men at Blytheswood—whether their major and the beautiful lady Rebel shared more than a dinner table. Obviously not, the shrugs said. Or he wouldn't leave her standing in the cold snow.

Leanna had forgotten them. She stood staring after the Yankee major with desolation in her eyes. Chase, no, she tried to send the thought to him. Chase, you can't believe what you just said. Can't you understand what I did? Not that I *wanted* to, but that I *had* to. I *had* to, Chase, despite everything I feel for you.

"You need a hand, ma'am?"

The voice startled her and she turned too quickly, stumbling again on her weakened ankle. Fresh pain shot up her leg. She tried to hide it, raising her head and squaring her shoulders and trying to see the soldiers clearly despite the tears in her eyes.

"Here. Climb on up." One of the other troopers kicked his horse forward, bumping the first and obviously not caring. He only smiled to the other man's frown. "I'll keep you warm on the ride back."

"Stop it, Banks, you shouldn't—"

"Shut up. You ain't no officer to give orders."

"Banks, you're looking for trouble."

"Comin' up, lady? Or you planning to walk home?"

Leanna paled, glancing at the other two men. Neither one met her eye. If they didn't approve of their comrade's coarseness, still they weren't ready to battle him for her sake, either. She closed her eyes in abject misery, turning away for answer. She started to walk, trying to ignore the ever worsening pain in her ankle. Banks reined his horse against her shoulder, following her, step after slow step.

"You only go for Yanks with shoulder straps?"

Her face flamed and she clenched her teeth, struggling another step.

"You took to the major's lap cozily enough when he hauled you up out of the river that day."

Pain shot through her ankle again, and Leanna turned on the man baiting her, her eyes flashing anger and humiliation beneath the gleam of tears. "Your major's a gentleman! You aren't. Now leave me alone!"

Banks only laughed, leaning down from his saddle to cup Leanna's chin in his hand in a sudden, rough grip. She cried a protest, raising her hand to slap at him. "Yip! Yip! Yippeee!" He only laughed again, mocking the Rebel yell. Leanna stumbled and fell to one knee as he released her unexpectedly, then began to turn his horse around toward her again. She was frightened suddenly, as well as angry. She tried to jerk to her feet and only stumbled again, catching her boot heel in the overlong hem of the riding skirt.

"Banks, that's enough." One of the other troopers had finally had it. He pulled his horse in front of Banks's and dismounted, turning to offer Leanna a hand. "Here, Mrs. Leighton. You can take my horse. I'll lead you back."

Leanna mumbled a tearful thanks, trying and failing to maintain any show of dignity. She could feel Banks's eyes burning on her still. Blytheswood was miles away, Chase was lost to her forever. She let the Yankee soldier push her up to his saddle and then she gave in to the desolation that wrenched her heart, dropping her face down into her hands to cry, wishing she'd never heard of Mosby, code books, or Major Chase Courtland.

"Propriety will have to suffer, then, Jewel. I want to speak to Mrs. Leighton alone."

Jewel rose from her chair by the open door, taking a stubborn stance. There was a terrible grimness in the major's face, like she'd never seen on it before. But Leanna was her last baby now. She wasn't going to lose her to this war, too. Not while she drew breath. "You ain't coming in here, boy. Not over my dead body!"

"Move aside, Jewel."

"Miz Leighton's in bed still and she ain't—"

"Damn it! I said get out of my way!"

"It's all right, Jewel." Leanna closed her eyes momentarily, the blood draining from her face. But she kept her chin high. "Please let him in." Her voice was soft but there was something in it that weakened Jewel's iron resolve. A plea, almost. And a terrible, terrible despair.

Chase looked up from the black woman's face into Leanna's. She was in bed still. That, at least, had been the truth. Jewel wavered another second, then grumbled an anxious protest and waddled through the door, risking a last backward glance at the girl in the bed. "I'll be right out here in the hall if you needs me, chile."

Leanna didn't even hear her. All her attention was focused on him. On the dark pain in his eyes, the grim, silent strength of his white-edged jaw. He took a half-dozen steps forward to stand beside the edge of the bed.

"I'm leaving for Winchester. I'm liable to be several days. I'll need your sworn word you won't try anything else—at least while I'm gone."

Leanna looked up at him where he stood barely out of arm's reach by her bedside, and her heart sank even lower than it had been before this entrance—something she hadn't thought possible. Amber brown eyes once so very warm were now equally that cold. Her lip began to quiver and she bit at it to restrain tears. "Yes, of course. You have my word."

"Good." He turned even as he spoke, starting back toward the door.

Leanna sat up and made a desperate grab for his hand, missed it, and cried softly aloud in a choking sob. "Chase!"

The anguish of her voice touched him—echoed deep where it hurt the worst, and involuntarily he checked his step.

"Chase, you must listen to me. I found the book purely by accident. I didn't go looking for it. And I didn't know what else to do, what else I *could* do. Oh, Chase, for God's sake, forgive me!" Leanna tasted the salt of tears as she spoke, heard her voice breaking and was helpless to prevent it. She stared beseechingly at his back, broad, darkly blue, rigidly set.

He only nodded and started forward again, still not turning around, not looking back. Leanna watched him helplessly as he reached for the brass knob, opening the door, to walk through it. "Chase, please!" He offered no sign of having heard her. Only the soft click of the closing door broke the silence and Leanna closed her eyes against fresh tears as she listened to the measured rhythm of his bootsteps fading down the hall.

It was a week to the day before Jonathon opened his eyes with any kind of consciousness. Doc Lacey sat on the edge of the crisp linen bed, smiling faintly, but only a vague blur to Jonathon's eyes. Behind him stood a young woman, also blurred, but there was a certain softness in her face that reminded him of Whitney, and he frowned, making the effort to clear his vision.

"Feeling better, Major Penley?"

It was the man who spoke, not the woman. It startled him and he redirected his gaze to find the speaker. Feeling better? Was he? Yes, he thought in sleepy surprise. Yes, he was. He tried to say so and couldn't.

Only a soft, slurred sound came out of his mouth. He frowned, embarrassed, beginning to try again. Greater pain was coming with greater consciousness, and he reached instinctively to touch his belly.

"No, no, Major. Hands off." Doc Lacey chuckled, deflecting the young officer's hand. He held the young man's drowsy eyes for a moment, his smile fading as compassion softened his amusement. "I know, Major, believe me. I know it hurts. But you won't live unless you eat, and you won't eat if you're always asleep from the morphine."

Jonathon made the effort to concentrate. The Yankee doctor's words echoed as if in a tunnel, distant, far away, each word a puzzle to be slowly solved. Finally, he understood, and nodded once, even that small effort exhausting. Doc Lacey reached a hand to his shoulder in understanding, then gestured Susan closer.

"Beef soup. I want you to eat all of it." He moved to let the girl take his place, not noticing her quick blush at the touch of his hand on her arm. He stood close to her as she spooned the first few mouthfuls into the CSA major's mouth, not realizing his hand rested still on the girl's slender shoulder. At last, he noticed. Surprise changed to a kind of gentle amusement and he glanced at Susan's face. She didn't seem to mind at all. What a pretty girl, and a wonderful nurse, he thought. He knew by now she was Chase's fiancée and had, of course, said nothing to her of Chase's love for Penley's sister. And he'd keep silent, too. Still, if Chase weren't in love with Susan, perhaps. . . .

"Well, I guess I'll go send that telegram I've been waiting to send," he commented finally, watching her face. "To Chase." Her expression didn't change and Doc Lacey smiled faintly, pleased. "Perhaps afterwards we could celebrate together with a late supper. I'm afraid I've worked you awfully hard these past few days. We'll make it a token of my extreme appreciation."

Susan blushed and nodded awkwardly, unable to hide entirely the smile that instantly curved her mouth. She didn't look at him, but Doc Lacey touched her shoulder once more as he turned to go. 'Merry Christmas,' he thought he'd say. 'Pleased to report from Washington that CSA Major Penley is still alive, and contrary to earlier rumor, looks liable to remain very much that way.' He didn't think he'd mention Susan. That could wait for another time.

Chapter Ten

On Christmas Eve in Philadelphia, soft white snow was falling. The wet cold made Joshua Courtland's chest pains worsen, so he observed the holiday near a warm fire, with aged brandy and a fine cigar. 'Peace on Earth, Goodwill toward Men.' It seemed a more distant dream than ever these days, and carolers singing of such sweet wishes struck him as sadly naive. But most of Philadelphia, like the other Northern cities, was celebrating gaily this year. Satin gowns and extravagant champagne suppers were once more the norm in holly-draped mansions glittering in the dark, for December opened the social calendar. The less wealthy sang, and ice skated on frozen ponds. Some ate chestnuts roasted by street-corner braziers. Almost everywhere in the North, people rejoiced. The tide of the war was turning at last.

Below the Mason-Dixon line, the Christmas of 1863 wasn't quite so merry. Not dismal either, for hope was still high and the people had a deep abiding faith in God to see their just cause eventually triumphant. Lieutenant Colonel Stewart Leighton shared dinner with a local judge and his family and a dozen other of Jeb Stuart's officers who hadn't gone home for the holiday. They served an eggnog, light on eggs, heavy on brandy, and then discussed plans for raiding the next Yankee payroll headed for Culpepper.

Whitney had helped Miranda onto a chair to hang her homemade stocking on Cool Spring's high mantle. The tree was trimmed this year with pinecones and tattered bits of ribbon, but Mandy, who remembered no other Christmas, thought it fine indeed. Corn for popcorn had gone to the army. Cranberries were unobtainable. But the baby had kicked in Whitney's belly for the very

149

first time today, and except for her continuing fears for Jonathon, the day had been a truly fine one.

On Christmas Eve, Blytheswood was quiet—exceptionally quiet, as snow falling tended to make a place. The house was dark and Leanna laid staring at the canopy of her bed. Chase had been five days in Winchester. He'd arrived home this evening, late, after she'd retired to her room. She'd heard his boot steps in the hall, coming from the stairway, and had shamelessly closed her eyes and prayed he would come knock at her door. He hadn't. He hadn't forgiven her. Even after the passing of the long, long days. And pain that had finally begun to lessen had seared her soul with new agony. Fresh tears trickled silently to fall on an already wet pillow. How could she love him this desperately? How could it hurt so badly to have done the only honorable thing she could do? Honor had done this, she found herself thinking. Throw honor to the winds, then. It couldn't be right to live hurting this badly. She must somehow make him understand.

No light showed beneath the crack of his door, and for a moment only, Leanna hesitated. Then she reached for the knob, knocking softly as she swung it open to step inside. Chase glanced up from the edge of the bed, startled by the sight of Leanna standing shadowed in silver moonlight. He stood up slowly, saying nothing, only watching her without a sound. She had caught him undressing. His coat and shirt lay discarded on the cane chair, his boots dripped melting snow onto the bare hardwood floor. Her eyes sought his in a silent plea. His answer was coldness and a wariness almost tangible.

"Is there only one way I can prove myself, Chase?" The room was so silent, her words seemed to echo. She heard her voice begin to break and made a redoubled effort to keep it steady. "To try to undo the damage I've done? You seem convinced I only pretended to love you because I was playing spy for Mosby." She drew a deep breath, raising her chin, and started to untie the bodice ribbon on her winter gown. "Will this convince you otherwise?"

150

"What's the price this time?"

Leanna's fingers faltered on the ribbon, but she forced herself to hold his eyes. "No price, Chase. There never was a price. That's what I came here to prove."

"Damn you, Leanna, have you no mercy?" Pain flashed on his face as he turned away. "You know I'm in love with you. If it were only myself, God help me, I'm not sure I wouldn't let you have whatever it is you want so badly. But not other men's lives. I won't give you them."

Leanna felt the sting of tears as she walked toward where Chase stood with his back to her in the darkness. His broad shoulders were shadowed in the moonlight, muscles pale gold against black. She reached out to touch him. "I don't want the lives of your men, Chase. I don't want anything but you."

"This is what you want still, I gather." He stepped away from her with something like a shudder, reaching down to the bed. He thrust something at her as he turned. "Take a good look at it before you give it back. And make up your mind that's the last you'll ever see of it. Regardless of what you offer in trade."

She stared at the thing he'd offered, taking it with a trembling hand. The book. Blacker than ever in the night-dark room. More awful, more sinister than a demon. She could only stare at it for a long moment, unable to speak. She flushed fever hot, then terribly, terribly cold. "In one breath you say you love me, in the next, you call me a whore." She thrust the book back at him with revulsion, turning on one heel toward the door. He caught her before she could leave, pulling her roughly around by the shoulders.

"Just tell me why. If you're so damn eager to serve the Confederacy, why not at least sell yourself higher? For something that might make a difference!"

"Mosby told me to get the code!" She said it without expression, meeting his eyes without apology. Even that terrible secret seemed trivial now. "I was only trying to serve my country—the same way you serve yours. I didn't go looking for that book. I found it while I was

151

cleaning. And I thought I could balance the scales a little for falling in love with a Yankee, for cuckolding my husband with him. That code book would have given the South a chance again! Something to fight back with! My brother gave his life for that—my husband is out there prepared to do the same. Should I have stayed warm and safe in your arms and said the hell with everything else I believe in?"

He gave her a startled glance. As she spoke, a strange expression played on his face. Leanna didn't notice. She'd closed her eyes, feeling more numb than anything else—half sick where she felt at all. In was no use, she realized now. There was no way to convince Chase of the truth. This had only made it worse, convinced him further she was what he'd guessed. It was over then. There was no way back.

She shook her head slowly, defeated. "I'm not apologizing for what I did any more than I expect you to apologize for fighting for the side you believe in. I only came in here tonight because I hurt so badly I couldn't bear it. And I had some silly notion that I could make you listen—make you understand that I love you, I loved you then, I do now. That what I did was in spite of what I feel for you, not the other way around."

"Taking the code book, you mean?"

"Yes." There was a strange note in his voice but she hardly heard it.

"What if I'd called your bluff tonight? What did you want from me this time?"

She glanced up at that, meeting his eyes for a long minute. "It wasn't a bluff. Just the opposite, in fact. But I don't expect you to believe me any more."

"Perhaps I should." He raised his hand to the ribbon of her bodice, wrapping it slowly around one hand. It startled her, but she made herself stand still, refusing to cower. The ribbon was half untied already from her own hand. A single pull and it was loose. Leanna began to tremble, but she made a desperate effort to conceal it. She'd never seen Chase like this—he was dangerous. Tall, powerful, silent. The room was dark. Everyone else in the house was asleep. It was cold, for he hadn't bothered to light a fire. She fought against a rising sense of fear as his hand slid up her gown to cup her breast, his thumb moving against her nipple. She trembled harder, unable to repress it any longer, and closed her eyes. "Don't hurt me, Chase. I beg you." Tears began to slip down her face and their humiliation forced her finally to lower her proud head.

Chase watched her face in the darkness, caught the gleam of the tears and slowly dropped his hand. "Did you really believe me capable of hurting you?" He raised his hand suddenly to her chin, forcing her head up as she opened her eyes. For a moment, he said nothing, only studied her, silent, dark and grim. "You'd make a lousy spy, my love. Take my advice and don't pursue it as a career."

Leanna stared at him, not even daring to breathe. Somewhere in the house, a roof beam creaked.

"Forget about Mosby. Forget about what he wants of you. There is no code book. There never has been one. There never will be one."

She felt even sicker. "But—the book I took from you?"

"It is not a code cipher, Leanna. Had you bothered to even glance through it, you could have seen that for yourself. It's my officer's log. It could have hurt in the wrong hands, but not too badly."

"But, but the way you reacted!"

He shook his head once sharply. "Leanna, listen to me. I have nothing here with me that could be of any significant benefit to your Southern armies. Nothing at least that could make any real difference in the war. Think about it, for God's sake. I have two hundred men. I'm fifteen miles from the nearest Federal encampment. Would they risk anything of any importance by sending it here?"

She stared up at him. "Nothing?"

Chase raised one dark brow and released her. "Sorry, my dear. Nothing."

Leanna stood motionless, searching his dark eyes,

studying his face. So many emotions were surging inside her, she could not identify any one without confusion. "But can you forgive me then, Chase? For what I tried to do?"

Momentary pain flickered in his eyes. "I love you, Leanna. Let that be enough."

She closed her eyes with a deep sigh, not knowing what else to say. It wasn't perfection, but it was a start. Just now, she was grateful for even that much. Without thinking, she lifted her face up to Chase's, seeking his warmth and feeling a sweetness spread through her as his mouth covered hers. She clung that way to him for a moment, outside the world and all its painful choices. Her body began to press to his, her breasts felt the familiar warmth of his bare chest and began to throb in eagerness, and she raised her arms to encircle the broad muscles of his back.

"No." Chase broke the kiss and raised his hands to disengage her arms. He shook his head and stepped away from her. "No, not this way, Leanna. Not again while you're torn between two masters. I just can't do it. It tears me apart inside. Maybe something will change. Maybe by the end of the war . . ."

"I can't wish Stewart's death . . ." Leanna's confusion showed in her eyes.

"I know."

". . . or the South to lose, either. I believe in our cause too greatly."

"I know that, too."

"But I love you, Chase. More than I'd ever thought possible."

He only nodded once, taking another step backward. "Go to your own room now. I'm trying, but I'm only human. Don't ask too much of me, Lea."

She reached only a last time to lay her hand wistfully over his, then nodded and turned to leave. It was one of the hardest things she'd ever made herself do. And small comfort to her to realize that, just as Doc Lacey had once warned her, she and Chase were in some ways too much alike. Both of them put a limit on the love

154

each could offer the other. For her it was Blytheswood, and the cause of the Confederacy. For him, a commitment to the uniform he wore. She could not help but fear the future and the agonizing choices it must hold. For neither she nor Chase could truly win a war waging it each against the other. One of them would have to lose.

Christmas day found Leanna hanging evergreen boughs and holly. The Yankees had brought them by the armful, almost pathetically eager to see a real, Christmas-decorated house. She understood a little bit. And resented them for it, too. It had been much easier to hate Yankees when they hadn't been human to her.

Delicious smells were coming out of the kitchen. Jewel had somehow cajoled the last supply wagoneer to give her a whole loaf of real white sugar and Christmas baking was suddenly a reminder of previous years, pre-war years, when sugar was taken for granted, and plum puddings and hard sauces were nothing very special.

Chase was outside somewhere. She'd seen him go from her bedroom window. A patrol was due back from Front Royal and it was his habit to be outside to meet the returning men. She heard horses in the driveway now, the click of the front door, and a draft of cold air. Her heart beat faster, but she busied herself intently with another sprig of holly.

"Leanna?"

Boot steps sounded on the floor of the dining room, muffled as they reached the fringed square of carpet. She closed her eyes, praying she would not find hatred again in his eyes when she turned, and drew a deep breath. "Oh, Major. Merry Christmas." She had to make herself meet his eyes. Relief swept her to see his expression and for an instant she didn't move, only enjoyed the lack of enmity. "Jewel has some cider heating in the kitchen if you need a warm-up."

"She wouldn't let me in earlier. I gather she's making something special." But he smiled as he said it, shrugging.

"I'll get it, then. Have a seat."

"Major Courtland?"

Both turned to a trooper who leaned in the dining room doorway, holding something out in his hand. "This came over the wire for you, Major."

Chase frowned momentarily, taking the telegram, saluting to the departing trooper before he began to read it.

"What is it?" Leanna prayed it wasn't bad news. The death of a friend—or transfer orders. She climbed down from the chair to walk slowly toward him.

"It's from Doc Lacey in Washington." He read as he spoke. "He wants me to come up to see him there to—" His voice faltered suddenly. He reread the thing swiftly to make sure there was no mistake. Then he smiled faintly, and turned to hand it to her. "Merry Christmas, Lea. He's found your brother, Jonathon."

"You're being a damn, stubborn fanatic, Major Penley!"

"It runs in the family," Chase sighed softly, raising one brow as he turned aside. Susan was still a good distance away, standing and talking with Whitney. She couldn't hear the discussion. "Your sister, at times, exhibits the same traits."

Doc Lacey noticed Jonathon's sharp glance at the Yankee officer and hastily moved between them. Didn't Chase realize how his expression changed when he spoke of Leanna? Any fool could see he was in love with her. And Jonathon Penley was no fool. That was one complication they didn't need. "Your only alternative is a prison, Major Penley. And with the condition your wife is in—"

"My duty remains the same, Doctor. I'll be exchanged eventually and I'll be able to go back and—"

"Duty? What kind of duty do you have to your wife, Major? Your family? If Mrs. Penley doesn't stay here where—"

"Whitney can stay. She won't be in prison with me. Then after the baby is born—"

"That baby will never be born! She'll lose it worrying about you rotting in a prison camp! A goddamn waste is

156

what it is! Of both of you! I can't believe I wasted so much time and energy patching you up."

"Now, settle down, Roger," Chase interrupted his friend with an impatient frown. "Be sensible, Major. You might get exchanged, yes, but not for months. Maybe never. I've heard rumors already of eliminating the exchanges for prisoners of war. You damn near died once already for your Confederacy. I don't think you owe them any more. And I'm a soldier, like you are. I think I'm seeing things in a valid perspective. If you'd accept parole, give your word you won't fight against the Federal government, you'd be free to take your wife and daughter up to Philadelphia for the duration of the war. I cabled my father and he's willing to offer some sort of work for you at the bank. Whitney can stay at the house. It's only a couple blocks from the university hospital, and—"

"Hire me as a clerk, you mean? Or to dump wastebaskets and sweep the floors? I think not, thank you."

"You can hardly expect to be offered the vice presidency, Major. And as your alternative is a prison camp, I suggest you make an effort to swallow a little pride."

"Thank you, Major Courtland, but this discussion is at an end. I've made my decision." Jonathon studied the Yankee officer's face as he spoke. Why make any offer at all? Why did he give a damn about a Confederate officer he'd never met? And what had he meant about Leanna, anyway?

Chase sighed and shrugged, frowning, frustrated, defeated. Doc was right. It was a waste. The return of Jonathon Penley wasn't going to help the CSA. Only God could at this point. And he hoped He would choose not to. "Well, I've done my job, anyway," he shrugged. "I've delivered one Penley safely to you, Roger."

Doc Lacey only grunted, furious and grim. Damn war. Damn 'honor' business. One was as lethal as the other, apparently. "Well, thanks for that, anyway, Chase. I'll keep a good eye on Whitney for you."

He wasn't thinking and he didn't notice Jonathon's quick frown at his words.

'For you'? Just what the hell did his family mean to Major Courtland?

"One more thing, Chase, while you're here in Washington." Doc Lacey turned away from Jonathon, speaking softly and sparing a single swift glance to be sure the women were out of earshot. "I'd like to speak to you a minute about Susan."

Chase's quick glance showed his surprise. "Susan? Has she been a problem for you here at the hospital?"

"No, no. Nothing like that. As a matter of fact, she's a wonderful help, a good nurse. But we've spent a great deal of time together these past few weeks and, knowing how you feel about Mrs. Leighton—"

"What I may or may not feel about Leanna Leighton has no bearing on Susan and me. For one thing, as you well know, Leanna's already married. For another, I wouldn't have given Susan a ring in the first place if I weren't at least fond enough of her to be quite sure I can be a better-than-adequate husband to the girl."

Anger flashed on Chase's windbrowned face as he spoke, and for a moment, Doc Lacey was too startled to respond. It wasn't like Chase to be quick-tempered. Defensive, maybe, he decided. Perhaps he'd been getting pressure of some sort already from either of his own or Susan's family, and was assuming Doc Lacey was doing the same. "No, Chase, you're misreading what I'm trying to say. Quite the contrary, actually. The more time I spend with the girl, I find myself becoming very—"

"Major Courtland?" An orderly interrupted. "Sorry, sir, but you're carriage is waiting below. You'll miss your train."

Chase was still frowning as he turned to nod a curt acknowledgement. "Sorry, Doc. We'll have to continue this another time."

Doc Lacey reached to grab Chase's arm as he bent for his gloves and swiftly began to turn away. "Chase, if you'll just give me one minute, I'd very much like to—"

"Another time!" The anger flashed openly on his face this time, and Doc Lacey released his grip. Chase moved

158

hastily, pausing only briefly by the women to say his farewells. Doc Lacey noticed the warmth of Whitney's goodbye, the awkwardness of Susan's. No, she wasn't in love with Chase, either. At least, he didn't think so. Still, as long as the two were engaged to be married, it was almost as great an obstacle as if they were actually married. It was still impossible for him to court the girl. Impossible for her to allow him to do so.

Chase didn't even stop again to speak. He merely waved, and even the gesture was tight and tense with anger. Damn, he thought, watching Chase's familiar, long-strided walk out the doorway. If anything, he'd probably only made matters worse, today, starting the conversation and not being able to correct Chase's impression that what he was offering was a lecture, poorly disguised. He turned back into the room with a soft sigh and a half frown lingering on his face. Jonathon Penley was laying in front of him, and the half frown turned to a full one. Damn, he thought again. Nothing today had turned out as he'd hoped it would. Not one damn thing.

Chapter Eleven

Winter in Virginia is a mellow season. It moves slowly, at a pace of its own—refusing to be hurried, but without much violence. Snow falls often enough to be pretty. The ground is muddy after it melts. The sun shines often, and in the Valley when the mountains take the wind, even the winter can be warm. But this was a cold one, and by the middle of January, Blytheswood's pond had frozen hard enough that Yankee soldiers cut blocks of it to store in the underground, stone-built ice house. Covered with straw, it would last most of the year. February stayed cold, colder than usual, and the top of the ground froze in places. The troopers had to hammer a hole in the horses' water buckets every morning, and sometimes the water pump froze. Troops on both sides shivered the cold, monotonous days away. The Yanks in Culpepper had better blankets and better food. By March of 1864, Lee's veterans by the Rapidan River were desperate for shoes and boots, and scurvy was rampant in the ranks.

The deep South doesn't get much winter, and hundreds of miles away from the fighting lines in Virginia and Tennessee, life still followed a more mellow pattern, an echo of prewar days when courtesies and cotton were king.

In Savannah, Georgia, Chase's sister Elinor lifted the hem of her satin azure gown as she stepped into the drawing room. She noted Thomas Wilson's quick glance at the ankle she deliberately showed, then dropped the hem again to take a seat on the Chippendale settee.

"You don't mind if I join you, gentlemen?" she purred demurely.

Wilson looked startled, but in true Southern chivalrous fashion offered a quick bow and an equally quick denial. "My exquisite pleasure, unless your husband objects."

The viscount only raised a brow and shrugged. "Her husband has learned not to."

Elinor hid a smile, concentrating on arranging her satin dress artfully. She'd known Wilson wouldn't protest. He wanted the guns and ammunition they'd brought in on the *Gypsy*. Only a small portion of their cargo, but the South was desperate for weapons and shot. The ankle shown hadn't been to convince him, but to entice him. He was young and good-looking in an earthy sort of way. It had been a long voyage, out and then south of Bermuda, waiting for the Federal ships of the blockade to disappear long enough to risk a dash into the Savannah Harbor. She was bored silly with Hadley. And with the confinement of the ship, she hadn't dared enjoy any of the young, brawny sailor lads. She had Hadley pretty much where she wanted him, but his possessiveness made him dangerous when it was aroused. It was Wilson's house. He would find a way. Maybe even tonight.

"Cotton for your return trip?" Wilson seemed astounded. "Well, of course, we have plenty, but how do you propose to get it out?"

"Oh, the blockade, I know. But Elinor's father has good connections in Washington. She knows what part she's to play if we should get stopped and searched."

"Caught in a storm, Mr. Wilson," she offered in her low, throaty voice, half laughing. "We needed to refit the ship and take on fresh water most desperately."

"I see."

"I need cotton for my mills, Wilson. This damn war's gone on interminably."

"Perhaps if England would recognize our Confederate government—"

"Don't start that nonsense. Why should they do that? Oh, the aristocrats sympathize. But the lower classes, the masses—well, it's a pity your General Lee didn't

161

conquer Pennsylvania last summer. That would have helped."

Wilson choked on his brandy. "Conquered Pennsylvania? You mean Gettysburg? We weren't trying to conquer the whole *state*, Lord Bennington, just—"

"Oh, don't talk war!" Elinor pouted. "I'm sick of it."

"Yes, talk money," Hadley smiled. "She likes that subject better."

"Money?" Wilson hid surprise. He'd expected an aristocrat. This man was more like the damn Yankee merchants. "All right, money. We'll give you cotton for a return trip to England, but if you would consider—ah—bringing more guns and ammunitions, powder especially, on the next run . . ."

"There won't be a next run. I'll have what I need. It's a big ship."

"Yes, but cotton mills aren't as profitable as a certain kind of shipping could be."

"You mean running guns, don't you, Mr. Wilson?" Elinor eyed him with curious intensity. "How profitable *is* the ammunitions business?"

"Very."

"For example?"

"For a good rifle, a profit of five hundred to one thousand percent. A shade less for powder, cartridges . . ."

Elinor's eyes opened wider. "Five hundred percent?"

"Or more."

"Oh, Hadley . . ." She smiled at her husband, beckoning him over. "If I could—say, free a bit of my father's money, invest it in such a business, you could stay in the South to manage it from this side, I could stay with father in Philadelphia, and perhaps—"

"You'd run black-market guns to the South while your own brother fights for the North?"

"Is my 'own brother' at all concerned about what this war is doing to me, to us, Hadley? I told you in London, dear. I don't intend to be poor."

"I personally would prefer to be rich again, also."

Elinor smiled faintly, nodding. "Why don't you discuss the details then with Mr. Wilson?"

Hadley hesitated. He risked a single sidelong glance at his wife's face, struck as he always was by her extreme beauty. He held no illusions any more that Elinor loved him—she was, by some flaw in her nature, he thought, unable to love anyone. That had disturbed him deeply at first. By now, he had adjusted to it. It had not changed the fact that he was in love with her, whatever she was. And she would not stay with him if there were no money. And no money was about what there was. He had concealed from her the true depth of their financial ruin. Still. . . . "Elinor, my love, if we should be caught, think how humiliating, and especially if your father—"

"I'll take care of my father. Don't worry on that score. And I grew up with the business, remember? I know how to divert a little capital so that it will never be missed."

He hesitated another moment, then sighed agreement. He turned and missed Elinor's sultry glance at their young host, missed Wilson's returning glance and slow nod. "All right, Mr. Wilson. Let's discuss specific details."

"Oh yes!" Elinor moaned approval, her face flushed in the darkness of the closet, her whole body trembling with eagerness. Wilson's hands roamed in bolder exploration, slipping beneath her dressing gown to find bare skin. Breasts high and full and remarkably firm filled his hands and he dropped his head to her neck, smelling the strange musky odor of woman and expensive perfume mingled together. He kissed her hair, her ear, then her throat, feeling her lips at his ear, nipping once almost painfully, murmuring encouragement and giving directions.

"Hurry . . . Hadley won't be down there very long. . . . Oh, yes, there . . . do that again . . . oh, yes . . ." He'd dropped his hand to her hips, reaching to caress her milk-white buttocks, then sliding quickly to the front of her. She pressed eagerly at his hand as he touched her, hot and wet and wanton. A faint shudder of passion shook Wilson's body—he had never known a woman like this, so bold, so unashamedly passionate. Her hunger fired his own and he clutched at her eagerly, exploring her with growing greed.

She moaned again and pushed herself harder against his roving fingers, pressing herself down on them as they found her dark entrance. Haste only added fuel to this stolen fire. Wilson knew they could not have more than a few minutes, and if Lord Bennington caught him with his wife, the guns were lost—but it was harder to remember that with each passing second. Elinor rocked her hips against his hand, hot juices dripped from her to run down his palm like tiny rivers of flame. He began to tremble with eagerness, dropping his other hand from her breast to fumble hastily at his trousers. He wished they were in a bed together with hours to spend. But even now, Hadley might be climbing the stairs, walking in the hall. . . .

"Hurry, Thomas, hurry!" Elinor reached to help him with his trousers, slipping the buttons with practiced ease, her slender hand diving inside to find his engorged manhood and drawing it out toward her. Her thumb rubbed the tip of him until he moaned a kind of begging sound for her to stop. She teased him more by drawing him against her, rubbing the hair of her hips over his swollen member, smiling faintly in the darkness. He was putty in her hands, completely helpless. He would do anything now to satisfy the craving she'd so carefully built. Wilson fumbled almost pathetically at her, trying to draw her hips over him. Elinor artfully manuevered so he could not, raising her hands to pull down on his shoulders. "Kiss me, Thomas. Kiss me there first."

He dropped to his knees in blind obedience, seeking her and sucking greedily at her with his mouth. Elinor moved her legs into a slightly wider stance, running her fingers deep into his blonde hair to pull him tighter against her, arching her hips slightly toward him. She closed her eyes as she felt his tongue pressing upwards into her, his teeth hard, his hands pulling at her buttocks. She rotated herself slowly against his face, feeling the sure pleasure building into wild hunger. What more should she ask of him, she wondered? How much time did they have left?

His kisses were desperate already, his teeth nipping at her as all rational control fled his mind. His swollen member ached and throbbed between his legs, pointing upward to the dark mysteries above it. He pulled his mouth away from her and began to stand, grabbing her buttocks with one hand, himself with the other to guide himself within. She moved away, turning around to his searching thrust, feeling it slide between the cheeks of her buttocks and squeezing to hold it there. Wilson moaned in desperation, pulling himself out of that teasing trap. His hands were no longer gentle on her, his body no longer tolerant of game playing. His breath was ragged gasps against her face as he turned her to face him again, his arms tightening to hold her still while she writhed in feigned distress. His eyes were half open, glittering, unfocused. Elinor knew he was no longer aware of her but only of himself, like a wild bull maddened by the rutting season, desperate, angry, determined to ease the demands of a body aroused beyond mercy. She felt him pressing at the inside of her thigh and struggled harder while she smiled. He grunted as he pulled her closer, fighting to keep her hips still for a swift upward thrust. He was almost crushing her but that pleased her, inflamed her greedy passion further. He pulled her down while she pushed upward, her bare feet arching against the soft carpet of the small closet they stood in. He groaned again, louder with each futile upward drive that failed to impale her on his swollen flesh. Suddenly, he dropped his arms from around her back, reaching one behind her hips, the other to one thigh. He stepped forward at the same instant, slamming her shoulders against the closet wall and lifting her one leg with his arm. Elinor sighed and closed her eyes in anticipation of ecstasy. Now, she thought. Now.

It came then as she'd known it would, driving up into her like a battering ram, hard enough to lift her off her feet, crushing her back against the unyielding wall. He was huge, hot. He felt like rock more than flesh. She'd judged him well-endowed before dinner, eyeing him with a practiced eye. He was at least as good as she'd guessed, maybe better. Her flesh received him greedily, closing around him and pouting dark and wet as he withdrew to thrust again. She moved against him, clinging to his shoulders with breathless pleasure. He impaled her again, with frenzied desperation, withdrew and thrust again, harder and harder, his hand on her buttocks to move her now as he willed. She no longer made any pretense of struggling. "Oh wonderful, that's so good . . ." she whispered in ecstasy, limp in his arms, feeling only the steady, relentless surging of his body inside hers. "Oh, good, Thomas! Now more, more, Thomas! Harder, harder! Oh, that's it! Oh, yes, yes, yes!"

He drove into her the last time with a shuddering groan, staggering suddenly beneath the weight of her as he climaxed like an exploding rocket. Elinor came on him at the same moment, biting her lip to withhold an ecstatic cry. She could feel the hot juices of his body shooting into her, bathing her and himself as well, felt her own body's joyful release, the sticky wetness that began to seep out as he grunted once more in stunned ecstasy, his arms growing limp around her. She pulled herself carefully off of him as her feet touched the carpet again, sparing only a last moment to touch his shoulder and the soft velvet of his dinner jacket. Then she left him, hurrying to her own room just down the hall. She'd no sooner closed the door behind her than she heard Hadley on the stairs, finishing his brandy and the last cigar that had allowed her time for such frolic. She smiled and drew the sheets higher over her naked body before he came in. Perfect, she congratulated herself. You've got the timing down just perfect.

March brought change in Philadelphia, too. Magnolias weren't blooming as they were in Savannah, but gray snow melted from cobbled streets, the ice disappeared from Wissakickon Creek and the Susquehanna River, and shipping activity began again on the winter-gray Delaware dockside. A military black sheep named Ulysses S. Grant had finally made good in the Western Theater and earned a reputation as a resolute, relentless fighter. Abraham Lincoln had been looking for just such a man for a long time. Now that he'd found him, he promoted him to General in Chief of all U. S. Armies and moved him east to match wits with the seemingly unbeatable Robert E. Lee. Within days of his promotion, Grant did two things—met General Sherman in Nashville to arrange a concerted drive against the CSA that spring, and eliminated exchanges of prisoners of war.

The first affected no one just yet. The second left both North and South reeling. Northern families wanted their captured men returned. Southern families needed them, for the CSA was already desperately low on manpower and the cessation of exchange would cripple them further. For Jonathon Penley, it had been the end of hope. Three futile months of rotting in a Yankee prison—blankets crawling with lice, more maggots than food in the food, overcrowding even in the officers' quarters to the point that everybody stunk and everybody knew it and nobody cared after a while because they forgot the smell of everything else.

Now, he stood in the spacious parlor of the Courtland's Philadelphia mansion, looking at a trio of portraits, gilt-framed. Two young men in Federal uniforms—one he recognized as the cavalry major he'd met in Washington, the other was draped with black ribbon. It gave him some slight satisfaction seeing that, a kind of grim pride. But it didn't come close to balancing the agony it cost him to stand there, and he nodded once toward the center portrait simply to break the tension of the silence.

"And that one?" It was of a beautiful young woman, hanging above the piano on the papered wall. A woman with a rather strange smile.

"My daughter, Elinor." Joshua concealed any expression his face might have shown by turning away, reaching to open the cigar box. "A cheroot, Major Penley?"

Jonathon flushed. "Not major, any more. I've given up my right to claim that title."

Joshua glanced swiftly at the young man. "Because you accepted parole, you mean?" The silence was answer. Joshua felt a frown gathering and made an effort to shrug it away. "From my son's letter, I don't see that you had much choice, once General Grant eliminated exchanges of prisoners of war."

"Everyone has a choice. Everyone always has a choice," Jonathon disagreed with anger, turning sharply on one heel. *Damn*, he hated this! Swearing parole. Abandoning any hope of escape or exchange to once more serve the CSA. Dependent on a Yankee's hospitality—his whole family, it seemed, shamefully unable to provide any longer for their own.

"Major Penley . . . Mr. Penley," Joshua's frown crystallized. "Let's not argue with one another. I'll be quite frank with you—I'm no more pleased at this turn of events than you are. My son wrote and requested I help you and your family in this manner. I felt obliged to assent. But my oldest son fell at Shiloh under Confederate bullets. My youngest son is hardly out of danger of the same fate. Please, don't aggravate a difficult situation."

To say nothing of his other troubles, he thought worriedly—Elinor's unexpected arrival two nights ago, a board meeting at the bank that had ended unpleasantly, and pains, more chest pains this morning when he'd received the telegram that had turned out, thank God, to be *from* Chase, not about him. Joshua still wasn't sure exactly how he'd let his son talk him into this damnable situation. But Chase had asked, and he hadn't had the heart to refuse him.

As if the world weren't complicated enough! Just last night he had had to agree to contribute money, twenty thousand dollars' worth, to Roland Hodges and that damn coalition. Plans were in motion to buy eight key Congressmen, their influence and their votes. Contributing money to something he so thoroughly detested had been bad enough. Worse was seeing the list of who they were buying. Two of the eight were men he knew, men he had, up to now, believed far above this sort of thing. It was hell getting old, he thought. You saw too much of the seamy side of everything; ideals fell faster than wheat before a thresher. After sixty years, he guessed he should have accustomed himself to it, but he hadn't. It still hurt. It probably would until he died.

And now this. Some strange Confederate officer, stiff-necked and barely cordial, standing in his parlor like it was the vanguard of an army attack. "We might make an effort to avoid each other as much as possible, Penley. It might be easier on both of us. I'm a busy man and I haven't the time to spare to play host to you. You will be going to the bank every morning with me, though, and I expect a fair day's work from you on whatever task I see fit to assign. I hope to hell you can add a list of numbers if you need to."

Joshua waited grimly, letting his words sink deep into the young Virginian's head. He watched him covertly while pretending to watch the taper he raised to light his cigar. Anger flashed in Penley's blue eyes. A muscle twitched in his lean jaw. But he didn't argue back. Joshua let the silence hang as long as he dared, then nodded, turning to walk briskly onward again, gesturing as he moved. "The kitchen's that way . . . dining room, ballroom behind, library—that's mine, I'll ask you not to use it without permission; servants' quarters, drawing room, dayroom, the foyer you've seen. Upstairs, bedrooms. I'll put you in the one at the end of the hall."

Jonathon nodded, trying to follow the overquick description. He didn't want to humiliate himself further by having to ask twice. He frowned in concentration, marking the invisible rooms in his mind. A young woman's voice sounded unexpectedly from behind him and he turned, startled, and found the woman of the portrait staring directly at him."

"Ah . . . our resident Rebel, I gather."

Joshua tried to force a nonchalant expression. But nonchalance and Elinor just never mixed easily. They didn't now. "My daughter, Mr. Penley. Elinor, Lady Bennington."

"Pleased to meet you." Jonathon shifted his gaze when she didn't. A faint, instinctive tremor flamed briefly in his loins. She was stunning. And it had been many, many months.

Elinor stepped forward, letting her eyes rove leisurely over the handsome stranger. "Pleased as well . . ."

Joshua caught her gaze and frowned. There was a familiar tightening sensation in his chest and he spoke quickly, hoping to relieve it. "Mr. Penley's wife will be joining him in a few weeks, Elinor. She's expecting a child next month."

"Oh? Your first?"

Her voice was like satin, Jonathon thought. Soft, cool . . . strangely sensual. "No, ma'am. I . . . we have a daughter as well. A two-year-old."

"I loathe children." But Elinor laughed as she said it and neither man knew exactly how she felt. It was a routine feeling for her father—a novel one for Jonathon. Puzzled, he glanced back at her. She smiled—trying to be friendly, perhaps. The English were somewhat sympathetic to the Southern cause. Maybe she would be an ally if he let her—more so than her stiff-necked dyed-in-the-wool Yankee father. He smiled hesitantly in return.

Joshua watched, frowning, ever more uneasy. "Come on, Mr. Penley. I'll show you the stables outside." He exited the room without looking back, relaxing only slightly to hear Penley's boot steps immediately following. Why, Elinor? he found himself thinking as he led the young Confederate out of the drawing room and down the long, oak-paneled hallway to the rear of the huge house. Why do I feel I know you so little? Less now than ever. My little girl, who used to sit on my lap to coax candies from my pockets—where in the world has she gone?

Chapter Twelve

"If I only gots one more week to feed you, I gonna fatten you up good." Jewel shoved another plateful of cookies at a trio of young officers. She didn't notice Leanna's entrance into the dusk-shadowed kitchen, nor the fear that suddenly widened her violet eyes and drained the color from her face. "You all gonna be gone by the fifth, you says, so I'se gonna . . ." At Leanna's soft gasp she turned, remarkably agile for such a big woman. Spring had finally come to the Shenandoah Valley and thawed winter's stiffness from Jewel's bones. Outside, the redbud was blooming—the cherry trees, too. Yellow forsythia and purple wisteria colored the land amidst the lime green of spring pastures. "Oh . . . Miz Lea . . ." Jewel began to smile, moving toward her. "I didn't know you was . . ."

"You're leaving?" Leanna sought Captain Grier's eyes, reading the answer before he could speak. Chase had been gone to Winchester for three days. He'd only come back tonight in time for dinner, and said nothing. She turned for the door in a rush, too distraught to try to mask her emotions.

Jewel watched her exit with a quizzical gaze, grumbling aloud as the door slammed and bounced behind the girl's flight. "Now tarnation! What the devil be getting into her?"

The young officers exchanged silent looks, and suddenly, Jewel read the meaning in their glances. How had she missed it, knowing the girl like she did? All winter then. Those soft, sweet smiles, the renewed radiance of those beautiful violet eyes, the occasional tears. . . . You're a dumb old woman, she scolded herself worriedly. Now what the devil was the chile gonna do?

Leanna ran into the gathering dusk of April's later sunset. More shadows than light lay around her but she hardly noticed, hauling her skirts high to run in search of the Yankee major. He hadn't told her. Would he ever have? Or would he simply have ridden away one morning and never returned?

Music caught her ear, coming from the campfires near the Yankee-built shed. She turned involuntarily toward it, slowing her step, realizing only now she was out of breath—as much from dread as from running. The singing drew her inexorably, but she moved slowly now, suddenly almost afraid to find him. If the Yankees' choice of song meant anything—

"Oh Shenandoah, I'm bound to leave you," a clear, sweet tenor voice rang through the gathering night.

Leanna stayed well back in the shadow of a huge oak, slowly dropping her skirt back to the ground. Tears filled her eyes, her heart pounded in her breast. The soft melancholy strains of a mouth organ grieved in the growing darkness. Chase's deep baritone took up the second verse.

"Oh Shenandoah, I love your daughter. Away you rolling river . . ."

Some of the other men in the small circle joined in, others sat staring silently into the dying flames of the fire. Chase, by some sixth sense, felt her presence. He looked up over the others' heads, not moving from his seat on the log stump, but his voice faltered before the last bars of the old song and the other men finished without him.

"Oh Shenandoah, I love your daughter. . . .
But away, I'm bound to go. Across the wide Missouri . . ."

It was true then. Leanna felt the last of her hope fading slowly before the expression in his dark eyes. She waited until the last melancholy notes faded in the darkness, echoed a moment, and then softly disappeared. Then she turned awkwardly away, stumbling as she moved, trying to run before she humiliated herself

172

completely. Evening had come unnoticed. The first star shone in a sapphire sky, the shadows had claimed the earth. She ran over the dark fields for the edge of the creek, the willow where she'd played as a child. Now like a wounded, wild creature, she ran for it to hide her grief.

"I thought I might find you here, Lea." Someone ducked under the low, trailing branches and stepped inside.

It was Chase, and she threw herself at him, circling his neck with her arms. "No, Chase! Don't leave me!"

"Don't say that! Don't ask that of me, Lea. I beg you."

"But you said we'd have months yet—months. Oh God, I love you so!"

He held her closer, burying his face in her hair. "I know . . . I love you too, wrong as it is for both of us. But we knew it would come to this. We've known it all along."

"Chase, I can't bear it. I thought I could, but I just can't. She drew back from him in a sudden motion, staring up into his shadowed face. "Take me with you."

He shook his head, a sudden gleam of something like tears in his own eyes. "You couldn't do that. Even if I said yes."

A sob caught in her throat and she closed her eyes helplessly. "You would if you loved me."

"Oh God, Leanna, don't do this to me . . ." He jerked out of her arms, starting to turn.

"Chase!" She reached for him desperately. "Chase!"

She threw herself into his arms as he turned, sobbing and moaning, holding him with the strength of desperation. His arms tightened around her, crushing her to him, moaning his own agony. Leanna pulled his head down to hers, seeking his lips. He groaned out loud, making a last effort to move, then covered her mouth with an urgency of his own. Nothing had ever felt more right. Leanna's heart lifted in dizzying joy. She yielded in his arms, her body molding itself to his. All the laws of God and man not withstanding, this was what she

173

wanted, what she needed. Perhaps love was its own honor, oblivious to all else. "Oh, I've been wrong, Chase, all this winter . . ." She kissed the thick waves of his dark hair as she spoke. "I've wasted all our time . . ."

He only moaned for answer, his arms trembling as he held her. He turned his head as she spoke, taking her lips again under his, pulling her closer to him. His lips brushed her cheeks, her forehead, her closed eyelids with soft fire, his hand seeking her breast and closing over its throbbing fullness. He would pay for it afterwards in pain, but just now he was helpless to deny its sweetness. Leanna sobbed out loud, but with joy this time, not sorrow. He bent suddenly to lift her in his arms, his lips still claiming hers as he started the long, dark walk back to the main house. Leanna clung to his neck, the broad muscles of his shoulders, kissing him feverishly as he walked, nuzzling his neck, the thick curls where his hair touched his uniform's dark collar, breathing deep of his scent, the dear, blissful warmth of his skin.

Neither of them noticed the lights burning in the parlor of the main house. Chase shouldered open the front door and started for the stairs, tightening his hold on Leanna to lift her higher.

"Major!" Jewel froze a dozen steps from them, staring, then reaching to jerk the parlor door closed. She paled in shock, forcing herself forward to block the stairs. "For God's sake, chile, have you lost your mind?"

Leanna heard her as if from an incredible distance, and slowly forced open her eyes.

"Good God in heaven, what you two think you're doin'? Don't you know them Yankee pickets just brought Colonel Leighton in here with them not ten minutes ago? You hear me, chile? Your husband! He's standing not ten feet away from you behind that parlor door!" Jewel grabbed desperately for the Yankee's arm. "Good God, man, put her down! You cain't take a woman whose husband's in the same house!"

"Stewart? Home?" Leanna's heart froze in her chest; she had met Jewel's glittering black gaze for only a

174

heartbeat before the black woman looked away. Stewart home? But that was impossible. He was with the army on the other side of the Blue Ridge mountains.

"Pickets have brought Colonel Leighton in?" Chase felt an abyssmal coldness seeping through his body, quenching the fires Leanna had lit. Even as he spoke, he lifted his head away from Leanna's and slowly began lowering her to the floor. Barely beyond his arm's reach was the closed parlor door. Muffled voices were drifting through it.

"He ain't with the army no more." Jewel spoke to the Yankee instead of to the girl. Inside her, there was such an ache of shock and sorrow she couldn't meet Leanna's eyes. "He been wounded and discharged. Captain Grier's got the papers he brung to prove it." Chase let go of the girl altogether and Jewel pushed forward to wedge her bulk between them. "They's all waitin' in there for the Major to get back. Seems *nobody* knew where you was."

Chase started toward the parlor door, took two steps, and then turned back toward Leanna. But Jewel stood in front of the girl, her black eyes glittering as they met his. "Maybe you ain't heard what I said, Major. Miz' Leighton's husband's home. He's the only man got any rights to her."

He looked over her head to seek Leanna's eyes, holding them for a long moment while no one moved. A kind of helpless shock lay written on her face, and a lingering softness mixed with deep longing. But she didn't speak. Didn't even try to move from behind the wall Jewel had made of her body. Only moments ago, she was thinking, she had been prepared to throw everything away. Her name, her husband, even her beloved Blytheswood. In that first, terrible instant of facing a future forever without him if she stayed, she'd been willing to lose everything else for his sake. But not now. The moment had passed.

Her head was once more in control of her heart. She held his eyes for what seemed an eternity, and read the question that burned there in his dark eyes, and was helpless to give him any other answer. "He's my husband," she whispered brokenly at last, and turned her head away. A moment later, she heard the quick step of his boots toward the parlor door and the abrupt click of the brass knob being turned.

"You got to go in, chile," Jewel gave her a gentle push as she moved to one side, and Leanna didn't turn back to notice the tears that glittered in the black woman's eyes as she spoke. "You got to go in there, too." The trouble she'd long ago anticipated had finally come to Blytheswood. Now, as then, she didn't know what she should have done to prevent it. Maybe nothing. The whole world was falling apart, and maybe there wasn't nothing she could have done to help her chile from being caught in its ruin. God help them all, she thought. What was gonna happen now?

". . . not done in the South, Major. In fact, under normal circumstances, nothing less than a duel would suffice to repair—"

"Stewart!" Leanna froze in the doorway, staring at her husband and moving forward again in a sudden rush. "In God's name, Stewart, what are you—?"

"I was just explaining to the Yankee here my—displeasure, Leanna." Stewart's blue eyes were coldly angry as he glanced at her, then back to meet Chase's dark gaze. "To find my wife out walking with another man—alone."

"And I explained that my position here is hardly of a social nature." Chase spoke softly, low and even, but Leanna had heard that tone in it before—the night of their confrontation over the 'code book'—and she began to tremble where she stood. "If you're that anxious to shoot me, perhaps you should rejoin your army and do it from there."

"I have no doubt such an occurrence would suit your purposes, Major. You would be once more unchallenged in your control of my house, my servants, my brandy—" Stewart gestured coldly toward the decanter that stood on the breakfront by Chase's elbow. "Perhaps, even my wife."

176

Leanna paled to ash, too mortified to even voice the protest she had every right to voice. Neither man looked at her, but she could feel the angry tension surge higher in the room, and the other officers were markedly silent.

"I am not overworried about your 'challenge' to my authority, Colonel." Chase only shrugged, and turned to pour himself a portion of the fine, aged French brandy Stewart had just gestured to. "If you'd take the trouble to look around yourself, you'd find I have well over two hundred men quartered here. More than sufficient, I would say, to subdue any undue resistance from a Confederate officer too 'unwell' to continue discharging his duties to his army."

"This is still my home, and if you were any sort a gentleman you would accede graciously to my proprietorship."

"But I thought it was a well-known fact down here that Yankees aren't gentlemen." Chase raised the brandy snifter and took a deep swallow. Flaunting it, Leanna would have said. "I wonder very much whether you Confederates are, either. If I were to judge by you alone, Colonel, I would have to guess not."

"Major Courtland, please!" Leanna interrupted with a single, anguished glance in his direction. His eyes met hers for only a fraction of a second, then swiftly moved on beyond her. But she'd read the dark pain in them—the anger and the frustration both. She ached in silent empathy. Oh God, how to choose. *Who* to choose. When either choice would be a betrayal.

"The discharge papers are genuine, I think, Major." Captain Grier stepped forward, looking up from his examination to hand them back to Chase. "That's the CSA seal, all right."

A muscle twitched once in Chase's jaw as he glanced down at the paper in his hand. "Wounded the fifth of March . . .?"

"Wounded in action," Stewart corrected as he began to walk toward Leanna. He reached first for a cane, and limped slightly as he moved. For the first time, Leanna noticed the trousers of his uniform were bloodstained.

The left leg was cut open to mid thigh. Bulky bandages showed beneath the cadet gray of the outer cloth, and she started forward in quick guilt. While she was here, falling in love with a Yankee, her husband had nearly been killed.

"Wounded in action against your Yankee cavalry troops, Major," Stewart smiled humorlessly at Chase over one shoulder. "While cutting to pieces a rather poorly organized raid on our capital. An assassination attempt, I understand, aimed at our President and his cabinet officers. A typically shameful Yankee maneuver."

"You're believing your own CSA press propaganda, Colonel. And I'll only warn you once that discharge or no, I won't listen to your insults. I have the authority to confine you here if I choose. Or to send you packing."

"Must we fight the war right here in my parlor?" Leanna interrupted desperately. Please God, help me, she prayed. Help me know what to do. "Please, Stewart, if you've been discharged, leave the war back on the battlefield. Major Courtland has treated us all very generously while he's been here. Can't we, at least, be civilized enough to repay that with some courtesy?" Her hands trembled as she spoke, her face was ashen, but she tried to force a smile, not knowing how dismally she failed. "Have you eaten, Stewart? Perhaps I could bring a tray."

"Upstairs, if you would. Tell Jewel to prepare one." Stewart started for the door, still limping, glancing one last time at the Yankee major's face, unrelenting enmity still cold in his eyes. "I'll ask you to join me as well, Leanna. If the major here can spare your attention."

Chase flushed, his dark eyes sparking anger, his mouth grim and suddenly edged with white. He nodded stiffly and turned away. Leanna threw him a last, beseeching glance as Stewart waited for her in the doorway. Chase didn't look at her and she had to go, her steps slow but nonetheless toward Stewart. He was her husband, she told herself again. He was still her husband. There was no other choice for her to make. "Good night, Major . . ." she murmured in soft pain as she stepped out through the door Stewart held open for her, and walked slowly toward the stairs. Chase did not answer and only silence lay around her as she took her husband's arm to help him upstairs.

". . . but your discharge said . . ."

"Don't be a fool, Leanna," Stewart sat on the bed, unwrapping the bandages with careless hands. "That was almost a month ago. I came home to find out what was happening. And to find out why Major Mosby never heard anything from you about—"

"Mosby! You only came home because they sent you? Because I wasn't reporting what I was supposed to be?"

Stewart glanced up with a frown, puzzled by the sudden sharpness of her voice. "I didn't say I didn't welcome the chance, Leanna, if that's what you mean. Of course, I was anxious to come home—for a lot of reasons. Not the least to see you."

His blue eyes held hers, searching them, and Leanna paled again, dropping her gaze guiltily.

"It's been damn near a year since I've seen you." Stewart's expression softened as he studied the girl. She was beautiful still . . . his wife. He smiled faintly. "I've missed you."

Leanna shrugged against tears that sprang to her eyes. She'd missed him, too, until Chase. . . . "You certainly didn't give that impression earlier."

"Should I have been pleased? To find you out walking unchaperoned with another man? A Yankee, no less." He rose to his feet to walk toward her, lifting one hand to tuck black wisps away from her face. "Leanna, I know you're young. But you know better. You can't do that sort of thing without people talking."

"People talking!" Leanna turned away from his hand in renewed anger. "I've had more important things on my mind than worrying about people talking."

"Nothing is more important than maintaining your reputation. As long as you're my wife, the honor of your reputation reflects on the honor of—"

"Of yours? And what about you, Stewart? Coming home here under the pretense of being too badly wounded to serve in the cavalry anymore? Tricking Major Courtland? What kind of honor is that?"

"For God's sake, Leanna, what's gotten into you. They're only Yankees! It doesn't matter what *they* think." He stared at her in genuine bewilderment, exasperated, but struggling to understand. She had changed somehow. He sensed that. He didn't know exactly how, or what to do with it, but he could feel a difference in the woman who stood before him, and the adoring, obedient girl he'd married. He frowned again, puzzled, reaching once more to touch her face. "I was pleased to hear about Jonathon." He tried a different subject. "And Whitney, too, of course."

"Jonathon took parole, Stewart—just this week. They're going to stop the prisoner exchange, and it was senseless for him to rot in a prison camp."

Stewart was startled. "Parole? He's coming home then?"

"No. He's—for Whitney's sake, he's going to remain up North until the baby's born. Doc Lacey thinks it may be twins."

"Doc Lacey?"

"Yes, the doctor I wrote you about who—"

"Oh, the Yankee." Stewart shrugged dismissal.

Leanna glanced sharply at him, but held her tongue. Bright moonlight gleamed in from the window to add to the oil lamp's light. Stewart's hair shone dark gold, touched now by silver she didn't remember seeing last summer. His face was leaner, darkly weathered. It occurred to her as a shock that he was handsome, but practically a stranger to her, familiar only in that he matched the picture by her bed. Other than that, she knew this man very little. Stewart glanced up at her suddenly as he reseated himself on the bed.

"Will you help me, Leanna?"

She froze, paling. Mosby again. "Stewart, I—"

"Take that end of the bandage if you will. I'll unwrap it from this way."

She took it, trying not to show her relief. A wound did lay under the bandage, an angry-looking red crease, but healed enough so it didn't bother her too badly.

"Saber cut," Stewart explained almost absently, looking at her face instead of the wound. "Not the first—nor, I imagine, the last."

She glanced up to see a faint, half smile on his mouth. It triggered a memory. That smile was familiar and it made him less a stranger. "You never told me you'd been wounded before."

"I saw no reason to alarm you needlessly."

The faint smile remained on his face, and Leanna offered one of her own, remembering he'd smiled just that way the day they'd been married. A good day. Her father had been there. Jonathon and Whitney, too. The war had not yet quite begun.

"I wish you'd told me."

"Why?"

"Because I should know more what's happening to you. How you are. How you feel. How the war is . . ."

"Why should you know that, Leanna? That's the point of this as far as I'm concerned. Women shouldn't have to know about such things."

"Maybe that was true before the war began, but since then, what with running Blytheswood, getting the crops to market, dealing with the various armies that have fought in the Valley here, I—"

"That will be over soon, I promise you. Things will go back to how they were."

There was a new grim sort of stubbornness in his voice and Leanna fell silent, only flinging him a single startled glance. Go back? How could they? Even if the South won, the war had happened. It had changed things, changed her, irrevocably.

"God, it's been a long day. Why don't you dress for bed, Leanna? I'm half asleep just sitting here."

Confusion rose. The part of it that felt like relief shamed her for its rising, but she said nothing, only nodded and obeyed, keeping her back to him awkwardly as she undressed. That at least was postponed then. It would have been hard if he had asked for her; repellent after she'd been in Chase's arms only a couple hours earlier, to give to her husband what she had so longed then to give to her beloved Yankee.

"Good night, Stewart. I'm glad you're home." Guilt forced the words and her heart ached in renewed confusion at the pleasure she saw in Stewart's blue eyes.

"Good night, then."

He smiled once more, drowsily, and was asleep a moment later. But it was hours later before Leanna could get to sleep. Almost against her will, she'd found herself listening for Chase's familiar boot steps in the hall. They never came. Wherever he was, the pain was too great to permit him sleep.

"Yes, I fought at Fredricksburg. It was a Saturday morning, early. Cold, I remember. Cold and foggy."

"And Chancellorsville? In May?" Stewart smiled faintly, a humorless smile, a challenge. Leanna felt it instantly, glanced up at him and then at Chase. They had only sat down to dinner moments before. It was starting already. She'd tried to get Stewart to agree to eat in their rooms with her, but he'd refused. Now she saw why. Chase's eyes darkened from golden amber to deeper brown, but he held Stewart's gaze steadily. They were fencing—only with words instead of swords. An unholy competition. Leanna felt the muscles of her stomach begin to tense painfully.

"Chancellorsville . . ." Chase raised one dark brow slowly, then nodded. "Dowdall's Tavern, by the Wilderness Church, in the woods . . ."

"We defeated you there, too."

"We were outnumbered. Most of our cavalry was off South with General Stoneman."

"Your army lost seventeen thousand men, Major. Outnumbering our infantry two to one."

"Our cavalry redeemed itself in June at Brandy Station."

"That was a draw."

182

"And March of '63, at Kelly's Ford? Did you get any of the coffee we left for General Fitz Lee that night? In his camp?"

Stewart flushed faintly, but managed a nod. "One for your side, Major."

Leanna sat helplessly, keeping her eyes on her food. She'd given Stewart her seat, thinking to avoid any confrontation between him and Chase over the other head chair. Maybe it had been a mistake. Neither man was even making a pretense of eating any longer. They were staring at one another coldly down the length of the linen-and-crystal-set table.

"But that was Fitz Lee, not Jeb Stuart," Stewart amended with a faint smile.

"All the same army, isn't it?"

"All the same country, I thought you were going to say. That is why you're fighting, isn't it? To ensure the destiny of the glorious Union?"

"Gentlemen, please . . ."

Stewart only shrugged to Leanna's plea, still smiling faintly as he glanced down to take a forkful of perfectly done roast pork. Leanna risked a single, beseeching glance toward Chase. This was the first she'd seen him all day. He had taken a patrol out last night. Deliberately?

"Yes. That's why I'm fighting." Chase's deep voice was softer, more controlled. Leanna risked another, split-second glance at his face. Tension flickered along the hard edge of his mouth, but he said no more. She knew with a deep, aching anguish how hard it must be for him, sitting here, unable to object to Stewart's claim to the woman he loved, but he had heard her plea. Unlike her husband, he would try, for her sake.

"What was it your President Lincoln called it this fall? At Gettysburg? A government of the people, by the people, and so on and so forth."

Chase said nothing, staring at his food, eating as if alone.

"I assume you were in the fighting at Gettysburg,

speaking of the place." Stewart continued in a grim voice. "You must have enjoyed it."

Enjoyed it? Despite himself, his hand faltered, his fork froze in midair. He remembered the desperate mounted fight between the two opposing cavalries, crashing headlong into each other's lines at a full gallop, sabers high and flashing in the July sun, men shouting, dust and sweat and blood everywhere, bugles calling, horses screaming. Jeb Stuart's troopers, exhausted from their disastrous roundabout ride, weary but desperate, trying to break through the Federal cavalry to attack the unprotected rear of the main army. Enjoyed it? "No, Colonel. I didn't enjoy it. Did you?" He looked up at last to meet Stewart's cold eyes.

"I don't usually enjoy getting defeated, Major. I prefer winning."

Chase studied him. Was there the sense of a message somewhere in that cryptic phrasing?

"How about chasing General Lee's departing wagon train? Was that more fun?"

Chase realized suddenly the point of the conversation. Stewart had sensed Leanna's lack of enmity toward him, toward the occupying Yankee troops. There was a reason he was driving home how many times they'd clashed, stirring her deeply cherished Confederate conscience. Oh Lea, he thought bitterly. Damn him. Damn this war.

"No, Colonel, I didn't enjoy that either. . . . By the time we went after the wagons, it was July 5th. We were riding through fields where the infantry had fought days before. Unburied dead, Colonel, four days in the hot sun . . . in some place the bodies were too thick to get around so we had to ride over them. The horses hooves made crunching sounds, and clouds of black flies rose up at the disturbance of their feast. We leaned over our saddles, most of us, and threw up as we rode. No, I didn't enjoy it, I don't enjoy any aspect of war." Chase laid his silverware on his plate with a soft clink.

"If you'll excuse me, I believe I'll check in with my sentries outside now." He didn't look back as he rose and left.

Leanna stared after him in sick anguish. Chase. . . . Oh, God, the horrors he had seen. Doc Lacey's words came back suddenly to haunt her, speaking about the war at Gettysburg. How it would be even worse this spring. Good God, *worse*? And later, 'Don't kill him, Leanna. Don't let him throw his life away to gain nothing!'

"I'm sorry, Leanna," Stewart's voice was faintly angry. "I had no idea he would tell such a disgusting story with a lady present."

"Disgusting? Tragic, I would have said. Terrible." Leanna dared not meet the eyes she felt on her. She stared sickly at her plate instead, closing her eyes briefly. She suddenly longed to hold Chase, to kiss all that hurting away. If she were only free! "He's never spoken of it like that before. You goaded him into it."

"A gentleman would never—"

"Is it like that really, Stewart? Is it as horrible as he says?" There were tears unshed but gleaming in her violet eyes as she raised them to meet her husband's.

Stewart seemed startled, then looked away, shrugging. "It can be sometimes."

"How do you keep from going mad?"

"You don't care after a while. You learn not to care about anything but your own survival, I guess. Or maybe you don't. Maybe we all do go a little insane . . ." He looked at her suddenly, a strange look, almost bewildered.

He needs me, Leanna realized with a shock. I knew Chase did, in his way, but Stewart does too, maybe more. Because Stewart is liable to lose everything else that's important to him, while Chase, with a secure home, fortune, fiancée. . . . She forced a smile to cover the anguish of her thoughts. "It's all right, Stewart. Let's not talk anymore of it just now."

He returned her smile and reached unexpectedly for

her hand, holding it tight. "We must beat the Yankees, Leanna. The Confederate cause is worth any sacrifice."

Is it? She could not help but wonder, unable to resist a last, wistful glance outside to where Chase was mounting his horse in the evening's sunset. I hope it is, she answered herself. I hope to God it's worth this one.

Chapter Thirteen

Joshua concealed his astonishment over the young officer's quick progress. Only a few days had passed. It was the evening of the second of April and already Penley was balancing account books like a veteran. Joshua thought that had been a stroke of genius, assigning the long held Southern deposits to him—an extra check to balance the greed of certain board members if the senior Courtland met an untimely end. Who would be more diligent in protecting those investments than an actual Confederate? He smiled smugly, glancing over the young man's dark head to the clock on the mantle. Perhaps the young man had his uses, after all.

"Ten o'clock, already, Penley. You've put in more than a fair day's work. Quit now."

Jonathon nodded, finishing a last calculation before closing the ledger. What a mess. Why didn't those two last figures come out right? Joshua Courtland would hardly assign accounts to him if he were embezzling from them. The figures must be wrong. "Yes, I'll finish up tomorrow. My brain's getting a little foggy, I guess." He started to rise, caught a step away from the couch by Joshua's voice.

"Cigar? Or some brandy?"

Jonathon stopped in surprise, glancing toward the old man. Up to now he had barely spoken. "Thank you. Perhaps another time."

"Oh, don't be stubborn. Yankee brandy swallows the same as Confederate." Joshua caught the boy's eye and studied him a moment. Fair, he decided. Maybe just a touch more than fair. He had to admit the young man had an intuitive grasp of the banking business. Not that he'd intended to involve the Virginian in that. At least, not at first. The Southern deposits were one thing—they were frozen accounts, no way for even the most ignorant bumbler to mess them up—but beyond that he'd never considered allowing some strange Rebel to assume that kind of responsibility. Now he found himself reconsidering. Why not, he thought? God knew with Josh Jr. dead and Chase away in the Federal cavalry, he could certainly use the help. If the young Confederate were capable, which he seemed—surprisingly—to be. *And*, he reminded himself heavily, *if* he were trustworthy. That would be much harder to discern. "I'm not one much for praise, Penley. My own sons—son—would tell you that. Take a brandy and a cigar in lieu of that and you'll be the better for it."

"Thank you, sir, but you yourself were the one who said we were better off avoiding each other as much as possible. I think perhaps that's still the best idea." Jonathon turned, reaching to the table to collect the ledgers. It was an arrogant thing to say and he knew it, but he could only swallow so much. And since coming North, he'd swallowed about his limit. Joshua Courtland had extended his hospitality, perhaps, but he'd done it begrudgingly. That much he'd made clear.

"Pretty hard to avoid each other when we're living in the same house and working at the same place." Joshua raised one gray brow. "I know I did say that once, but I was a bit miffed that first day. Quite a lot besides you was on my mind. Cranky, you might say. Old men like me get cranky, sometimes. Young men like you don't understand."

Despite himself, Jonathon smiled faintly, and hesitated on his way out the door. Cranky was an honest name for it, he thought. He remembered his own father and his grandfather before him.

"One thing especially, I confess, has aroused my curiosity about you," Joshua moved to hand the young man a cigar, not giving him a second opportunity to refuse it, nor wanting to leave him in a position where he had to ask. He didn't think he would do that, and lighting up his own while the Confederate stood there without one seemed unnecessarily rude. "Where did you learn to balance books like you do? I was most surprised."

Jonathon allowed a small, very dry smile, to touch his mouth. "We Southerners aren't quite the idiots we're reputed to be. We have banks and businesses, too. Even running a good-sized plantation is quite similar to running any other business. Books need to be kept. Income has to be balanced, obviously, with expenses. The principles are the same."

"Indeed?" Joshua grunted noncommittally. The young man's arrogance bothered him, but he couldn't say he doubted his reply. He really had never thought of it that way. Score one for the Confederacy, he decided drily. Another Yankee miscalculation. He glanced at Jonathon's cigar, still unlit, and gestured curtly toward the matches on the desk. "Going to light your cigar, son? Or have you Southerners found a way to smoke one without that?"

Jonathon's smile faded, but he turned to take the match. He would have liked to have refused the fine cheroot. He almost had. But it had been nearly a year now since he'd last enjoyed one, and what the hell purpose could be served by a rude refusal of this eminently civilized old man's tobacco?

Joshua watched the young man strike the match, and his eyes narrowed sharply. It had seemed to him that Penley's hand was shaking slightly. Well . . . tough position to be in. The thought occurred to him as a surprise, and he considered it a second time, more slowly. "Help yourself, of course, any time." He gestured to the fine rosewood box and then turned to include the brandy decanter as well. There was a moment's awkward silence, and he cleared his throat rather gruffly, conscious of a sudden faint sense of being angry with himself. He prided himself, usually, on being a fair man, or judging people by their insides rather than and not according to various bigotries. The suspicion he hadn't offered the young Rebel here the

189

same consideration bothered him somewhat. "You like the bank work? Ledgers and such?"

Jonathon glanced over his shoulder, sharply. For a moment he was taken aback.

"I'm sure it's no secret to you that this damn war has left me in a difficult position. You Rebels have taken both my sons away from me—one permanently—and just when I most needed them. If you like the bank work and you seem capable of doing it, you're welcome to do more. We'll talk more about it in a couple days, see how you're doing with what you've already got."

Jonathon nodded slowly, thinking the old man was trying to offer a concession, maybe. Thinking he probably ought to say thank you for it, at least for the effort that so obviously lay behind it. But, damn it, he *was* good at this sort of work. He could more than carry his share of a fair load if Courtland wanted to give it to him. The Yankee would be adequately repaid for what he seemed to consider only a generosity. Still, he reminded himself, it was generosity of a sort. Better, too, than dumping trash and sweeping the hallways, which was what he'd been doing up to now. He tried to balance the two thoughts and ended with a compromise. "Thanks for the cigar, Mr. Courtland."

Joshua nodded once, and then again, mostly to hide a faint, begrudging smile. Sounded like the boy had never said the words before, so stiff were they in coming out. "Why don't you take a seat for a minute, if you're not too tired. I'll pour us a brandy."

Jonathon frowned faintly, hesitating, then nodding acceptance. He'd taken parole. Perhaps it was time to try to leave the war behind him. He sat somewhat awkwardly back down, conscious of the silence, and struggling for something to say. "Have you heard from your son lately? I was wondering how my sister is faring."

Joshua shrugged, but not unkindly. "Chase was never much at corresponding. The last letter was barely a note." He paused a moment, wondering how much more to say. He could hardly tell him what he thought he'd read between the lines of the last few letters, that Chase had fallen in love with the Rebel's sister. His *married* sister. "Everything's well evidently. He didn't send any more specific news.

Jonathon nodded.

"One thing puzzles me, if I may ask," Joshua turned to offer the brandy. "I understand Blytheswood is the original family plantation in the Valley. Why then did your sister inherit that one and you the other?"

"Cool Spring, you mean?" Jonathon was momentarily taken off guard. But the Yankees were more outspoken with things than the Southerners. He'd noticed that to his shock before. "Well, it was my doing, in a way. I spoke to my father at some length about it before he died. Leanna has always been deeply attached to the place, far more so than I. We used to spend most of the year in Richmond, move to the Valley in the summer. I preferred the city, but Leanna always lived and died to get back to Blytheswood. I don't know why, really. I had a grandmother a bit like Lea, though. Even in Richmond, in one back corner of the formal gardens everyone had to have, you'd always find her growing tomatoes or watermelons . . ." Jonathon was unaware of his smile as he said it, remembering her well. Feisty, beautiful even at sixty . . . thoroughly eccentric. "Maybe Lea takes after Grandmother Douglas. Crazy for the open country."

"Sounds too much like my son," Joshua grunted. "Something he'll have to get over now his brother's gone. He'll have to be here running the bank."

There seemed little else to say suddenly. An old Yankee, a young Rebel. Jonathon hurried his brandy and nodded once more. "I'll go up now if it's all right. I have a lot of things to do tomorrow."

Joshua nodded absently, as Jonathon left. The conversation puzzled him though, reawakening an old, but still unanswered question as he climbed the stairs and started down the hallway. What was Chase Courtland's interest in the Penleys, anyway? Not Whitney, obviously. Leanna was married—and happily, too, from all he'd heard. Though Stewart hadn't been home very often, true.

"Jonathon?"

He checked his step, startled, turning. "Oh, Lady Bennington." She was dressed only in a sheer, pale-green silk dressing gown and the nipples of her breasts showed clearly through the light fabric. He averted his eyes hastily—but not before a surge of desire tingled in his loins. He could feel himself hardening in his trousers, and frowned at himself, embarrassed. "I was on my way to my room. Sorry if I . . ."

"Don't be sorry," Elinor smiled, glancing back to check the stairs for her father before continuing. "My husband's not here with me, you know. I get bored at night. And lonely. Don't you?"

The desire surged hotter. He swallowed and ignored the rising urge of his body. Could she mean the brazen invitation he thought she meant? "Lady Bennington, I'm a . . . guest in your home. I hardly . . ."

"Are you made of ice, Major? I hadn't guessed so." Elinor stepped forward, raising her hands to rest on his shoulders. A cloud of heavy, intoxicating perfume wafted from her. Jonathon breathed once of it and began to feel the tingling in his loins heighten to a demanding throb. He closed his eyes and forced himself away from her, frowning with effort.

"Another time, perhaps, then." Elinor let him go, only reaching one hand out to run her finger wistfully down the front of his starched white shirt. She continued down to the buckle of his belt, smiling a little wider as her eyes noted the physical reaction he couldn't hide. Jonathon began to sweat, trembling, clenching his jaw. Oh God, how good it would feel to be with a woman again, to bury himself deep inside her. Remember Whitney, a small part of his brain prompted. But even when she arrived at the end of the week, she would be too far along with child to—share his bed.

"Good night, then, Major Penley. Until another time."

Elinor was gone in an instant. Only the thick, sweet smell of her perfume lingered. Then it, too, was gone.

Jonathon forced a deep breath and hurried for his own room before he changed his mind. The Courtlands were proving to be a very unsettling family, he thought shakily. Thank God his own was in better shape.

Leanna sat alone at the dining room table, her back to the warm morning sun that shone in through the bay windows. It caught in the crystals of the chandelier overhead and tiny rainbows flickered among the hand-painted roses of the wallpaper, shifting and turning in a colorful dance. She watched them thoughtfully as she finished her coffee. Boot steps sounded out in the foyer and she turned, surprised to find Chase rather than her husband coming into the room. "Morning, Major." She offered a smile more gentle than she could allow words to be, cocking her head to one side to study him as he paused in the doorway. He smiled faintly in return, but raised one hand to his head, shielding his eyes from the overbright sunlight that streamed through the white chintz curtains.

"Too much brandy last night?" She rose to her feet as she spoke, meaning to call Jewel in. Since Stewart's return, and by his command, Blytheswood was once more being run according to prewar rules. Married women did not share even a breakfast table with another man unless chaperoned. Especially not a Yankee.

"If it's any consolation, I believe my husband is in worse shape. He isn't downstairs yet." She noted the faint, grim smile that touched Chase's mouth as she turned to call for Jewel. She'd been right then. When the second brandy had been poured in the parlor last night, she'd seen the ever-present tension between the two men flare again. She'd guessed the evening would turn into a drinking duel. Obviously it had. "Jewel, Major Courtland is down for breakfast. Would you come in, please?"

"How's a body to be in two places at once all day long?"

Leanna could hear her grumbling as she waddled out, dough sticking still to her fingers. Jewel looked at the

Yankee major as she entered, but avoided meeting Leanna's eyes—as she'd avoided meeting them since that first shocking night of Stewart's return to Blytheswood. But the expression Leanna had seen flare in them then was forever burned on her memory, shaming her—shaming Jewel, too, she thought. As if it were somehow a shared disgrace.

". . . making breakfasts while I'se playing chaperone to you two, and knowing all too well, they both needs the—"

"Never mind, then," Leanna interrupted. Her face flamed, but defiance flashed along with the guilt in her eyes. "I'll make Major Courtland's breakfast myself." She turned in an abrupt motion, glancing once more, almost apologetically, toward where Chase was sitting. He didn't catch her glance. He was holding his head wearily in one hand, and she ignored Jewel to touch his shoulder gently as she passed, suddenly very conscious of how deeply she was torn. How much of last night's drinking had been to keep Stewart downstairs, away from his wife? And how much to numb the pain of the past few days?

"Oh, Leanna . . ."

Stewart's voice sounded from the doorway and she turned with a guilty start. Good God! Had Stewart seen her hand on Chase's shoulder?

"Have I missed breakfast?"

"By about three hours," Jewel answered before Leanna could, making no effort at tact. Leanna cringed, sensing trouble from a new quarter before Stewart even replied.

"I won't tolerate your uppitiness this morning, Jewel. You're to show respect to your masters—or else."

"Employers, Stewart, please. Remember, Jewel is not a slave."

"What's the difference? Go make my breakfast." Stewart scowled as he took a seat, he too turning his head back against the sunlight.

"Major Courtland's, too, Jewel, if you don't mind." Leanna spoke softly, her gaze beseeching the woman to argue no more. Men with hangovers tended to have little patience, and with emotional tension already seething just below the surface, if a shouting match between Stewart and Jewel began. . . .

"I don't need breakfast." Chase began to rise to his feet.

"Hush and sit down," Leanna's voice had more of an edge to it than she'd expected and she colored faintly, feeling Stewart's smug smile. "And you should eat, too, Stewart. Look at what a gorgeous day it is outside. The sun's so—"

"Still leaving tomorrow, Major?" Stewart interrupted and Leanna fell silent, puzzled at the sharp glance her husband gave her as he spoke.

"Or the next day. Whenever we get the urge."

Leanna began to frown uneasily, trying to catch Stewart's eye. Mosby again? Would they try to plan an ambush if they could find out enough information? She flushed suddenly, remembering it was she who had told Stewart April fifth, never dreaming then that it might not be something he shouldn't know.

"Tell me, Major, how long a trip is . . ."

"Stewart, please," she interrupted nervously, noting the quick frown on his face. "Don't spoil such a lovely day by being quarrelsome."

Stewart's gaze sharpened suddenly, but then he nodded, smiling again. "Very true, Leanna. Forgive me, Major. It is a lovely day, isn't it? If this darn leg were more healed, I'd offer to take you riding, dear."

"Riding?" Leanna was startled. Ever since he had come home to find her out walking with the Yankee officer, Stewart had been decidedly unpleasant whenever Chase was around. Suddenly, he seemed altogether different. Ready to forgive and forget, perhaps. She smiled back warily. "That would be lovely, Stewart. Thank you."

"Breakfast here." Jewel's face was impassive as she set the dishes on the table. "You can help yourselves. I got kitchen work to do."

Chase was silent, taking some food and passing the rest.

195

"Perhaps, if Major Courtland's planning to ride a patrol today, you might accompany him."

Leanna's smile faded and she dropped her eyes back to the table. No, Stewart, she thought. I won't ride along and then report where the pickets are to you, even if Major Courtland were naive enough to let me, which he isn't. Thank God. I don't want to have to make that choice again: Him—or the CSA.

"I wasn't planning to ride a patrol today. Sorry." Chase glanced at the Confederate colonel with a frown, then quickly at Leanna, less unkindly. For a moment, there was silence at the table, punctuated only by the sound of the men eating. From Leanna, there wasn't a sound of any kind.

"Although if your wife is truly that anxious to ride, I have a few free hours later this afternoon. I'd be glad to offer my company then."

Leanna felt her heart lift in hope, trying desperately not to show it. If Stewart would only. . . .

"Not unchaperoned, I'm afraid, Major." Stewart shrugged disapprovingly. "You forget you're in the South. We're very careful with our women."

"I didn't mean alone. I'll detail some troopers to go with us."

Leanna dared to raise her eyes, stealing a glance at Chase. It startled her to see the intensity on his face as he watched her husband. Suspicious, she realized instantly. As well he should be. But if they could only have a few more precious moments together, what harm could it do?

"That sounds reasonable. You may go if you'd like, Leanna."

She was careful to control her smile, murmuring her thanks in a soft voice. The rest of the meal passed with surprising pleasantness.

With him, even silences were sweet, Leanna found herself thinking as they rode side by side through the sun-dappled forest land. The horses' hooves made soft plopping sounds in the April mud, birds chirped and made rustling noises among the budding branches overhead. She kept her eyes on Chase most of the time, terribly aware of the passing of minutes that now could never be replaced. The strain of the past two days showed on his handsome face. His eyes were dark, expressionless when they'd met hers, his mouth unsmiling. How different from their rides together before Stewart had arrived home, when they had been so much freer with one another. She glanced back at the detail of troopers that rode with them, deciding they were far enough away to risk speaking openly. "Are you still leaving the day after tomorrow, Chase?"

He gave her a strange look, shrugging. "Yes. Is that what you were supposed to find out?"

Leanna drew her reins in in surprise. "What?"

"It was very obvious, the scene at breakfast. You casually mention how you'd like to go riding, I offer to accompany you and your husband agrees without a moment's pause. Strange, don't you think, for a man who hasn't let you out of his sight for the past two days—especially near me—to suddenly be so acquiescent."

Leanna had been staring at him, speechless at first, a slow, disbelieving anger gradually reddening her face. She felt her lip begin to tremble and didn't risk a reply, only turned her mare's head back toward Blytheswood's main house. "You needn't accompany me then, Major. I can find my own way back." She ignored the sting of sudden tears and put her horse into a canter, a reckless gait in these thick woods, with tree roots, exposed outcroppings of moss-slicked rock, low-hanging branches. She had become an enemy again. She'd seen it in his eyes.

Chase was slow to follow her, partly because he was not sure if he should. A sudden movement along a tree limb caught his eye and he grabbed for his rifle, calling a startled warning to Leanna. His cry was drowned out by a sudden feral growl above her. She looked up in alarm and had the split-second impression of something hurtling down from a tree bough overhead. She screamed as it hit into her with a stunning thud, knocking her sideways from the mare's back. A single shot cracked. The mountain lion turned in midair with a vicious snarl, snapping at the air. Another shot sounded as she hit the ground, her fall cushioned by the spring growth of new-leaved saplings. For a moment, she lay dazed, choking for the breath the fall had knocked out of her, rolling slowly to a stop. As she lifted her head, the open, bared-teeth snarl of the dead cat lay inches from her face. She screamed and scrambled backwards before she realized it could no longer threaten her. Then she slowly pushed to her feet, staring wide-eyed at the still twitching predator.

"You're all right, Leanna?" He arrived at a gallop and resisted the impulse to run to her. The carbine still hung from his right hand as he glanced beyond her to check the mountain lion. It was dead, and he realized suddenly his hand was shaking in reaction. Having to shoot the damn thing so close to Leanna's head like that. . . .

"Come on." He forced himself to turn away, torn between suspicion and his love for her. Beautiful Rebel. Dangerous, dangerous woman to love. "Whatever game you're playing almost got you killed. We'll go back to Blytheswood before you—"

"There's no game."

"The hell there isn't."

"Damn you, Chase, how can you be so sure and be so wrong."

"I've lived with this for three years now! I've gotten good at war—good at killing." His eyes were bitter, mocking his own words. "Wonderful quality, isn't it? Of course, it has certain advantages, too—like being practiced enough with a rifle to shoot a mountain lion in midair. One of the drawbacks, though, is that you develop a gut instinct of when something smells, Leanna. And this smells—to the heavens!"

"But you must trust me, Chase, or you wouldn't have come."

"Trust you?" His eyes touched hers briefly, anger

and hurt all mingled together. "Trust you, Lea? Dear God, I wish I could!"

"Then you only came because—"

"I was hoping you'd tell me what it is. What is he after, Leanna?"

There was a long silence. Leanna held his eyes, searching them, not sure whether to hit him or hold him. Finally, she managed a trembling smile, shaking her head. "You had me fooled, Major Courtland," she murmured finally, with a bitterly sad smile. "I thought you came because you loved me."

There was a silence, long and pained.

"I do—more than you realize." His voice was weary, defeated, and he turned away from her to reach for the reins of his horse. "If I didn't love you so desperately, I wouldn't be here. I shouldn't be, but I couldn't give up the chance to prove to myself you might love me as much as I've come to love you. That you'd tell me what it is he's up to."

"Stop it, Chase, for God's sake . . ." Her voice faltered and she reached for his arm. It felt like a knife had turned in her heart at the bitterness of his words. "I do love you! How can I tell you something I don't know?"

His eyes swung to meet hers, searching their violet depths.

"Chase, it's a beautiful day. The sun is so warm. The wildflowers are all in bloom. The trees are just budding. I wanted to go riding. And I wanted a few more moments with you. It was that simple."

"And your husband's approval?"

Her confidence faltered and she dropped her gaze uneasily. "I don't know. I guess I've tried not to think about it." She took a deep breath, forcing her eyes up to meet his. "You're right not to trust him, Chase. Don't trust me, either. Not entirely. Don't tell me anything you wouldn't want to read in the newspaper."

A faint smile flickered on his mouth and Leanna reached up to touch his arm. "As for this morning—the riding . . . maybe I'm a fool, but I can't really believe he'd use me this way, Chase. He loves me in his own way."

"Yes, I believe he does. In a fashion, anyway. As long as you obey all the rules." He was already turning around, glancing over her shoulder at the soldiers who were just now catching up. He glanced back at the dead lion, gesturing the troopers toward it to explain the shots.

Leanna had been watching him with a puzzled look on her face, wondering at his words. All the rules? What did he mean?

"I hate to say this, but we've got to get back, Leanna. I don't dare leave Blytheswood very long now with your husband roaming around free, knowing he's up to something and not knowing what."

She nodded, daring only a last touch of her hand on his. "I love you, Chase. That's all I wanted to say anyway."

"I love you, too, Lea. God help me, but I could murder your husband. I've wanted to. I want you that badly."

She tried to see his eyes to see whether it was a joke—however bad a one. But he was looking away. Whatever his eyes held she couldn't tell. And only pain showed on his handsome, sun-darkened face.

"Here, Leanna. I'll help you up."

It was over. She realized that with a sudden terrible pain. They would not have another chance like this to speak. In a day or two, Chase would be gone altogether, riding out of her life and back into the war. All that would remain for her at Blytheswood was a memory that would grow ever dimmer over the years. She stepped forward, only nodding because she couldn't trust her voice to speak, and tried to ease the agony in her heart by concentrating on reseating herself in the saddle. A beautiful little clearing lay just ahead. The soldiers with them were riding toward it, too close now to risk their overhearing. She noted with a dull sort of uneasiness that Banks was one of them. He met her eyes boldly with an obvious leer as he rode past and she flushed, looking away.

"What is it?"

"Nothing really. Just that soldier on the right . . ."

"Banks? Has he been offensive this winter?" Their horses stepped out into the open sunshine. Chase raised one hand to shield his eyes against the sudden, blinding glare, frowning as he spoke.

"Not really. Nothing worth mentioning."

"You should have told me, Lea. I could have disciplined him for it. Now that we're leaving in another day, I . . ."

Shots rang out with the suddenness of summer thunder. Leanna's mare half reared in panic and she grabbed desperately for her reins to control her. The Yankee troopers, well used to war, were off their horses already, running back toward the trees for cover. One, mounted, whirled to ride for aid. Two of the five remaining fell as they ran, rolling to a stop in the long grass. Leanna screamed and raised her hands instinctively to shield her face as a bullet richocheted into a nearby tree limb, and splinters of flying bark hit her hair.

"Leanna, get down! Get off your horse!" Chase shouted over the confusion. There was the high whine of bullets, the loud rustle of horses running in the knee-high grass. She didn't move, too utterly stunned to react even if she'd heard him. He spurred his horse forward, leaning out to grab for her, hauling her out of her saddle and dropping her to the ground.

"Stay low! Get into the woods—there behind that fallen log!" Leanna stared a moment up at him, white-faced, frightened. Then her brain began to work again and she whirled on her heel, running for the log Chase had pointed to. He reached beneath his right leg to pull the loaded carbine free of its saddle straps, starting to raise it. His horse screamed suddenly as a bullet hit it, rearing in pain. Leanna saw the animal begin to crumple before it hit the ground and she cried out in alarm, starting to her feet. Chase jumped free of the wounded animal, stumbling a step from the force of his momentum as he hit the knee-high grass of the clearing, running for the woods, crouched low. An instant later, another volley of shots echoed and he half turned, stumbled, and fell hard in the grass a dozen yards from her.

"Chase!" Leanna lifted her skirts and began to run, no longer conscious of the bullets or the danger. A terrible fear overwhelmed everything else, her mind contained only one thought. God no! Don't take him from me.

"Chase!" He was still as death; blood covered his left shoulder in a widening circle. She tore at the buttons of his uniform, sobbing with urgency as her fingers fumbled with a seemingly endless number of them. She ripped the last few with the strength of desperation, reaching inside to feel for a heartbeat. Oh thank God! For a moment, she only closed her eyes in numb relief, feeling the strong, if somewhat erratic, beat beneath her palm.

"Leanna! Get back to your horse. They'll be back in force and we have to be long gone."

She lifted her head and stared. Stewart. Here in the woods? How? Why? He was supposed to be back at Blytheswood.

"Leanna, didn't you hear me?" He loomed suddenly huge above her, reaching down to grab her shoulder, shaking her. "Hurry now."

"But, but I can't . . ."

"I'll check these saddlebags." Stewart dismounted, speaking over his shoulder to more men who were appearing out of the woodland shadows into the open sunshine like ghosts taking physical shape. "You don't need to do this—you go on, Leanna, and get Jasmin. I'll check his pockets before I leave."

She felt her mouth dropping open, all the blood draining from her face and she shivered with a terrible, abysmal coldness. Oh God, no! She stared at the nightmare scene around her as if awakening from a dream. The beautiful little clearing was still with a deadly silence. Four dark-blue bodies lay amid a mocking gaiety of wildflowers. Chase had been right. Stewart had used her in some ghastly plan, and assumed, when he found her searching Chase's pocket, she was as much a ghoul as he was.

"No, I'll search him." Her voice was remarkably cool, and even while astonished at it, she congratulated herself. "I'll only be a minute."

"But, the way you are with blood . . ."

"I'll manage," she replied curtly, bending back to make a show of a search. He stood watching a moment more. Leanna felt his eyes on her, felt it when he turned away. She saw her hand, saw scarlet blood drying to a reddish brown, and shuddered helplessly, closing her eyes against a dangerous dizziness. Please God, help me. The wound must be bad or he would be conscious. If I can't stop the bleeding, he'll die before the others get back with help. Spider webs. Doc Lacey had mentioned using them to staunch a wound. That would take much more time than she had. Stewart would be done in a minute. Only wildflowers and grass lay around her. A piece of her petticoat, then, and to hell with propriety! If she could rip it in time, without the others noticing. . . .

The Confederacy's poverty worked to her advantage, she thought bitterly, as the overworn cotton fabric ripped easily in her hand. She wadded it hastily and reached beneath the blood-soaked jacket to press it to his shoulder. The blood felt warmer, wettest there. Thank God she couldn't actually see what she was doing. She held it with her hand as long as she dared, pulling more fabric free to fashion a crude, overhasty bandage. Better than nothing. Pray God, good enough. Chase, I didn't know. Will you ever believe that now? I swear I didn't know he had this planned.

"Leanna, aren't you done yet?"

Stewart was back. Leanna managed a brusque nod and rose to her feet. "Nothing here." She couldn't look at him. Neither could she look at Chase lying unconscious on the spring-green carpet of the ground. She picked her long riding skirt up in one hand and reached for her mare's reins. What was Stewart going to do now? He couldn't be going back to Blytheswood.

"I'm sorry, Leanna." She was startled to feel Stewart's hand on her elbow as he began to help her remount the skittish mare. "This wasn't exactly how we had planned it. But one of the Yankees caught me this morning going through Courtland's papers. I was determined not to leave you behind and there was no other way."

She nodded, careful not to look at him. She felt sick suddenly. Cold. Nauseous. Chase's blood covered her hand.

"They're coming!"

A half-dozen men instantly ran for their horses. Stewart literally pushed Leanna into her saddle, then turned to run for his own horse. Could she try to escape? Would the other Yankees ever believe her innocence now? Or would they hang her in cold-blooded retaliation?

"Come on." Steward leaned to grab one of her reins, pulling the mare after his own horse. She hesitated a last moment, then set heels to the mare's flanks, following the others. Whatever Stewart was, he was still her husband. Whatever he had done, it had been for a cause she too should have been willing to make any sacrifice for. Something deep in her heart turned cold and dead. She rode without looking back. The war had come to Blytheswood after all. And as Doc Lacy had prophesied on a long-ago, black December evening, it had taken an ugly, ugly turn indeed.

Jonathon's face paled as he read the telegram. He refolded it quickly, hoping his hand wasn't shaking. "Mr. Courtland?"

Joshua looked up, absently. "Just a moment. I've got some figures here to finish."

"It's from my wife in Washington. She won't be coming up tomorrow after all." He swallowed against a sick feeling, steeling himself for a blow. "It's your son, sir. He's been wounded." He reached out to hand over the telegram. Joshua paled and seemed to gasp for breath.

His hand, when it moved, reached not for the telegram but for his heart where redoubled pains had begun to grip it.

"Brandy . . ." he managed to grunt.

Jonathon's hands were shaking as he grabbed the crystal decanter and poured a stiff drink. Oh God, don't die, don't make *me* a murderer, too. Leanna, my sweet and lovely sister, what have you been brought to?"

"Here, Mr. Courtland." He held the glass to the man's mouth and tipped it, spilling a little in his haste. "Steady now. Your son's not in any danger." He accused himself in an agony of remorse. Damn stupid, Jonathon. Telling him as he had—so bluntly! A man of Courtland's age. "He's in Washington, that's all. Doc Lacey's treating him for a shoulder wound, that's why it will be a few days before he can bring Whitney . . ."

"Let me see it." Joshua lifted his hand to push the brandy in the young man's hand away, drawing a few deep breaths before looking for the telegram. They were easing now, the pains. . . . He closed his eyes in grateful prayer, drawing a deep breath. Thank you, God, for a little more time. The telegram lay fallen on his desk and he fumbled with his spectacles to be able to read it.

DEAR JONATHON STOP MAJOR COURTLAND WOUNDED IN GUERRILLA ACTION NEAR BLYTHESWOOD ON APRIL THIRD STOP LEFT SHOULDER NOT SERIOUS STOP DOC LACEY TREATING SO WILL DELAY OUR ARRIVAL PHILADELPHIA STOP SOME QUESTION LEANNA INVOLVED IN ACTION STOP COLONEL LEIGHTON APPARENTLY OPERATING NOW AS INDEPENDENT PARTISAN—SPY? WANTED AS SUCH BY FEDERAL AUTHORITIES STOP AWAIT RESPONSE WHAT TO DO NOW STOP WHITNEY.

The pains eased further and Joshua raised his eyes to the young Rebel's face. It was pale and closed tight, his eyes staring at the carpet design. "Wire her to come as soon as Doc Lacey can spare the time."

Jonathon shook his head, a tight, angry gesture. "We can't presume on you any longer, sir, not now."

"It was your brother-in-law, not you, Penley—and your sister, if the girl was involved at all, which I tend to doubt." Jonathon flung Joshua a startled glance. Joshua chose not to explain. He didn't think it was anyone else's business but theirs. "We have learned, in our family, that women are sometimes difficult to control. We don't judge you by what your sister may have done. As we hope you wouldn't judge us."

Jonathon felt heat creeping up his neck. Elinor? Oh God! Did the elder Courtland know somehow about the other evening?

"Chase is all right. That's the important thing to me. I'll wait to talk with him before I make some overhasty, unfair judgment."

Jonathon managed a nod then, beginning to turn away. His hands were shaking badly. He put them in his pockets and cleared his throat before he spoke. "You're all right now, sir? I mean, for me to leave you?"

Joshua lifted one brow in resignation, just nodding. Then he changed his mind, catching the young man at the door. "Penley, what you just saw—I mean, my physical infirmities—I would much appreciate it if you'd keep that to yourself."

Jonathon was startled again, turning to question the older man with his eyes. "But you should see a—"

"Doctor, yes, of course. But I don't need to." Joshua hesitated a moment more, then finally sighed, spreading his hands in an irritated gesture. "Perhaps I should be completely honest with you. I have had several attacks of this sort. I know from my own father what they are—and what they mean. I am a man whose time is running out. This war has come at a bad time for me. You might as well know because you may have to deal with several more such incidents with me. But my son doesn't know, nor my daughter.

"Nor," he managed a wry smile, "the directors of the bank board or . . ." He thought of Hodges and the others. That hellish coalition. But that was far too secret to name. "Or anyone else. Repay my hospitality by keeping my secret, please, Mr. Penley. It's important to me. Very important." He thought again of the coalition. The King Rats, as he called them privately. Those captains and those kings who turned the world to a tune of their own, regardless of the misery they caused. "Important to a good many people," he finished softly. "More than you could ever imagine."

Chapter Fourteen

"Jewel sent this along from Blytheswood." A paper boy cried the news outside on the Washington street as Doc Lacey turned to pick up a lace-edged length of worn cotton cloth. It had been washed, but the dark stain of Chase's blood still marked it. "Apparently, she took it off your shoulder when she first dressed your wound. It looks like a piece of woman's petticoat to me. I assume she meant it as some sort of message."

Chase reached for it with his right hand. His left hung in a muslin sling still to ease his shoulder. He shifted his weight on the narrow hospital cot and wished his head felt a little clearer. If Jewel had taken the trouble to send it on, it could belong to only one person.

"Leanna's?"

Chase frowned, setting it aside. "I imagine so."

"Seems rather illogical for a woman who sets a trap to mind its closing."

"*If* she set it."

Doc Lacey paused at that, turning to face Chase and raising one brow in slow surprise. "You think she *didn't?*" He studied his friend a moment, considering. "I gather, then, that you're in love with her still."

"I gather you think I shouldn't be."

"For God's sake, Chase, she's married, she's Confederate—she may very well have just tried to murder you! Not to mention the fact that you do have a fiancée here at this very hospital who's as fine a woman as any I've ever known. You seem to have trouble even remembering her!"

Anger flared in his voice, but Chase didn't seem to notice. Between loss of blood, the concussion, and the lingering effects of the morphine, his head was pound-

208

ing too badly to catch subtleties. He had only closed his eyes with a frown and raised one hand to his head. Doc Lacey turned briefly away, fighting his anger. He had no right to be angry for Susan Stratford's sake. No right even to feel what he felt for her. He controlled himself with an effort, reaching across Chase for the blood-stained cloth. Stick to the subject, he ordered himself. Deal with the problem of Susan later when Chase has a half a chance of thinking clearly.

"I'm just afraid that if you keep on believing this romantic fantasy about Leanna that you'll give the Leighton's another chance to finish the job, someday."

Chase pressed his hand harder against his eyes, but it didn't ease the pain. If anything, it worsened with the effort of trying to think. What if Doc were right? He usually was. What if he *were* just believing what he wanted to believe, thinking with his heart and not his head? Christ, it wasn't as if Leanna hadn't betrayed him once already—and that time beyond any shadow of a doubt. As clear as yesterday, he could remember reaching down for her in the December snow, watching the book slip out from beneath her cloak. And *if* Doc were right? He could forgive her, somehow, for trying to kill him. But for those four of his men that he'd buried, if she'd acquiesced to their murder, he couldn't.

"Chase, at least admit that the evidence shows—"

"Damn the evidence! She wasn't involved!"

"Chase, for Christ's sake, everything I've heard says that she was!"

"Leanna might do a lot of things for the Confederacy, but not that! You knew her, damn it!"

Chase fell suddenly silent. Doc Lacey saw Chase's eyes shift from his face to the doorway beyond, saw his expression change, and quickly turned. "Oh, Susan, it's you."

Her smile was rather obviously forced, and she moved slowly, hesitantly, into the room. "I have the feeling I'm interrupting an argument. You must be feeling much better, Chase, to risk talking back to your doctor. I hope you'll be better humored with your nurse." She laid her hand briefly on Chase's good shoulder, avoiding Doc Lacey's eyes. "What's the problem?"

Chase hesitated a moment, then shrugged, gesturing down to the bed. "Maybe I'm just ready to get out of this."

"I'd be more sympathetic to a wish to get out of this bed if you'd stayed longer in one at Blytheswood." Lacey was irritated by Susan's affectionate gesture and angry at himself for it. Later, he reminded himself. They would settle later what Susan's position would be. He turned away with a frown, unnecessarily curt. "Twenty-four hours? Was your schedule all that important?"

Despite the cloud of pain, Chase's gaze sharpened. "Yes, it was. Should I have risked getting the whole battalion ambushed?"

"Well, you've about ten days before you're required to report to General Sherman in Tennessee. Plan to spend most of that time convalescing either here in the hospital or at my place." He started out, not looking around. "I'll be back later. I have other patients to check on."

Chase watched him out, conscious of Susan's hand lying lightly still on his shoulder. Was it only the damn morphine, or was something really wrong here? Roger snapping at him, Susan obviously strained.

"Don't mind Roger—I mean, Doctor Lacey." Susan blushed at her slip of the tongue and hurried on to cover it. "He's mad at you for pushing yourself so, Chase. That shoulder was bad enough, but you whacked your head, too, when you fell. I could still feel the lump three days later." Silence followed her words. Chase was frowning at the door where Doc Lacey had exited.

She glanced uneasily at the ring Chase had put on her finger and forced herself on. "Chase, last night when you arrived, you were feverish so I stayed up with you. Chase, who is Leanna? You said her name over and over again, but I couldn't understand what else you were saying."

It had come out in a rush and, for a moment, Chase

was too startled to reply. He glanced at her quickly. Her eyes were locked to his, her face pale. "She's Whitney's sister-in-law."

"Oh, Mrs. Leighton." Relief and despair mingled in a jumble of emotion. Susan forced a little smile. "Oh, yes. Of course. She was with you when you were shot. That makes sense now." How could she explain to him what she had thought—hoped, maybe—about the gentle way he'd murmured her name.

"Susan, I—" Chase started, then stopped, looking away, shaking his head. "Oh, never mind." His head was throbbing again badly. Too badly to tackle that problem just now. How easy it would be to just tell her the truth. Tell her he'd only ever loved her like the little sister she'd seemed—Ben's sister, his closest friend until he'd died in his arms at Chancellorsville. Tell her he'd given her the ring because he didn't like to sour the hope he'd seen in her eyes as the war drew only days away, and because there'd seemed no reason then that he shouldn't someday marry her. Never dreaming there'd be a Virginia woman named Leanna Leighton who'd complicate things so greatly.

"You must be tired, Chase. I'll go."

He opened his eyes with a start. He hadn't remembered she was still there, he didn't remember closing his eyes. "Sorry, Susan, I didn't mean—"

"It's all right, Chase." She squeezed his shoulder gently as she rose to go. "It's the laudanum. It does that."

He *was* tired suddenly. No, weary. Why couldn't life ever be simple? The woman he had, he didn't want. The one he wanted, he couldn't have. Did you know, Leanna? he asked himself. Did you know he was going to try to kill us all? Susan left and he closed his eyes to the vivid, unsettling dream of the opiate painkiller. In every one of them, there was a beautiful woman with violet eyes.

"Chase," Joshua smiled in the bright morning sunlight, rising to offer his hand to the tall young officer just

211

walking in the door of Doc Lacey's Washington apartment. "Glad you finally made it back. It's good to see you, son."

Chase paused, startled, his hand freezing halfway up to his hat. "Father, good morning." He offered a surprised but genuine smile, closing the door and moving toward Joshua with a quick stride. As he reached to take his father's hand, their eyes met and held, exchanging a greeting of warm, mutual affection. Just for a moment, neither needed words to speak. War or no war, they had remained close. "I didn't know you were coming down to Washington. I would have met your train."

"I didn't want you to trouble yourself—better you should enjoy what few hours you get off from this damn war. Besides, trains are unreliable these days. I just took a cab."

"When did you get in?"

"Last night."

Chase flushed faintly, his smile turning rueful. "Oh. Then you should have wired ahead. I was—"

"No apology needed. A young man—long war. I quite understand. Celebrating your release from the hospital. I was pleased, really, to find you so well recovered."

"The wound wasn't all that serious."

"Thank God. It could have been." Joshua paused a moment, then eyed his son intently as he continued. "Chase, the reason I came to Washington, aside from seeing you, of course, was to find out what happened exactly. Down in Virginia. Do you mind telling me?" He could see his son's smile freeze before Chase turned a half step away.

"A guerrilla ambush. But we're not sure—"

"Not the newspaper account—yours. I could have stayed home and read the war reports, otherwise."

"Well, what exactly—"

"The girl, Chase. Was she involved?" Joshua's voice was soft, but the question deliberately blunt. He watched his son's averted face and saw dark pain flash there,

212

answering the question he hadn't yet asked. He kept his own face impassive, but inside, he swore in silent dismay.

"Her husband was. One of my officers was nearly killed interrupting his search for military papers. But Leanna, Mrs. Leighton rather . . ." He frowned and turned away entirely with an abrupt gesture. "It's done. I don't suppose it matters whether she was or not."

"Doesn't matter? I'm afraid I don't agree with that. It may have slipped your mind for the moment, but I've got her Confederate brother living at my house, her sister-in-law coming—"

"Penley's been a problem for you?"

"No. Not exactly. I expected him to be a liability—actually he's become something of an asset. Surprised me, I confess, but he's got an intuitive grasp of the banking business."

"Why make changes then?"

"Because if his sister tried to murder you—"

"She didn't," Chase flung his father a single, swift glance. There was a warning there and a short silence followed.

Joshua nodded once in the silence and made an effort to soften his voice. "Chase, what the devil is going on? Don't you owe me an explanation? Maybe I was reading more into your last few letters than I should have, but I was guessing there was something between you and her. Was I wrong?"

"What could be between us? She was married."

"Damn it, Chase!" Joshua felt pains gathering and tried to relax, trying not to show them on his face. "I'm no child to be fed moral pablum! I've lived long enough to know 'should' and 'is' aren't always the same thing! I want the truth! It's what I came all the way here to get!"

"All right. I'm in love with her! Is that what you wanted to hear?"

"No, hardly what I *wanted* to hear! A married woman? A Confederate woman, no less! I suppose she's in love with you, too?"

"We didn't plan for it to happen."

213

"No one ever does." Joshua shook his head, turning for his seat and waving Chase to take one as well. The pains lessened as he lowered himself back to the worn leather couch and took a deep breath. Chase hesitated a long moment and finally sat, his eyes dark as he stared down at the shining black leather of his high boots. Joshua glanced at him finally and sighed. Damn this war. Damn it. "As long as you think Mrs. Leighton was not involved, Penley and his wife are welcome to stay."

"Thank you."

The silence grew longer. Joshua tried not to be angry. He glanced finally at his son again and what he saw on his face made his heart ache in redoubled anguish. It was time he changed the subject. "Elinor's home."

Chase looked up, startled.

"Who knows?" Joshua shrugged. "I don't know where the good viscount is either. Elinor says he's in England. I have my doubts. But where else would he be?"

Chase said nothing. Elinor home? With Leanna's brother?

"I figured they'd keep an eye on each other back home. I won't be gone long anyway."

Chase nodded, not speaking any of his thoughts aloud. "And you, father? How are you holding up?" He studied him as he spoke, more concerned by the question than he would let on. And he decided his father didn't look well—not as well as he would have hoped to find him, anyway. The war was taking a toll on all the Courtland men.

Joshua only smiled faintly, shrugging. "You were always the only one of my children who asked that, Chase, as if you meant it, anyway. Thank you for that, at least." He smiled. "I'm fine, of course. Looking forward to the war's end and having you home. You're off now with Sherman, I hear."

"You hear right."

"Want me to pull some strings? Would you rather stay in Virginia?"

Chase glanced at him, wondering if he were making some oblique reference to Leanna. "No, I'm happy to go. I'd rather not be in the Valley to see it torched. It's beautiful country and most of the people are Dunkers and such—not even involved in the Confederacy. And east of the Blue Ridge, Grant's going to wage a wicked war."

"But he's good, Chase. He'll get it ended."

"If he stays sober."

"That's greatly exaggerated, those drinking reports. He's a fine man."

Chase shrugged. Grant had been caught napping at Shiloh and his brother had died for it. And he'd seen Lee in action, his brilliance at defensive strategy. He'd wait and watch before deciding how a good commander Grant really was. "He's brought Sheridan with him to head his cavalry. From what I recall Josh saying, I'm not sure I'd like Sheridan much."

"You'll be under Kilpatrick with Sherman. Is that any better?"

A faint smile curved Chase's mouth. "The devil or the deep blue sea. Kilpatrick's like Custer—interested in making a big splash to further future political careers. 'Kill Cavalry's' got his eye on governor of New Jersey, I understand."

"His leaflet-dropping nonsense—that raid on Richmond—was a disaster."

"I know."

"Dahlgren's son was killed."

"Well, I've got to fight under someone, Father," Chase's smile widened slightly. "Any suggestions?"

"You liked Buford, at Gettysburg."

"But he's staying under Grant."

"You're determined to go with Sherman, then. I give up. Word is he's heading for Atlanta, did you know that?"

"No. Atlanta? That's the CSA's main railroad center in the deep South. They'll put everything they've got into protecting it."

"Exactly what Grant and Sherman think. But the CSA can't concentrate on *two* points at one time. They're

215

hoping it will weaken the armies enough at both Richmond and Atlanta to—"

"Mr. Courtland. Chase." Doc Lacey forced a smile as he entered and interrupted. "I see you finally found each other. Washington nightlife apparently hasn't suffered from the war."

Chase turned at his friend's entrance. Damn. There it was again. Roger had been ill-humored all week. This last comment—like so many others these past few days—had been innocent enough, but there was a nasty edge underlying it.

"Forgive our intrusion on your home, Doctor. Chase and I were just going out to get breakfast. Care to join us?" Joshua rose and smiled kindly.

"No, thanks. I have some work here."

"I've only got another day, Roger. Come with us," Chase reached to catch at his arm.

"No, I won't." Doc Lacey jerked away, angry, first at Chase, then at himself. Hell. It wasn't Chase's fault he'd fallen in love with the man's fiancée. "No, not just now." He managed a friendlier smile, but still shook his head. "You go on."

Chase hesitated a moment, then shrugged with a frown, and walked toward the door. Joshua glanced at the young man curiously, then followed his son, catching him outside on the stairs. Chase's face was grim and dark and he asked no questions as he walked beside him.

This had been one hell of a week, Chase was thinking. Roger's infernal moodiness, the question of Leanna. . . . For the first few days, laudanum had clouded his mind too greatly to think straight. For the last few, Leanna had taken precedence over Roger. His father's reaction had surprised him. Relieved him, really. He'd expected worse. 'We didn't plan for it to happen . . .' 'No one ever does . . .' That summed it up so neatly. Cutting through all the pain, all the guilt, all the confusion.

"Chase," Joshua had stopped suddenly on the stairs, reaching out to grasp his son's arm. "If there's anything I can do to help—"

216

Chase saw the genuine concern in his father's eyes and checked his own step momentarily, thanking him with a faint smile. "No. Thank you, though. I can handle it on my own."

Father and son stood a moment on the stairs, exchanging a wordless glance. To Joshua, there was a certain pride in it, also a kind of sorrow. The changing of the guard, he thought to himself. His son was a man full grown.

He turned wordlessly toward the bright Washington sunshine, finishing the stairs.

Outside, the cherry trees were blossoming. The Potomac was broad and silver in the sun. Workmen were refurbishing a new white marble dome on the Capital Building, and carriages clattered over cobblestones and pieces of wood scaffolding as they manuevered around the mess. He looked at it closely, fixing it in his mind. And he wondered where Chase would be that day long in the future when his own son would turn to him as Chase had now, and startle him with the knowledge that the reins had passed to younger hands.

That's the cart in front of the horse, Joshua, he told himself. There's a lot of fighting yet between then and now. And even without the war, Chase needs a wife before he can have a son. Remembering the look on his face when he's spoken of Jonathon Penley's sister, Joshua suddenly found himself wondering whether Chase would ever have one. That reminded him of Susan, and the fact he'd made up his mind to speak to him about her. It was more important than ever Chase should set a definite date to marry the girl.

It was hot that mid-April night, as Philadelphia spring nights could occasionally be. Jonathon Penley left the window open and lay in bed under only the crisp white sheet, staring up at the dark ceiling with a thoughtful frown. Why didn't those figures work out? Outside, a carriage rattled by on the street-lamp-lit street, a dog barked back in the stables, but they were only the normal night sounds of a city house, and they no longer intruded on Jonathon's consciousness. No matter how many times he checked the figures—he'd even gone down to the vault personally and counted the notes there on deposit—they still came out wrong. The ledger showed some two hundred thousand dollars in frozen CSA assets. The actual money figure was more like a hundred and seventy five thousand.

Had Joshua Courtland embezzled from his own bank? If so, why give the books to someone else to check, for God's sake? And if not Joshua, who? Who else even had access to the vault? None of the other employees. Not even the board members. When Jonathon had gone in, he'd been with another bank officer and even so, a guard had stood most alertly by, and he'd needed Joshua's written permission to do that much.

He closed his eyes to the puzzle, but it refused to go away. Who? Why? And most importantly, what to do about it? Confront his host with the discrepancy, which, no matter how tactfully he phrased it, was going to sound like an accusation? When Whitney and Mandy were due back with him tomorrow? To be houseguests until the baby—babies?—were born at the nearby University of Pennsylvania Hospital? God, he couldn't risk it. Whitney needed that Yankee hospital, those bright young Yankee doctors. He might lose her otherwise. And nothing was worth that. But what to do then? If he didn't say something soon, and the money were missed later, would someone not wonder whether *he'd* done it? For his own pocket or to aid the poor CSA coffers? What of Joshua's heart condition? If he were confronted by the fact someone had embezzled those funds. . . .

Sleep came eventually, but no answer. Outside, the street lamps were trimmed low; even the stables were quiet. Downstairs in the foyer, the imported English clock chimed three, and its mechanical moon dropped lower into its painted ocean. Gilt filigree hands moved with a smooth whir and the floorboards near Jonathon's bed creaked beneath the step of a woman's bare foot.

Elinor smiled faintly in the darkness, a beautiful, but somewhat predatory smile. She'd enjoyed Wilson so,

218

down in Savannah. And Jonathon Penley was far handsomer—lean and tough as the army tended to make a man. Clean shaven—which was a shame as she enjoyed the sensation of bristling whiskers. But a faint scar traced a white line along one temple, in contrast to his black hair and sun-darkened face, and that intrigued her. That, she decided thoughtfully, looking down at him as he lay sleeping, at his muscled shoulders and arms that showed above the edge of the sheet, plus one more thing.

He was a challenge. There was always novelty in that. And a deep satisfaction . . . when she won. He was trying to keep at arm's length from her. Dinner had been amusing in that sense—frustrating in so far as he'd succeeded with remarkable diplomacy. The true Southern gentleman. She smiled wider. Honor bound to his big-bellied twit of a wife. Probably adored her and the whining little brat she'd be bringing, too. Ah honor! Thank God she'd escaped the clutches of that particular virtue. God knew the rest of the family had inherited it in sickening degree.

Downstairs the clock chimed three-fifteen and she drew a last deep breath, smoothing her light silken nightgown tighter over her breasts. The familiar tingling feeling began to spread in her loins and she lifted the nightgown's hem high to climb agilely into the sleeping Rebel's bed.

Jonathon stirred uneasily in his sleep. Jeb Stuart was riding in his dream, his bright yellow sash waving, the scarlet-lined cape flapping in a wind Jonathon couldn't feel. He took his plumed hat off and held it high. Gilt spurs gleamed on high, over the knee black "jack" boots. Bugles drowned out what the General was saying, and suddenly the singing started as it always did—men singing as they rode into death. The corps started off and Jonathon tried to follow, but something was holding him back . . . something cool and smooth like silk . . . and the scent of a woman close. Whitney? It must be.

Whitney needed him. Jeb Stuart must ride without him, then. He turned over, murmuring her name, and

Elinor smiled, slipping her hand beneath the sheet. The dream began to change. The scent of heavily perfumed flowers surrounded him—magnolia, maybe? Gardenia? Summer, it must be, then. In the deep South. He could feel a woman's hands on him, light fingers on his chest, running down over his taut belly. His body responded instinctively, he sighed his pleasure. The wet warmth of a woman's lips brushed his, moved across his face to nuzzle his neck. Perfumed hair fell across his face and he inhaled its fragrance gladly. He hardened quickly, a throbbing that surged greater with each heartbeat, and the dream began to fade to half consciousness. Now he could feel the soft sag of a fine mattress beneath his back, the crispness of lightly starched linen, the warm weight of a woman's body pressed over his. Her fingers found him beneath the sheet and began, deftly, to stroke him, hastening his full arousal. She nuzzled his bare neck with a smile, pleased at what she felt beneath her hand. This would be worth the effort she'd made. Good Lord, these Southerners—she should have stayed in Savannah and sent Hadley back North.

Jonathon half groaned, forcing his eyes open with a quizzical frown. Where the devil was he? And what the hell was going on?

"Hello, Major." Elinor's words were a murmur against his ear, her tongue flicked out to trace it as she finished speaking. She shifted her weight slightly above him, reaching to drop the shoulder strap of her gown to free one breast to lie against his mouth. The dark nipple rested against his lips, its inviting peak waiting for his tongue. He frowned harder, beginning to turn his head away. Good God! It was Lady Bennington, Courtland's daughter.

"Oh, don't be a spoilsport," she scolded with a teasing smile. Her eyes glittered like emerald jewels in the soft light as she pushed herself up to sit straddling his chest. Jonathon tried to sit up, couldn't, and raised his hands to begin to lift her. Elinor only turned with a soft laugh. Jonathon's hand found her breast, firm and full, and involuntarily his fingers closed around it. Lightning seemed to pierce his body. He groaned the effort of resisting, and in that single moment of weakness, Elinor moved again. He arched his back helplessly as she kicked the sheet lower and bent over to take him in her mouth. The wet heat of her tongue caressed him and he closed his eyes, unable to move any longer, fighting for a last moment of rational control. He'd been too damn long without a woman. Since September. Eight months. Oh damn . . . Whitney. . . .

Elinor's white teeth nipped at the very tip of him, gently, then her lips took him in full again. Jonathon groaned surrender. The hands he had reached down to try to force her away held her now instead, tangling in her golden hair. Elinor smiled in satisfaction as she felt the change. His hips arched toward her. His swollen manhood pulsed against her tongue. Good, she thought. Now the fun can begin.

"Do you like this, Major? Does it feel good?" Jonathon only moaned and Elinor almost laughed. She didn't need to ask whether any woman had ever done it for him before. She knew that answer. She herself had only learned the trick from a *very* fabulous, *very* exclusive Parisienne courtesan. Even Hadley had been a bit ruffled when first she'd tried it. My, though, the wonders it worked. . . .

"No, just lie still." She had begun to draw her head away and he had followed her helplessly with his hips. He obeyed the gentle pressure of her hands more than her words and she knew he was beyond thinking. She bent and caressed him once more as a reward, then slowly slid her hips toward his. It wouldn't do to prolong this encounter too greatly, she knew. If she let him slip once from this pinnacle of blind need, she would lose the young Rebel. She lifted herself over his jutting spear and impaled herself with a single, practiced thrust, a half sigh of pleasure escaping from her lips. She felt Jonathon grow rigid instantly beneath her, his muscles glistening in the moonlight beneath a film of sweat. His hands reached for her, starting to move her hips over his. She allowed it for a moment, then deftly twisted out of his grip with a soft laugh, lifting herself from him. "Not so fast, darling," she scolded. "This isn't all for you, you know." He reached blindly for her and Elinor only laughed again, sliding across the bed and raising one knee to block his immediate attempt to follow. He rolled over, his eyes half open, unfocused and desperate. She held her arms out to him, then closed her legs tight as he came to her invitation. He was trembling hard now, his body hot and heavy over hers, his mouth covering hers and plunging within in a frenzy of desire, then lifting to nip at her neck, less and less gently as she continued to thwart him. She could feel his rigid member thrusting at her closed thighs, penetrating only far enough to touch the entrance to her, tickling her pale brown hair, and he groaned each time he lifted himself to thrust again. He was doing exactly what she wanted of him, albeit not purposefully, and hot waves of throbbing fire surged in Elinor's loins as well.

She felt his weight on her shift suddenly, taking her by surprise, for she had been lying back on the pillows, quite content with the proceedings. She opened her eyes with a sense of alarm, too late. Jonathon grunted a hoarse demand even while his hands reached down to part her thighs wide open. She struggled a moment against his greater strength without success. Then she saw his lean hips lift high over her gaping entrance and suddenly drop, plunging into her to bury himself to the hilt. She cried out but not in pain, writhing beneath him only in greed. It was marvelous. He was taking her with all the savagery of a wild stallion, forcing her to lie still beneath his plunging masculinity. She had no control over him any longer and the novelty of that was enough to drive her own passion to the brink. She felt herself bursting around him as he impaled her again and she whimpered in an ecstasy of pleasure. He shuddered suddenly in her arms, grew absolutely still within her, then groaned, shuddering again, moving convulsively in a last thrust before he lay still above her. Elinor closed her eyes and drew a deep sigh of satisfaction. Then, before he could quite recover his senses, she pushed his weight away from her, slipping from beneath his arm to start back for her own room.

Jonathon rolled away from where they had lain, groaning again in helpless despair. The pleasures of his body faded quickly beneath the anguish of realization as his head began to clear. Oh God, what had he done? Elinor had begun it, yes, but by the end. . . .

"Good night, Major. Pleasant dreams."

He raised himself on one elbow without speaking a word and saw her smile as she slipped soundlessly out the door. Whore, he thought, watching her go. And what does that make you, Jonathon? he asked himself. He had no answer, but he lay sleepless for long hours wondering. Whitney would be arriving today, and Miranda, their daughter. He would be hard pressed to keep this guilt from ruining the long-awaited reunion. Oh God, I'm sorry, Whitney, was all he could think, over and over again. I'm so sorry, love . . . so very sorry.

Chapter Fifteen

"I'm sorry," Leanna overheard one woman saying to another. "I'm so sorry to hear that. He was a fine boy. But we must go on, you know. The cause is far greater than . . ." The woman wandered slowly away, and she made no effort to hear anymore. It was an all too familiar conversation these days—familiar and true. The cause *was* far greater than anything else—even greater than Chase. She'd been on the verge of forgetting that this winter. It had taken Richmond to remind her again.

She took a glass of champagne punch offered wordlessly by a formally dressed Negro slave—one who hadn't escaped, obviously, in January, when another slave had nearly burned the house down doing so. Then she slowly turned to survey the ballroom of the Davis's Richmond home. They called it the White House of the Confederacy, a deliberate taunt to the Federal one in Washington. Those who had seen both declared this one finer. The long room here was bright tonight with crystal chandeliers and cut spring flowers, a rainbow of shining ball gowns and the brass of men's dress uniforms. The band was just finishing "Bonnie Blue Flag" and some of the dinner guests were singing along. Beautiful, she thought, proudly. Touching. Both gallant and defiant. The Yankees might have beaten the South to her knees, but her spirit was yet unbowed.

"Mrs. Leighton?"

She turned with a start, blinking against sudden tears misting her eyes. "Oh, General Lee." She'd seen him earlier, recognizing him first by his brother, Smith Lee, who'd stood with him. Smith had been a friend of her father's. "You must excuse me." She quickly wiped her eyes dry. "The music was so moving."

He nodded once, graciously. "I'd ask you to dance, but that's a marching song. Perhaps they'll play something of a better tempo later."

"It's been so long anyway since I've danced. I'm not sure I remember how." She managed a faint smile, hoping that had not sounded like a complaint. "I don't recall seeing your wife, General. Is she here?"

"No, I'm afraid not. She's no longer able to attend these functions. Hasn't been since the war began."

Unfair, Leanna thought. The flower of Confederate manhood—tall, handsome even now in his fifties. Everything the South said a man should be. But his wife, Mary Custis, was an invalid; had been practically since their marriage. Yet the Lees shared a noted mutual devotion. "I'm sorry to hear that. Truly I am."

He smiled rather distantly, offering his arm. "I understand you have had quite a winter. Surrounded by enemy troops, yet you've emerged obviously unscathed. I wish I could say the same of myself in such situations."

Leanna smiled at his obvious gallantry, hoping to hide the quick pain in her heart. "I found them courteous in the extreme."

"You were very fortunate then. Who was commanding?"

"Oh, I—I'm sure you wouldn't know him." General Lee continued to look at her and she forced a faint smile. "A cavalry major. Courtland."

He shrugged pleasantly. "Gentlemen often prefer the cavalry—on both sides." He stopped by the punch bowl, and Leanna dropped her hand from his arm. Stewart turned from where he stood speaking with several of Lee's staff officers, saw Leanna, and excused himself to start toward her.

"You're returning to your home in the Valley, Mrs. Leighton?" He offered her another glass of punch and Leanna refused it politely. The champagne was already making her light-headed.

"No, we can't, I'm afraid. My husband—"

"Oh, that's right. That guerilla action. I had forgotten." Was that disapproval she'd glimpsed momentarily in his eyes? He'd glanced away now and she couldn't tell. "We may be staying in Richmond, or . . ."

"We're at the Spotswood now," Stewart offered his arm to Leanna with a faint smile, a courteous nod toward the general. "Leanna's father had a townhouse here, but with housing so acutely short, it's been occupied for the past two years with government personnel. Until we know how long we may be staying . . ."

"Nothing wrong with the Spotswood Hotel," Lee offered a polite smile in return. "President Davis stayed there and ran the government from it for several months."

Leanna said nothing. The five-story hotel had once been one of the glories of Richmond—its high-ceilinged, elegant bar *the* favorite meeting place for Richmond's notables. But the Spotswood, like the rest of Richmond, had suffered in the war years. Even here, if one looked too closely, the men's uniforms showed careful mending, the ball gowns were several years old. Sugar was sorghum, coffee was rye, and she thought it likely the roast beef had brayed rather than mooed while it had lived.

President Davis turned in a doorway, gesturing. The tall, silver-haired general was gone with a pleasantry. Unobtrusively, other high-ranking Confederate officers melted away from the dancing, moving upstairs to conduct a war session in Davis's paneled offices. The president did not usually stay longer than a few hours at these parties—too much else to do—and the general and his staff were leaving tomorrow for the front by the Rapidan River. War could not be long away now that the winter's thawed mud was beginning to dry, and they must be there when the new Federal General Grant made his first move.

"A pleasant party."

Stewart's comment seemed strained and Leanna glanced at him quickly. "You don't approve?"

"The president approves, obviously—and General Lee. Good for morale. It seems a bit unrealistic to me."

"Is it?" she wondered out loud with a thoughtful

smile. "It's about all we really have left to fight on, I'd say. Morale. Pride. Our determination not to give up to 'those people,' I believe General Lee calls them. Our resolution to continue living on in our own way."

"Much of Richmond disapproves."

"Yes, they're at home knitting and sewing for the troops. Worthy gestures, no doubt, but so is this."

Stewart smiled faintly, glancing sidelong at his wife. Even in a borrowed, two-year-old gown, she was the most beautiful woman here. For that alone, he would forgive her for almost anything. "Plus," he continued in a lower voice, "Most of the really best Richmond families snub Mrs. Davis's parties for other reasons. Socially, she's not quite top rank and she hasn't the good grace to accept that fact."

Leanna threw her husband a swift, sharp glance, irritated to see the faint, smug smile that played on his lips. Odd how she had fallen out of step with the social hierarchy she used to accept so completely. Maybe it was a function of spending the winter with the Yankees, their lack of attention to it. It was very much a part of the South, and part of the world she loved so dearly, but still she found Stewart's attitude annoying. "Well, I think Varina is a lovely woman, and we're lucky to have her at such a time." Leanna moved restlessly away from the punch table, frowning. "How can people be so petty in the midst of something this important?"

Stewart shrugged, neither knowing nor, in truth, caring very much. What other people did rarely bothered him. Their motivations for this or that, he found unimportant. Action counted. And winning. He glanced at the now empty doorway through which President Davis and the officers had gone. "What did you think of our fair-haired General Lee, my dear?"

Leanna began to frown and caught herself. It was just Stewart's way to speak so flippantly. "I—well, I found him a bit awesome, actually. I like him. I admire him to no end. But he seems so far above all this. So distant, so cool and so grand. I think he's marvelous, but I'm a little afraid of him at the same time."

"His troops adore him."

"Do they?" She smiled faintly, shrugging. "I'm not surprised. He's done wonders with what pitiful little we can give him to fight with."

"Breeding shows. The Yankees don't see that, of course, nor understand. It's all money with them. But many of our best officers are from the best old families—Lee, Stuart, Jackson, Johnston." Stewart turned as he spoke, offering his arm. "Care to dance, Leanna?"

He said it so abruptly that it startled her. She guessed he'd done it purposely. They'd fought that first night after the ambush that had wounded—killed?—Chase Courtland. They had spoken only superficially since. She had the feeling he was asking for a decision now. Where did she stand? She looked up at him, at her Confederate husband. In uniform again, gray cloth with a yellow collar for cavalry, two stars denoting his rank of Lieutenant Colonel. Gold braid on his yellow cuffed sleeve, a fine dress sword on the belt at his waist above his sash. His blond hair and mustache lightened by the sun that had darkened his face and hands. Part of the world she'd grown up in and belonged in. Why can't I love you like I loved him, she asked herself? I ought to. Perhaps, in time, I will.

The band was finishing "Dixie" and beginning a Virginia reel. She nodded finally, banishing the memory of Chase Courtland to some dark, locked-away place of infinite pain. "Yes, I'll dance, Colonel Leighton," she managed a smile as she answered and reached one hand out to take his. "I'd be most honored."

"This is—astounding, Jon!" Whitney's face had paled ever further as she'd watched the bustling activity of Philadelphia during the long carriage ride home from the train station. Joshua had suggested he be dropped off at the Rittenhouse Club. Jonathon had taken the opportunity to drive his wife the long way home. It wasn't a pleasant sight for Confederate eyes, but he wanted his wife to know the truth.

His eyes were grim as he nodded, and he reached

wordlessly to take her hand. Miranda was exhausted by the adventure of the train ride from Washington. Just now, he was relieved to have her asleep.

Robust prosperity lay all around them. Produce for sale in the markets, shiny new carriages pulled by sleek, well-fed horses, jeweler's shops doing a thriving business, women in gorgeous new gowns, theaters, restaurants, lecture halls, grand hotels like Green's at eighth and Chestnut, a billboard advertising P.T. Barnum's travelling 'Grand Colossal Museum & Managerie', men's clubs so crowded the air inside looked solidly packed with black top hats. People laughed as they promenaded around the park of Rittenhouse Square. Young men *not* in uniform were a common sight. Finally, she saw a small group of Federal suited soldiers going inside what looked to be an upper crust gambling house—or worse—but other than that, there was little sign of war here in the northern city. "My God, Jonathon!" She thought of the South, the cruel shortages—most especially of prosperity and young men—and her heart began to feel a coldness stealing upon it.

"Yes, I know exactly. It's like a totally separate world, isn't it? As though the war hasn't touched them." Jonathon drew the carriage to one side of the street and halted the horses, gesturing as he spoke. "There by the river, Whitney, for block after block, are manufacturing mills—shirts by machine, shoes, clothing, blankets, linens, everything. And where that smoke is, the heavy industries—ironworks there bigger than Tredegar in Richmond, and a half dozen of them, not only one. The're laying suburban and rural railroad track, Whit—expanding the system. You know the South hasn't produced a single new tie in three years? Not one. Up here they've got more than they know what to do with. There's the business section, Front to Fifth and Market to Vine. Where the Courtland bank is. Look at the people. Look at the men they've got left—not even in the army yet. And food—they're producing enough to sell whole boat loads of it to England, while we're starving at home."

229

"I thought it was only Washington, because it was their Capitol . . ." she murmured, awestruck, ashen faced. "At least there were soldiers there—hospitals and . . ."

"Washington's their war city, apparently. Not Philadelphia. Not Boston, not New York. I went to New York last month with Mr. Courtland, to the Wall Street Stock Exchange and to Broadway. They were mourning the fact that ice skating was stopping for the summer—something called roller skating is the new thing. Oh, and picnics. They're making toys while we're taking the nails out of our houses to make cannon shot. And the parties there . . . the luxuries. . . . Good God, it made me sick. Mr. Courtland, too, I think, though he didn't say anything, at least to me. Grand-balls. Extravagance heaped upon extravagance. The North must be making a bloody fortune on this war, and most of the people seem to have forgotten it's even still going on."

Tears misted Whitney's eyes as she stared helplessly around her. "It hasn't touched them at all?"

Jonathon shrugged bitterly. "Some of them, yes. Those with family involved. Some women nurse or roll bandages. Other than that—tobacco is a little short, I understand. Cotton, of course, though it seems to turn up whenever it's needed to keep textile mills running at a profit. Paper is a trifle short, but newspapers are still printing—and not on recycled wallpaper either. Higher taxes on whiskey have turned some of the people to beer. That's about the extent of the privation."

"They have grain enough to use it for beer . . ." Whitney sighed, closing her eyes and shaking her head. "It's like a dream . . . or a nightmare. I'm not sure which." She forced her eyes open and tried to keep her head up, very conscious of Jonathon's hand over hers and very glad of its strong grip. "And the young men . . . that's the most awesome to me, Jon. I can't remember the last time I saw a young man at home who wasn't in uniform."

"Even the old men, at home. Like the Lee family. Fathers and sons both."

"Yes, and here . . ."

"Most of the wealthiest families haven't sent their sons. Not like home, is it? They buy them out of the army up here—hire a substitute. The Courtlands are unusual, I've found, in more ways than one. Both sons enlisted. The older one died already at Shiloh. But Mr. Courtland's younger business acquaintances—Carnegie, Mellon, Pullman, Jay Gould, Marshall Field; here in Philadelphia, Wanamaker and Widener—they won't go themselves. They're too busy making fortunes profiteering. They think Mr. Courtland's crazy, Whit; I overheard them laughing behind his back in New York." Jonathon looked around for a long minute, then shook his head. "We're done, Whit. I mean the South is. I knew it as soon as I got off the train out of prison camp and saw all this. We're at rock bottom. They haven't begun to do more than scratch the surface."

Whitney made no reply. There was nothing she could think of to say in either rebuttal or denial. Besides that, her throat was painfully constricted and she was making a desperate effort not to cry, not to be angry, not to be any of the things she felt just now like being. What a waste, was all she could think of. All their fine young men dead at home. Jonathon almost. Farms ruined. Colleges shut down. They'd never really had a chance, had they?

"I've surprised myself by liking Joshua Courtland. I think you will, too." Jonathon clicked the horses to start forward again and avoided his wife's eyes as he spoke. He was remembering Elinor just now—the other Courtland sharing the house. One he doubted Whitney *would* like. Please God, don't let Whitney ever know what happened last night. "He's a fine man, I think . . . at least he tries to be. The—ah—his daughter is there, too. Lady Bennington."

Whitney didn't reply and Jonathon glanced sideways at her, afraid he had already betrayed himself by the strain of his voice. She was sitting silently in the late April sunshine, just looking around her. Tears kept rolling down her face to splash their warm salt in Miranda's dark curls, and Jonathon spoke no more, just hurried the horses home instead.

White flour was three hundred dollars a barrel, meat five dollars a pound, ordinary corn meal twenty dollars a bushel. Everything else nearly unobtainable at any price—candles, matches, cooking utensils, linens, furnishings, cloth, leather, soap, bedding, dishware, kettles, oil, coal, wood, paper, pens, ink, needles, pins, boots, salt, whiskey, medicine, shoes. Rumor said the soldiers in the field had scurvy from poor rations. The Richmond *Enquirer* wasn't admitting it, but Leanna noted that most houses had gardens for produce now instead of for pretty flowers. Depressing, she thought—also strangely uplifting.

She was too used to the Valley and all its bounties, largely untouched by the ruination elsewhere. Living in Richmond laid the war in her lap. It was frightening. And it was also beautiful. Inspiringly so. In spite of everything, the will to fight on was unwavering. Not a person in the city was unaware of the uphill battle the CSA faced this spring, but the South was right, their cause was just, and God would see their sacrifices ultimately rewarded. Other than 'Crazy Betsy' Van Lew, a Yankee sympathizer who kept a bedroom in her Richmond mansion always ready for a Union general, the people of Richmond were uncomplaining as they struggled and staggered beneath the burden of carrying the spiritual and military weight of the whole Confederacy. The bread riots of last spring had gone for good. This spring of 1864 was the South's last hope and everyone knew it. People tightened overworn belts and straightened stooped and weary shoulders. They sang brave and gallant songs like "Lorena," "Dixie," "All Quiet Along the Potomac Tonight," and "Bonnie Blue Flag."

The churches were crowded every Sunday. Men in uniform were almost all Leanna saw out the window of the Spotswood Hotel anymore, soldiers and women dressed in black. There were few carriages, even fewer horses to draw them—the army's desperate need had taken both. Shops were closed down, some boarded up. Restaurants were few and those still open offered poor fare. The theater had been mostly closed for two years. Fresh produce arriving in the city went with military guard to ensure its safety. Few women were abroad during the day—they gathered in one another's parlors to knit, sew, and roll bandages for the coming campaign. Leanna was rolling one now—it had become practically second nature.

She glanced at the clock on the bed stand. Four o'clock. April 17th. Whitney's baby was due about a month from now. But after the ambush that had left Chase Courtland bleeding in a forest meadow, she could only assume Whitney would be back at Cool Spring, dependent once more on the incompetent care of one of the Valley midwives. And Jonathon was probably back in a Yankee prison camp, if he still lived at all. And Joshua Courtland, who would have offered the Virginia family sanctuary despite the ongoing war and personal bitterness—what would he be doing now? Maybe burying his last son and cursing the Penley name. It had all gone wrong, somehow. And worst of all, there was the nagging suspicion she had only herself to blame for the mess. She sighed, setting the bandages aside with a restless gesture, and moved to sit on the bed.

They were invited tonight to a reception at Mrs. Robert C. Stannard's salon—an invitation with more cachet than one from the Davises themselves. But Stewart wasn't home yet—he had been summoned this morning to the Confederate White House. Leanna wasn't sure that one hadn't prompted the other—there was some competition between the two social circles—but Mrs. Stannard enjoyed the home-field advantage and her receptions were considered even more elite, limited to the very best blood of the old Southern families.

Leanna's family earned such an invitation. The first Douglas had landed in Portobacco, Maryland, in the

mid sixteen hundreds and owned the original Blytheswood with full baronial privileges. In the mid seventeen
hundreds, the family had moved to the Fauquier region
of Virginia. Two centuries of a gentrylike association
with large land holdings, a tradition that was the basis
for the Southern aristocracy, ensured Leanna's place at
Mrs. Stannard's. Stewart's family was equally good,
but Charleston, South Carolina—based. In the old, prewar society days, he would have carried a letter of
introduction to break into Richmond's inner circle. But
the war had changed the system somewhat; the barriers
were no longer impenetrable. Now, having married a
Penley was enough. That and being a high-ranking
Confederate officer. For usually, in the South, social
standing and military rank went hand in hand.

Leanna lay back on the hotel's over soft bed, letting
her thoughts wander. Richmond held memories of hap-
pier days than these—memories of childhood, of parties
and balls, of the first time she'd met Stewart—some
three years ago—when Jonathon had brought a half-
dozen young officers into their Richmond parlor. The
best and the brightest of the Confederacy's young men,
officers early trained in either the Virginia Military
Institute or at West Point. So many of them buried now
at nearby Hollywood Cemetary.

She could remember how gloriously handsome they'd
seemed, dressed in brand new gray uniforms, sabers
and brass buttons shining. Dashing and invincible. Stewart had been charming but somewhat cool. He was
older than Jonathon, and had seemed more a man, less
an untried boy, and a little dangerous because of that.
His blue eyes had shown interest as they'd flickered
over her lovely face and slender body. Leanna had
blushed and fallen instantly in love. Ah, those glorious,
hopeful days, when they'd all been sure of their cause,
their right, sure of a quick victory. The bands had
played, the brand new bars and stars flew, speeches of
commitment stirred Southern souls, the April sun shone
as the troops had marched through the Capitol square in
review. . . .

She knew him better now, her enigmatic husband. She'd been with him more these past two weeks than in the previous three years. He was still as handsome as he'd been that day that was now an eternity ago. Still strong and tall and straight. He was still charming often, but now Leanna had seen beneath it. There was a certain reserve as well—an aloofness, almost a coldness. And a moodiness that sometimes troubled her. Maybe not moodiness, precisely; perhaps he was only sometimes preoccupied, she amended carefully. Generally, he was indulgent in the extreme toward her, considerate and attentive. Other women looked at him, he rarely looked back. Courtesies were unfailing. She'd found he liked her a little more serious than she actually, by nature, was. Humor, like lovemaking, he preferred at his own initiation. Yet she did not doubt he loved her. He thought nothing of having risked his life in the field for three years—yet it angered him to see his wife's efforts to replace a silly needle that had broken. He resented the war's intrusion on her life, not so much on his own. He was a puzzlement, she decided. Truly a—

"Napping, dear?"

Leanna sat up, startled, offering Stewart a smile as he shut the door behind him. "No, just thinking."

He smiled as if he found that faintly amusing. "Well, we're due at Mrs. Stannard's though, aren't we?"

"What went on today at your meeting?"

"Nothing earth shattering." He smiled, but as he turned away, Leanna caught a glimpse of the distance in his eyes. It was one of those times, apparently. Thoughts for Stewart only.

"Better hurry, Leanna. We don't want to be too late. It would be rude."

She held her questions for another time and stood up, nodding. Then she took a few steps toward where he stood by the window to offer a single kiss. He smiled as if startled, and for a moment, a kind of indulgent pleasure replaced the distance in his eyes. It returned though as Leanna turned to begin dressing for evening, and his blue eyes were unusually grim as he watched the cloud-covered sun set over the Confederate capitol. It seemed like an omen and did not improve his humor any. If he accepted the position President Davis had pressed upon him today, what in the world was he going to do with Leanna?

Chapter Sixteen

April warmed quickly to May. The first of the month was a Sunday, and the churches of Richmond were filled with women, government personnel, children, and old men. Most of the soldiers had left to join Lee in the Northwest. St. Paul's was especially crowded today. President and Mrs. Davis were among the worshippers and Leanna and Stewart sat in a pew farther back. Outside, intermittent sun shone on the white marble of the Greek-columned church. Its high, lancelike spire gleamed fitfully, a brilliant white. Inside, the sermon was political and inspiring, as sermons in Richmond these days tended to be. It was amazing, Leanna thought with a wry smile, noting the standing room only crowd at the church, how quickly a war revived religious faith.

Religious faith was running high in the Yankee camps as well. It always did when troops were looking at the end of winter's monotony, and the resumption of the war in earnest. Now, while Leanna was attending church in the distant Confederate capital of Richmond, Chase Courtland was tipping the brim of his black, felt hat against the drizzle that showered the Chattanooga Federal camp.

It was a warm rain, preferable to the dust that would otherwise be rising from the traditional Sunday morning troop inspection he was conducting from horseback. In the army, things were a little backward. The first consideration was given to the main event at hand, the waging of war. Church services were delayed until the afternoon. And Chase guessed that the chaplain's outdoor service this afternoon would be well attended, despite the weather. That was the surest sign of all that even the enlisted men knew the army was about to move toward Atlanta. He smiled faintly and returned his captain's salute as one troop wheeled and turned in ranks at the hand gallop. Flashy, he thought. The Federal cavalry had finally come of age. They would need that maturity, too, if Confederate cavalry genius Nathan Bedford Forrest deviled General Sherman's supply lines on the road into Georgia. From what he'd heard, Forrest was every bit as tough a foe as his Virginia counterpart, J.E.B. Stuart.

In Washington, Captain Roger Lacey, Staff Surgeon at one of the two dozen Federal military hospitals there, was on duty this Sunday morning, and he heard the light tatoo of familiar footsteps suddenly sound in the corridor behind him. He turned with an eager smile. "Susan!"

She halted a half-dozen steps from him, her face unnaturally pale.

His eyes flickered to her hand and his smile died. The ring was still there. For a moment, he said nothing, trying to imagine what had happened.

"I couldn't tell him, Roger. Forgive me."

Silence gathered. Down the hall echoed the creak of the soup cart being wheeled into a distant ward. Doc Lacey managed a nod, finally, looking up to meet her eyes. "That's why you stayed so long in Philadelphia."

Susan flushed faintly, shrugging. "That last night, here, Chase's father came to dinner with us. Before I had a chance to speak to Chase alone, Mr. Courtland asked quite bluntly whether we'd yet set a wedding date. It seemed . . ." she made a nervous little gesture, unable to hold his eyes any longer. "It almost seemed as if something odd was going on. Chase gave his father a very strange glance. And didn't say anything at all. And Mr. Courtland murmured something I couldn't quite hear, something about it being more important than ever . . ." As she paused, only silence answered. She waited a moment, hoping, then forced herself on, barely above a whisper. "Chase stared at his father for a moment. Then he turned to me and apologized for being able to spend so little time with me that past week. And asked if I would consent to marrying on his next leave." There was a long silence this time. The soup cart creaked again, louder, coming this way. Somewhere a man groaned.

Because of Leanna Leighton, Doc Lacey was thinking. Because neither Chase nor I will hurt Susan by admitting he's in love with another woman. And, of course, Chase has no idea how I feel. It's all gone wrong. "Susan," he began, almost desperately.

A single tear slipped down her face, she shook her head. "It's decided, Roger, please. I spent these past weeks making the arrangements. Whenever he gets home again, we'll marry."

He loves another woman. It would be so easy to say it. And so cruel. Wouldn't it?

She turned awkwardly, brushing dry a last tear. "Well, Doctor, have you no surgery planned? Have I come all this way for nothing?"

"You should have let me talk to Chase, Susan. As I wanted to do." He took a single step forward.

"No."

The determination in her voice startled him, made him almost, just for a split second, doubt she loved him.

"Please, Roger, for the love of God, don't make it harder. I am Chase Courtland's fiancée. Any time the vagaries of war next allow, I shall become his wife. Unless you swear to accept that as unchangeable fact, I shall leave now and seek a position in another hospital."

He stared at her for a long minute. In midnight blue, she looked pale as the death he'd grown used to dealing with. Unchangeable fact. For a moment, he hated Chase Courtland with a terrible hatred. Then it passed, leaving numbness. "I have surgery scheduled this afternoon, Miss Stratford. I would be honored if you would assist." He turned away as he spoke and walked toward a stack of newly laundered butcher aprons that lay piled in the hall. He hoped his hands were shaking less by the time he had to use the knife.

*   *   *

In Philadelphia, church had ended and it was a balmy, still afternoon of lazy inactivity. Jonathon bounced a laughing Miranda on the goose-down mattress of his upstairs bed, then reached for the magazine he'd come up to fetch. Whitney, by doctor's orders, did not take stairs. She stayed below in the dayroom Joshua Courtland had ordered prepared before her arrival. They spent a lot of time in that room, the three Penleys, trying to intrude as little as possible into the Courtlands' home. It was easier in many ways. As confederates in a Yankee house, they could speak more freely. Mandy could play without her parents fearing she might break a porcelain vase or scratch imported Chippendale furniture. And Jonathon could avoid the all too lovely Lady Bennington.

"When the baby comes, you can sleep up here with me for a week or two, would you like that?" Jonathon hoisted his daughter high in one arm, turning to reach behind himself with the other to close the door.

Miranda frowned, cocking her head. "Mommy will miss me."

Jonathon hid a smile, somberly shaking his head. Ah, the egocentricity of a little child. . . . "But daddy will be lonesome, love, if you won't say yes. You're my girl, aren't you? You'll keep me company."

Mandy smiled, reaching her arms around his neck for a hug. Her dark curls tickled his neck and Jonathon chuckled, kissing her and then moving her to where her hair couldn't tickle so. God, how many nights had he lain in the cold, lonely darkness of a camp bed, listening to some unknown trooper singing "Lorena" or "All Quiet Along the Potomac Tonight" and found the courage to go on by thinking of Whitney or this sweet babe three years old this month. He'd missed so damn much of her infancy with the war. Well, not this time, he reminded himself. This time daddy won't be coming home a virtual stranger to his own child.

"Happy first of May, Major. It used to be a pagan holiday, you know—May Day. Involving fertility rituals, I believe."

Elinor suddenly blocked his path to the stairs and Jonathon's smile died. He met her eyes over his daughter's dark curls and read teasing mockery in their green ice.

"Here, darlin'. Go on down to Mommy. I'll be down in a moment." He kissed Mandy as he set her down on the blood red Oriental runner of the hallway, forcing a smile as he urged her to go. The little girl went happily. Lady Bennington was not a favorite of hers. Jonathon watched her to the stairs to be sure she took the railing as he'd cautioned her a hundred times to do. You could never be too careful with children.

"You've been locking your door at night, Major. Afraid of things that go bump in the night?"

"Lady Bennington, my wife is downstairs waiting for me. If I might excuse—"

"No, not just yet." For an instant, something dangerous flashed in her emerald eyes. Jonathon felt it rather than saw it and frowned. The hair on the nape of his neck prickled. Like the war. The same feeling of riding into too quiet woods, of danger as yet unseen, unknown. "I thought you enjoyed yourself that night. Was I wrong?"

Jonathon kept her gaze, unsmiling. "You'd call me a liar if I said no. So why ask?"

She smiled faintly, reaching to stroke his arm. "Because you've avoided me so deliberately ever since. Why don't you leave your door open tonight? It's a holiday of a sort after all. I know some lovely pagan games we can play."

Jonathon swallowed against a sick fascination and shook his head. Pagan games—they would suit her. She reminded him of that sort of semidarkness, the frenzy, the partial cruelty of such things. An elemental spirit. Amoral, tempestuous, brazen. Dangerous to set free to walk the surface of the earth. "Lady Bennington, I don't blame you for what happened between us. I accept responsibility for it." This was exactly what he'd

241

dreaded—and avoided so carefully these past weeks—a confrontation so blunt, so ugly.

"Well, I'm bored." Elinor was no longer playing. Her hand fastened on his wrist, his eyes glittered ice. "I can hardly find such convenience as you offer elsewhere here, Major. My father watches far too closely. You're a guest in my home, after all—you and your *enceinte* wife. One brat will shortly be two, squalling in the night, no doubt, like an alley cat. Perhaps you should reconsider your alternatives to remaining here—prison, for example, or—"

Jonathon pulled his wrist from her grip, his face drawn and pale as he began to shoulder past her in the narrow hallway.

"How dare you walk away from me while I'm speaking to you!" She stepped to block his way, raising one hand in temper.

Jonathon caught it instinctively before she could use it, then reached for the other as she began to raise it. Elinor laughed suddenly, and stepped against him. She smiled up at him as she pressed her breasts to his chest, her hips beneath a voluminous skirt to his.

"There now, dear Major, that doesn't feel so bad, does it?"

"Elinor!"

She paled at that voice, jerking her hands from Jonathon's grip overhead and stepping hastily away. "Oh, Father! I was just showing Major Penley a new dance step. It's all the rage in Paris."

Joshua froze in the doorway of his room. He was half sick, angry, humiliated, and mostly, desperately sad. Oh God, Elinor! He sought the young Rebel's eyes and felt his chest pains immediately flare. Jonathon held his gaze, which made it worse. Apology lay in the young man's eyes, shame, too, but not the same kind of guilt he'd seen for that half second on his daughter's face. He closed his eyes and gestured him to go on down the hall. "Excuse us, won't you please? I want to speak to my daughter privately."

Jonathon hesitated a moment, then nodded, forcing

242

himself to move. He trusted Joshua Courtland's fairness. He wouldn't be judged guilty without a chance to speak. Not that he gave a damn what happened to himself, but he was desperately concerned for Whitney just now, and for their unborn child—so precious, so precariously clinging to life. His heart felt like wood in his chest as he reached the stairs to descend, his stomach constricted sickly. What price would he have to pay for one night of weakness? What punishment would be meted out to Whitney for his sins?

"Daddy!" Miranda's tiny feet were running with a desperate beat on the pinewood flooring of the back hall. He heard her before he saw her and began to run on the stairs. "Daddy!" She burst around the corner and despite himself, Jonathon froze, his breath catching in his throat. An instant later he'd begun to move again, reaching for the child as she flew up the stairs. "Mommy said to find you! Mommy has a real bad tummy ache!"

Involuntarily, Jonathon turned on the stairs, pulling the child up in his arms as he glanced at the elder Courtland. Joshua still stood ashen-faced and shocked in the hall above. For an instant, no one moved or spoke. Then Elinor shrugged and started toward her own room without a backward glance. Joshua forced a deep breath and looked after her only once as the door closed behind her, then looked back down the stairs. He started toward the young Rebel with sudden haste.

"It's only a few minutes to the hospital, Jonathon. Go order the carriage up. Leave Miranda here with me, and then we'll get your wife ready to go."

Jonathon nodded, handing the frightened child to Joshua. He wanted to say something, but he didn't know what and there was no time now to think on it. He hesitated for a moment, trying, raising his eyes to find Joshua's meeting his.

"It's all right, son," Joshua managed in a murmur, tightening his arms around the little girl who had begun to cry now very softly. "Go get the carriage. I'll tell your wife we're almost on our way."

Jonathon nodded, reaching briefly to touch Mandy's

hair in reassurance, then running for the stables. A few minutes later, Whitney was in his arms and he was lifting her up to the carriage for a dash to the hospital.

The twins arrived quickly. Jonathon had been at Whitney's side for Miranda's birth, but the doctors here would not allow his presence. He waited instead in a small room, with Mandy and Joshua Courtland. Silence was omnipresent. Even the little girl said nothing, only clung to her father's hand. Occasionally, muffled voices could be heard, and once, the distant closing of a door.

"Mr. Penley?"

Jonathon turned, startled to find himself looking at a doctor not much older than he was. But look at Doc Lacey, he reminded himself. These young Yankees were a new breed. Age didn't increase value anymore.

"I'm afraid I have some bad news for you." The young doctor sighed as he spoke, shrugging his own frustration. "Your wife has delivered twins, one girl, one boy. The boy was born blue and we couldn't revive him. I haven't much hope, either, for the girl. I'm sorry, I truly am."

It felt like someone had punched him hard in the gut. For a moment, Jonathon could only stand silent, accepting the man's words. All for nothing, then? All his agonies when faced with the choice of his wife's welfare or the Southern cause . . .? His rank, his home, his honor. . . . He'd lost everything else to gain nothing? "And my wife?"

"She'll be fine, I'm sure." The doctor looked briefly less grim. "Good thing she was here. You would have lost her otherwise. The second twin was presented breach. We practice Semmelweiss's approach to childbirth so I'm confident there will be no infection, but we had to turn the baby before we could deliver him. Badly managed, the labor would have been protracted and your wife would likely have hemorraged." He paused a moment, sighing. "One out of three isn't much, but we tried. God, I swear, we really tried. There just wasn't much we could do."

Jonathon nodded, forcing a smile. "I'm sure you did,

sir. Thank you." He still felt wooden inside. At least Whitney was all right, he told himself. At least he had her still. God, what else could he have done? What other choice could he have made?

"If I might make a suggestion—is that your daughter there? With your father?"

Jonathon frowned, confused, turning to follow the doctor's gesture. Joshua Courtland stood a half-dozen steps away, Miranda in his arms. "No, not my father—a friend."

Joshua stepped forward, shifting the little girl's weight to offer his hand. "Joshua Courtland, doctor. Pleased to meet you."

The young doctor returned the handshake. "Sorry we couldn't do more." Doubly sorry, now, he thought. 'Courtland' had rung a bell. He was a very generous patron of the medical school here.

"I'm sorry, Jonathon," Joshua turned, handing the child to her father.

"I think you might take your little girl in to your wife for a brief visit, Mr. Penley. It might make all three of you feel better."

"Thank you, sir," Jonathon nodded. Amazing how these courtesies came without thought. The product of a lifetime of training. No matter how badly you hurt inside, on the surface. . . .

"The surviving twin is with your wife, but I wouldn't get your hopes up, nor let your wife do so either. In fact, it would be more practical to delay the boy's funeral for a few days to—"

"I'll deal with that," Joshua spoke hastily. He'd noticed a suspicious glitter in the young Rebel's eyes. Hadn't he been through enough today without discussing such necessary, but such coldly final details? "Go on in to your wife. Go see your little girl."

Jonathon managed a nod and took a better grip on Mandy, starting into the hospital hallway.

"Is my mommy's baby here now, Daddy?"

Joshua winced at the child's question as she disappeared through the doorway with her father. He could not hear Jonathon's reply, only an indistinguishable murmur. Damn, he thought, surprised at the grief his own heart ached with. When had he taken the Confederate family so deeply into his affection, anyway? He felt like it was his own child that had been so cruelly disappointed today, not some Rebel stranger.

"Mr. Courtland, you shouldn't encourage—"

"Oh, hush, Doctor," Joshua frowned, "leave them have a few minutes. The girl isn't dead yet. Let them bear that grief when they must." He felt a sudden stab of pain in his chest and frowned harder at it, reaching one hand up and turning to look for a chair. "Get me a brandy, Doctor, please. Bring a couple glasses. That young man could use one later, too."

The doctor frowned but shrugged, noting Courtland's hand gesture and the pallor of his face. He returned in a moment, apologetic. "It isn't the best brandy, I'm afraid. We keep it for medicinal purposes."

Joshua grunted, taking a stiff swallow. The pains eased. What a day, he thought. What a damnable day. Elinor. Now this. The kind of day he wouldn't miss when he was laid in the Courtland burial plot, six feet under.

"Are those heart pains, Mr. Courtland, that you're having?"

The young doctor began to lean over him and Joshua waved him away with a disgusted gesture. The doctor frowned, hesitating, then finally shrugged.

"Now about the twins," Joshua spoke with a sigh, keeping one eye on the doorway for Jonathon's return. "You can't imagine what that young man has gone through to try to save those babies—and his wife, too, of course. I don't want another word spoken to him about embalmers or burials or anything else. You leave that to me. Understand?"

The doctor nodded and Joshua grunted in satisfaction. Damn, he thought again. After all this, a cruel bit of luck. Unfair, he decided. For all God's wisdom, today was a mistake. What must young Penley be thinking? That he should never have brought her North after all?

Never have made the choices he'd made, the sacrifices of honor and pride both, accepting parole, accepting the Courtlands' charity?

"The twins were not developed fully," the doctor said defensively in the silence. He felt badly, too. But people expected miracles from his profession. A profession far too ignorant still of far too much. "Even for being almost a month premature, the boy especially was—"

"They're starving in parts of Virginia. Not in the Shenandoah where Mrs. Penley was, but I'm sure even there they are lacking certain things."

"Perhaps with the double drain on her body, yes." The doctor sighed and stood up. "Anyway, before I go back to my other patients, I must stress again to you that if Mr. Penley has any doubts, you must assure him he did the right thing having her here to deliver. I didn't like to emphasize that and frighten him after the fact, but some women are built better for childbearing than others. Mrs. Penley is not. Twins . . . well, under optimal conditions, I would have grave doubts. She'll need good care for any further pregnancies as well." He began to turn away. "Oh, are they planning to return at once to Virginia?"

Joshua blinked, taken aback. He hadn't thought about it, actually. He'd assumed so, but now. . . . "I'm not sure." He found the idea dismayed him. Silly, foolish old man, he scolded himself. But the house would be so damn quiet again if they did. Only Elinor. . . . He'd miss the boy at the bank, too. Ever since he'd witnessed Joshua's heart problems, or maybe in guilt over Chase's ambush, Jonathon had willingly, quietly, taken over more and more of the work there.

"Well, if they are, I'd suggest not leaving for a month or two at least. Should any postnatal complications arise, Mrs. Penley should remain near here until then."

"You might mention that to them."

"I will."

"Tell them, too," Joshua shrugged, a little embarrassed, "tell him to stay as long as he—"

247

Jonathon reappeared and Joshua rose hastily, eyeing the young man's ashen face.

"I wanted to bring Mandy back out before . . ." Jonathon met neither man's eyes. He kept his own on his daughter's dark hair. Another doctor appeared in the doorway, gesturing to the first. Joshua turned to touch Jonathon's arm.

"Is it Whitney, son?"

He shook his head, praying he wouldn't humiliate himself by beginning to cry. Oh God, it wasn't fair. So tiny, the baby. Never even a chance. It was horrible enough to see grown men die in battle, but this was infinitely worse.

"Here, I'll take Miranda with me. You stay as long as you like." Joshua forced a smile, reaching for the little girl. "Want to come with me, sweetheart? I'll bet we can find a pony ride in the park. Or maybe a nice, new doll."

"Like Mommy's?" Mandy brightened.

"Yes, just like that one." He took the child and walked away without looking back, intent on keeping her attention, her eagerness to go. He missed Jonathon's quick glance of gratitude, the surprise and thanks that mingled together. He stood watching the older man and the now smiling Mandy, half frowning in puzzlement as he watched them out the door.

"Mr. Penley. You're coming back in to be with your wife?"

When they take her dead baby away from her, Jonathon finished the thought with a fresh stab of impotent anguish. Whitney, I'm sorry. God, what else could I have done to spare us this agony? "Yes, I'm coming." He turned on his heel and followed the doctors back inside.

But the tiny girl clung tenaciously to life. Hours became a day, one day two, and two days three. Joshua Courtland lay in bed the third night, astonished to find himself praying for her life. Had she died the first day, it would have been hard enough. But now, when she'd made such an effort, showed such a terrible, incredible will to survive—that pathetic struggle against such odds, was enough to break your heart.

He decided on his own to proceed with her twin brother's funeral the next day. Maybe if they stopped expecting her to die and started expecting her to live, God would take pity on such faithful souls.

They'd named the baby Bonnie. Joshua didn't ask, but he suspected it might be a reference to the 'Bonnie Blue' flag her father had fought and nearly died for, the flag he'd had to forsake for the child's sake. He couldn't admit it—his Union League fellows would probably be horrified—but he'd decided he approved of the name. Like the newborn baby, and against all odds, the Confederacy itself had survived. Like the newborn baby, it should have died, and simply, but by sheer stubborn determination did not allow itself to do so. It was a good name for the tiny girl.

Joshua did not attend the infant boy's funeral. Whitney was still in the hospital bed. Jonathon went. And Joshua knew what agonies it cost a man to bury a firstborn son. But Joshua was busy with Miranda, taking her and her doll for a pony ride in the park. Funerals were not for three-year-olds. The war had made the world a grim enough place without that.

"Another, Grandpa-pa Courtland!" Mandy began to plead as soon as the ride ended, her blue eyes wide and radiant.

Joshua smiled, beginning to nod. He'd said earlier it would be the last, but. . . . "All right, sweetheart. Just one more."

Lord, how she reminded him of days long past, he thought. Days when he was young yet, the children little. Before the war. Before Josh's death. Before the coalition's ugly plots. He'd simply taken her over these past few days, to give her parents time to grieve and time to heal. He'd done it as a favor and found it was a pleasure. The ride ended and he started toward her.

"Again! Again!" She clutched the saddle with one hand, the new doll with the other.

How pretty a child she was, Joshua thought. Like Elinor a bit, such big eyes and ruffles of petticoats everywhere. . . . He started to smile and nod to let her go again. How many times had he given in to Elinor's pleas like that? What had he always said? 'You're so pretty, my darling, no one should ever say no to you.' His smile froze on his face, a sudden cold shudder touched his soul. Good God, had he learned nothing from his own daughter? Would he do it again with this sweet little girl as well?

He started forward toward the pony, reaching for Miranda to lift her off. The pony took a step before he got there and a cool sweat broke out on his palms as he grabbed the child from the saddle. It had seemed for an instant the whole world had turned upon his getting to her before the ride began. "No." He said it sharply, meaning it as he'd never meant it with Elinor. "No, sweet. I said that was all."

Mandy blinked and began to frown. Her mouth gathered in a trembling pout. She met Joshua Courtland's eyes for a moment and finally dropped her head, giving a little nod.

I've learned, Joshua thought. Thank you. God. I won't do it again, I swear. He smiled, reaching down for the little girl's hand. "Want an ice cream, sweetheart?"

Her smile came back as radiant as ever and she nodded her head so hard her curls bounced. "Yes, Grandpa-pa. Dolly, too?"

"Dolly, too," he agreed with a smile, starting back to the carriage. "Dolly, too."

Chapter Seventeen

Chase barely had time to wire a reply to his father's telegram before the Federal Army of the Tennessee broke camp to begin marching south into Georgia. A huge army. Invincible, he thought. One hundred thousand men, twenty-five hundred wagons. What could the South have left to stand against them? And once Grant moved on Richmond. . . . He glanced northward over one shoulder, caught the involuntary motion and smiled wryly at himself. It was a bit too far away to see Richmond. Or Philadelphia, where his father had wired from. The telegram had saddened him some, made him restless. It had reagitated thoughts of Leanna for one thing, not that she was ever entirely off his mind. He'd be content, Chase tried to tell himself, if only he knew where she was. Knew she was all right. This way he feared for her everywhere—the Valley, Richmond, a half dozen other places. Pray God she'd have the good sense not to get caught somewhere between the two colliding armies.

"Major! Move your troops on!"

A staff officer called the order, waving to him from the hilltop. Other thoughts faded as Chase wheeled his horse and raised a gauntletted hand to signal his men forward. Saber rings jangled and leather cracked. Dust rose and horses snorted. The march to Atlanta had begun.

Grant had moved across the Rapidan River on the fourth, and clashed with the Confederates on the fifth in dense woodlands known as the Wilderness, northwest of Richmond. On the sixth, Chase and the rest of Sherman's army began their long march South. On the seventh, the first wounded of the spring of 1864 campaign began to arrive in Richmond.

At least it wasn't like it had been in '62, following the Battle of Seven Pines. Then all of Richmond had been one immense hospital, the wounded cared for on every street, in every home. The war had come of age and there were hospitals now—twenty-eight of them, actually. Chimborazo was one, high on one of Richmond's seven hills, one hundred and fifty wards there alone. And this May of 1864, drugs and supplies were still available for wounded Rebels. They would run out later. By mid year, Richmonders would be burying the dead literally naked to conserve clothing for the living. But this day in early May, both the hospitals and the city were coping easily.

Leanna didn't volunteer for service as a nurse. She rolled bandages and helped organize relief missions, but she would have been useless in a hospital with fresh blood pooling around stacks of amputated arms and legs. And worse. Stewart kept such stories from her as best he could, but he was at the Confederate White House most days now and the women whispered among themselves. Whispered of men burning alive as the Wilderness's dense undergrowth caught fire from exploding shot and spilled powder; of the wounded trapped in the flames, unable to move from them, shooting themselves in desperation as the fire licked at their tortured bodies, of mass confusion as the smoke grew denser, companies opening fire on their own men or wandering blindly, point blank, into enemy artillery fire to be blown to bloody bits. War was hell. The Yankee Sherman had said it, and Leanna agreed. The more so as she lived ever more intimately with it.

On the eighth, Lee won the foot race to Spotsylvania and entrenched there. On the ninth, Sherman's army reached Dalton, Georgia, and made its first unsuccessful attempt to flank General Johnston's Rebels, trying to pass unhindered on to Atlanta. Chase and his cavalry sat guarding the wagon train, a mile from the skirmishing infantry. In Virginia, other Federal cavalry was more active. With Grant's approval, his Western cavalry commander, Colonel P.H. Sheridan, took off cross country on a long raid aimed directly at Richmond. In the dark morning hours of the tenth, General J.E.B. Stuart led his Confederate corps on a desperate dash to try to intercept the Yankees. Stewart and a handful of other couriers rode out from the Capitol with orders from a worried Jefferson Davis, trying to find the Confederate cavalry before Sheridan's Yankees did. Awakened from sleep when they'd come to fetch her husband, Leanna waited behind, seeing a side of war she hated with a deep passion. Enforced inactivity. Nothing to do but wait, wonder, and worry. The day of the tenth seemed a hundred hours long. She found herself straining her eyes to see if Yankee blue yet darkened the northern horizon, wondering, if they came, whether Major Chase Courtland would be among them.

In Philadelphia, Jonathon Penley sat in the Courtland parlor, the wicks of the lamps turned high, a faint odor of camphor and kerosene burning from them. Joshua Courtland was out for the evening. Elinor, too. And he was using the opportunity to catch up on bank work that had been sorely neglected in these ten days since the twins' birth. It was late now, nearly midnight. Mandy had been asleep in his bed upstairs for hours. Jonathon was tired, too, worn out from grief and worry more than anything else. But the longer he worked, the more concerned he grew, and the prospect of sleep grew ever dimmer. Something was most definitely awry at the bank. The figures for the frozen Southern accounts showed a greater discrepancy than ever. Another ten thousand dollars was missing, or the vault inventory of notes, paper currency, and bullion was seriously off. He doubted that was the case.

He checked his figures a last time, frowning at the totals that said more to a banker than words ever could. He would have to say something to Joshua Courtland about it. He could no longer justify further delay. Whitney was being well cared for at the University of Pennsylvania's Hospital, little Bonnie's life was more in

God's hand now than in his. Miranda was Joshua Courtland's darling. So if the bank matter rebounded on himself and sent Jonathon back to a Yankee prison camp, he could afford to take the chance now.

The front door opened behind him and Jonathon turned, gathering his notes. If it were Lady Bennington returning, he would go out the other door and up the servants' stairs. But if it were her father, then the moment of confrontation had come.

Joshua Courtland frowned as he laid his silver-tipped walking stick to one side and set his top hat down on the bench. It had been a bad night, a supper meeting of the coalition that always made for an unpleasant evening. Tonight, they'd been discussing politics, specifically Abraham Lincoln's renomination at the Republican convention next month. Seward and Stanton, respectively Secretarys of State and War, were radical enough anti-Southerners to reassure the coalition members. They might still back McClellan and the Democrats in the general election, though. They would wait, lurk in the shadows, Joshua rephrased disgustedly, to see which carcass offered the better cooking. Disgusting, how callous men could be in the face of. . . .

"Oh, Jonathon." He stopped in surprise at the parlor door, glancing beyond the young man to the mantle clock. "You're up late." He frowned suddenly, remembering what the evening had temporarily made him forget. "It isn't your little girl, is it? She hasn't—?"

"No." Jonathon shook his head hastily. "No, I was just catching up on my work a bit. Sorry to have fallen so far behind this past week or so, but—"

"Quite all right." Joshua smiled faintly, relieved. "I have myself." He started toward the brandy decanter, speaking over his shoulder. The evening had left a bad taste in his mouth. Maybe brandy would help. He frowned slightly, remembering what had puzzled him earlier. Hodges had been joking about the rifles he produced for government contracts—something about what he did with his surplus and the few that didn't pass the Federal's most cursory inspection. He'd glanced at Joshua with a very strange smile, as if at a joke Joshua, too, must be in on. Now what the devil . . .?

"Mr. Courtland, excuse me, sir, but there's a problem with the Southern accounts." Jonathon fairly blurted it out in his nervousness.

Joshua grunted dry amusement, pouring a brandy for the young Rebel without asking, turning to hand it toward him. "If you're going to ask me to unfreeze them and disperse the funds, my dear Virginian, the answer is no. If the Federal government didn't hang me, the board members would." Jonathon didn't smile. He didn't meet the older man's eyes, either. He took the brandy rather awkwardly and Joshua's own smile faded. "I've had a rather bad night, actually. If it's something that can wait, Jonathon . . ."

"It can't." Jonathon set the brandy to one side without drinking it. There was no tactful way to say this, no way to soften the shock. He settled himself for a confrontation and handed Joshua the accounting sheets. "I should have said something before this, I know that. There's money missing from these accounts, a lot of money. It was about twenty-four thousand before. Now it's thirty-three." Nothing but silence, absolute, breathless silence, answered his statement. The clock in the foyer chimed half-past midnight and one of the burning lamps popped and sputtered softly. He glanced at Joshua Courtland's face and found the man's eyes fixed on his, an unspoken question lying in them. Jonathon squared his shoulders as he spoke. "No, sir, I'm sorry. I won't deny I took that money."

Joshua felt pain flare as anguish stabbed his heart. Damn you, boy. After all I've done for you, after all you and your family have come to mean to me. "You mean you took it?"

Jonathon flushed, and swallowed hard to even answer. "No, sir. I mean you'll have to make your own judgment on that. On whether you think I did, or I would, steal from your bank."

If it were any other account, I'd never doubt you, Joshua wanted to say. But you labor under divided loyalties, like your sister, maybe, when she quite possibly helped to ambush my son. "I wish you'd just tell me you didn't do it. I'd try very hard to believe you."

Jonathon shook his head and looked away. He had paled, but a white edge of tension along his firmly chiseled jawline bespoke an unyielding position.

But Joshua had seen the pain flash in his eyes before he'd turned his head. Seen it, and grasped at it, like a drowning man at a life raft. "You damn Southerners and your damn pride! Honor won't feed your family, Penley." He reached out suddenly to grasp the young man's arm. "For God's sake, son, you know how fond I've become of you! You know I don't want to believe you would do it. Unbend that honor enough just to give me your word."

"My honor may be all I have left after this damn war!" Jonathon raised his eyes again. Now anger flashed in them openly. "I've already compromised it beyond any point I would have once dreamed possible! You say it won't feed my family, but by the time you Yankees get through with the South, it may have to!"

Joshua's eyes narrowed. "You'd challenge me in Virginia to a duel, wouldn't you? Even for asking."

"You're damn right I would! And I would here, too, except for what you've done for my wife and daughter!"

"Honor is a funny thing," Joshua spoke in a grim, hushed voice. "I don't believe it's that different in the South than here with us 'Yankees.' Most men find honor a luxury rather than a necessity, I've found. As soon as it becomes inconvenient or dangerous,"—or unprofitable, he'd like to have said—"they dump it in the nearest wastebasket. Why don't you, Jonathon?"

Only silence answered and he sighed, suddenly very tired, feeling infinitely old. "If you'd been where I've been tonight, seen what I've seen in my lifetime, maybe you'd understand, but that's all right. Maybe if there were more men like you, less of the others . . ." He was rambling and he caught himself, frowning as he dropped his hand curtly from the young man's arm. "Go on to bed then. I can talk to myself without you here to listen to me." He stared down at the papers Jonathon had handed to him, trying to concentrate on them. It was hard. He wanted to cry. Or hit him. Maybe both. Thirty thousand dollars? It wouldn't hurt the bank. Joshua himself was a millionaire, most of it liquid. He could cover the loss personally with no one the wiser. Damn that boy, Chase, for getting him into this. He was another one. Stubborn like this. Every bit as proud, and bound to honor. Not unlike his father, he acknowledged bitterly, thinking of the evening he'd just spent in the faint hope of thwarting that band of greedy jackals.

"I'm sorry, sir."

Joshua blinked and looked up, startled to see Jonathon still standing where he had been. He'd thought he'd left when he'd told him to. "Go on to bed. I'll study these sheets and discuss it further with you in the morning."

Jonathon shrugged, reluctant to leave. Was he being merely stiff-necked, he asked himself? He could remember wondering at first if Joshua Courtland had taken the money. Now, if Joshua thought he'd done it, wouldn't that leave the real culprit free to strike again? That wasn't right either, to repay the man that way.

He frowned, stepping forward to gesture at a point he'd marked on the balance sheet. "There." He cleared his throat awkwardly as he spoke, avoiding Joshua's eyes. "That was the figure you first gave me for the accounts. But it didn't tally with individual account totals of deposits on hand. It was about eighteen thousand off. By the time I went down to the vault personally to check, it was closer to twenty-five. Then just this week, it's changed again. Just over nine thousand more if the deposit tallies are accurate."

Joshua grunted, trying not to look at the boy who'd stepped to his side. Compromising. That in itself, he guessed, a terrible, painful effort. He knew suddenly, as clearly as if God had told him, that Jonathon Penley hadn't touched that money, wouldn't have if he were starving. "You have dates for any of these?" he questioned in a carefully neutral voice. "It might help us know who's doing it."

Jonathon shrugged, shaking his head. 'Us.' "Not specifically. But I can give you the week, maybe, on this." He gestured to the middle one. "April 5th, about."

Joshua nodded, putting the date in mentally. There was no pattern that he could see. Too many holes and not enough substance. He sighed, handing the sheets back to Jonathon. "I'm tired, son. I'm not as young as you are. Let's work on it some more tomorrow, shall we? I'll have the guard at the vault doubled for the next few days as a precaution."

Jonathon nodded, hearing dismissal in the older man's voice, this time ready to obey it. He murmured a good-night and turned for the door, suddenly aware of how exhausted he truly was. The last thing on his mind as he fell asleep though was not Bonnie, as it had been for the past ten days, not what hope or lack of it the doctors had offered that day, but the balance sheets that refused to balance. Who besides Joshua Courtland would have access to the Courtland Bank vaults?

Elinor read Hadley's letter that Roland Hodges had given her. His men had brought it back from Virginia when they'd left behind twenty crates of brand new breech-loading rifles, just south of the Maryland border. Mosby's Confederacy, they were calling it now, that part of Virginia between the Rapidan River north to Maryland. He'd been promoted again. And he and his force of about two hundred men continually harried the Yankee troops west in the Valley—where Sigel was finally making a move—and east toward Richmond.

The rangers' legitimate function of harassing communications and disrupting supply lines was only one small part of Mosby's activities. He also kept a vital lifeline open to the North for black-market guns, ammunition, drugs, and other necessities of Confederate survival. The war against such guerrillas turned briefly vicious earlier in the year. A Federal order had come through authorizing the hanging without trial of any Rebel caught behind Union lines, wearing a Union uniform, caught in the act of making war against the Federal government.

Chase had not followed that 'suggestion' when he'd commanded at Blytheswood. Too many legitimate Confederate soldiers wore captured Federal uniforms these days out of necessity—it was that or go naked, sometimes. Other officers had agreed with Chase. In April, the order had been revoked. But a trace of that brutality remained on both sides. Mosby and other raiders ambushed outposts and picket stations, harassed civilians, shot stragglers, burned wagon and railroad trains, captured, killed, sometimes mutilated sentries and couriers. It was only symptomatic of the larger war and the ugly turn it had taken. Confederate high command was morally aghast at such activities. But they turned a blind eye, needing too badly what the raiders provided.

That suited Elinor. Mosby's little empire was the easiest way to trade guns for money—lots of it. Hadley reported over ninety thousand in cash already—gold, not CSA paper currency that was being deflated this spring at a horrendous rate. Hadley wrote of missing her. Of being feted in Richmond, but of the shortages there, the consequent lack of life's amenities. Elinor could see he was bored and restless and ready to quit. The Confederates had kept their part of the bargain. Cotton for Hadley's mills had been slipping out of New Orleans all this spring. But Elinor had no intention of letting anyone quit yet. This was far too profitable. As far as she was concerned, it was physically impossible to become too rich.

She'd had to wait tonight. Roland Hodges had had an earlier supper meeting to attend first. Then he'd met with her to assure her of the success of the last foray, give her her husband's letter, and take the money for the next shipment. She'd momentarily considered making a play for Hodges—she was that bored. But he was fat and old. She wasn't that desperate yet. Pity the handsome young Rebel sharing the house wasn't more fun.

Well, maybe another time, she thought. Some night when her father wasn't around. She might press Jonathon a bit harder then. Hodges's young Irish stable boy brought her carriage around and she started to climb inside it, pausing with one slippered foot already on the mounting rung. She glanced thoughtfully over one creamy, bare shoulder and smiled over the puffed sleeve of mint green silk. He smiled back and she turned out of the carriage. The night wasn't going to be a total loss after all.

It was late and dark in Richmond. Street lamps stood unlit—coal and oil were too scarce any longer to spare for them. Leanna slept restlessly in the hotel bed, plagued with dismal dreams. A faint breeze, almost as hot as the balmy, still, mid-May air, puffed at the curtains by the open window. Stewart trimmed the wick of a small lamp the desk clerk had lent him to light his way up four flights of the Spotswood's stairs and the pitch black hallway with its fading flowered wallpaper, and opened the door quietly.

"Stewart?" Leanna rolled over slowly, opening her eyes. For a moment, it confused her—the sudden intrusion of light, her husband's presence. Then she remembered. He had returned. They had stopped the Yankees then. She sat up with a beginning smile, feeling relief bloom sweet as the summer's first rose. He half turned at her word and her smile froze as quickly as it had come. Dark stains shadowed one side of his gray coat. "Stewart, you're hurt!"

"No, I—" Stewart caught her hand as she reached up toward him. He glanced down as if puzzled and began to frown. "Oh, this. It must be J.E.B. Stuart's." He spoke slowly, slurring the words. It was an effort to think at all. "He took a mortal wound in the fighting. We brought him back to Richmond with us."

Leanna froze, her hand limp within her husband's. She only stared at him, faintly confused, hoping this was another bad dream. "Not the General!"

Stewart's shrug was infinitely weary. He turned to begin undressing in the low, flickering light. "We barely managed to stop them at all. We caught them at Yellow Tavern, just a handful of miles away. General Stuart

took a bullet in his stomach. The fighting was exceptionally desperate."

"Oh, no!" A portion of the South would die with
J.E.B. Stuart. Just as Robert E. Lee epitomized the
mature Southern aristocrat—morally faultless, abound-
ing in dignity and quiet courtesy—J.E.B. Stuart embodied
all that was best in the South's young men. Daring to
the point of recklessness, placing esprit before material
advantage, chivalrous, dashing, gallant, heroic. She'd
met him at Mrs. Standdard's one night, once or twice at
the Davises'. Charming, witty, good-natured, proudly
determined. Now he was dying. Good God, even if
they finally won the war, would they have anything of
value left?

Stewart was fumbling at his coat buttons, his fingers
clumsy with fatigue. Leanna watched him in the darkness,
finally reaching one hand up toward him. "Here, let me
help." She could keep Chase Courtland out of her
thoughts most of the time, but he was always there, in
one dark corner of her soul. It made her twice as attentive in ways like this, trying to make it up to Stewart,
somehow, for loving him less than she should. "You
look exhausted." Leanna spoke gently, reaching to brush
at the streak of dirt with her finger tips. "Have you
slept? Or eaten anything since you left?"

He shook his head, shrugging his jacket off as she
finished with the buttons. "There was no time."

"I'll go down and find something for you in the hotel
kitchen."

"No, don't bother. I'll sleep now. Eat in the morning."

Leanna hesitated, then nodded, deciding not to argue.
She reached to touch his hand before extinguishing the
low burning lamp, felt him flinch and glanced down in
the semidarkness. "Your hand?"

"Only a scratch . . ."

She leaned across him to turn the lamp up higher.

"They still won't abandon Richmond. They won't
leave . . . they won't listen to anyone trying to tell
them . . ." Stewart spoke in a soft murmur, as if to
himself. "The President thinks we must keep Richmond,

261

but if he'd only move, shift the Capitol to another city in the deeper south . . ."

Leanna glanced up, confused. This was unlike him, this rambling kind of speech. He must be exhausted beyond belief. "What, dear? Are you speaking to me? Give up the city to the Yankees, you mean?"

Stewart frowned, glancing over as if surprised to find her there. He took his hand away to rub it wearily over his eyes. "Yes, give it up, for God's sake. Let them have the damn place. It's the only sensible way. We can't defend it any longer, we barely stopped the Yankee cavalry tonight, and now we've lost Stuart. We've been fighting this war all wrong, from the beginning. We can't beat the Yankees in a stand-up slugging match. They've got too many men, too many weapons. Our only hope is small groups with high mobility. Stonewall Jackson should have taught them that, to strike and move, use the terrain we're familiar with to our advantage. Look what he did in the Valley that year, with sixteen thousand against sixty thousand. But the President won't move the Capitol. He's going to tie the army down here, in trenches, like a feudal siege."

Leanna felt a whisper of cold fear touch her heart. "But we do need Richmond. It's become the very center of—"

He interrupted her as if she hadn't been speaking at all. "I've accepted a position on the President's staff, as Military Adviser." He spoke if he had remembered he had something else to say and was running out of time to say it. "I'll be going to Atlanta in a day or two to report to him on General Johnston's performance. Sherman's army is headed there, we understand from intelligence reports. Johnston has the CSA command. And you know the President distrusts Johnston." He reached wearily to extinguish the lamp. The room was plunged into total darkness and Leanna's astonishment was concealed. For a moment, she could say nothing. She slid over to let Stewart lie down, sitting beside him with one hand resting on his bare shoulder. When had all this been decided?

"Well, that's fine, Stewart," she managed finally. She even forced a smile, but it was lost in the darkness. "I've always wanted to see Atlanta."

Stewart reopened his eyes with a frown. "No. You'll be going to Charleston."

The forced smile faded. "I beg your pardon?"

"Leanna, please. You're my wife and you'll do as I say. You'll be going to Charleston. You'll stay with my family there."

Leanna felt resentment flare and she withdrew her hand. She didn't want to go to Charleston, and she didn't want to stay with his family. They were practically strangers for one thing—she'd only ever met them once. And then, to be perfectly frank, she hadn't much liked them. Stewart's mother had made no secret of her mixed emotions concerning Leanna as a daughter-in-law. The family was good enough, but it was Virginian. And Virginia was Northern enough in her mind to be suspect. She'd have preferred a South Carolinian, or failing that, a Georgia or Louisiana belle. Someone from the *real* South.

Stewart sighed and reached for her hand in the darkness. "Don't pout, Leanna, please, not tonight." Silence answered him and he frowned. "Leanna, you can't stay in Richmond. It's only a question of time until the Yankees surround the city, and then you'd be trapped here."

"I'll go back to Blytheswood, then."

"No. Sigel's troops are already marching in the Valley. I learned that just tonight." Fatigue put an edge in his voice he might not have meant to have there. "I've gotten space for you on a train tomorrow. I'll see you off before I go."

There seemed nothing else to say. She lay back down beside him in the darkness, listening to his breathing as he fell quickly asleep. She was trying hard not to be angry. Trying not to resent the way he ordered her life. In prewar days, she wouldn't have questioned it. Husbands were like fathers, in that sense. They made all those decisions. But since the war, since Chase. . . .

What had Chase said that day in the woodlands, just before the ambush? 'As long as you obey all the rules . . .'

He'd been right. She hadn't realized it then. How had he known Stewart better in those few days than she who had known him for years? She wondered suddenly what Stewart would do if she *didn't* obey all the rules. If she defied him, for instance, and returned to Blythes-wood? To her astonishment, something like fear rose as her answer.

Leanna took her seat in the crowded car, listening to the sounds of coal being shovelled into the front engine, of steam puffing louder. The green and gold fabric covering her seat was worn through in half a dozen places. Half the windows were broken or boarded over. The overhead iron luggage racks had long since disap-peared into munitions furnaces to recast into field artillery. She was lucky to even be on a train, she decided silently. Most of the few remaining cars had been detailed to the army for moving troops, carrying the wounded, ship-ping food supplies. The engine's chug quickened. The car began to vibrate and the wheels to screech on glisten-ing silver track. Charleston, she thought. She regretted suddenly that she hadn't been more forceful this morn-ing with Stewart about it. What could he have done if she'd simply refused to go?

"Leanna!" Stewart appeared suddenly, hurrying down the narrow aisle. The car rocked more violently and he stumbled against the edge of her seat, leaning into it for balance as he reached one hand out toward her. "Come on, Leanna. Before the train begins to move."

Other people in the car stared curiously at them. Leanna didn't care. She was conscious only of an enor-mous sense of relief, grateful Stewart had relented after all. She pulled hurriedly at the wide hoops of the skirt she had wedged into the narrow seat space. The young man next to her pushed to his feet to give her more room. His wrong-handed salute caught her eye.

"Colonel Leighton, hello. Going to Charleston?"

Stewart glanced up with a frown. The man looked

vaguely familiar, but half the Confederate cavalry did now. Then he noticed the young man was missing an arm. The sleeve of his gray uniform was neatly pinned up. He managed to nod and force a faint smile, careful not to look at the disfigurement. "No, Lieutenant. Last minute change of plans." It made him feel half sick, it always did. It was all he saw anymore. Deformed men—or dead ones.

"I'm going home to the reserves. Keep the Yanks up here, though, will you, sir? I've seen a bellyful of them."

"There, I'm free." Leanna got her skirts out and stepped into the aisle way, reaching for Stewart's arm. Stewart saluted the young officer and started instantly for the doorway, pulling Leanna after him. The shrill shriek of the engine whistle echoed down the track, people behind them braced themselves for the jerk of forward motion. Usually he slowed his long stride for her, but he didn't now. Leanna had to hurry to keep from being pulled off her feet. She glanced over her shoulder to see the young lieutenant's eyes still on them, and managed a quick smile of thanks, wondering briefly what he must be thinking. It wouldn't have hurt Stewart to be a little friendlier with the poor man.

"I got a telegram from my sister. Both Mother and Aunt Patricia are down with a fever. They don't know what it is or how serious it may be. But you obviously can't go there." His jaw was clenched, his blue eyes dark with anger and Leanna glanced at him sidelong, taken aback. "You'll have to go with me to Atlanta. I've no time now to make other arrangements. Maybe once we get down there . . ."

Leanna barely had time to nod. Stewart turned and lifted her down the iron steps and onto the train platform. She'd thoughtlessly clasped his hand. At his grunt of pain, she remembered to look down at it. "Stewart, I told you this morning to get that hand tended to."

"J.E.B. Stuart died. I felt I ought to be there."

She bit her lip, nodding. "I'll tend to it then. As soon as we—"

"The President wants to see me. We'll have to go

directly there. I'm late already." He turned to wave to a conductor. Leanna saw him sliding her trunk away from the car and rebolting the door, then he waved back and signaled the engineer. The engine gave another shriek. Sparks began to fly as metal wheels turned on metal track. She took a hasty backward step as the train began to move off to Charleston. She hoped the fever wasn't smallpox. The coast was notorious for it. And with medical supplies so horribly depleted. . . .

"I'll find a cab, Leanna. You'd better wait here. I won't be very long."

"Colonel Leighton?"

A well-dressed slender man in his early forties tipped his black hat. Stewart turned with a frown of irritation. "Oh, Lord Bennington. This is my wife, Leanna."

"How do you do?"

She knew he was English before he bent gallantly over her hand in a half bow. Bennington, she was thinking. I know I've heard that name before. . . .

"Ah, such lovely women you Confederates possess." Usually Hadley didn't mean that. He'd been disappointed, actually, to meet the famed Southern belles. Ugly as toads, half of them—compared to his Elinor, anyway. But this one was an exception. "You're going on a trip today, Colonel?"

"Yes. But this afternoon it seems." Stewart hesitated, glancing toward Leanna. He could leave his wife momentarily in the English lord's care while he hailed a cab on the street outside, but she was looking at the man strangely, too closely to suit him. "If you'll pardon me, sir, I'm in a bit of a hurry just now. My wife and I have to find a cab for the President's mansion." He tipped his own hat and reached to take Leanna's arm.

Leanna managed a farewell smile, giving up trying to place the name. The man didn't seem at all familiar. She was sure she'd never met him, and she was more concerned with her own thoughts just now. As Stewart hurried her on, she kept her chin high and worked at not showing her thoughts on her face. She'd felt a moment of genuine joy in the train car when she'd first

266

seen Stewart hurrying toward her, something very close to love for him, when she'd thought he'd changed his plans to accommodate her wishes. But now that she knew of his sister's telegram, it had faded. She kept trying to love him like she had Chase Courtland. Trying to pretend, almost, that he was Chase—only dressed in Confederate gray instead of the hated Yankee blue. You're a fool, Leanna, she told herself, Chase Courtland's probably dead and buried. You made your choice the day you rode away from Blytheswood. And Stewart Leighton is not the same man, no matter how hard you close your eyes and wish he were. It's not even fair to expect him to be. She had the sudden feeling the world had all gone wrong these past years—and a sudden, panicky fear that there might be no way, ever now, to make it right again.

Chapter Eighteen

Nights in the Deep South have a rhythm all their own. Dusk falls slowly and deepens to a velvety darkness. Leaves rustle unseen in night breezes. Owls hoot and insects vibrate. The air is heavy with humidity and the faint, elusive scents of magnolia, camellia, roses, and honeysuckle vines. This night, the Federal cavalry horses tethered in between the gnarled old oaks were restless. They added the muffled sounds of hooves stamping on spongy ground, soft snorting, and the creak of the long rope. What little silence there was to a Georgia night, the bugle call shattered at three-thirty A.M. sharp. In the darkness, Chase Courtland rolled from his camp bed, reaching for his boots as he opened his eyes. It was habit by now and no great accomplishment. How many midnight reveilles had he answered in just this way? There was a little moonlight coming in the flap of the tent—that helped some. It showed his spurs in a gleam of dull gilt and he reached to strap them on over his boots. New Hope Church, May 25th. Johnston wasn't giving way to the Union advance like he had at Dalton, then Resaca, then Casswille and finally Allatoona Pass. New Hope Church was more defendable. The Confederates were strongly entrenched and the Union's usual flanking manuevers were hampered by the terrain and the mud of spring rains.

It would be a fight then. Sloppy, sharp, likely protracted—Sherman was determined to go straight ahead. Chase reached for his revolver and tightened the buckle of the belt he'd loosened to sleep in. A moment later, he was bending over for his saddle, hoisting it up over his forearm, the familiar smell of horse and leather strong from it as he ducked under the tent flap without a backward glance.

Amazing what bizarre behavior could become normalcy after three years of war. Hardly anyone spoke. Even the horses seemed used to such midnight saddlings. Men appeared mostly dressed, incredibly awake. Coffee and hardtack helped. The battalion formed in the shadowed darkness with a minimum of confusion. A staff officer cantered by, returning a silent salute a few minutes later, checking to be sure all troops were in correct positions before returning to General Sherman.

Chase watched the crisp, black silhouette of the officer disappear back into vaguer darkness and glanced over his shoulder at the men of his own command. Only one troop of the battalion had come along with him from the Shenandoah. He'd put them directly behind him. He knew Captain Grier and even most of the enlisted men—they were used to him and vice versa. They'd learned to recognize his voice shouting orders above the din of battle confusion, and the other three troops could follow the center's lead. So all was well. Captain Grier saw his major's habitual prebattle check and smiled in the darkness, saluting that all was in readiness.

Chase turned back in the saddle, surveying the slowly graying field below where long lines of infantry were appearing. Behind him a horse stamped, a canteen jingled. To his left a hundred yards, the regimental battle flag snapped once in a gust of warm wind. They were normal sounds and he paid them no attention. Hurry up and wait. It was the army's way, the curse of a few commanders who fouled up their orders, a crucial unit that had failed to be properly assigned. Confusion more than glory was the war's real companion, all the recruiting posters and newspaper accounts aside.

He let his thoughts drift to Leanna as he often did before a battle. He'd found it the only thing powerful enough to keep his mind off the brooding of waiting for that sudden bugle call. Not that he feared death anymore. That had ended with Gettysburg, with the hell of that

269

terrible fight, the realization of the war changing, the honor of its conception slipping away in the bitterness of burying slaughtered armies. Briefly after that, he'd feared living. Feared endless repetition of the hell of battle, of meaningless killing, with no end and no worthwhile purpose.

Leanna had changed that. Most men carried tintypes, or letters, or a lock of hair. He carried one, too, of Susan. He'd felt he ought to after committing himself to marry her on his next leave. It was in his inside pocket. If he were killed, someone would tell her it had been there. But it wasn't Susan's picture he looked at at these times. Nor Susan's face he saw engraved within his mind. It was Leanna's. Not at her most beautiful necessarily, which he had found initially surprising. It was the odd moment actually, where a certain smile had just barely curved her mouth, or that peculiar set of her eyes just before she began to frown. Moments he had not particularly noted at the time, but now, despite time and distance, maintained an incredibly powerful hold on him. He had begun to wonder after a dozen waiting, dark nights like this whether it was quite normal for him to remember her as he did, to feel so strongly about a woman he would never see again, a woman he probably should never have seen at all. He wondered whether he was in love, or insane.

He smiled wryly at the idea and shrugged. Insane probably. Weren't they all? What sane man would be sitting where he did, waiting for a bugle to send him forward to shoot and kill men he'd never known and had nothing, essentially, against except different color uniforms and different ideas about how they all ought to govern themselves?

Why hadn't he fallen in love with Susan instead? It would have been so much simpler. Especially now. Had Susan been the wrong woman? Or merely appeared at the wrong time? Maybe he'd loved Leanna as he did because of loving her when he did. When nothing else had mattered much anymore. When there had been a kind of bleak recklessness raging within him and nothing inside left to protect. He'd given her his soul because there was nothing else to give it to, and reclaimed it in some strange way when he'd thought to lose it forever. Not that loving her was without pain. Quite the contrary. Of all he'd heard written or sung about it, no one had described love the way he'd found it to be. Less a joy than a hunger. A relentless, ever-aching need for her. A quiet strength that could turn to a swelling surge of terrible anguish, a desperate all-consuming cry of his soul for hers. Yet, perversely, he cherished it as he cherished nothing else, the pain notwithstanding.

Overhead, dark clouds began to obscure the faint light. The air grew heavier, ominously still. A thunderstorm gathered slowly on the graying horizon. I love you, Lea, he thought to her, with a faint frown. Regardless of all the reasons I shouldn't. Regardless of the madness going on all around us. Wherever you are, I love you still.

The gray dawn came and with its feeble light, the train shrieked to a stop at another ramshackle station. Leanna gave up trying to sleep and fanned herself with a folded piece of newspaper. How did the native Georgians stand this humid heat? And it was only the end of May already, the worst yet to come in July and August. Beside her, Stewart was reading a month old copy of *Southern Illustrated News*. He'd smiled a greeting, but didn't bother to look out at the stop. Leanna only did out of habit—and boredom. They'd been weeks on various trains, slowly working their way down to Georgia. The Confederate transportation system was in ruins. This one was the worst yet. A mail run. It seemed to stop more than it moved, all night long. Luckily, from what she'd seen of it, Georgia was a pretty state. Low mountains in the north, wide rolling hills. The reddest earth she'd ever seen, even redder than the red parts of Virginia west of Richmond. Pines and hardwoods, a few mountain laurel and rhododendron late losing their spring blossoms. Acre after acre of cotton fields, tobacco growing, peach orchards and peanut vines, a few fields of corn and other grains. Not many people. But it was early yet, and life slower this far south. Plus, the morning sky was threateningly black as she craned her head to look upward from the window. Maybe the heat was from the storm. Maybe it would be less oppressive after it finally rained.

The dark blue of a Yankee uniform suddenly appeared and she turned her head sharply as the train began to clank and groan forward again. Something in the way the man stood made her breath catch in her throat. Her fingers tightened convulsively over Stewart's arm. Dear God! Chase?

"What is it, Leanna?"

The captured Yankee officer turned even as Stewart spoke, and she shook her head, seeing it wasn't. "Nothing, I—I was just startled, seeing him . . ."

Stewart followed her gaze, moving restlessly in his seat. "Oh." He smiled grimly, watching the retreating station. "Just a Yankee prisoner. No need to fear him. He's unarmed. And surrounded by three Confederates. Kind of a nice change, actually. Usually it's the other way around, we who are virtually weaponless and outnumbered."

Leanna's racing heart was finally slowing, the blood draining back into her ashen face. She managed a nod.

"Probably on his way to Andersonville Prison," Stewart spoke in a satisfied tone, smiling faintly. "You might see some others along the way this morning."

The station disappeared behind the train. Small farms lined the track again. Leanna finally trusted her voice to speak, and reached to touch her husband's sun-browned hand. She forced a smile, and nodded to a deep red, furrowed field outside the train's dust-smeared window. "Look, Stewart . . . working their farm in this terrible heat . . ." Two women and a man bent over hoes, a young child walked behind, hand scattering seed. "Maybe that will be us someday. After the war. If the Yankees should win."

Stewart frowned instantly, unamused. "No, Leanna.

I don't intend to do that the rest of my life, so I don't intend to let the Yankees win."

Leanna glanced at him startled, her smile fading. "I was only teasing." She frowned slightly as he looked away, frightened by what had flashed in his ice-blue eyes. Such coldness. Such ruthless determination. She eyed him sideways as the train rumbled on. She'd never seen that in him before. Was it something of the war's leavings, or something he'd always had? Something she just hadn't seen before? 'Obey all the rules' flashed into her mind again. Despite the heat, she felt an irrepressible chill.

"Colonel Leighton?" An aged, uniformed train guard hurried down the car aisle, apprehension written plainly on his wrinkled face. He waved a telegram paper in one hand. "This was waiting at the last station."

Stewart stood up, still frowning. He read the paper and nodded once. His mouth settled into grim lines that, by now, seemed habitual to Leanna. "New Hope Church? How far ahead is that?"

"About five miles."

"According to this, we still hold the position."

The guard looked startled. "Yes, sir, but by the time we get there, Yankees may be—"

"Aren't your instructions to get this train into Atlanta?" Stewart snapped impatiently, his blue eyes flashed. "Aren't you carrying supplies and ammunition for Johnston's army?"

"Yes, sir, but—"

"They aren't liable to do him much good if you stop them on the wrong side of the Yankee line, are they?"

The aged guard flushed. "No, sir."

"Well then, I suggest you worry a little less about what the Yankees may be doing and a little more about what we're going to do. Don't make any more stops. Don't stop at New Hope Church either; take it through the station at top speed. Even if they're holding it by then, the Yankees will have a difficult time trying to stop a locomotive going full steam."

"But they might derail—"

"We'll just have to hope they won't think of that, won't we?"

The guard flushed again but nodded, saluting crisply. Leanna watched, saying nothing. She agreed with Stewart's decision. She'd known this wasn't a pleasure trip. That earlier glimpse of something unknown in him, something frightening, was eclipsed by something admirable. Officers needed to make instant decisions— and aggressive ones. She'd learned that by watching Major Chase Courtland this winter. Learned what made a good officer. Funny, she thought. She hadn't realized they were at all alike. Stewart turned and glanced at her almost apologetically. "Sorry. Looks like the heat may not be our only concern."

"I understand. I agree with you."

Stewart smiled faintly, giving her that strange look he sometimes did, as if debating whether to take her opinion seriously. "You'll stay down, clear of the windows if there's any shooting. I'd better stay here with you, I think." He unsnapped the holster of his Le Mat revolver and drew it out, drawing the hammer back, flicking the chamber with one finger to check its load as the cylinder turned. He glanced up satisfied. Damn those Yankees. They were everywhere now. "Don't you worry, Leanna. I won't let the Yankees get you."

Leanna said nothing. She could have assured him she wasn't afraid, could have reminded him she'd spent a long winter surrounded by Yankees and no longer considered them all first cousin to the boogie man. But she didn't. It made her think of Chase—too much made her think of Chase. She kept silent for fear of betraying herself.

Stewart's smile faded as the second station flew past the train windows. Two more, he counted mentally. He gestured her away from the window as a distant boom sounded ahead of them. Thunder? Or cannon? He frowned, no longer trying to act nonchalant for Leanna's sake. He knocked a thick glass window pane out with the revolver's butt, then turned it in his hand to cock the hammer. The way things were going, this would be the last train to Atlanta from this direction. He hoped to hell the Yankees didn't think to try to fire the station if they held it. The powder in the fourth car would go off like a bomb. For himself, he didn't care. Getting captured by Yankees would be worse. But he wished Leanna were somewhere else—Charleston, where she should have been. So he wouldn't have had to choose between a responsibility to her, and a responsibility to win this damn war any way he knew how. Johnston had to have this train!

Chase's battalion was ordered into the fight with shocking suddenness. A staff officer appeared, screaming and waving, disappearing again in a puff of artillery smoke. The Rebels had made a reckless counter attack from their entrenched position. The Federal infantry had wavered, and begun to crumble. The cavalry had to break Confederate momentum. Their own infantry needed time to regroup. It was a suicidal assignment for cavalry to go against infantry's massed firing power, but that was war. Chase didn't question the order, just spurred his horse forward. For a moment, all was screaming confusion on the field. Thunder and artillery fire boomed together overhead. Acrid smoke drifted across the meadow in long black wisps. Revolvers cracked and sabers swished and fell, sometimes with a cold ring of metal returning metal, sometimes with a meaty thud that left blood on silver blades. Horses screamed and some fell, the shrill yip of the Rebel yell punctuated the Union cry of 'Charge' and the brassy notes of the bugle. The gray line halted, bracing itself to meet the shock of collision with galloping cavalrymen, then dissolved into a milling, confusing open brawl on the storm darkened field. Only a dozen yards behind the last Confederate trench, an outdated steam locomotive rattled on uneven track. It flew through the rear of the melee with only a single shrill shriek of a whistle to mark its passing. Chase hardly even saw it.

Leanna watched cautiously from a window corner as the battle appeared with incredible abruptness—a shrub-covered hill, a stretch of open land, a single fence post, and then men in an incredible, surging mass, locked together in a fight to the death. The sound of it erupted simultaneously, muffled by train wheels clattering, the scene itself obscured by puffs of smoke that hung motionless in its midst. A bugle sounded the cavalry's retreat. Federal infantry was ready to charge. Chase shouted the order hoarsely from a dust-dry throat, raising his bloodied saber high and wheeling his horse, crouching low in the saddle against the bullets that would be aimed after dark-blue backs. Lightning flashed in the storm-dark sky. The rain started in a burst of slashing waves, falling sideways in a sudden gust of wind. Thank God, Chase thought. It would help them get the hell out of there.

Leanna blinked involuntarily against the blinding flash, startled by it, not realizing what it was until rain began to pelter the roof of the car and wet the windows. Chase Courtland galloped by only half a hundred yards from her, taking his command back to the dubious shelter of the scrub-covered hill. Leanna never saw him. She had turned to watch Stewart instead. His handsome face was contorted in a frown of apprehension as lightening flashed again closer to the speeding train. If it hit the powder. . . .

He jerked from his stand at the window, running for the doorway to call an order to the engineer. They were through the battle now, out of that danger. But with the storm, even if lightning didn't hit the explosives, water on the tracks could make such speed suicidal. Leanna watched in confusion as he forced open the car door and reached for the iron hand hold to jump the treacherous hitch. The words of his shouted order were lost in the roar of more thunder. She glanced back to the window but by now, the battle was only a distant, water-splotched blur through the trees. From what little she could see, it appeared the Yankees were retreating. A reassuring sight.

Stewart came back in, offering a grim but somehow congratulatory smile as he raised one hand to brush the rain off his hair. "Next stop, Atlanta." he assured her.

He smiled wider and leaned over the seat to give Leanna a quick kiss. It was a most uncharacteristic gesture for Stewart and touched her very deeply. She raised her hand to link her fingers through his, squeezing them and offering a very genuine smile in return. "Well done, Colonel Leighton. Very well done, indeed."

Jonathon had loosened his tie and unbuttoned the stiff, starched collar of his shirt as he read the early June Sunday paper. He laid it aside now with a frown, laying his head back against the hard, hand-carved cherry of the Chippendale settee. Then he closed his eyes wearily. Was everyone's private world as complicated as his own had become? Did everyone in the world walk, talk, sleep and breathe with this many secret thoughts churning through their minds? Was everyone bedeviled by a thousand hidden anxieties, a thousand unanswered questions? Was everyone essentially unknown to another, existing in worlds no one else could begin to fathom, only pretending as a ritual courtesy that any one man could truly begin to know another?

There were so many things to balance now, to juggle. The bank problem. The questions of who, how, why? How had it become Jonathon's personal responsibility anyway? Why should he feel he owed it to any Yankee to solve questions plaguing someone else? Didn't he have enough problems of his own? Leanna. Where was she? Richmond, maybe? How deeply had she been involved with the guerrilla ambush on the Federal troops? Blytheswood and Cool Spring. Angus, and Jewel, the Valley, the War.

According to the newspapers, a virtual slaughter in eastern Virginia. Twenty thousand Yankees lost at the Wilderness battle alone. More at Spotsylvania. Seven thousand in a half hour at Cold Harbor early this week. Northern editorials called Grant a butcher. But he was forcing Lee's Army of Northern Virginia back, mile by bloody mile, toward Richmond. Relentless, inexorable, unstoppable, Jonathon guessed. Lee might delay him; he could never defeat him. Let the Federals lose three or four to every Confederate one. Grant could replace dead soldiers. Lee could not.

And there was Sherman in the deep South, inching toward Atlanta, the CSA's major railroad city. Sigel had moved finally in the Shenandoah Valley and gotten beaten by CSA General Breckinridge on the fifteenth of May at the Bushong farm in New Market—less than a mile from Cool Spring. But Breckinridge had used VMI cadets to do it. Children. Literally children. Thirteen- and fourteen-year-olds, not even shaving yet, dying in a war Jonathon knew was unwinnable for the South . . .

Hunter now, replacing the inept Sigel, moving down the Valley, vengeful, burning as he went. Cool Spring and Blytheswood were both virtually abandoned in his path, the spring crops not planted, a whole year lost even if he could leave tomorrow to tend to them—which he couldn't, because of what he owed Joshua Courtland, and because of the too tiny, too fragile little girl he'd brought home from the hospital only a few hours before, today after church. Sleeping now with her mother in the dayroom, absurdly small in the Courtland's borrowed cradle. And Elinor, Lady Bennington. Amusement and a dangerous secret gleaming in her green eyes whenever she looked at him. God only knew what she was liable to say or do. Now, with Whitney here, he could only pray she would have the decency to—

"Jonathon?"

He jerked, startled at the light touch of a woman's hand on his shoulder, bolting upright and turning on the seat.

"Oh, I didn't mean to startle you so." Whitney withdrew her hand with an apologetic smile. "I suppose I shouldn't have disturbed you."

"No, no, I was just a million miles away." Jonathon's smile was genuine, relieved, and he moved over on the settee, raising his arm to welcome his wife next to him. "I thought you were sleeping."

"I was. Then I woke up and I was lonely for you." She sat down with grateful adoration shining in her soft gray eyes. How handsome Jon was. How dearly she

278

loved him. And marveled that he seemed to love her so dearly in return, when she seemed to offer only problems—unable to bear his son alive for him, unable to take over Cool Spring as Leanna had Blytheswood, so competently, so easily. "I'm sorry if I interrupted—"

"You interrupted nothing," he assured her, tightening his arm around her shoulders. He turned his head to brush her chestnut hair with a kiss. "You're feeling all right?"

"Fine," she smiled. "And Bonnie took the trip well. What were you thinking about?"

"A million things." He shook his head, then smiled wider, turning to look back to her. "I guess I shouldn't say that, should I? Women want to think we men only think about them. I was, too. At least partially."

"Only one thought out of a million?"

"Two or three, maybe." He laughed to her teasing, meeting her eyes and holding them for an instant.

Desire flashed momentarily in them and Whitney felt her own heart pounding quicker in instinctive response. It had been a long, long time. "Have you decided yet about going home?"

Jonathon's smile faded slightly. "No. The bank problem isn't solved for one thing. For another, there's no way I'm taking you and the children back to the Valley when there are Yankee armies crawling all over it."

Whitney turned her head suddenly, listening, then rose quickly to her feet. "Someone's home. I hear a carriage outside."

"And I hear Bonnie." Jonathon rose with her. "Are you ready to hire a wet nurse? I could ask Mrs. Eaton to—"

"No." Whitney spoke more sharply than she'd meant to. She tried to mellow it with a quick smile, but she could not conquer a secret superstition—that until she was sure the baby would live, she had to nurse her herself—feed Bonnie her own desperate determination that she must live. It sounded insane, even to her. "Another week, Jon, if you wouldn't mind at night. She's growing so well."

279

"All right, love. Whatever you wish."

The front door opened and Whitney started out the other doorway. At Bonnie's soft, mewing cry, her milk had let down. It had begun to show on her dark green dress. Jonathon stayed to gather the bank papers he'd begun working on for tomorrow's board meeting. "I'll be right in, Whit. You don't mind, do you?"

"Of course not. I'll leave the door unlocked."

He frowned as he glanced at the bank sheets. He and Joshua had agreed not to mention the missing money at the meeting tomorrow. For all Joshua talked about the board members, the Courtland family really owned the bank—eighty percent of it, anyway. No reason to stir up trouble, especially when there was no explanation yet. Who besides Joshua could get into the vault unguarded? Probably the Courtland sons when they had been here. But one was dead. The other was down in Georgia.

"Lady Bennington." Jonathon spoke a greeting curtly as she entered the parlor. "If you'll excuse me, I was just . . ."

"Your wife sleeping?"

How did she manage to make even that innocent question an invitation? Jonathon flushed slightly, frowning. "No, she's waiting for me in her room."

"Is she the patient type?" Elinor enjoyed baiting him almost as well as she would have enjoyed a repetition of his services in bed. Denied one, she would take the other. "It's a lovely day to play outside. Croquet, or some other game." She ran her fingers lightly down his arm, feeling quick tension in those lean, strong muscles.

"Excuse me." Jonathon turned, walking away to her soft laugh. He bent over the table to pick up the ledgers, suddenly frowning in startled thought. Elinor. Joshua's daughter. If her brothers would have access to the vault, wouldn't she? God no, it would kill her father, he thought at the same instant. Please God, make it anyone but her.

Out in the hallway, Whitney forced herself to turn around and tiptoe silently back to her room. She had heard Elinor's voice and thought to invite her in to see the baby before she began to nurse. Women always loved infants. She'd been a little surprised when Lady Bennington had never come to the hospital. Now she felt trembly and half sick. Stupid. How stupid of you, Whitney. Lady Bennington was not interested in her baby. She was interested in her husband. Bless Jonathon for his reaction.

But her hands were shaking, her palms damp as she went over the cradle to pick Bonnie up. Whitney had few illusions about herself. She could not easily compete with Lady Bennington's stunning beauty. Leanna could have, Jon's sister. But not her. Especially not after bearing the children, puffing her waistline—with her breasts now swollen and heavy, dripping milk. She could hardly leave this room.

Jonathon stepped through the door behind her, laying the ledgers to one side of the bureau and coming up to stand behind his wife. One hand rested warmly on her shoulder and he kissed her hair softly as he watched her changing Bonnie's wet gown. "I love you, Whit."

She bit her lip against tears that threatened in her eyes and nodded. "I know, Jon. I love you, too." She said no more, but made an instant decision, praying God would not punish her for it. It was time after all to find a wet nurse for Bonnie. "Are you sleeping downstairs with me tonight, Jon?" She didn't need to look at him as she spoke. She felt the pressure of his hand on her shoulder tighten slightly, felt his heart against her back increase its beat.

"If you're sure it's not too soon . . ."

She smiled, turning her head to catch his darkening eyes, thinking it was an ironic choice of words.

"Yes, I'm sure," she murmured softly. "It's not a moment too soon."

"I know Stanton and Seward side with us, but that damn 'rail splitter' has the final say and he'll hamstring us eventually—you mark my words."

Joshua concealed a smile of bitter satisfaction, only

nodding in what others could assume was disapproval of Lincoln's determination to protect the wayward Southern states. Thank God for the President, he thought. A rare and gentle genius.

"But I have news that may mitigate that fact." Roland Hodges enjoyed the instant silence of surprise that followed. He picked a letter up from the table and waved it—a touch of sheer melodrama. Even Joshua stared at him expectantly. "A little note to cheer us all. The President is not a well man. So says one who ought to know."

Joshua willed his heart to continue its beat unchanged, sent a prayer of fervent denial to the heavens, and shrugged to Hodges's announcement. He glanced sharply at the letter he held, desperately curious. All he could see was the seal of the War Department on it, part of its address at 17th and Pennsylvania Avenue. Stanton? Eckert? Baker, maybe, Stanton's chief of secret investigations.

"He grows gaunter by the day," Hodges read from the paper with a smile. "More easily fatigued, headaches more common. As he sits now in a Cabinet meeting, legs crossed, his raised foot trembles quite noticeably. The squinting, too, of his left eye increases . . ."

"Squinting and trembling." One man snorted in exasperation. "Neither is terminal."

A murmur of assent rippled around the table. Hodges frowned, piqued.

"But a disease of some sort, maybe. These may be symptoms of that."

"I thought we had decided to support Lincoln's renomination. Isn't the convention convening tomorrow? A bit late now to switch horses, isn't it?"

"If he is ill, that would only be to our benefit, wouldn't it?" Joshua spoke coolly, shrugging feigned unconcern. "The less he's able to do, the freer Stanton and Seward would be to control things."

"Stanton told me he favors military occupation of the South. Government in perpetuity of martial law.

Administered, naturally, by the War Department—and select friends."

"Here, here to that!"

"I wish he were running for President."

"He may, in essence, be—if Lincoln is actually failing," Hodges pointed out.

"But Seward won't tolerate Stanton's dictatorship."

"Then give Seward the war with England he's been wanting so dreadfully. He's only jealous of Stanton's power these past few years. He'd like a war in *his* department. We'll need one somewhere eventually anyway. It's only good business."

"Give our unemployed soldiers something to do." Someone chuckled softly.

"I must point out, gentlemen—not in any attempt to burst your bubble—but we haven't won *this* one yet." Joshua managed a smile, drinking a huge swallow of brandy before he spoke. Sick. That's what it made him. Every time he had to attend one of these damn meetings. He'd almost skipped tonight's, deciding after these long months that the coalition was mired in its own vested interests, unable to be the unified—and hence truly dangerous—force he'd first feared they'd be. Only a collection of selfish, quarrelsome old men. But now, oh God, what if Lincoln were really ailing?

"My son is in Georgia just now—finding the CSA far from beaten. What say we repledge our support to renominate the President simply because he has the best chance of getting the South conquered just now. See how things go before the election this fall?"

"Ah, true, Joshua." Henry nodded, smiling almost proudly at his friend. "You're invaluable to us, you know. You level-headed bankers."

"Renominate Lincoln."

Hands rose quickly around the table. There was no reason to bother counting—it wasn't close.

"Same time, two weeks from now?"

Joshua nodded as the others did, already rising to his feet and making his farewells. Most would stay, smoke a cigar or two, drink brandy and play cards. He never

283

stayed. They no longer expected him to. He made appropriate conversation to Henry, who followed him out, standing with him at the club's front door while the doorman called the carriages. But the only real thought in his mind lay unspoken until he'd climbed inside his elegant new Concord and swung closed the black-lacquered, spring-lock door behind him. "God, don't let us lose Lincoln." he murmured then, closing his eyes and shaking his head. "If we do, we lose the whole war. No one else has the power to stop Stanton and the others from trampling the South, pressing every last penny out of it. The Union will be as lost as if we'd never fought at all. Don't let that happen, God, not after all we've given to try to prevent it."

After all *I've* given to try to prevent it, he thought. My oldest son, maybe my younger one as well. That seemed like it ought to be enough. But if it weren't, God could take him too. It wasn't maudlin. It wasn't self-pitying. Joshua was used to the debits and credits of banking. He assumed God worked the same way.

Chapter Nineteen

"From Chase, I assume?"

Susan glanced up, startled, guiltily folding the letter she held. She made herself stop. Made herself look him in the eye instead as she nodded. "Yes, it is."

Doc Lacey shrugged and turned away. "He's well, I hope."

"Yes."

"Coming home on leave?"

There was a heartbeat's silence. Susan put the letter away. "No, at least he doesn't say so. It's a terrible fight down there, Roger. He says the army, or some portion of it at least, has fought almost every day. I'm worried about him. I can't pretend I'm not."

"Why should you pretend anything?" Doc Lacey's eyes flashed bitterness. "You're his fiancée still, aren't you? You ought to worry about the man you're going to marry."

"Roger, please!" Susan turned away and blinked once at gathering tears. He said hardly anything—at least by words. But, every day, for months now, she had read hurt and anger in his eyes. "He thanked me for the picture. He said he carried it into the last fight."

He may carry your face in a picture, my dear Susan, but not in his heart. Leanna Leighton holds that place. Fools, he accused bitterly. The world is populated by them, and you're as great a one as any. But he hadn't told her before. He didn't tell her now. He wondered if he ever would. What if he hurt her for no reason? What if Chase Courtland died in Georgia and never came home to marry her?

"Washington is hotter than I would have thought." A single tear had dropped. Susan brushed it away, pretending it was from the heat. "The poor men in the wards must be miserable."

"They are." He glanced at her and his anger slowly faded. In her high-necked, dark-blue dress, she couldn't be comfortable, either. Yet she came every day, and worked ungodly hours, as he did. Grant's butchery this spring outside of Richmond had filled every hospital, land and sea, to overflowing. And she never complained. He did, frequently. "I'll take you out later. Hire a boat to go out on the Potomac. It's always cooler there out of the city itself, with the water . . ."

"No," Susan shook her head sharply and moved away from the window's glare. "No, I think not. Thank you, anyway."

She moved on down the hallway, slender and strong, and silent. Doc Lacey sighed looking after her, allowing her to gain some distance before he started after her. Outside, the newsboys cried the latest rumors of Jubal Early's progress toward the Federal capital. Many of the Washington inhabitants were already hysterical enough to be moving out of the city. As he stood there, yet another overloaded carriage went clattering past. Funny, he thought, as he started to follow Susan back to the wards. Funny, but he was far less concerned with the Rebel menace of Jubal Early than he was the Atlanta campaign. He found himself hoping the Confederates there would continue to keep the Federal advance to an agonized crawl.

In July, the Georgia sun was blazing hot. Most afternoons, Yankees and Rebels alike declared an unspoken truce and sought refuge in the cooler shade of the low-wooded hills—fighting with voracious black biting flies instead of one another and trying to conserve energy for the next day's battle. Sherman continued his methodical, chesslike flanking movements. The Rebels withdrew slowly to a nearly impregnable position on Kennesaw Mountain. A frontal assault on June 27th had been a Federal disaster. After two days of burying dead infantry, the Union forces resumed a flanking strategy

286

instead. By the 3rd of July, Johnston withdrew to his Chattahoochee River defenses only ten miles from Atlanta. And Chase, riding a long, dusty, sweating patrol, got his first distant glimpse of the city they were marching toward. It was becoming obvious to everyone that Confederate General Joe Johnston was no man's fool. He would avoid any confrontation with an overwhelmingly superior Yankee army. Keep them moving in their slow, crablike pace instead—five miles sideways for every one mile forward—wearing themselves and their horses out in the ungodly heat. Cavalry General Nathan Bedford Forrest would continue to pick away at the overlong supply line running down from Tennessee. Between the two of them, the Union army might collapse under its own weight.

Even if that didn't happen, the spring had started too promisingly for the North. Now Sherman was getting nowhere, Grant was stuck outside of Petersburg in a seemingly interminable stalemate with Lee, Hunter had been soundly defeated in the Shenandoah Valley by General Jubal Early—one of Jackson's old lieutenants— and now a Confederate offensive was moving north down the Valley to menace Washington itself. Union cavalry under Sheridan, riding to raid the Valley, had been beaten by J.E.B. Stuart's successor, Wade Hampton, at Trevilian Station, only days after Forrest's cavalry of three thousand trounced a Union force of eight thousand in Mississippi. The Northerners had seen victory firm within their grasp this spring. Now they'd seen it slip again, the CSA struggling back to snatch impossible victories from frustrated Union armies. The people were not pleased. Lincoln's reelection was beginning to look doubtful. And the usual outcry had begun—to replace generals, to send out peace feelers, to do something, anything, to get this war ended.

In Philadelphia, printed broadsides posted on store fronts and park trees reminded the people that war still dragged on and that this was an election year. The newspapers spoke of little else, either. Jonathan avoided confrontations which could have been ugly by saying as

287

little as possible on either subject. Joshua Courtland's awesome social prestige shielded the Confederate family somewhat, and the Courtland mansion at 16th and Locust was a bastion of tolerance. Joshua would allow nothing less. Still, there remained an acute awareness of being a stranger in a strange land, and only Miranda had wholeheartedly adopted the Yankee city as home.

"Jonathon."

He glanced up, startled, not pleased to find Lady Bennington gliding through the doorway of his office at the bank, satin skirts rustling, the sweet smell of gardenias preceding her. The bank was a Greek revival, marble-fronted, massive oven in the humid heat of the Philadelphia July day. The cobblestoned streets outside at Fourth and Market radiated heat in waves. Opening windows only let hotter air in and Jonathon had unbuttoned the vest of his black business suit and loosened his starched collar. Now, as Elinor appeared, he reached up to rebutton both.

"Working through the lunch hour?"

Jonathon shrugged for answer, meeting Elinor's deep green gaze with a wry smile. "I've found Yankees seem to enjoy lunch better without a Johnny Reb sharing their table," he answered finally, watching her with a distant smile, a wary eye. He and she had established a kind of uneasy rapport, an understanding each of the other. Not friendship exactly. More of a truce.

"Not this Yankee." Elinor stepped closer.

He only shrugged. "At least your father should have his lunch in peace. We imposed on you already—too much."

"You haven't imposed on *me* nearly enough." Her green eyes gleamed with invitation, holding his.

Jonathon felt involuntary response stirring in his loins. He smiled faintly to conceal it even though he knew well she knew how she attracted him. "You are, at least, honest in your own way, Elinor."

"When it suits me."

His smile faded. "Yes, I have no doubt of that, either."

288

"Hardly anyone else is here just now, Major. Why don't you put your papers aside for a minute."

Jonathon sighed almost regretfully, shaking his head. "Don't you get tired of being told 'no'?"

Elinor smiled, leaning over the desk toward him— deliberately, Jon guessed, letting the bodice of the pale green gown gap to show the soft shadows of high, full breasts. He shifted his gaze, but not without an effort. He smiled, nodding once in recognition of the near success of her ploy.

"I've never met anyone quite like you, Major," she murmured aloud, thoughtfully. "I begin to understand why your countrymen continue their ridiculous fight. You don't know when giving up would be to your advantage." She raised one perfect brow in half-mocking admiration and straightened up, turning for the door. She turned in the doorway, smiling once again faintly. "One thing I know, although you may be too much of a gentleman to admit it, even to yourself—I can do a lot more for you between the sheets than your sweet little lady of a wife can. I'll wait."

Jonathon frowned and she smiled wider, stepping out to close the door behind her. It was easier now—now that he had Whitney back. But not effortless. There was such an extreme sexuality about Elinor—something that once tasted, was hard to entirely forsake.

Go check the bank vault, he ordered himself angrily. Get your mind on something else.

The guard nodded as he walked by. Jonathon didn't stop to make pleasant small talk for a moment as he usually did, only stooped to scrawl his signature on the clipboard. Elinor's lay on the line above. For a second, his hand froze there, an involuntary chill rose up his spine, then he finished and stood aside. The guard opened the massive metal door casually as if it were only a normal day. Inside, four smaller vaults stood, silent and closed. He went directly to the third and turned the two keys required to open it, then reached for the metal lock box that contained the Southern deposits. As he opened it, a faint whiff of what smelled like a hot summer night in the deep South rose up. Gardenias . . .

He didn't need to count the currency. He just stood looking at it, feeling sick. Where there had been eight packets neatly lying, now there were seven. Damn it, he thought. Goddamn it. You incredible, beautiful bitch! Now he would have to tell Joshua Courtland. And God knew he didn't want to do that. He wished suddenly he'd left for Virginia about this time yesterday, or better yet, never heard the name Courtland.

Joshua didn't come back to the bank after lunch. The humid heat made his heart pains worse. Jonathon knew it must be that. Everyone else had been told a 'headache.' Elinor had met him for supper after that. So Jonathon had bided his time, gotten Mandy settled upstairs, and waited now in the parlor with a brandy, dreading the few, terrible words he had to say to Joshua Courtland.

Carriage wheels rattled outside, the sound loud through the open windows, mixed with the faint, sweet smell of summer honeysuckle. Elinor's soft laugh drifted through on the warm breeze, puffing the white sheer curtains, but she went directly upstairs as she entered. Joshua's footsteps came toward the parlor. For a moment, Jonathon's resolve nearly broke, a cold sweat broke out on his palms, and the brandy glass nearly slipped from his grip. Oh God, he thought. What am I going to say?

"Jonathon!" Joshua's smile was genuine as he stepped into the parlor and found the young Rebel there. "Lovely night, isn't it? I love the smell of July."

Jonathon nodded. His hands were trembling, but he smiled too, reaching for another glass. "Virginia smells even better—at least I remember it that way. Brandy, sir?"

Joshua nodded. He laid his walking stick and tall, formal black hat to one side, stepping forward. "Speaking of Virginia, I had a letter today from my son, Chase. He complains the campaign is too slow and the Georgia summers are too hot."

"The more so when you're suited in dark blue, I imagine. I never had much trouble in gray."

If Jonathon's voice was strained, Joshua didn't seem to notice. He chuckled as he turned around. This was a standing game between him and the young Rebel. Teasing the other about being on opposite sides. It was far less strained than trying to avoid the subject altogether. Less chance of an explosive argument, too, than if they discussed it seriously. "He also says he's sick to death of peaches."

"If the whole army feels that way, I'll write to President Davis and suggest they manage another crop of them."

"The CSA works miracles, now?"

"They have been for years. We've still got Richmond, haven't we?"

"Touché." Joshua chuckled, sipping his brandy, a relaxed smile on his face.

Jonathon glanced at him and took a deep breath. It's about your daughter, sir, that beautiful whore you see only with a doting father's eyes. She's the one taking money from—

"Chase asked after you and your family, Jonathon, I gathered he hasn't gotten my last letter, telling him how splendidly Bonnie is doing, and how great a help you've become at the bank. Speaking of that, I was thinking just this afternoon that I've never discussed an equitable financial arrangement with—"

"Joshua, I've something I must tell you." Jonathon interrupted before he lose the courage to speak at all. The older man blinked, startled, and his age began to show suddenly on his face. For a moment, silence was loud. In that instant, Jonathon's resolve broke. To the sudden fear in the older man's eyes, he managed a faint smile. An apologetic shrug. "I was telling your daughter earlier, I've decided it's time we returned to Virginia."

Joshua Courtland blinked again, no longer smiling. "Because of the way the war's going?"

"No."

"Because you're unhappy at the bank?"

291

"No, sir."

There was silence. Joshua raised one gray brow. "Elinor then. It's got to be Elinor."

For a moment, Jonathon felt the blood drain from his face, his stomach turn over sickly. Good God, he knew. Joshua knew it was his daughter stealing from the frozen accounts. An instant later, he realized it wasn't so. It was Whitney, he meant—the obviously strained relationship between the two women. "No, sir." Jonathon shook his head, turning away. He understood suddenly that he could never tell Joshua the truth. Never. "No, sir. It has nothing to do with Lady Bennington. I think Whitney's homesick. I have a lot of matters at Blytheswood and Cool Spring, too, that need my attention. And now, while the Valley is once more in Confederate hands, my first duty seems obvious."

"But Doctor Lacey said he'd asked after Blytheswood. Some of the officers under Hunter had headquartered there briefly. He said it sounded as if Jewel was running it to perfection."

"I know that, but . . ." Jonathon only shrugged, stiffly, making it a wordless denial. He was thinking as he spoke. His announcement about returning to Virginia had surprised him, too. Why, he wondered? Do you really want to return? Or was he afraid to be around when Elnior was caught stealing from her own father, threatening everything he'd spent a lifetime building— his bank, his fortune, his good name—and not giving a damn while she did it. There was no doubt in his mind, Joshua Courtland *would* catch her. He was too smart. Too sincerely concerned. God help them both.

"Well, I'd, ah . . ." Joshua shrugged and cleared his throat. All the old, terrible weight of running the bank alone began to descend upon him. It felt as if it was smothering the life breath out of his lungs. "I promised Miranda a party next Sunday, in the garden. You'll stay for that, at least."

Jonathon suddenly felt like crying but he nodded, avoiding Joshua's eyes. "Of course, and I'm sorry, sir. I truly am. If it were just myself . . ."

"I've been expecting you to leave, Jonathon. Don't feel as though you need to apologize. This was never planned as a long-term commitment on either of our parts." Joshua said it brusquely to conceal his disappointment. Why had he ever assumed the young Virginian would stay? Chase, I need you home, son. I'm too old. I can't do it anymore all by myself—the bank, Elinor, the wretched coalition so gleefully discussing the President's failing health. Why won't this damn war end? Good night, Jonathon. See you at breakfast."

"Good night, sir." There was so much more Jonathon would liked to have said, more explanations, something to soften the pain Joshua had mostly managed to conceal. But men didn't speak together of such things. Not even a man he liked as well as the older Courtland, not even the man he owed such a debt to. Maybe it was for the best. Nothing he could have said would have changed anything, anyway. That was the most damnable part of all.

Jonathon frowned suddenly, turning to lay his unfinished brandy aside with a sudden movement. You're a damn fool, he accused himself. You never needed to tell Joshua at all. There was a far better way to stop Elinor from stealing from the bank.

He hurried on the stairs, but soundlessly, not wanting either Joshua or Whitney, downstairs, to hear the direction of his steps. He didn't knock at her door, just opened it and stepped inside.

"Major?"

She had been undressing from dinner. Long, honey-blonde waves fell free down her nearly bare back. Her white silk camisole showed high, pale, perfect breasts about a sky-blue ribbon as she turned. "Unannounced is better than not come at all." She unfastened the snaps of her hooped petticoat as casually as if he weren't there. The low-burning lamp flickered in the window's breeze, shadows darkened and changed on the wide bed behind her. Its red velvet canopy was the color of fresh blood, white roses stood in an emerald vase. She smiled. "I wasn't expecting you for another week or so. Not that I'm complaining. Is poor little Whitney 'indisposed' tonight?"

He frowned, taken aback. He understood her reference but, as a matter of fact, Whitney hadn't been 'indisposed' as women regularly were, though she'd weaned the baby weeks ago.

"Cat got your tongue?" She smiled, stepping closer. Gardenias floated around her in a thick, sweet smell. Remembering that scent in the bank vault, Jonathon felt nearly sick. He drew away.

"This isn't a social visit."

"Oh. Maybe it could be."

"You're taking money from your father's bank. I want it to stop. I want you to replace what's been taken. Swear you'll do it or I'll tell your father before I leave for Virginia this week."

Something cold flashed momentarily in Elinor's green eyes, something darkly dangerous beneath the still waters of an emerald pond. Then it was gone. "Do, Major. Tell him, I mean. It's the only honorable thing to do, isn't it?"

She smiled and Jonathon stood silent, startled, returning her gaze. Why should her lack of denial surprise him? Yes, an ordinary person would deny it, at least try, but he knew well that Elinor was no ordinary person.

"Of course, Major, you realize it will pain my father deeply, if he believes you, as it will pain your wife when I tell her of what's passed between us." She smiled more brightly, as if amused, raising one brow. "Will she believe me, do you think? Or shall I be trying to remember something *specific* to offer as proof?"

Jonathon felt the edges of a trap snap shut as he stood returning her stare. She'd called his bluff on telling Joshua—raised him by threatening to tell Whitney of Jonathon's own guilt. And he didn't *doubt* she *would* without a blink of an eye. Whereas he had already realized, he could not expose her. "Unless I wait until Whitney is safely back in Virginia, Elinor. And then speak to your father."

294

She didn't look worried, merely shrugged and stepped forward, raising one hand to the top button of his shirt. "Go ahead if you want to. It will hurt him far more than it hurts me. I may not even be here that much longer." She raised her eyes to catch and hold his. In the shadows her face was sculptured perfection, her golden hair gleaming like a halo. She moved closer so her breasts lightly pushed against his chest, and slipped the button open. "Now, if you're quite through threatening me with exposure of my horrendous crime, dear Rebel, let's finish our discussion in more pleasurable fashion." She moved her hand to the second button, smiling faintly, swaying her hips forward to brush his. "I might be willing to make a different sort of deal. How badly do you want me to stop taking that money?"

Jonathon stood still, forcing himself to remain motionless. His mind warned him to run. His body, beginning to stir under her assault, cried to yield. Either would please her—and amuse her. Indifference, though, if he could manage it, might weaken her defenses. "Why, Elinor?"

"Why not?" Her voice was husky, soft, her fingers starting on the third button. "Why take the money? Or why tell Whitney?"

"Why be what you are?" For an instant, her fingers froze, a strange expression flickered across her face.

Elinor raised her eyes to his and dropped her hand. For a moment, she stood motionless, reading his eyes, then suddenly slapped him hard across the face. Jonathon only shrugged, raising his hand to touch the blood on his lip. "Be warned, Elinor. The decision is yours. I'll do nothing now, but if you persist, if you take more from that vault, then here or from Virginia, I'll find a way to stop you. Do you understand me? I may tell Joshua. I may write your brother Chase instead. But I'll do something. I owe your father more than to let you continue stealing from him, because if you do, eventually he's going to catch you himself and that would be even worse for him."

She stood silent a moment, watching his eyes. "Have you met my brother?"

Jonathon was startled again, thrown off balance. No further anger. No more threats. A whole different subject.

"You'd get on famously, if you haven't already met him. You're a great deal alike." She smiled again, but a kind of amused cruelty gleamed in her eyes. "Brothers and sisters, as they say . . ."

He had the feeling she meant far more than she said, but the point of it eluded him. He frowned faintly, warily, watching her. Brothers and sisters? Chase Courtland and Leanna?

Elinor slipped the last of of his shirt buttons open and slid one cool, slender hand within to caress his muscled belly. Jonathon flinched at her touch, but she seemed not to notice. He gritted his teeth against a surge of dark passions and stood still. It was incredible to him, at the age of twenty-six—a husband, a father; what he'd been through in the war, in the hospital, in that godawful humiliation of a prison camp, to discover this dark side of himself now. To know so clearly what she was and to want her still in spite of it.

"Stay, won't you, Major?"

It was a gentle plea, surprisingly soft. Almost like a child's. In spite of himself, Jonathon's will weakened and he looked down at the lovely contours of her too-perfect face. The dimness of the low-burning bed-stand lamp only heightened her exquisite beauty. Her lips were moist and full, invitingly parted, her emerald green eyes shaded almost to shyness by long, thick lashes. Rounded shoulders the color of new cream, and breasts he knew too well the soft perfection of.

"Good night, Lady Bennington." His voice was husky with the effort of restraint, he shook his head as he turned away. Quick as a cat, she curled her fingertips into claws and raked the bare skin over his ribs as she withdrew her hand. Jonathon grunted in pain, jerking away in reflex quick enough that only one narrow furrow was pinked with blood. He frowned a wordless warning as he stepped away, beginning to rebutton his shirt. Elinor's eyes flashed anger, her mouth curled in an unpretty pout. For a moment, she looked every bit of her age and decades more. "Remember what I told you," Jonathon murmured in a deceptively soft voice. "You'll find I don't make idle threats. You leave your father's bank vaults alone—or else."

"Good night, Major." Elinor's eyes were green ice, undaunted. She stepped past him to open the door.

His mouth was set in a grim line as he nodded once and stepped wide around her out into the hallway. "Good night." The door shut behind him, loudly, but he didn't look back. He was confused and baffled—by her, by his reaction to her, by the situation. All the more reason to leave for Virginia, he thought to himself. Being caught in the middle of two warring armies was beginning to look like child's play compared to the intricasies of the situation here.

Whitney heard Jonathon's footsteps out in the hallway and brushed hastily at the tears in her eyes. She couldn't be, she told herself with the sinking feeling of a conviction no longer secure. She was hardly over the twins' birth—had only stopped nursing a few weeks before. But she'd had no monthly flow since. And this morning, that awful, faint stir of nausea when she'd sat down to breakfast. Oh please, God, I mustn't be pregnant. Not again. Not so soon. Swollen and misshapen. Sick every morning. The perfect Lady Bennington only waiting for the chance. . . .

"You're still up, Whit?"

Jonathon's voice sounded strained, but she dared not look at him too closely to guess why. She didn't want him to see the telltale redness of her own eyes. She'd cried far too much these past weeks as it was. Men lost patience with a woman forever weeping. Even men who loved their wives as dearly as she knew Jonathon loved her. "Just going to bed." She reached to turn the lamp out, knowing he could undress by the faint glow of the outside moonlight, knowing he couldn't see her face too well.

Jonathon was relieved. He turned to one side as he unbuttoned his shirt, hiding the oozing blood of Elinor's nails. "I love you, sweet."

"I love you, too." Her voice broke, but he seemed not to notice. Maybe the click of opening the armoire door had covered it.

"I was just thinking, now you're well enough, would you prefer we move upstairs? Mandy could take this room?"

Upstairs. Closer to Lady Bennington's room. Was that good or bad?

"Or maybe there's no reason to bother." Jonathon finished undressing and came to sit on the edge of the bed. It creaked under his weight, and the mattress tilted slightly toward him. Whitney reached her hand out to touch his bare knee, thinking again how handsome he was, the more so in moonlight. His hair black in the darkness, his finely cut face shadowed, the muscles of his bare, lean body a beautiful interplay of softness and strength. No wonder Lady Bennington desired him. He didn't look at her, but reached to take her hand. "I was thinking today, this afternoon—"tonight, he thought to himself ruefully, when I could feel myself wanting that beautiful whore—"that maybe it was time we went back to Virginia." He managed a smile, glanced briefly over to see her eyes widen in startlement. He tightened his hand over hers. Please, Whit, don't argue.

"That problem at the bank, Jon? The money missing. That's solved?"

"No, but . . ." That's one of the problems, Whitney. "But Joshua will be able to solve that if anyone can. I'm not doing anything about it here any longer, anyway."

"You've told him already?"

"Just this evening," he shrugged apologetically, turning his head for her eyes and holding them this time. "I would have waited, spoken to you first, but . . ."

"That's all right, Jon. I understand." *Virginia. If she were pregnant, there'd be the same problems—no doctors in the area with the necessary training, no hospitals, no medicines. . . .*

"The Valley's in Confederate hands again. It might be now or never in that sense. When Early retreats as he'll have to do, the Yankees will follow him up the Valley, and if Cool Spring and Blytheswood are both still essentially abandoned . . ."

"I know. I've thought the same thing. Virginia it is then. The sooner the better." She started a smile, found to her surprise it was effortless even though tears started to her eyes. *I love you so desperately, Jon. Enough to risk the baby if there is one. Enough to risk dying, myself. Just to get you away from her.*

"You're sure?" He frowned faintly, catching the glimmer of tears. "Whitney, if you're afraid of the armies—"

"I'm sure. When?"

"This week, I think. No sense delaying it beyond Mandy's party."

Whitney nodded, keeping her smile. For a moment, fear threatened and she forced it away with iron determination. *I've been enough of a problem to him, caused him to make enough decisions he would rather not have made. I won't do that again.* "That sounds wonderful, Jon. I couldn't be more pleased."

His frown disappeared, a gentle smile took its place. "I must confess, home sounds awfully good to me. By this time next week, we'll be carrying our things up the stairs and chasing dust and cobwebs out of the old place."

"And planting crops."

"And chasing livestock."

I'll never be able to carry this baby with all the work we'll have to do. "Once a 'damn Reb,' always a 'damn Reb' I guess." She leaned forward to kiss his hand, her

299

chestnut hair falling over the warm ivory of his bare leg. He reached one hand down into it and bent over to return her kiss. It might be a bittersweet homecoming, but he would never guess that, she swore to herself. Not even if it cost her life.

Chapter Twenty

Atlanta lay hot and lazy in the mid-July heat. As morning turned to afternoon, traffic on its dusty streets dwindled, windows were closed and drapes drawn to keep the morning's cooler air inside. Shades were pulled down on shop windows and iced tea and lemonade were brought out from back kitchens to stand sweating in parlors on silver trays. It was a peculiar place, an odd mixture, caught by the declaration of war between being merely the railroad terminal it had begun as and the fashionable city it might have become. Inside one of its quaint, tall and narrow townhouses, Leanna sat sewing, trying to ignore the familiar but still oppressive heat, startled suddenly by Stewart's loud exclamation of disgust. Since arriving in Atlanta in late May, his humor had markedly improved. The war had been going well for the South. Now though, apparently, something major had gone awry.

"He should have gone into Washington that first day! Lee should have abandoned his defense of Richmond and slipped north to hit the city from the other side," Stewart's blue eyes flashed anger as he tossed the telegram down on the parlor table near where Leanna sat. "They've lost the chance of a lifetime! They could have burned the city to the ground!"

She paled, pricking her finger with a mending needle no longer very sharp, then frowned at both the instant of pain and Stewart's words. "Burned it? Burned Washington, you mean? But the women and children, the hospitals there . . ."

"Damn the women and children. They're Yankees, too, aren't they? Why should we be so careful of them anymore? The Yankees aren't of ours."

"That's the very thing you hate the Yankees so desperately for doing, Stewart. Now you're saying we should be doing it, too?"

"It's time we faced facts, my dear." Stewart's eyes, when he turned back to her, were pale-blue ice, and Leanna felt a shudder run up her spine between her shoulder blades. That terrible coldness, that ruthlessness. . . . She had seen it before once—where? "We're fighting under enough of a disadvantage. We can no longer afford gentlemanly warfare."

"General Lee seems to be doing all right," she pointed out in a quiet voice, holding her husband's eyes and trying not to be afraid of what she saw there.

"Oh, yes, our good cavalier general. Limiting warfare to opposing armies only. Shades of a medieval jousting challenge. Honor above all."

There was a bitter quirk to his mouth as he spoke. The train, Leanna remembered. Stewart's expression had been much the same as he'd looked at the captured Yankee officer on the platform. Not compassion. Only cruelty. An utter lack of human feeling.

"Fighting so honorably is losing us the war."

"I thought honor was what this war was all about." Leanna laid her sewing down in her lap, conscious of how fearfully her heart was pounding, how loud its beat was in her ears. "A commitment to a just and honorable cause. To resist the Northern invasion of a new country with every legal and moral right to its independence." Stewart said nothing, but his expression didn't change. When Leanna continued to look at him, he only shrugged. "If we abandon our commitment to honor, we defeat ourselves. The Yankees won't have to bother."

"You ignore the fact there's a war on. One we happen to be losing. Chivalry is a disadvantage in warfare. The Yankees know that. Look at Grant in Virginia. Sherman here. Honor be damned if the tactical advantages dictate that. So they're doing their job, the job of any good soldier—getting the war won for their side."

No, she thought. Chase was a good soldier. And he didn't sacrifice women and children to be one. "You would have approved of the Yankees burning Blytheswood then, Stewart? Burning our fields? Slaughtering our livestock?"

His face took on a strange expression, but he shrugged. "On a personal level, obviously I'm glad they didn't."

"Major Courtland seemed able to combine both honor and efficiency as a soldier." God, how it struck at her heart just saying his name aloud. She held Stewart's eyes, making a desperate effort to conceal her thoughts.

"Did he?" Stewart shrugged as he turned away. "I said I was glad he didn't burn the plantation. I didn't say I approved of that decision in a tactical sense."

Fear touched Leanna's heart. Her eyes opened wider. For a moment there was silence. Her voice, when she finally spoke, was almost a whisper. "I'm beginning to think being a very good soldier is a very terrible thing to be."

Stewart replied with a quick sigh of exasperation, turning to face her once more. "If we lose this war, honor won't keep Blytheswood for you, Leanna. It won't keep Cool Spring, or the Richmond house. It won't keep my plantations in South Carolina or the Negroes working the cotton fields there. You won't be able to eat your honor when there's no farmland giving harvest! You won't be able to wear it when winter comes and you're sitting there shivering!" He frowned as he spoke, anger plain on his face, his mouth grim and set. "Honor is a luxury, Leanna! One I'm more than willing to give up if it means keeping everything else!" He stood staring at her for a long minute, his eyes cold and strangely calculating. Finally, he spoke again, more quietly, still watching her shock-paled face. "And what about you, my dear. Sitting there so horrified at what I'm saying? What's more precious to you? Your conscience? Or Blytheswood?"

She didn't answer. Really, she couldn't answer. I don't know, she thought fearfully. God keep me from such a choice. . . . So this was the full measure of the horror of war. Not only the tangible destruction—homes, fields, livestock, the terrible cost of human lives. This, too. The intangible destruction. The ruination from the inside out. She understood now as she hadn't then, suddenly remembering Doc Lacey's warning on a cold December evening. 'You'll have to answer that question yourself, Mrs. Leighton. We all will.'

Stewart's hand startled her as it dropped lightly to touch her hair. "Sorry, sweetheart. I forget sometimes you're just a woman." His mouth was curved in a familiar, distant smile. His blue eyes no longer held anger, but a remote sort of tolerance. "It's my job to make decisions like that. I'll take care of the war. You just worry about getting your mending done." His smile widened briefly and he touched her shoulder before he turned away. "Big night tonight. General Johnston himself's coming in from outside the city. He'll be at the party for a while with us. I'll be meeting with him after dinner but you'll stay in the ballroom. I'll assign a couple of junior officers to keep you dancing."

"Is he going to surrender Atlanta to the Yankees, Stewart? Without even making a stand somewhere?"

"That's not for you to worry about, dear. You let us menfolk handle such unpleasantries. I'll tell you if or when it's time to pack."

Stewart smiled back over his shoulder as he disappeared out the parlor door. She heard his boot steps on their 'borrowed' townhouse's oak-planked floor. A moment later, the front door opened and she watched Stewart's straight, well-formed, golden handsomeness through the sheer dotted swiss of the ruffled curtains at the parlor windows. But a fear she'd never felt before kept gnawing away and the homey little townhouse with its pretty wrought-iron railings and airy French doors and chintz-covered Heppelwhite didn't satisfy her sudden desperate longing to be home—at Blytheswood. The only place in the world that had ever been home to her in her heart. I'm afraid of my own husband, she thought with a start of shock. Afraid of what else he'd sacrifice in his ruthless determination to win what had become obviously—to him, at least—a very personal war.

Chase adjusted his ocular glass on the top of the hill, looking toward the city. Peachtree Creek was about four miles ahead and below. He could just see its silver ribbon through the scraggly, tall pines and overgrown weeds and scrub that lay between him and it. It was a pretty day. The sky was bright blue, with scattered white clouds that looked like puffed cotton, only cleaner. It was a relief when the sun went under one, a break from the baking Georgia summer sun. The date was July 15th. It had taken two and a half months to get here, along the Western and Atlantic Railroad from Tennessee. He ran the place names through his mind in a familiar litany. Ringold, Tunnel Hill, Dalton, Rocky Face Ridge, Resaca, Oostanoula River, Calhoun, Allatoona Pass, New Hope Church, Dallas, the Mountains—Pine and Kennesaw, Marietta, the Chattahoochee River . . . two and a half months to here. And here, Chase decided silently, lowering the glass, they looked likely to stay for awhile.

The Rebels had dug in practically under the shadow of the city itself, their backs to supplies and arms, their faces grim and stubbornly set toward the distant dark-blue Yankee line. He sighed and raised his forearm to wipe the sweat from his hatband off on his dust-covered sleeve, then raised his hand to wipe the dust off his face and resettled his hat. This hard red clay made the damndest mess.

"Shall I give the men the go-ahead to break out their tents, sir?"

Chase smiled wryly, grunting an answer as he began to turn his horse. "Tell them to build houses, the way I see it. Johnston isn't going anywhere. And until he does, neither are we."

Miranda's party on Sunday was a huge success. Joshua Courtland had made sure it would be. He's hired the pony-ride man from Rittenhouse Square and found a magician who produced rabbits from hats. Had she been staying in Philadelphia, Mandy wouldn't have had a Sunday free for months with the invitations extended to her that day. Sufficiently dazzled, the other children forgot she 'talked funny' with her Virginian drawl, forgot she was one of those 'darn Rebs' and courted her affection with frenzied zeal. Joshua watched with a grim smile. Perhaps we are born that way, he mused to himself. Perhaps I, with a sense of greater goals, am but a freak of nature. Maybe Roland Hodges better represents the true nature of man. Perhaps it's better she leaves tomorrow for Virginia, and won't have time here to learn what it really is that the other children so suddenly covet, what people, all her life, in this selfish world will actually covet—her success, and not her heart.

As the last carriage left and sunset streaked the sky with golds and reds to match the colors of the roses blooming along the outside walk, Mrs. Eaton, the housekeeper, took the tired little girl upstairs to go to bed. The adults gathered in the parlor below for a last evening together before the morning train trip to Washington, D.C. From there, they'd travel by special pass across one of the heavily guarded bridges out of the city, on into Maryland, and then finally down into the Valley itself. Joshua Courtland tried to conceal how badly he thought he was going to miss the Virginian family. His constraint, and the rather odd, strained feeling that had persisted among all of them all week long since the night Jonathon had announced the departure, lent an awkward air to the superficial good-will of the farewells.

"Yes, we're all ready, I think. You haven't, by any chance, a tintype of yourself, do you, Joshua? Miranda will miss you dreadfully, and she made me promise to ask." Whitney managed a smile, trying not to cry. "Better yet, promise to visit."

"Visiting in the midst of warring armies is hard enough on younger men, dear." Joshua tried to make light of his refusal, smiling. He caught Jonathon's quick, knowing glance, but didn't react to it. A trip to Virginia, even assuming it didn't kill him, simply wasn't in the cards. He

306

could not risk the time. Lincoln *was* failing, the coalition already plotting a successor if he withdrew from the Presidential race. Now, without Jonathon, more of the bank work, too, would fall to him. "I'm not sure about a picture, either. I've none on hand, but I could send one, I suppose, if the mails ever get through."

"I have this little one." Elinor was bored and restless. God, those oh-so-precious farewells! She opened her locket with an overly abrupt gesture, stepping forward. "Lord knows I don't need it."

There was an instant of strained silence. Whitney glanced covertly at Joshua's face, embarrassed for him by his daughter's tactlessness. Almost at once, Elinor seemed to catch herself, smiling and reaching out to touch her father's arm.

"I treasured it, of course, in England, but now that I'm here again, living with him, I hardly need my father's picture hung around my neck."

Whitney murmured a strained thank-you, avoiding anyone's eyes as she reached to take the oval miniature Lady Bennington held out to her in such graceful disdain. She always did that to her somehow, Whitney thought. Elinor always managed to make her feel like an awkward school girl, as ladylike in comparison as a field hand would be. She saw her glance toward Jonathon with a different smile, and tried not to show she'd seen it. "I'll put it in here," Whitney spoke aloud, mostly to avoid the silence. "I have Jon and Leanna in here now." She raised her gold locket to snap open the clasp. "Perhaps when we get home, I'll buy a locket for Mandy and give the picture to her then for it."

"You have one of Jonathon's sister?"

Whitney glanced up, startled by the intensity of the older man's voice.

"Might I see it?" Joshua reached as Whitney took the locket off her neck. Jonathon gave him a strange, puzzled look, but he didn't notice. He studied the face in the rather formal, overposed miniature curiously. The dark hair lent a resemblance to the young man standing beside him, but there were differences, too. A sort of wistful look about the eyes that even the formality of the pose didn't quite hide. A combination of strength and softness around the young woman's mouth. Joshua smiled faintly and nodded once in understanding. Sad as it was, he thought he could understand his son's choice. "Very lovely," was all he said aloud, looking down at the open locket. "Very lovely, indeed."

"So this is the face that started it all?" Elinor glanced over her father's shoulder only briefly. She smiled and shrugged. "I expected more."

Whitney felt hot color rising, but she managed to speak softly. "Leanna is a beautiful girl, Lady Bennington. And a very dear sister. If you—"

"I'm not criticizing anyone," Elinor shrugged again, smiling more widely as she glanced toward where Jonathon stood frowning faintly. "I'm just saying I prefer the brother to the sister. Which is to be expected, I suppose. Chase and I agree on very little."

"Elinor," Joshua frowned a warning.

She smiled and began to turn away. "All right, all right, dear Papa. Chase can chose whomever he likes to warm his Virginia winters. What do I care?"

Jonathan went rigid. He felt Whitney's hand touch his forearm and he shrugged it off.

Joshua frowned harder. "That's crude and nasty, Elinor. You forget yourself," he snapped icily.

"What do you mean?" Jonathon interrupted, staring at Elinor's back. She paused a moment, then turned, smiling, raising one brow, her eyes sparkling with amusement. She was no longer bored.

Joshua closed the locket and stepped toward the young Rebel. "Jonathon, please!"

"What the hell do you mean saying that?" Jonathon felt feverishly hot. Not Leanna. Not his sister. Penley women were above suspicion.

"Well, why else do you think you're here, for God's sake?" Elinor almost laughed. "Think we're running a way station for pregnant women and captured Confederates? You sister bought your ticket in the most elemen-

tal of ways, dear Jonathon. Had that really never occurred to you?"

Yes, it *had* occurred to him, Jonathon realized, but
denial had begun in the same split second. He'd been so
sure of Leanna!

"That's not true." Joshua was ashen with fury. "Elinor,
I won't tolerate this kind of thing!"

Jonathon hardly heard him. He had turned to Whitney,
catching and holding her eyes with a furious question.

"Jon, we're leaving tomorrow. Please, just let it *be*!"

"Damn it! I have a right to know! I confess I wondered in the beginning why some Yankees—strangers to
us—would suddenly be falling all over themselves offering such generosity. Did you know all along? Did you
know from the beginning that Leanna was whoring
with some damn Yankee?"

Whitney's eyes blazed. She raised her hand and
Jonathon grabbed it, painfully hard.

"Didn't I have a right to know, Whitney? Exactly
what kind of deal it was?"

"There was no deal! Especially none as filthy as
that!" Whitney jerked her hand free with a struggle, her
eyes full of tears even while she trembled with anger.
They'd been so close . . . leaving tomorrow. Why couldn't
it have been left unsaid for just one more day? "You
know Leanna better than that! Or you should! Now
you know the Courtlands better, too."

"My son fell in love with your sister," Joshua grimaced against chest pains rapidly getting worse. He
stepped forward, taking the young man's arm and holding it despite an immediate shrug of anger. "But that's
all there was, Jonathon. He fell in love with her and for
her sake asked me to aid you and your family." He tried
to take a deeper breath and couldn't, and spoke anyway,
desperate to make Jonathon understand. "Don't leave
for Virginia thinking I, or we, are like that, son. I'm too
fond of you."

Jonathon clenched his jaw, glancing involuntarily toward the three gilt-framed portraits he'd noticed the
first day he'd arrived. The older son, dead. Beautiful

Elinor, with that strange smile. And Chase, whom he knew only as Major Courtland. The Yankee officer who'd occupied his sister's home, and saved his daughter's life, he reminded himself with an effort. The portrait showed only a young man, there in his dress uniform, with a certain kindness in his brown-glazed eyes that appeared at odds with the weapons buckled around his dark frock coat's waist. He felt Whitney's hand on his arm again and nodded this time, stiffly.

"They couldn't help what they felt, Jon," Whitney murmured softly. "Stewart had been gone so long." She said no more than that, but waited for the subtle change of Jonathon's face. Yes, he knew what remained unspoken. He had served in the field with his brother-in-law for over two years. He'd grown to know Stewart Leighton more than well enough. "Knowing Leanna, and as well as I grew to know the Major, I don't believe there wa anything dishonorable in their conduct. I just don't believe it."

Jonathon nodded once more. You were deliberately blind, he acknowledged to himself. You can't entirely blame the others. No wonder Joshua had been so sure Leanna had not been part of the partisan ambush on the Yankees. No wonder Whitney had been so sure last winter that neither Leanna nor Blytheswood were in any real danger despite the two hundred and some enemy soldiers crawling all over the place. You'd have known it too, Jon, he told himself, if you'd bothered to think it out.

"I certainly didn't mean to stir up such a royal fuss," Elinor spoke sweetly, glancing over her shoulder as she seated herself on one of the matching green velvet settees. The peach of her gown made a startling contrast. The gilt-framed mirror on the floral fabric wall hung at an angle to her there. By some quirk, when Jonathon glanced toward her, it gave the impression there were two of her, and he frowned. "The way you were so quick to jump to such conclusions," she raised one brow, smiling, "one might think you had a guilty conscience yourself."

Joshua frowned again. Whitney paled but bit her lip,

refusing to look at either Lady Bennington or her husband.

"*Have* you a guilty conscience, Major?" She smiled wider, her green eyes gleaming with laughter as they held his. "Perhaps if you do, this is the time to air it."

The last of his anger faded as Jonathon turned to stare down at her. Elinor was enjoying this. As she hadn't enjoyed the children this afternoon, as she hadn't enjoyed the earlier pleasantries. There was mocking amusement in the eyes that stared back at him, and more—a wordless, taunting challenge. Go on, she dared him. Strike back at me for saying my brother used your precious sister like a common whore. Go on and tell my father what I've done, and watch how fast I tell sweet Whitney of other things.

The ticking of the mantle clock was loud. A carriage rattled by outside. The room brightened abruptly as the street lamps outside were lit. Still no one spoke. Jonathon felt a sudden, gut level revulsion at the thought of leaving tomorrow, leaving Joshua Courtland alone with this destructive monster.

"If you've something to say, Lady Bennington, then say it." He met her challenge finally, speaking in a level voice.

Elinor shrugged daintily, still smiling. "I'm only saying, we all have our secrets, don't we? Everyone in this room." A heartbeat of silence followed. Everyone was conscious of secret guilts, wondering, just for an instant, how she could possibly have divined them. "You and I, for example, my dear Jonathon. Just think of all that has passed so pleasurably between us, before your far-too-pregnant wife could manage the trip—"

"Elinor! I will hear no more filth from your mouth! Daughter or not, while you live in my house, you will control yourself!" Joshua jerked to his feet, ghostly pale in furious horror. "You've done enough damage already, or tried to, with your filthy insinuations! Slandering your own brother was bad enough without dragging—" A terrible, searing agony interrupted him. He choked for breath, staggering and trembling still in a fury he

311

could no longer express. The room began to lose its focus. He grabbed instinctively for the wood frame of the chair as he began to weaken. "Jonathon!" he managed to croak, choking and wheezing on even the single word.

For a stricken instant, Jonathon couldn't move. Thoughts came too fast, contradicting themselves, leaving a numb, chilling confusion, a desperate urgency to do something without knowing what. But what seemed like hours was actually only moments. Elinor's smug smile froze on her face. Whitney stared in stunned horror. Jonathon leapt forward, catching the stricken man in his arms as he began to fall. "Get me the brandy!" He ordered it over his shoulder, easing Joshua onto the chair and ripping at the tight collar and the tie he wore. "Whitney, move for God's sake! Get the brandy! Then run for the servants' quarters! Tell them to fetch a doctor."

Joshua's hand clenched feebly over his. Jonathon nodded again and again, relieved to hear the sudden sounds of people moving behind him. Whitney, her own face nearly as white as Joshua's, thrust a filled glass into his hands and he put it quickly to Joshua's mouth. An instant later, he heard the back door slam, the cry of voices outside, someone running toward the stable. "It's all right, Joshua." He tried to assure the older man confidently, hiding his own fear, the sick trembling of his own hands. "No, don't try to speak. I'll get you upstairs. And the doctor will be here in a moment." He nodded once more, no longer sure whether the older man was entirely conscious. His face above the salt-and-pepper whiskers was turning a terrible bluish gray. Jonathon blinked, realizing with a distant sense of astonishment that there were tears in his eyes. One ran from the corner of his eyes as he closed them. Jesus, I'm sorry, he thought. My fault. All the confrontations. I forgot. In my anger I just forgot. Oh God, don't die! Please, for the love of heaven, after all you've done for us, don't die!

* * *

312

It was well after midnight, the big stone house softly speaking with the sounds it only seemed to make this late at night—the hissing of the gas-fed chandeliers, the creak of timbers settling in the roof, far away the scrape of a chair being drawn over bare floors in the servants' quarters behind the kitchen. Whitney sat silently in the darkened parlor watching Jonathon standing at the bottom of the shadowed stairs. The doctor had come down at last. He and Jon were speaking in voices too low for her to hear, but it occurred to her suddenly that the doctor was dressed all in black, even to his tall black top hat. He reminded her of the undertakers that had seemed omnipresent on the Washington streets, with twenty-four Union military hospitals there, they'd been in great demand through these terrible years.

Jonathon nodded a last time and thanked the man. He managed a weary, faint smile as he turned toward the parlor where Whitney sat waiting, and stepped inside. "He says he thinks Joshua will live. He hopes there's no damage to the brain, but it's too soon yet to be sure."

"Oh, thank God!" Whitney reached out to grip Jon's hand. In the darkness, her eyes sparkled with tears of relief. For a moment, she closed them, drawing a deep breath, tightening her grip on Jonathon's hand as the silence lengthened.

"Whitney, I think it's pretty clear that we can't even think of leaving for home for the time being."

"No, we mustn't go now. I understand that already, Jon." She kept her grip on his hand as she glanced up, trying to smile. "Joshua will need you now, and we've quite a debt to repay."

For a moment, he said nothing, only held her eyes, searching them. How had his world come apart so quickly? Leanna and the Courtland son, Elinor's cruel admission, Joshua's sudden attack. He felt Virginia fading away, like a sweet dream, hard to recall upon waking. It was almost as if, in his mind, he heard the door back to it slowly closing.

"Is Lady Bennington sitting with him?" Whitney turned away, dropping Jon's hand awkwardly.

Jon's eyes followed her with a silent question. "Yes, I think so."

"She should be. She caused it."

Jonathon shrugged, his eyes dark and grim as he watched his wife's back. "Maybe partially. I certainly didn't help. And I knew Joshua had heart problems before this."

"No, it was her." Whitney's voice was a whisper and she half turned, glancing superstitiously up through the solid parlor ceiling toward where Lady Bennington sat. "She's wicked, Jon—very, very wicked. I don't think she'd really care if she did kill him."

He felt the short hairs on his neck begin to rise and shrugged at such foolishness, frowning as he spoke. "You don't know the half of it, Whit." She threw him a quick glance, fear lying in her eyes. "It's one of the reasons I was anxious to return to Virginia. She's the one taking money from Joshua's bank."

"Oh, no!"

"Oh, yes, I'm afraid. I threatened to expose her to her father. I'm not sure she'd care if I did. But I couldn't do it to Joshua." He shrugged, still frowning. He felt his wife's eyes on him and forced his head up to meet them. His guilt was bad enough without adding cowardice to it. "And Whitney, about the other things she said, the business about my—"

"I don't believe her." Whitney spoke almost too quickly, paling. She felt the sudden nausea of fear; her heart beat faster, but with a dull, dead beat.

"But Whitney, I have to—"

"No, Jon." She shook her head as she stepped toward him. "I've known for some time she was after you. Please, listen to me for a moment. What she implied tonight about you and her is just part of a vicious, senseless desire. She wants to ruin us, Jon, don't you see that? It isn't just that she wants you either. At least not entirely. It's our relationship, our love for each other. She wanted me to doubt that, but I don't. God above, what more could you do to prove you love me than what you've done already? Coming home through the war as you did, whenever you had furlough, even when you had to ride forty-six out of forty-eight hours to do so? Telling me this winter to do what Doc Lacey said, to come to a Yankee hospital? I know how you love Virginia and the South. I know how badly it hurt your pride to admit the Northern hospitals were finer. Then taking parole, living here as another man's burden, taking Joshua's orders, swallowing *more* of your pride. But I needed you with me this spring. And you knew that and never once have I heard you complain." Her voice fell to a whisper, barely above a breath. "Even when I gave you, for all your troubles, only a dead son and a sickly daughter . . ."

He frowned and stepped toward her, starting to speak a denial. "No, Jon, I mean it—every word. I don't believe what Lady Bennington would like me to. And I don't ever want to discuss it again. You'll stay here now because you must, and I'll stay here with you, because I love you. Nothing can ever change that. Here or Virginia—it doesn't matter any longer."

She reached her hand to him and he took it in silence, hesitating a final moment. Then he nodded, managing a faint smile. "We'll stay then, at least until Joshua is well enough, or the war is over and Major Courtland gets home." Even as he said it, he wondered. The tone of his voice was sure enough, outwardly confident. But the words sat strangely on him. He hungered for Virginia, but with a vague sense of affectionate memory. Beautiful, rich, green, rolling homeland, now ravaged by war, reddened with blood. He wondered if it would ever really be home now again. He sighed, feeling as if a decision had been made that he wasn't entirely aware of. Whitney's hand tightened over his and he glanced down to meet her gaze.

"Now you'll be taking Joshua's place for a while at the bank. Now you can stop Lady Bennington from taking any more money, without even telling him."

"But we'll need our own place, Whit. I can't do that and continue to live here."

"The carriage house is vacant, Jon. It's not as grand as Cool Spring, but it's homey." She smiled faintly.

"I'll ask Joshua as soon as he's well enough." He smiled finally, genuinely and without effort. It was a feeling oddly like coming home. "Ever guess I'd end up a Yankee banker, Whit?"

She laughed softly, shaking her head and turning away toward the stairs, not letting go of his hand as she moved. "Let's go up now, Jon, and see how Joshua is doing." As they left, she couldn't resist a glance over her shoulder to where the three portraits stood, silently watching, atop the piano. Odd, she thought. While Jon was away fighting, Chase Courtland had appeared to lend the Penley women his strength and protection. Now, with him away, Jonathon stood where the Major would have, caught between father and daughter, wrestling with the problems of a family he'd never heard of this time a year ago. And God only knew where Chase Courtland and Leanna were now, the two who had begun this odd entanglement and now seemed the ones free of it.

Elinor appeared suddenly, a shadowed figure atop the stairs, and Whitney tightened her grip on her husband's hand. Don't ever get complacent, Whitney, she warned herself. Things are far from resolved just yet.

Chapter Twenty-One

By the time Joshua Courtland had recovered to the point where Jonathon could think of taking his family home to the Shenandoah Valley, the chance to do that was gone. He did not know it, and that was probably a blessing, but Jubal Early's Rebels had been turned back the very outskirts of the Federal Capital, and his at soutward along the silver Shenandoah River marked the last time CSA troops would ever securely hold the once solidly Confederate Valley.

Confederate luck, which had seemed once more invincible in June and early July, began to weaken with each passing day of that last desperate summer. Grant's troops endured the humid Virginia heat and epidemics of every conceivable kind to keep the seige rock-hard around Richmond and Petersburg. Robert E. Lee's weakened army could do no more than hold its ground and pray the coming Presidential election would find the fervent Unionism of Abraham Lincoln defeated. And meanwhile, all around the Army of Northern Virginia's heroic defense of Richmond, the Confederacy was slowly crumbling.

A last desperate appeal to Europe failed. France backed down on a semipromise of recognition to the beleagured Southern government, fearing such a declaration might lead them to war—England, spoiling for such an opportunity to gobble French interests, might join the Yanks. France could not afford to fight a war on two fronts. Supplies of all kinds, already pitifully scarce in the spring, grew ever scarcer in summer as Federal warships closed most of what few ports had remained even semiopen. Of the many privations, none was more anguishing than the lack of medicines and vaccines for the fevers that always devilled the South in summers. Charleston reeled beneath a smallpox epidemic that raged like a wildfire and spread all throughout the swampy Low Country. Soldiers wounded in the field, Yankee prisoners included, found only home-brewed whiskey for antiseptic or anesthetic, and even the drunkest man felt the agony of losing a limb to the surgeon's hacksaw. Compassionate souls who would have sent such medical supplies down were defeated by War Department's edicts that forbade it. In the heat of the Washington summer, as the bloody war dragged ever on, Lincoln's health, too, was failing, and Secretary of War Stanton grew ever more powerful as the Presidential hand of restraint grew weaker.

In Georgia, the Confederate High Command had made a disastrous mistake. Jefferson Davis, ever suspicious of the brilliant but arrogant Johnston, had replaced his general with a subordinate, John Bell Hood. Hood promised daring action, which was what Davis, from the distance of Richmond, had decided was just what the situation called for. On July 20th, the new General's reckless attack at Peachtree Creek had failed. On July 22nd, the second did, too. On July 28th, when Hood's third attack at Ezra Church finished the issue, Stewart Leighton had left Atlanta in a desperate effort to reach Richmond and the CSA President. He was hoping to convince Davis to rectify his error before it cost the Confederacy the city itself.

Leanna had been left behind, once more, as in Richmond, trapped in a city being assaulted by Yankee armies. Much of the same horrors repeated themselves. Food and everything else were fearfully lacking. Things once taken for granted—a pin, a needle, a length of cloth—were virtual treasures. And the groans of the Rebel wounded drifted on the very air of Atlanta. In the terrible heat of the Deep South summer, they were cared for outside in open-air wards, in parks, in freight depots, anywhere there was room, waiting for space on the few rusted, rickety trains still running. The question always was where to take them, because by the end of July, Yankee troops ringed seven-eighths of the city.

All throughout it, Leanna had stayed in Atlanta, awaiting her husband's return. Weeks passed with no sign of him, no word. But Southern communications systems were in shambles by now and she paid little attention to the lack of communication from him. The Federal bombardment of the beleagured city began in August, while the CSA cavalry was still making a last few, futile strikes on Sherman's supply lines. The first shell into the city hit a little girl walking her dog, and the hatred of the Atlanta people toward the enemy army outside their walls intensified to a frightening pitch.

Leanna shared only some of the uncompromising viciousness. Blytheswood was still her secret heart, and the Yankees hadn't harmed it last winter when they'd taken it. Hadn't harmed Blytheswood—or her, either. She didn't realize how great a care Chase Courtland had exercised to shield them both. She only knew she did not share the same blind, hysterical terror that most of the city felt. If she was lonely at night, sleeping by herself in the over-wide, unfamiliar bed of the Atlanta townhouse, at least she was not overly afraid, and nightmares of Yankee troops swarming into the city did not too greatly disturb her sleep.

The first of September was hot still in Georgia; the windows of the city townhouses were left open to gather the cooler night breeze. Suddenly, the distant patter of carbines firing and then the single, sudden roar of an explosion from the Confederate arms depot shattered the night. The sound woke Leanna from a dreamless sleep. She opened her eyes with a start and rolled over toward the window. Another roar exploded, closer this time; the sky behind the printed chintz curtains flared bright as day. A thunderstorm, she thought. But unlike lightning, the glow didn't fade. Fire, she realized a fearful instant later. Atlanta was on fire!

"Susannah!" Leanna grabbed for a dressing gown, throwing it on as she ran for the narrow, dark stairs.

"Atlanta's burning! For God's sake, Susannah, where are you?"

The small room off the kitchen was silent, black. Leanna froze disbelieving at the doorway, searching the emptiness of the slave girl's room. "Susannah?" She hurried to the back door, and found it unbolted from the inside. As she touched it, the door swung shut with a faint click. Another roar sounded outside, then the deafening clatter of horsemen galloping on the nearby cobblestoned main street—iron horseshoes ringing on uneven stones, men shouting, revolvers cracking. She'd heard that sound before, back in Virginia. Cavalry. It must be. But Confederate? Or Yankee?

Yankee, she answered herself, hardly believing it even while she knew it must be true. Atlanta had fallen then, sometime during the night. There had been rumors for days, but there were always rumors in the midst of war. She hadn't believed them. But the CSA army must have slipped out of the long besieged city, southward, the only direction left for them to go. Abandoning Atlanta before the Yankee noose could tighten completely, or a second Union cavalry raid could succeed where the one of ten days ago had failed—to cut the army's last remaining line of supply.

Leanna started back through the darkened house at a run. She didn't pause at a window to check the color of the uniforms she would find outside—the slave girl's absence was proof enough they were no longer Confederate gray. Damn that girl, she thought as she reached for the stairpost to pull herself around. She could understand the slaves' longing for freedom, and the Federal troops promised that, yes, but to leave at midnight, the door left wide, not even so much as a—

"Let's try this one!"

Leanna froze on the first stair, whirling at the sudden sound of voices in the darkness outside, voices with the nasal twang of Yankees. An instant later, she screamed, flinging one arm up to shield her face. Front windows shattered. Glass knives shot inward to splinter on the bare floor or thud softly on the carpet runner. One

320

nicked her wrist, but she hardly felt it. The front door gave a single, protesting groan and then exploded inward, slamming the inside wall so hard that porcelain vases rocked on the tiny, delicately carved hall table, rocked a moment, then fell, adding their cry to the chaos of destruction that rose up around them. Sudden torch-light streamed through the darkness. Leanna blinked once, then screamed again, turning to make a scram-bling effort on the stairs. One glance had sufficed to show her all she'd needed to see. These were not the same kind of men who'd knocked so courteously on Blytheswood's front door. Stewart had left a revolver for her to use. God, why hadn't she thought to bring it downstairs with her?

"I caught me a Reb!"

Leanna felt rough hands seize her from behind. She turned before the light dressing gown ripped and left her naked, raising one hand to strike at a face she could hardly see in the darkness. The instinctive terror of a trapped animal seized her, fanned by the shadows, the shouting, the suddenness. She screamed and struck again, struggling against the grip that was dragging her too easily back down the stairs.

"A gen-u-ine Southern belle!"

Loud whoops of triumph and raucous laughter echoed eerily. Four or five Federal soldiers stood grinning like gargoyles in the shadowed hallway. She sobbed once as she screamed, kicking at the soldier's leg without seem-ing effect.

"Let me see that, Corker. Oooh-ey! That's a fine one."

The sour smell of rotgut whiskey reeked from them. That and worse. Old sweat. Filth. And the acrid stink of gunpowder.

"Let go of me!" Leanna tried desperately to regain her dignity. Tried bravado as a last defense. The sol-diers had been a long time without a woman; 'Uncle Billy' Sherman had ordered every last female to stay behind at Chattanooga. Their eyes were gleaming now in undisguised lechery at the girl half dressed, and wriggling most provocatively, in the flickering torchlight. A terrible fear had gripped her soul. "Damn it, I'm no soldier for you to manhandle! Where are your officers? Where are your orders? How dare you break into innocent people's houses?"

"Innocent people?" The man holding her laughed like a maniac, grinning over one shoulder to his equally amused comrades. In his drunkenness, he staggered a step, his shoe heel coming down on Leanna's bare foot. She cried in pain and shoved him away with her free hand. "We was told this was a hiding place for Reb ammunitions, there missy! We're doin' our duty and searchin' the place. Ain't we, boys?" Laughter sounded again behind him, but scattered now as each one started in separate directions, looking for something worth looting. "You got any weapons concealed about your person, Miss?" He stuck his face closer to hers, leering, his eyes dipping down to the shadows of the gown's loose fitting bodice. He raised one hand as he spoke, grinning even wider. "Maybe I better check for some."

Chase pulled his horse up at the corner of two wide streets, glancing over his shoulder at the fires that lit the Georgia sky a dozen or more blocks away. He could hear the cries of men from over there, but he didn't think the soldiers had much chance of dousing the fires. The Rebel cavalry had set them last thing before they'd abandoned the city and they'd gotten too good a start on the cotton bales and abandoned army supplies before the Yankee cavalry had ridden in, surprised to find the usual defenders gone from their trenches, surprised to find not a single skirmisher left between them and the sleeping city. What had begun as a routine midnight raid at the CSA lines had turned into a long, astonishing canter into the city itself. They'd cut Hood's last railroad line only yesterday. And Chase guessed the CSA general had decided to get while the getting was still good.

"Major, any word from headquarters yet?"

Chase turned in his saddle, shaking his head. They'd

sent couriers to General Sherman as soon as they'd guessed the situation. But no orders had come back yet. That was normal for army communication.

"Well, we've got a problem, I'm afraid." The young captain eyed the nearby streets uneasily. Here and there, windows were brightening with light. "Some of the soldiers we came in with are celebrating already. On their own, if you understand my meaning."

Chase frowned down the residential street to his right. Even as he watched, a group of two or three men appeared briefly out of the bushes and disappeared back again without a sound. He gestured toward them, calling to an officer behind him. "Take a patrol, Lieutenant." He nodded the direction. "No burning or looting until we hear from headquarters. Try to round up our over-anxious infantry friends, would you?"

He turned his horse around, pulling hard at the reins to keep the animal from bolting in that direction. The horses smelled smoke. That and the night's shadows were making them restless. "Let's split the men into patrols, Grier. I don't think we're liable to meet the kind of resistance we'd need troop strength for. And Rebels or not, I hate to see soldiers let loose on civilians—especially in the dead of night." He glanced at his captain, and they exchanged nods. Grier was a good man. Not many of them were left anymore. "Meet back here at four-thirty. We should have orders from General Kilpatrick or from Army Command by then."

Grier saluted in acknowledgement. Chase returned it before he turned his horse again, gesturing his portion of the troopers forward to cover the dark street at a cautious canter. There was some faint grumbling from the men at such an order, but they obeyed it, drawing their carbines and searching the shadows for looters.

Atlanta was kind of a pretty little city, he thought, as it passed him by on either side in night-shadowed stillness, but hardly worth the blood spilt over it. He'd expected more, something more obviously urban. His horse stumbled once, and he drew the stallion down to a slower canter, gesturing his men to do the same behind him. The streets were wide and fairly level, but in the darkness it was hard to see any distance ahead, and an unexpected hole could break a horse's leg or a trooper's neck. Wrought-iron street lamps lined a good portion of the street they were riding, but they stood mostly dark— due, he guessed, to a lack of whale oil to light them. He doubted Atlanta had gas, yet, as most of the northern cities did. A dozen blocks comprised downtown—big banks, munitions warehouses, and stately, Greek-style government buildings, all interspersed by lots of trees and open land. Even at a slow canter, they were through the area in minutes.

Beyond them lay several blocks of townhouses, elegant, and mostly dark—just a few beginning to show the dim glow of candles or lamps being lit, the inhabitants finally aware of something happening outside in their night-shuttered streets. On the city's outskirts lay two-story brick mansions, with generous lawns and walled gardens, some girdled by ghostly gray picket fences he guessed were actually white by day. Some of these were overlaid with climbing flowers—roses, he thought, from the fragrance. Only a half-dozen of the streets were paved or cobbled; in most places, the beat of the horses' hooves was muffled by dirt.

Cabins and farm buildings lay only a few miles from the town square, and he drew his horse down to a trot as he entered that area. It was senseless to ride any farther; looters wouldn't be in this part of town.

It was a big city acreage-wise, but a town in most other respects—at least in comparison to the industrial cities of the North. He felt a startling surge of compassion for the Confederacy he was trying to defeat. Atlanta was only a town to him, but they considered it one of their major cities, its rolling mill, munitions works, and railroad yard irreplaceable to them, and desperately needed. His eyes were darkly without triumph, his mouth grimly set as he raised his hand to signal about-face. "We'll head back uptown, toward the depots burning." He started his horse forward, glancing over his shoulder at a door slamming open in a rundown cabin nearby, the joyful cry of 'Jubilee!' that roared suddenly from a black slave throat. The men behind him returned the cry happily, unconfused by sympathy for their failing foe. The exchange eased him some, but not entirely. Damn war, Chase thought to himself. Nobody's either entirely wrong, or entirely right, and the issues weren't getting any easier, much, to balance out.

"What the hell do you think you're doin', soldier?"

Leanna staggered as the Yankee was suddenly hauled away from her by a strong, gauntletted hand. Cavalry, she realized numbly, seeing the familiar glove. And thank God, an officer. . . . She raised her dressing gown higher around her neck and took a deep, trembling breath, leaning against the stair rail and closing her eyes in relief.

"I ain't no horse boy. The soldier snarled, drunk enough not to care who he insulted. "You ain't my officer."

"I am for now. What do you men think you're doing?"

"Looking for Rebs," one snarled. Leanna opened her eyes and glanced toward him in the flickering torchlight. The gleam of silver candlesticks showed beneath his half-buttoned shirt.

"The army's gone." The officer frowned at the ill-kempt crew that was regathering slowly and sullenly nearby. "I'm under orders to ride patrol—to prevent this sort of thing, at least, until there's some organization."

"Until you horse boys get first pickings, you mean. 'Kill Cavalry's' golden boys—"

" 'Uncle Billy' didn't give no order like that. He likes his boys to make these damn Secesh bastards squirm a little."

"That's enough!" A revolver glinted dully in the officer's hand. He waved it warningly toward the broken-in door. "Now get out. Rejoin your regiment. I'll put you under arrest if I catch you again."

"Give me a good-bye kiss, then, Missy."

Leanna jerked away with a cry of revulsion as the

drunken soldier grabbed for her a last time. The cavalry officer stepped between them, pulling the man away.

"I said get out, soldier. Now."

Another pair of troopers had stepped inside as the others filed out. Leanna noticed enmity in the exchange of glances and breathed a thankful prayer. That was the same for both sides then. Luckily for her, there was no love lost between infantry and cavalry.

"Sorry, ma'am." The young officer's tone was polite, but not genuinely apologetic. Leanna glanced at him swiftly. "If you're alone in the house, you'd best go to a neighbor's. Good night."

He started out. Leanna reached thoughtlessly for his arm. As he turned in surprise, his eyes flickered over her, and one brow was raised in speculation. She blushed at his expression. She'd forgotten she wasn't dressed.

"Wait, Lieutenant." Double bars on his shoulder straps gave his rank. As she spoke, she dropped her hand quickly from his arm. A momentary dizziness touched her and she forced it away. Her hand was strangely numb, but she needed desperately to know what was going on. "Just tell me, has Atlanta fallen then? What about those fires over there?"

"Army supplies. Lit by your own men, too. Don't curse us for it if the flames spread."

Leanna paled, but kept her head high, meeting his gaze. "I'm only asking whether it's safe to stay nearby or—"

"Holy Jesus!"

Both Leanna and the young, hard-faced officer turned as one. Torchlight flickered on a familiar face and Leanna gasped, her eyes flying wide.

"That's Mrs. Leighton!"

Leanna paled to ash and began to tremble. The trooper before her had been one of those stationed at Blytheswood. What was next? Arrest as a spy? Or would they merely abandon her to the likes of the drunken soldiers they'd just sent packing?

"Hot damn! Fancy that!" The trooper astonished her by offering a wide grin, stepping forward and tipping

326

his well-worn hat. "Now how the devil did you wind up in Atlanta?"

Suddenly, Leanna could hear no more. It was as if an ocean had moved inside her head, roaring in her ears. The trooper's face blurred and began to fade. Dimly, she was aware of a terrible weakness in her knees and it felt as if the room were tilting. The last thing she saw was surprise on the Yankee's face. He lunged forward to catch her as she fell.

"Oh, Jesus, is she hurt or something?" The veteran trooper looked up at the baffled officer as he bent over the unconscious young woman. "Jesus, look at this blood. The Major's gonna be madder'n hell, Lieutenant. He was mighty fond of this lady back in Virginia. We was quartered for the winter at her place."

The officer frowned, looking at the girl and back to the trooper. "You go fetch him, then. I don't know what the hell else to do with her, anyway."

The soldier sent to find Chase lost several hours searching for him in the confusion of the captured city, tracing him finally to the Army's temporary headquarters at Washington and Mitchell Streets. But there, an orderly guarded the door, and the soldier could only relay the message to him. The orderly, in turn, relayed it to a half a dozen others on its way up to where Chase stood debriefing, and along the way, it was heard by someone else who had reason to recognize the name of Leanna Penley Leighton.

Lieutenant Colonel Edward Drake had received a coded dispatch from Washington D.C.'s War Department concerning the very same woman, not three days before. Her husband, CSA Lieutenant Colonel Stewart Leighton was outside Atlanta, promoting partisan warfare more vicious than any before encountered. Perhaps— War Department thought had run, perhaps the man's wife would also be here. And someone in Washington wanted the woman—badly. Not, Drake guessed shrewdly, because of any connection to her husband's activities. The dispatch had had the feel of an animus more personal. Someone in the Department, or one of their friends, wanted Leanna Leighton put in custody—no more than that, at least for now. Simply placed under control, carefully kept in hand. Someone up North wanted to be able to say they held the woman in their power. Drake was used to such games. The secret power plays of the War Department were not unfamiliar to him. He had cooperated on other occasions before this one; he intended to cooperate on many more. He had his eye on the Senate, eventually. In return for such favors, Secretary of War Stanton would help him get there after the war.

As dawn broke over the smoking Rebel city, both men made their way toward Leanna's townhouse. Neither was aware of the other's interest in her, and their thoughts were as different as their motives for going there. To Chase, it was not a pleasant coincidence—no stroke of luck to have found Leanna so easily. It was, for him, the repetition of a nightmare he'd often had—that Leanna would somehow get caught in just such a position, trapped between the two warring armies. He knew he shouldn't care, but he still did. That only made it worse, somehow. It added the guilt of feeling he would betray Susan by whatever he might do to protect Leanna.

The dawn streets were crowded. Troops were pouring into the city from every direction, infantry and cavalry alike. For Chase, it had been a long night already, and this was the start of another day without even an hour's sleep to break the two. Not that he could have slept anyway, even if he'd had the time. The news of Leanna had awakened old agonies, rekindled old desires and old doubts. His mind churned with a hundred thoughts, most contradictory, all confusing and turbulent—anguished and elated, angry and afraid. He loved her still and had less right than ever to do so. Damn you, Leanna Leighton. Why couldn't you have been safe, somewhere in Virginia, out of my way? Why couldn't you have stayed simply a memory? God knows, even that had been agonizing enough to try to deal with. Now with her real again, flesh and blood, those beautiful violet eyes that could shine so softly or with such ice ... Leanna, did you betray me last spring in Virginia? Did you, damn it? God, I almost wish I could be sure you did. Maybe that would finally exorcise the devil that plagues me so.

Intent on the turbulence of the world within him, Chase spared little thought for the outer one. He didn't notice the other officer who rode up to the house just behind him. Drake checked the house address, then leisurely swung from the saddle, throwing the reins to a nearby soldier. He was already deciding how he should word the telegram he intended to send the War Department this afternoon. Whoever it was that wanted Leanna Leighton would be getting her on a silver platter.

Leanna woke slowly. A bearded, unfamiliar face bent over her. Her arm was stretched out tight, held by something. Instinctively she tried to pull it back toward her and the face frowned.

"Hold still. I'm almost done."

She blinked and turned her head, frightened and confused. The glow of early morning showed through the broken glass of the nearby windows. Black smoke snaked lazily upward in a distant place.

Horsemen suddenly galloped by outside on the packed clay street. It was the Cavalry in Federal blue. She remembered suddenly and gave a faint cry, struggling harder on the cramped parlor settee.

"All right. I'm finished."

Leanna snatched her arm away and sat up, aware of an instant wave of dizziness that threatened to take her off again. "Who are you?" She questioned instantly. "And what—?" The stark white of bandages circling her left wrist caught her attention and she frowned at her hand, momentarily silent.

"Regimental Assistant Surgeon Captain Wilkerson." He answered as he stood, and started for the door without looking back. "All right, Colonel. I'm through with the woman."

"Please wait. Can't you tell me what's going on?"

Leanna tried to stand to follow him, but she found her feet entangled in a cotton bed quilt someone had laid over her. She threw it off, then grabbed for it again in the same motion. She was in her dressing gown still. Bad enough last night in the darkness. Far more revealing in the full light of the rising sun. The Yankee surgeon left the room without another word, and Leanna felt a kind of hopeless, fearful confusion begin to rise.

Damn it, she thought, biting at her lip. What *was* happening? Yankees all over and no one to give her any news. Just then, two tall men in dusty dark-blue uniforms stepped inside the ruined parlor, speaking to one another in voices too low for her to hear. One pushed casually at the wreckage of a tea chair with his boot as he spoke, the other nodded in ash-streaked agreement, and gestured toward the settee. Leanna froze. One of the men was agonizingly familiar. That face had haunted her, sleep and waking, for over five months now.

"Chase!"

She only breathed the name but he seemed to hear, glancing up to lock his eyes to hers. For an instant, the shock of it overwhelmed everything. Atlanta faded. Stewart was forgotten. A sudden pounding of blood in her ears drowned out every other sound.

"Mrs. Leighton." It was the other man who spoke, a man she'd never seen before. He stepped forward and blocked her view of Chase. She stared stupidly, dazed, trying to make her mind function again. Finally, she glanced toward the stranger with an enormous effort. "You're feeling better I trust?"

Leanna blinked once, unsure what to say. Not that his question was a difficult one to answer, but the lingering shock of seeing Chase made her stupid and speechless.

"Lieutenant Colonel Drake, Mrs. Leighton." He tipped his black felt hat brusquelly. "War Department, Washington. I'm on temporary assignment to General Sherman's adjutant staff."

Leanna glanced almost involuntarily a last time to where Chase stood, but Lieutenant Colonel Drake still blocked her view of him. Why, she thought. Why didn't Chase approach her?

"I'd like to ask you a few questions if you're feeling up to it."

She looked back at him instantly, aware of an odd note in his voice, one that rang an instinctive warning bell. Virginia. The ambush on the Yankees. The code book—or what she'd thought was the code book at the time. Had Chase voiced suspicions of her to the Yankee high command?

"Can you speak, Mrs. Leighton?"

She flushed at his sarcasm, raising her chin. "Yes, I can speak, Colonel. If I choose to." It seemed to her his eyes narrowed, the faint smile that had been playing around his mouth faded.

"Don't be impertinent, Mrs. Leighton. Only courtesy keeps me from taking you into custody right now."

She managed to hold his gaze. "On what charge? And you'll forgive me if I ask to see your warrant."

"I don't need one. Understandably, you've been a bit out of touch for a few years with changing Federal regulations. 'Habeas corpus' has been suspended for some time. Now, one only needs suspicion, Mrs. Leighton. Your past conduct and your present associations are more than sufficient to justify arrest."

Despite herself, her eyes opened wider, her heart skipped a fearful beat. Chase chose that moment to step forward. Oh, God, she thought. That's why he's here. He's going to accuse me.

"Colonel Drake, I don't mean to make your job more difficult, but the lady *has* been under stress these past few hours. Perhaps you might give her a few minutes to compose herself."

"Maybe you're right, Major. I want to check something with my aide, anyway."

Leanna watched him, frowning as he turned. Thoughts and emotions tumbled turbulently together. Nothing made sense anymore. Drake gave her the feeling of something preplanned, something coldly calculated, but what about Chase? She glanced instinctively toward him and found his brown eyes locked to hers. For a moment, she could say nothing. Colonel Drake was entirely forgotten.

"You seem surprised, Leanna." Chase spoke softly, raising one dark brow as he held her gaze.

"I am." She had to force the words, and they followed a heartbeat's silence. Even so, they were barely a whisper. "I am surprised."

"To find me in Atlanta? Or to find me alive at all?"

The words stabbed deep in her soul. The bitterness he spoke them with was even worse. She shrugged and blinked once against the threat of tears, understanding now. The picture of a bloodstained Virginia meadow was suddenly clear in her mind, achingly so. Silence lingered but he stood, expecting an answer, and she shrugged as she spoke. "You shouldn't need to ask that. It wasn't as if I didn't care . . ."

"Care?" A strange half smile touched his mouth. He glanced at her a last time before looking away, surveying the wreckage of the parlor around them. War and its bloody destruction of things—and people, too. After all the times he'd defended her to Doc Lacey, his father, the war commission, it surprised him to feel such deep anger at her now. "Yes, I suppose you did care, Leanna. Enough to try to dress the wound. But not enough to stay behind."

I wanted to, she could have said. For a moment, she almost did. But it would only reopen old agonies, and reopen them needlessly. Nothing had changed. She hadn't changed. Nor had the lines drawn in blood that terrible day in April. "In case you haven't noticed, there's a war on, Major. People do get wounded—in all different ways."

He glanced back to her as if startled. She met his gaze silently, trying not to show he'd hurt her as badly as he had.

"Well, Mrs. Leighton, I hope you're more 'composed' by now."

Leanna looked away from Chase with an effort. She hadn't heard Colonel Drake's entrance. For a moment, she wondered whether he'd eavesdropped purposely. She spared a last, aching glance toward the Yankee major she both hated and loved, but he'd turned his back and stepped toward the shattered windows. She saw him kick aside a sliver of glass, watched him move away with a sudden feeling of anguish. "Yes, Colonel Drake. What is it you want to know from me?" She raised her chin as she returned her gaze to him, and tried to ignore the sick, thudding of her heart.

"Is this your house?"

The question took her aback. "Well, yes, I mean no, not entirely. We rented it from some people who'd chosen to leave the city?"

"We?"

"My husband and I." She didn't look again at Chase.

"Ah, your husband . . ."

Leanna frowned, confused by the faint smile Colonel Drake couldn't quite hide. This had the feel of play, over-rehearsed.

"But your husband isn't here."

Leanna said nothing. Was she betraying anything if she admitted that Stewart had gone to Richmond and not returned? "No, he's not," she said finally. "So if you're here looking for him, I'm afraid you've wasted your time."

"I don't think so, Mrs. Leighton. When was the last time you spoke to him?"

"You mean my husband?" She was genuinely confused. And stalling. Trying desperately to determine what the Yankee was getting at before she made some terrible blunder. She glanced again at Chase, but he had his back still to her, apparently uninterested in the proceedings. Oh God, she thought. Why doesn't he just come out with it and accuse me of whatever it is they've decided I've done?

"Where is Colonel Leighton, by the way? Where do you meet when you wish to communicate with him?"

"I don't, Colonel Drake. What is it you're really asking me? Whether I'm playing spy for Richmond?"

"Are you, Mrs. Leighton?"

"No." She flushed, trying not to show her fear. "And whether my husband is or not is a question you'd have to ask him, not me."

"We'd very much like to do that."

"Then you'd better press a little harder in your efforts to seize Richmond, gentlemen. Because until you've taken the capital, I doubt he'll oblige you."

Chase turned, frowning, flinging Leanna a single, strange glance. There was sudden silence in the room. Leanna was aware of it, aware, too, of the overquick beating of her heart. Her hand had begun to throb, and she felt light-headed again, cold and faintly nauseated. Colonel Drake was standing in line with the shattered front bay windows and against the glare she couldn't see his face well enough to read his expression. She raised her bandaged hand finally to shield her eyes.

"He's not in Richmond any longer." Chase spoke at last, stepping closer again to where she lay. "He's organizing the partisan resistance down here. Some of it's been pretty gruesome."

Leanna could only stare at him, open-mouthed. Partisan resistance? What was going on?

"I gather you didn't know that."

She was too startled to know what she should say. "Stewart told me he was sent here as a military advisor to the President. He said nothing about combat or killing. He did admire Mosby, I know. I didn't think much about it at the time, but he did speak about the way we were fighting the war—I mean, the way the South was fighting the war—at the same disadvantage as gentlemen trying to box in a street brawl . . ."

"Yes, the handicap of honor in warfare." Chase's voice had a strange note, but he shrugged and said no more.

"I don't imagine Colonel Leighton expected Atlanta to fall so abruptly. Very few of us did. We expected a long siege, actually, while Forrest, Wheeler, and groups like your husband's tried to cut our lines of supply from Tennessee. Then it would have been a question of which army ran out of supplies first—yours besieged here in Atlanta or ours outside the walls." Colonel Drake spoke softly, almost pleasantly, as if explaining something to a child. Leanna had the sudden sensation of smugness coming from him, a chilling feeling. She glanced at him swiftly, trying to think what she'd said wrong. "I don't doubt he'd have gotten you out of the city if he'd known. Lucky for us, he was just a bit slow."

Her eyes widened again. She stared at him. "You can't believe *I* am at work for Stewart?"

"It's insignificant, actually, Mrs. Leighton. Your husband's activities are well-documented. Merely the chance that you're involved, as a courier or an information gatherer, we'll say, is sufficient to make us wary."

"But I told you I had no idea of my husband's activities."

"I know what you told me. Nothing. Had you been more cooperative, perhaps your loyalty to the Federal government would be less in doubt."

Leanna paled in anger, sitting straighter on the settee. "I can't tell you what I don't know. As for my loyalties, they lie with the CSA, Colonel. I've never pretended otherwise."

"I think perhaps you'd better come with me." Drake smiled and Leanna paled further.

"Not willingly, Colonel."

"The War Department is interested in questioning you on other matters, also, Mrs. Leighton. An incident last spring in Virginia, for one thing."

Chase gave the adjutant a swift, frowning glance. The incident in Virginia was no longer under investigation. Leanna was not even mentioned in the final report.

"So willingly or not, Mrs. Leighton—"

"Am I correct in assuming you've decided to arrest her?" Chase interrupted softly.

His question caught Leanna as she had already begun to move from the settee. It startled her and she glanced up, too numb, too shocked to react any further. It was like a bizarre nightmare. Chase here. The accusations.

Stewart. The parlor all ruined, the settee and her dressing gown stained dark with splotches of blood from her hand. . . .

Colonel Drake turned as if surprised. "Well, not arrest, precisely. But I'd like to question her further." He paused to glance around the room with a faint smile. "I'm doing her a favor, actually. She can hardly stay here."

"But she's free, if you let her be, to find some other place."

"No, Major, that's hardly sensible. This city is attempting to quarter almost a hundred thousand troops. She'll find nothing else. Even if she did, I won't take the responsibility of seeing an unprotected woman cast adrift in such uncertain circumstances. She'll come with me, in custody, because she really has nowhere else to go. And I have no intention of letting her leave the city."

There was silence. Colonel Drake stepped forward to offer Leanna his hand. She looked at it sickly, and drew a deep, shaky breath. That was it, then. She knew what custody meant. Confinement for now, probably in some rat-infested warehouse by the railroad yards, and prison later. Not unlike Jonathon, she thought. Maybe it was ironic justice. Both Penleys. Beginning the war so favored. Honored and honorable. Wealthy, pampered, powerful. Ending the war, maybe their lives, helpless, in a Yankee prison.

"She can stay in my quarters."

Both Leanna and the Yankee adjutant turned, startled, at Chase's sudden statement. Drake looked almost angry at it. Leanna could only stare in surprise.

"I beg your pardon, Major, but I—"

"You say it's a matter of lacking other options, Colonel. I've just offered you one." Chase spoke calmly, hiding the confusion he felt. God, had she betrayed him at Blytheswood? Would he now be giving her the chance to betray him again? Maybe it was time, once and for all, to find out whether she had or she would.

336

"I don't think you understand. She'd be guarded most—"

"I understand. I doubt I'll even be there myself most of the time. Atlanta may be taken, but the war's hardly over. I don't doubt General Sherman will think up one or two things for us to do yet."

Drake frowned, no longer smug. "I can't imagine what—"

"Her brother, his wife, and their two daughters are living at my father's home in Philadelphia, Colonel," He glanced only briefly toward Leanna to see her shock. Two, she was thinking. The baby, then, had not been twins after all. And Chase's father had taken them in, despite what had happened in Virginia when—Stewart had led an ambush that had almost killed the man's son. All this time, she'd pictured Jonathon dead or in prison, Whitney dead or at least burying a dead child. Bless you, Chase. It had to have been you that helped them, in spite of everything we had done to you.

Chase had already shrugged and turned away, back toward the adjutant officer. "I doubt she'll murder me in my sleep, Colonel Drake. She'd hardly risk *their* continued safety. Would you?"

He's turned to her as he finished. Leanna flushed at the question, the bitterness that so obviously lay behind it. Chase smiled faintly as she shook her head, his brown eyes dark with pain. "Nice to find *someone* you care deeply enough about to place above the war, Mrs. Leighton."

She flushed again and bit her lip, turning her head away. Damn you, she thought. That was cruel—needlessly so. And you knew it, Chase, before you ever said it. She was staring down at the floor and she missed the expression that flashed in his eyes as he watched her.

"All right, Major." Colonel Drake nodded slowly, trying to feign good grace. This was unexpected, that there might be someone here to care what was done with the woman. "At least as a temporary measure, I'll agree to that."

Chase nodded stiffly, too intent on the turbulence of

his own emotions to bother assessing the adjutant's. Fool, he thought. Leanna Leighton is poison—and you just volunteered to take a lethal dose. God, I wish I loved you less, Leanna, I wish you were in Richmond, not here. And that I didn't give a damn what happened to you any longer.

"I'll assign guards, Major. And talk to you later, Mrs. Leighton. For now, good day." Colonel Drake turned on one heel to go.

Leanna turned slowly, dazedly, to start for the stairs. It was almost impossible to walk through the room. Debris was everywhere. The sterling tea service was gone, as were the candlesticks she'd seen last night in the soldier's shirt. The clock over the mantle had fallen and smashed on the marble hearth, cracking that. Tables were overturned, the china in the glass-fronted hutch was shattered. One drapery was simply gone, ripped off the rod. Now that she listened, she thought she could hear the sounds of people in the kitchen as well, emptying it. She glanced up at Chase, almost glad of the destruction—using it to better hate him, using it to try to kill whatever love might have lingered yet from Virginia. "So this is how you Yankees make war now. On women and children."

A muscle twitched in his jaw. "I'm not in command here like I was in Virginia." He urged her forward, toward the stairs. His hand on her arm was almost painful. "And, too, you may thank people like your husband and other partisans. They make this sort of thing look like schoolboy pranks compared to their tricks. We're all getting dragged down into the dirt in this war. It doesn't matter much anymore who started it."

She stopped at the edge of the stairs. More soldiers lounged in the ruined doorway, but she paid them no attention. "I heard Hunter burned the Military Institute in the Valley . . . and the governor's mansion." She said it deliberately, her violet eyes infinitely cold as they met his brown. She saw them darken and grow hard, and she felt a kind of pleasure mixed with the pain.

"And Rebel cavalry burned Chambersburg, Pennsylvania, last month." He let go of her arm and nodded stiffly toward the bedroom above. "Now go get dressed before I take you out of here just as you are. I have rooms assigned to me a few blocks from here."

She made no reply, but merely nodded, taking the stairs as quickly and as straight-shouldered as her weakened knees would let her. She looked straight ahead and concealed the tears that formed in her eyes. Damn you, Chase. And damn you, too, Stewart. Damn everybody who had thought the only way to resolve differences was to go to war. Honor had turned to infamy, glory to an ugly death. Nothing precious could survive this nightmare . . . nothing, nothing at all. She didn't exempt herself. She'd been one of them calling for Virginia to take a stand. For honor's sake. Thinking of it now, she smiled, forcing it, only so she did not dissolve into helpless tears instead. You'd have been better off going to Colonel Drake's Yankee prison, she found herself thinking as she gathered her things. Better than being too close to Major Chase Courtland once again. That was going to be an even worse kind of Yankee hell.

Chapter Twenty-Two

Whether by accident or by design, Leanna saw nothing of Chase in the next half-dozen days. Sentries were posted at the door below their upstairs rooms, Drake's men, she knew. They were unfamiliar, not men who had wintered at Blytheswood, and she made no effort to engage them in conversation. But overhearing them, she knew General Sherman had ordered all CSA civilians to leave Atlanta. Watching out her window on the fourth, she had seen signs of the mass exodus—weeping women, overfilled wagons, and bitter-faced men, escorted out into the Georgia countryside by armed Federal troops. By the sixth, she estimated at least half of the city's eighty-five hundred had fled. It was a bitter experience to have to watch so helplessly from a second-story window, one that more deeply crystallized her hatred of the occupying troops—Major Chase Courtland among them.

He had come back only once, for a few minutes that afternoon. She'd heard his boot steps, familiar still after all these months, on the stairs outside the small parlor's door. She'd gone into the bedroom, pretending to be asleep even though it was bright midday outside. The pantry door's click had told her he'd brought supplies with him. She hadn't gotten up to check until she'd heard him leave again. Then, hearing the heavy boot steps retreating back down the stairs, she'd turned her head against the pillow and begun, very softly, to cry.

"Pardon my disbelief, Major, but what makes you so sure Mrs. Leighton was not a conspirator in the Virginia ambush?" Lieutenant Colonel Drake fixed Chase with cold eyes, raising one brow.

Chase frowned faintly and glanced at Colonel Adamson, his brigade commander, a good officer and an old friend of his father's. He wondered which of those two things had made the man decide to sit in on the discussion. He hadn't known ahead of time he was planning to. The stenographer paused, glancing up at Chase's silence.

"Fair enough question, Major. Answer it." Adamson nodded.

Chase's frown deepened. "Personal things, actually, sir." He shifted his weight on the backless camp chair and recrossed his legs. It was stifling hot in the small canvas tent that was adjutant headquarters. Pitched in the city cemetery, no less. He glanced up to note Drake's reaction and found the man staring at him.

"Care to be more specific, Major?"

"Not unless you order me to be."

"All right. I'll make it an order."

"And I'll protest that order, Colonel, as an officer and a . . ."

"Gentlemen, please." The older Adamson gestured impatiently, shaking his head. "You, Colonel Drake, this is only an informal hearing, is it not? And you, Major, you might consider the possibility it could be less embarrassing for you to answer these questions than it would be for the lady in question. If Colonel Drake is unsatisfied, he can move to bring the matter to full trial. Then neither of you would have a choice."

A muscle flexed in his jaw as Chase shrugged. "We were having an affair."

Drake lifted one brow. "Flirtations are a woman's main weapon when spying is her game."

"It went further than that."

"How much further?"

"Damn it, Colonel," Chase's dark eyes flashed anger and he rose to his feet. "This is a hell of a thing to—"

"Sit down, Major and answer my questions! Or I'll put the damn woman under arrest, drag her in here, and ask her to answer instead!"

A tense silence filled the small tent. Adamson looked from one man to the other, but said nothing. The young adjutant smirked, but kept his eyes on his notebook.

Chase met Drake's cold stare angrily, trying to control a gut-deep urge to go after the son of a bitch. That would help no one—least of all Leanna. "I want this conversation off the record. Tell your scribbler to get out of here."

"My lieutenant stays." Drake's eyes narrowed unpleasantly.

"Then you can go to hell."

"Chase, settle down." Adamson spoke at last, quietly, reaching one hand out to shake his arm as he too rose to his feet. "I appreciate your reluctance to compromise Mrs. Leighton's reputation, but it could mean her life. Military judges are far less lenient with this sort of thing than they were a year or two ago. If you can convince Colonel Drake, the issue will be dropped. No one outside of this tent will ever know what's been said."

Chase's eyes moved back to lock with the adjutant's. "I'll need your word on that."

Drake frowned a moment, then shrugged. "All right. You have it."

A last silence followed and Chase gritted his teeth. "Mrs. Leighton and I were lovers."

"Once? Twice? Or regularly?"

"Regularly." Chase lied without so much as the blink of an eye. Drake would never understand if he tried to explain why they hadn't been. Instead of honor, he would suspect deceit.

"A well-kept secret, apparently." Drake raised his brow.

"We hardly advertised the fact, Colonel. She is a married woman, after all."

"And did she ever question you about military matters during those midnight rendezvous, Major?"

"No."

"Did she ever try to read your letters? Intercept messages? Communicate information to the enemy?"

Chase recalled a vivid mental image of Leanna lying on the slushy December snow, the black book dropping as

342

he lifted her in his arms. "No, never." For a moment, he was astounded he had lied. He half turned, shrugging to hide his reaction.

"What about when her husband returned home with a discharge, Major? Wasn't it Mrs. Leighton who led your patrol into her husband's trap?"

"Hardly," Chase flushed at the dual implication—first, that Leanna had conspired to murder; second, that he would have been so stupid. "As a matter of fact, she and I were riding last in the party, following the others. And she dressed my wound for me as well. Or tried to. That hardly indicates a wish to kill, does it, Colonel?"

"You were unconscious, if I recall." Drake made a show of leafing through some papers as if to check. "How do you know it was her and not one of the others?"

Chase smiled with little amusement. "I know the partisans wear irregular costumes sometimes, but I've yet to see one in a lace-trimmed petticoat. Have you?"

Drake's eyes flashed up to meet his and he flushed. Chase met his gaze and raised one dark brow.

"All right, Major. So much for Virginia. I'm willing to believe if she was sharing your bed, she might have been reluctant to see you dead. But as for this past month and Colonel Leighton's activities here . . . ."

"She didn't even know about them. She thought he was in Richmond."

"So she said."

"Prove otherwise." Chase only shrugged, not overly concerned about this part. He'd seen Leanna's face when he'd told her. He knew she hadn't known. Why the hell was Drake so devil-bent on convicting her of something?

Drake flushed again, angrily. "You're not making much of an effort to be cooperative."

"I'm not interested in seeing an innocent woman arrested because her husband is a renegade, and you're out to make a name for yourself by somehow connecting the two."

"And I wouldn't call a woman married to a CSA

343

officer, sleeping 'regularly' with a Yankee one very innocent!"

Chase went for him across the rickety camp table. Adamson moved faster, getting between them and shoving Chase backward. "Mind your temper, Major! That's an order!" He turned, glowering equally at the adjutant. "That was totally uncalled for, Colonel. I think I've heard enough to consider this matter closed." He turned back to Chase, waving toward the tent flap. "Go home, Major Courtland. Get some sleep before you bite somebody's head off."

"I feel it my duty to point out to your superior, Major, that you display a dangerous sympathy for an avowed Rebel," Drake snapped as Chase turned to go. "This lack of cooperation won't help your career any, my friend."

"I'm not interested in my career, Colonel." Chase shrugged coldly. "As soon as this war's finished, I hope to God I never see another uniform again."

"I'll warn you as well, my interest in this case is not resolved. I intend to keep the lady in question under a very close eye. And whatever you do with her at night, don't whisper any military secrets in her pretty little ear."

Chase turned on one boot heel, not replying. Adamson followed him out. Drake watched them go and turned to the young lieutenant, just finishing his transcript of the meeting. "Damned Rebel slut." he muttered. "She must be an awfully good ride to have our fine major so hot to keep her out of jail and between his sheets. But what Washington wants, Washington gets." Drake grunted a determined sound and stalked out. His last comment amused the young recorder, so he set it down as a postscript. This would make fine telling at the campfire tonight.

It was late afternoon before Leanna heard sounds of Chase's return. As he stepped in the door, she turned from the window to glance at him. Shadows ringed his eyes. Dust and sweat mixed together to make his solid blue uniform look patterned. Outside, the smoke from a burning house blackened the gray, overcast sky in a lazy spiral.

"I'm going to sleep for a while." Chase turned as he spoke, drooping his hat, coat, and gloves on a cane-backed chair with a weary gesture.

She watched him with a bitter smile. "Had a hard day harassing Atlanta's women and children?"

He glanced up, looking at her silently for a long moment before he replied. "Defending one, actually."

She frowned faintly, confused. For an instant, her eyes met his, trying to read an answer. Then she shrugged and turned away. "I was just on my way out to the market. I hope you don't mind if I leave now. I'm afraid if I delay, you Yankees may burn that, too." Behind her, where he stood, there was only silence. She ignored it, reaching to the table by the long couch for her gloves. "I could use some money, if you wouldn't mind. I'll repay you, of course. Consider it a loan."

"Repay me with Confederate dollars? Forgive me if I seem unimpressed."

Leanna flushed and glanced at him. "With Yankee dollars, then, Major. I'll write a note to my brother, Jonathon. You did say he was at your home. You can send it on with your own letters and I'm sure he'll make good my debts."

Chase raised one brow as if to argue further, then shrugged, wearily, turning toward the bedroom door. "There's money in my coat. Help yourself. Return what you don't use. Colonel Drake's men will go with you. Take my advice and try to at least be civil to them."

He didn't look back. Leanna stood watching as he shut the bedroom door behind him. It was such a small apartment. Only a kitchen, small balcony, parlor, and the single bedroom. Close enough quarters that, as she stood in the parlor, she could hear the click of the armoire door as Chase opened it, hear the sound of water splashing in the delft-blue washbowl, the creak of the bed as he sat on it to pull off his boots.

She turned quickly for his coat, picking it up off the chair. It was warm still. Damp with sweat. More worn looking than it had been in Virginia. The brass buttons were rubbed dull over the eagle's breast. The gold leaf stitched on his shoulder straps to denote rank were somewhat frayed. Her heart ached suddenly and her hand trembled as she reached into the inside pocket. A picture lay there, along with the Federal bank notes, of a pretty woman, soft and gentle-looking despite a severe hairstyle and high-necked gown. Susan, she realized with a shock. Maybe Chase had married her before he'd come on this last campaign. Best for all of them, perhaps, if he had.

She shoved the brown-glazed tintype back inside the pocket of the Yankee uniform, and dropped the coat back to the chair with an abrupt motion. It was getting late. If she intended to reach the markets still open in the war-held city, it was time—past time maybe—for her to go.

Time moves slowly in the deep South. Confined to the small apartment, weeks felt like months. Leanna saw very little of Chase, less of anyone else. That suited her fine. She'd learned in Blytheswood she hated Yankees better from a distance. She took comfort in rumored words of continued CSA strikes at the Federal army. They made her feel a little better as she stood at the window and saw the fate of the houses abandoned by fleeing civilians. Wanton destruction for sheer sport, possessions stolen, gardens trampled by horses' hooves— finally, the hellish fires.

The twenty-first of September was another hot day, a gray one, airless and stickly with rain that simply would not start. The white curtains hung limply on the inexpensive rod at the window. The heat of rolls baking and stew, all day long bubbling, hung in the kitchen and would not dissipate. Chase had been home some- time during the night. There was a chair cushion left against the couch's wood-frame arm, and a slim, dark cheroot half smoked lying in the ash plate. But he had been gone when she'd awakened and not been back since. That was not unusual. He was often gone days at a time.

The Yankees were busy still in the captured city—methodically destroying anything of CSA military value, riding patrols against a surprise attack from Hood's army that lay in trenches south of the city at Lovejoy's Station, or riding northwest along the railroad lines to keep Wheeler's CSA cavalry from breaking the track there. What few civilians were left stayed in as much as possible, walked quickly and fearfully when forced abroad, and ignored the catcalls and jeers of the Yankee soldiers, who seemed, literally, to crowd every doorway and lounge on the steps of every shop, tavern, and billiard hall.

And the days stayed oppressively hot. Unlike Virginia, September seemed to bring little change to the deep South. Leanna found herself ever more homesick, remembering the cooling breezes of autumn nights in the Valley, the last brilliant blaze of wildflowers and bright berries—lavenders and reds, the first hint of leaves turning to flame on the hillsides. She was tired of Atlanta, Tired of the war. Tired of confusion and Yankees and anguish. She wanted her life back. And she wanted to be happy once more.

Boot steps sounded outside the door, startling her. She'd barely turned before it opened, and then she froze. Lieutenant Colonel Drake stood there and wordlessly stepped within.

Leanna felt her heart begin to pound. There was a long silence he seemed disinclined to break. "Major Courtland isn't here just now," she murmured finally.

"I know. I came to speak to you, not to him."

There was another silence. Leanna began to feel half sick, her knees weakening. She tried to conceal it by squaring her shoulders and raising her chin. "About what?"

"I think you know."

Dimly, she was aware of the sound of another horse coming to a stop down below, the murmur of men's voices, a sudden quick staccato of boots on the stairs. "I don't think I should be required to tell you anything, even if I knew what it was exactly you want from me. I'm not a soldier, Colonel. I'm a civilian. Not even of your government. I told you that already."

"If that's your attitude still, I think you'd better come with me, Mrs. Leighton."

His mouth had an ugly look that warned it would be useless to argue. Better, she told herself numbly, to go willingly than to be dragged, kicking and screaming, by the soldiers he'd stationed below. Her heart sank, and she wiped her hands on her apron to hide their sudden trembling. "All right. I'll get my—"

"What the hell are you doing here?"

The door, unlatched, came open with a slam and Leanna jumped, smothering a cry. Chase stood in the doorway, furious, covered by an inch of Georgia red dust that testified wordlessly he'd just returned from patrol. He didn't look at her but at Drake, who turned on one heel, frowning at the interruption.

"Mrs. Leighton is coming with me, Major. To headquarters. You have no say in the matter."

"The hell I don't. I understood this matter was temporarily closed."

"I reopened it."

"Bring a written order then. From your adjutant staff general."

"Whose side are you on, anyway?"

"I spent the morning dodging her husband's bullets, Colonel. That ought to answer your question."

Leanna moved instinctively toward where Chase stood, dripping dust from his dark blue uniform onto the parlor's worn, floral rug. Fear emanated from her like a physical thing. He glanced down once, then raised his hand to take her arm.

Drake smiled humorlessly, his eyes narrowing as he noted the gesture. "She must be awfully good to make you so determined to keep her, Major." He strode past them to the door, turning there on one heel. Leanna had felt Chase go suddenly rigid with rage. She half turned, raising frightened, confused eyes to his darkly sun-browned face.

"I'll be back, Major, when I get my order. And then the whole cavalry won't stop me from putting her where she belongs on the gallows beside her back-stabbing husband. Better enjoy her well up to then. The way you're going, you might be swinging beside her." The door closed with a bang and Leanna felt Chase flinch, frowning as he stared after the departing officer. Too frightened to stop herself, she pressed against his side with a faint cry, inhaling acrid gunpowder and choking dust as she buried her face for a moment against the dark blue of his uniform.

"Hush, it's all right now." He didn't sound like it was, entirely. Anger and another strange note lingered in his voice. The frown remained. "I'm sorry." He released her abruptly as he turned away. "I met with Colonel Drake some time ago. I thought the issue was pretty much resolved. I think now I'd better write to my father and have him wire someone in the War Department. That way, if something should happen to me—"

"Oh, no, don't. Don't say it." The thought startled her, shocked her, and Leanna turned her head quickly to hide her reaction. Outside, the day was darkening—whether in dusk or approaching storm, she couldn't tell. The limp white curtain blew in a sudden gust of air, chilling the single tear that had slipped down her face. Thunder rumbled distantly outside the open window, and down the street came the sound of shutters banging shut. Leanna hardly heard them.

"Doc Lacey saw what the war was turning into. He tried to warn me, last winter. But I didn't understand him then. I thought it could never happen. Now look, day by day it grows ever more awful." She shook her head slowly, staring at spiraling smoke from a distant house. From the street below, she could hear the sound of Drake's horse cantering away. For some reason, it made her think of Stewart. "Go home, Chase. All of you Yankees. You aren't wanted here. Go home while you still can."

There was a short silence. Chase turned away. "I can't go home. Not yet anyway. I joined this army for a reason. I intend to see it through."

"Oh, yes, I'd forgotten how noble you are." She'd come too close to loving him again only a moment before. Now as she glanced at his shadowed, dust-streaked face, she hated him as bitterly as she had on that day so long ago when he'd first appeared at Blytheswood. "Yes, you've got a job to do, yet, don't you? Whipping the South to her knees. It should take some time yet. After you get done with the armies, you can work on the women and children. Or is that Colonel Drake's private assignment?"

"Don't blame me for what someone else does. I've provided you every possible protection."

"Guilt, Major? Or do you feel it's payment? Compensation for a woman who shared your bed?"

He turned his head sharply. Another roll of thunder echoed outside, but other than that, there was only silence. Meeting his eyes, Leanna felt a sudden shiver of fear.

"Payment, Leanna?" He spoke slowly when he finally spoke at all. He turned slowly to face her. "No, not payment. The gold locket I gave you afterwards was more than adequate wages, I think, for services rendered."

The locket she wore still. She'd told Stewart it was from Whitney instead. It felt suddenly heavy around her neck, and cold.

"When did you become such a bitch, my love? Here in Georgia? Or did I just fail to notice it somehow back in Virginia?"

She paled, but refused to look away, watching his handsome face growing ever darker in the deepening dusk of the approaching storm. "I haven't changed a bit, Major," she answered finally. She forced a half smile, a bitter one, and raised one black, perfectly arched brow. "It just served my purposed to lead you on back at

Blytheswood. I was hoping I could get information from you that we could use, and you know the old saying, the one about catching more flies with honey than with vinegar?"

She paused a moment, watching his face, wondering why this assault should feel so good and hurt so badly all at the same time. His expression never changed. "I remember you told me once I made a lousy spy, Major. You were wrong. I had you thoroughly fooled, didn't I?" Why Leanna, she asked herself dazedly? Why are you doing this to him—to yourself? Because I can't allow myself to love you, Yankee. And I hate you because I want to love you again so desperately.

"I see." Chase nodded once. He glanced down at the gloves he'd tucked into his black leather belt and slowly, almost casually, reached to take them out, tossing them to a chair. His hat followed. And he began kicking off his dust-covered boots. "Tell me, then, Leanna, why did you try to help me after the ambush? Why not just leave me there to bleed to death?"

There was a silence. Her heart was thundering in her breast and her breath was strangely short. He glanced up suddenly and her mouth went dry. Don't Leanna, something warned her. Don't press him any further. "I felt I owed you a little something." She managed another smile as she answered, almost helpless now to stop herself. It was like being in the grip of some ungodly compulsion. She could only hurt and hurt and hurt, knowing he would hurt back and welcoming that too. "Stewart didn't mind. You rode into our trap so dumbly he wasn't much worried about having to match wits with you again some time."

Lightning flared suddenly in the darkness outside. It startled her. Despite herself, she jerked. Chase glanced once at the window, then back, and began to walk toward her.

"Interesting theory, Leanna. One I'd believe except for one thing."

His hand gripped her elbow suddenly and she began to tremble. Not from pain. He wasn't hurting her—yet.

351

"Did you tell your husband we'd slept together? Did he applaud that sacrifice for the 'cause'? Or is that still a well-kept secret?"

"He knew before it happened. We discussed the strategy of it . . ." Her voice had begun to fail her. Don't Leanna. Don't sink this low.

"You're a damn liar. About that at least."

It was dark, almost like night in the small room. Leanna stared into the eyes above hers and shivered. They were dark too, darker than she'd ever seen them. Like black ice. "No!"

"Yes."

She felt his grip on her arm tighten, felt him move a half step closer to her. She didn't try to speak. She shook her head in unconvinced defiance.

"Do you think you're the only woman I've ever slept with, Leanna? Do you think I can't tell the difference between a whore and a lady?"

She couldn't reply. Her eyes were locked to his, helplessly.

"Did I only imagine it, Leanna?" His voice was a murmur, soft, suddenly throaty. His hand on her arm moved in a brief caress. "I don't think so. I bet my life on that fact in Virginia and strange as it sounds, I'd bet my life on it still." He lowered his head as he spoke, brushing her lips.

Leanna shuddered at his touch, her eyes closed helplessly. No, she thought. No, Chase, don't.

"You want to belong to Stewart, don't you? To your damn cause. But a little bit of you belongs to me. Or it used to." One arm slipped around her waist, and pulled her angrily closer to him. "Damn you to hell, woman. You think I like loving you? You think I wouldn't like to find a way to cut your face out of my mind? To forget I ever knew your damn name?" His arms tightened suddenly. Leanna's eyes flew open and she cried a fearful denial. The wind was gusting now. It made a howling sound in the trees outside. "Prove me wrong, Leanna. I'd like nothing better."

She saw him begin to drop his head. She cried out

again and tried to turn away. His arms only tightened harder, crushing the breath from her lungs. Then his mouth took hers, angrily, urgently, demanding and hungry with an unholy passion. She fought against him in sudden fear, trying to turn her head away. His mouth followed hers, and in spite of all the reasons it shouldn't have, she found her heart racing in unrestrainable response.

Darkness shadowed the small room like night. Only the occasional, still distant flash of lightning brightened it at all. But the darkness in her soul was worse, the shameful burning that craved just this, and would not listen to reason. She moaned faintly, suddenly limp in his arms, knowing the darkness had triumphed after all. His mouth was warm, his arms welcome. His body pressed to hers, familiar, beloved, and longed for.

Chase shuddered once as he bent to lift her in his arms. A moment later, the bed was beneath her as he followed her down, trembling, and as helpless to stem this forbidden passion as she was. Susan touched his mind briefly. Guilt followed, but was swept away by rising hunger. "Leanna," he murmured once, like a denial. War was forgotten. Honor, shame, guilt, ecstasy blended in turbulent confusion. Her lips yielded suddenly beneath his. He tasted the salt of tears as he took them now. Even that failed to dampen the fires.

Lightning flashed again outside, closer. She saw the symmetry of his shadowed face, the rippling strength of his shoulders, the touch of gold in his thick, dark hair. An instant later, it was dark again. She felt his head move beneath her hands, seeking her breast, his mouth on the rising nipple.

Lightning flashed once more, illuminating the room for another split second. Enough to see his eyes were closed, and she barely heard the thunder that rumbled nearby, shaking the clapboard house. The storm burst suddenly upon Atlanta. Rain fell in slashing sheets, drumming on the steep roof, blowing in to dampen the flying curtains. A storm of a different sort lay in her arms and Leanna felt herself drowning in its growing fury. It was as if, restrained for so long, now finally released, even he could not control its raging. She felt it take her like a whirlwind, felt an urgency of desperation trembling down the length of his body heavy on hers, his hands quick and strong, his mouth raining terrible fire with every kiss. Lightning flashed again, but she didn't open her eyes to it this time. Forgive me, God, she thought dazedly, and only once. Forgive me . . . I cannot stop him. I cannot even stop myself.

He moved above her and she could only moan surrender and yield to his intrusion. Nothing so terrible had ever held her so sweetly. Every fiber of her being ached and throbbed with longing. His fingers cupping the fullness of her breast tightened almost painfully, his heart pounded a racing beat against hers. She felt the heat of him pressed against her, the brief pause as he felt her warmth, then the fullness as he slid within. She cried aloud, a last, faint protest. Chase only moaned and moved again, rocking within her, hard and deep. Muscles rippled beneath her hands as she held him, and she clung to him, helpless to repress rising ecstasy. Every motion was pleasure in itself, building to a greater one. He dropped his head against her breast and Leanna held it there now, incapable of anything else. His arms around her tightened nearly to pain, his body plunging deep into hers, greedily, in urgent rhythm. She felt his arms slip down to hold her hips, raising them higher, and she cried out shameless pleasure, almost limp in the fury of his loving, lost in the gathering power of bodies merging into one. Her hips moved suddenly, convulsively, her hands clutched the bare warmth of his back with mindless need. She felt him raise his hips above her and begin to drop once more inside, then the world went momentarily dark, and ecstasy flared within like a lightning bolt, shaking her, coursing through her quivering soul with incredible totality.

She thought she cried his name, she tried to. It echoed in her heart like a thousand voices. Lightning crashed outside, but no one heard it. When Leanna felt the world finally, once more outside of her, Chase was lying still in her arms, heavy and motionless—only his thundering heart and uneven breathing interrupted the sound of the pattering rain. For a moment, she too was still, almost fearful of moving. But she opened her eyes, and blinked once slowly, and felt tears slipping down to roll across her temples and drop in her hair. She stayed that way a moment, breathing the smell of him—of maleness, of soap from his hair, of leather, and, faintly, of horse and Georgia dust. All she'd tried to tell him, all she'd tried to tell herself, had been a lie, but she'd lied for the sake of honor. No, not for honor. She lied for sanity's sake, for a sanity that had been swept away in a single, blinding instant of terrible need. I hate you, Chase. I hate you for making me know I love you still.

"Lea?" He raised his head at last, opening his eyes slowly. With one hand, he touched her hair gently, then began to shift his weight away from her. "I think I—"

His murmured words were drowned out by a sudden loud knocking at the door. Leanna jerked, startled, reaching for the sheet to cover herself. A deep scarlet flush began to dye her ashen face. Whore, she thought, in clear and growing horror. Despicable, traitorous, shameless whore.

Chase jerked away from her with a frown, reaching to grab his uniform. "Yes?"

"Major? It's me, Grier. A courier just brought a new order from General Kilpatrick. We're on patrol again tonight."

"Oh, damn!"

Leanna watched as he dressed, hurriedly, in a blur of dark shadows and an occasional gleam of golden brass. It got worse by the minute, not better. Her heart ached sickly. Her soul shrieked relentless accusation. Damn you, Chase. Damn you, damn you, damn you!

"I'm sorry, Leanna," He only paused at the doorway, glancing back. In the darkness, Leanna thought she could see him frowning. "I'll be back as soon as I can."

She looked at him a moment. And suddenly wanted to cry. And wanted his arms around her. No! No more!

Never again! "Don't hurry." The coldness of the words shocked even her. She turned her head away to hide her face, and shrugged. "One Confederate is still worth ten Yankees, Major. In *every* way." She flashed a glance to see his mouth harden in shocked anger, the sudden rigid tension of his broad shoulders.

"Damn you, Leanna. Damn you for a foul-mouthed, lying bitch." He began to turn on one heel, his eyes flashing.

"Major? You hear me?"

Chase jerked to a stop, frowning a long minute at where Leanna lay, knees drawn up, sheet to her neck, her black hair long and tangled around her bare shoulders and arms. She looked away, biting her lip to keep from crying. Go away, Chase, Go away from me. Go back to your damn war. I hope you die tonight. I hope you get killed. Maybe then, one day, I'll know a moment of peace again.

"I'll be back." Without another word, he turned on one boot heel and strode away from her into the lesser darkness of the storm-drenched shadowed Atlanta streets.

Chapter Twenty-Three

September did not pass easily for Leanna. Each day was slow and long; the nights, dark and filled with the distant noises of a city shuddering in an enemy's grip, were worse. Rifle and musket fire, the muffled boom of artillery, the crackle of flame, the pounding hoofbeats of Yankee cavalry riding patrols on the streets outside, all combined together to undermine what little confidence Leanna could still cling to. The threat or the promise of Chase's last words to her echoed mercilessly in the small apartment, haunting her day and night. Too often, she awoke in the wide bed trembling—thinking, or dreaming, that she'd heard his bootsteps on the stairs outside the door. Part of her feared he would return. Part of her feared he wouldn't. About this, at least, even Doc Lacey hadn't warned her, though he'd warned of nearly everything else. Another casualty of the war that had somehow raged out of control. Another casualty, but one whose wounds didn't show on the outside. And even thinking that, Leanna couldn't say exactly what had died that bitter night. Couldn't be sure whether to grieve or to celebrate its loss. Nor was she entirely sure it was as dead as she tried to convince herself it must be. There were those few haunting moments in the deep darkness just before dawn, when she'd wake from sleep longing for something, unable to be sure it wasn't for a Yankee cavalry major named Courtland.

In Philadelphia, September was passing for Elinor Courtland Bennington with far less anguish. She was faintly irritated, yes, because everything had been going so smoothly before, and since her father's heart attack life had become more complex. Joshua had assigned much of his load at the bank to the young Rebel and, unfortunately, granted Jonathon Penley a great deal of power there to enable him to fulfill such responsibilities. It made things difficult. She knew her father so well and personally wielded a great deal more influence with him than she did with Jonathon. Whitney frankly disliked her, an attitude that Elinor found in the main merely amusing, but as far as manipulating Jonathon, it was another stumbling block. Even her father, since his attack, had been strangely obstinate with her. He spent a great deal of his time now amusing the Penley daughter, Miranda, and Elinor suspected that at least a small portion of his affection toward his daughter had been displaced to the little Virginian girl.

The solution to the problem was obvious. She had to either gain some kind of control over Jonathon Penley, or she had to give up the black market activities that were proving so fascinatingly profitable. Roland Hodges would deal in nothing but cash, and with the young Rebel prowling the Courtland bank like some wild panther, cash was rather hard to come by these days. She'd thought ahead, luckily, when her father had first been stricken. She'd taken advantage of his incapacity to draw nearly twenty thousand dollars from his personal accounts. Gowns, she'd told him. Joshua had surprised her by protesting the extravagance with some heat. Usually, he indulged her more than he'd seemed inclined to of late. She didn't think she dared try such a trick again so quickly.

Washington had provided what ought to have been the answer. After witnessing Jonathon's reaction to her disclosures regarding Chase and the Penley sister, it had been obvious where the man's weak spot was. Gain control over Leanna Leighton and all her problems would be solved. Chase, too, should he ever prove difficult, would squirm under the same rod. Men were usually sensitive to threats concerning women they'd shared a bed with, even women they no longer cared for. It was an oddity of the sex and one she'd used to her advantage before.

The only problem now was time. She'd known well whose hand to grease in Washington: she'd known well it was the War Department she needed to enlist in her cause. That was all done already, the wheels already turning, the plan already set in motion. But if Washington couldn't give her Leanna Leighton before Roland Hodges was expecting his next payment, then she would be in trouble. That was the only real flaw in an otherwise excellent solution. She could not afford to miss a month's shipment unless she absolutely had to—but more essential even than that, she could not let anyone draw that connection between her and Hodges's surplus guns. Her father would forgive her almost anything—but not that. Not having lost Josh Jr. to the Rebels. It was a rather fine line she needed to tread in the next few weeks, but then, she assured herself, she was a rather talented lady, also. With a little luck, everything would work out just fine. She might hear from the War Department almost anytime now.

The last day of the month in Philadelphia was a cool one. Days with sunshine were still warm, not infrequently hot, but nights were crisp and mornings sparkled with a chilling dew. Consequently, a small, new fire crackled near where Joshua sat in an overstuffed chair in the parlor, waiting for supper and opening the letter from Atlanta that the housekeeper had just handed him. He forced himself to breathe slowly as his fingers fumbled at the envelope. The first attack, now months ago, had finally faded from his body, but not his mind. It had frightened him badly. Not because he'd almost died. He'd long ago resigned himself to that. But the timing of it had shaken him to his bones.

Jonathon was practically running the bank now—doing an excellent, almost an astonishing job, but he must eventually return to Virginia. And then there was Elinor, too. Lovely, troubling, the ever unknowable Elinor. And the coalition—Hodges and the others. For some time now, Joshua had known that most of them were not overly concerned about reunifying the divided nation come the war's end, but only last week had their actual ambitions been revealed. The Southern white aristocracy was to be disenfranchised entirely, for supporting the CSA government and the war. In their place would rise a new elite, one whose huge land holdings and personal fortunes would rival any of the ancient kings of feudal Europe. Power to the point that such 'barons' could thumb their noses at any challenge to their petty tyrannies, even one from the Federal government. It was a frightening future to consider. And the coalition members, the would-be new elite, were already drooling over whispers of how the South, once beaten, could best be carved up into such princedoms. Starting to firm up hard lines of allies and enemies in the Congress. Mentioning names of 'friends' who were high seated enough in government to make Joshua's blood run cold. Even if he lived, he was beginning to doubt that, alone, he could stand against them.

Abraham Lincoln could, so great a hold did he have on the people of the nation. But the other members of the group seemed unconcerned by the obstacle he could present to their ambitions. That nonchalance was not reassuring to Joshua—it hinted of even darker deeds yet to come. Plus there continued dark, sly hints of the President's failing health. Once the war ended, thank God, Chase would return, and he could pass his cares to his son's strong shoulders, and somehow, together, they would manage. But, though the reports grew more encouraging daily, the war still dragged on. And while it did, his old nemesis, time, remained an enemy. At least now, thanks largely to a handful of Union generals—Grant, Sherman, and Sheridan, who were forcing the long war toward a final end—and to a stiff-necked young Rebel named Jonathon Penley, he was beginning to cherish hope of beating that enemy and winning through.

Joshua unfolded the letter written in his son's fine, firm hand and smiled as he began to read it. Atlanta had fallen, he'd known that already from the newspapers. Chase was well; he never elaborated beyond that point. And . . . Joshua stared down at the letter with an exclamation of surprise, read a few words further, then pushed himself to his feet with a frown replacing his smile. Jonathon would be home at the carriage house, and it was still light enough outside for him to walk the distance over.

Whitney called to Jonathon from the kitchen, hearing the knock on the door. He gave Mandy a last grin, and bent over to Bonnie who lay giggling, kicking, and punching the air above her with an infant's clenched fist. She had defied the odds by surviving at all. Now, she was growing well. Trying to crawl already. And her bright blue eyes followed intently as he set Miranda off his lap and handed her the paper he'd been in the midst of reading aloud. It was an excerpt from an English book due out next year—a silly story about a girl named Alice who fell down a hole chasing a rabbit, and ended up in an underground kind of fairyland with Cheshire cats and Mad Hatters.

He was surprised to find Joshua on the other side of the door when he opened it. His first reaction was concern. But the older man gestured quickly, holding a letter aloft and smiling a somewhat strained reassurance. Joshua had not forgotten the first confrontation regarding Chase and Leanna Leighton. He could only hope such a scene would not be repeated.

"From Chase." Joshua moved a bit slower than he once had. It took him a minute to climb up the stairs and into the narrow foyer. "He's found your sister, Leanna, if you can imagine the improbability of that. She's in Atlanta."

"Atlanta? Georgia, you mean?" Jonathon stared for a moment, startled. Why in the world would she be down there? "Is she all right?"

"Chase says so, yes. For the moment, at least."

Jonathon had already begun to turn his head, meaning to call the news to Whitney. Something in Joshua's expression caught his eye, and the equivocality of the man's last few words sank in. He turned back, frowning as Joshua offered him the letter. He had the sudden feeling it was not entirely good news.

October brought changes to Atlanta. The autumn there was dry, and finally cooling after the long summer's hot sun. The remnants of Hood's defeated Rebel army made futile strikes at Big Shanty and then Allatoona Pass. Guerrilla groups like Stewart's prowled the countryside like hungry wolves, sniping from trees, shooting the unwary straggler, terrorizing the farm folk almost as badly as the hated Yankees. Widows, mothers with small children, the aged, the crippled, locked their doors at night and prayed to remain unnoticed by either side. In Virginia, Sheridan pursued Early's fleeing Rebels to Harrisonburg and then began, slowly, to withdraw northward, devastating the Valley as he moved. The rear-guard line of cavalry, following the dust clouds of marching infantry up country roads, rode with torches in their hands, and unknown to anyone else just yet, they left Blytheswood burning behind them. When it was over, the once beautiful Valley resembled a nightmare of devastation. The upper Shenandoah would feed no Rebel army this year.

In Washington, Lincoln, in the White House, was finally optimistic enough to smile when asked about the upcoming election between him and Democratic candidate, ex-General 'Little Mac' McClellan. His son, Tad, sat at the President's feet during Cabinet meetings and played with a most marvelous new mechanical pencil. And Mary Todd Lincoln's occasional fits of jealous hysteria were being carefully kept quiet, as were her debts for extravagant wardrobes. Vice President Johnson was occasionally getting drunk and embarrassing other government officials, and he remained where he was, living in rooms in the Kirkwood Hotel as there were no official quarters provided for vice presidents. The new dome on the Capitol gleamed in the bright October sun, rivaling the Washington Monument now for tourists. Cows grazed in the Presidents' Park by the still dilapidated White House—Congress would vote no funds to improve it—and most of the streets were soft and muddy with the autumn rains.

Philadelphia was a far more urban city. Jonathon didn't even glance at the sound of a carriage rattling by on a cobblestoned street. When Whitney came down from putting the girls to bed, she paused before a fire lit against the worsening chill of October night air. She glanced over her shoulder toward her husband, thoughtfully, then was careful to stare into the fire flames as she spoke. "You might write to Leanna while you've a minute free, Jon."

"And what should I tell her?" The words came slowly, with a bitter sound. "That Cool Spring and Blytheswood are burned nearly to the ground? That Jewel's dead—trying singlehandedly to keep the fire from spreading from the barns to the main house?"

Whitney closed her eyes in silent pain and shook her head. Jonathon had accompanied Joshua Courtland to Washington earlier this week in an effort to begin proceedings that should secure amnesty for Leanna. While there the War Department had offered the grim news, relayed from troops still in the Valley.

"No, not about that, Jon, not about Blytheswood." She shook her head once more in sorrow. "But write something. I'm afraid if you don't, she'll regard your silence as disapproval of the way she's accepted Major Courtland's protection." She phrased it carefully and tried not to sound uneasy. But Jonathon was silent behind her and her fingers began to play with the warm gold of her wedding ring as he didn't reply.

"And should I approve, Whit?" Jonathon spoke at last, softly. "Should I approve her accepting Chase Courtland's 'protection' as you call it."

"Jon, you cannot assume—"

"I'm not a fool, damn it! I'm not as naive as some schoolboy still in knickers who thinks it's all moonbeams and chivalry going on down there in Georgia, a handshake for a good-night. You were the one a few months ago who took such pains to impress me with how deeply they cared for each other! Now you want me to think, despite such a golden opportunity, they're above reproach?"

"Jonathon, please. People change. Perhaps Leanna or Major Courtland no longer even feel the same—"

"I saw a portion of the good Major's last letter to his father today. It was a codicil to his will, changing the major beneficiary. Now half his estate is to be held in trust for Leanna's firstborn child if she bears one within a year! Does that sound like they've changed?"

"Jon!" Whitney had turned from the fire to stare at him, ashen pale. "You read something addressed to Joshua?"

His gaze faltered under the accusation of her stare and he looked restlessly away, rising to his feet. "Not on purpose, I assure you. It was among some papers Joshua asked me to give his attorney. I had Mandy with me in the carriage and she held the envelope upside down. I saw it as I was collecting the papers to put them back. Leanna's name caught my eye."

"You still had no right to read that."

Jonathon shrugged angrily, his face hard. "She's a married woman, Whitney. And Stewart Leighton has been a fair husband to her. I can't sanction the way she's cuckolding him."

"Stewart never cared for Leanna half as deeply as Chase Courtland does."

"It's still wrong!"

Whitney's face grew distant and cold against the brightness of the fire flames. "Maybe one of the reasons you're so determined to defend Stewart Leighton is that you pressed the match so eagerly back in Richmond, in '61." She looked at him sidelong a minute, then turned back to stare into the fire. She had a habit of playing with her wedding ring when she was upset. She was doing that now. And Jonathon thought, before she'd turned, he'd caught the glimmer of unshed tears in her eyes. He watched her a moment, silently, then walked to stand behind her, resting his hands on her shoulders, and softening his voice.

"Whitney, love," he murmured placatingly, regretting his outburst.

"Marriage isn't a business proposition. Not in a

woman's eyes, anyway. It takes someone who's more than 'fair' to keep a woman's heart."

"Leanna was in love with Stewart."

"She was eighteen years old and she'd known him a week."

"She wanted to marry him."

"And that suited you well, Jon. You were anxious then to be off to war. You didn't want the responsibility of an unmarried but beautiful little sister."

"She wasn't my responsibility, anyway. Our father was still alive then."

"And dying of consumption already. You knew that, too."

There was a long silence. Jonathon sighed softly, frowning. Was it partly true? Had he been as self-serving as Whitney accused him of being?

"I'm only afraid someday you're going to change your mind, Jon." Whitney's whisper had a catch in it and she cleared her throat softly. "You're going to wish you'd behaved differently about this. You'll regret it. And I'm afraid then it will be too late." She turned under his hands and started toward the door, saying nothing more. Jonathon was equally silent watching her go, and only the hissing crack of the fire and the soft rustle of Whitney's crinoline petticoat combined to break the stillness. Finally, he sighed and turned restlessly to follow his wife. But outside the parlor's single window, a movement caught his eye. He turned, walking toward it and frowning into the night shadows outside.

A solitary figure walked alone outside in the darkness, following the flagstoned garden path toward the street. He watched, frowning. Then a cold gust of night wind blew the hood of her long cape back, close enough to the mellow golden glow of the street lamp for him to be certain of her identity. Elinor, Lady Bennington. He frowned. A cab rattled down the street and she raised one hand to hail it. The driver gestured and kept on going. Full already, or hired for the night. Jonathon saw Elinor's single furtive glance back toward the darkness of the Courtland home. Then another cab turned at the

365

corner and she pulled the hood of her cape closer and started toward it. This one stopped.

Jonathon watched in growing puzzlement. A barnful of assorted conveyances lay not six hundred feet away—carriages, coaches, gigs, a buggy. Why would any Courtland hire a dirty street cab instead? The driver dismounted to hold the door. It seemed to him Elinor climbed inside in an unusual hurry.

Ten o'clock. He glanced at the mantle clock, making a sudden decision. He grabbed his hat and coat, then paused to scrawl a brief note to Whitney. She'd left him angry. He ought to go talk to her first—tell her what he'd seen and what he'd decided to do. But there was no time. Not unless he wanted to lose all trace of the mysterious, midnight lady already closing the cab door.

He hurried out, keeping in the shadows until he saw her cab begin to pull away. Luckily, another was already turning the corner, its oil lantern lit for business, and swinging like a beacon from the brake pole, golden in the darkness of the cloudy night. Jonathon jumped in, closing the door and calling out the window with instructions to follow the first cab. The driver agreed without question, probably assuming some domestic travail or midnight rendezvous was afoot. Jonathon lit a cigar and noted the street signs passing as he rode a discrete half block behind her on the way to Roland Hodges's Delancey Street mansion. But the midnight outing answered no questions, only further confused the mysteries of the beautiful Courtland daughter. He returned home an hour later, chilled and more puzzled than when he had set out. The only good thing to come out of it was that he spent the rest of the evening with his curiosity piqued. And what Leanna was or wasn't doing down in distant Atlanta seemed less important by dawn.

Actually, Leanna wasn't doing anything much down in Atlanta. The days moved slowly still, with nothing to distinguish one from another. Chase had not yet returned since that stormy, bitter night now weeks ago.

366

Hood and Forrest had joined forces northwest of the city, posing a genuine threat to the Yankee supply lines and, consequently, his patrol had turned into an extended tour of duty scouting the Rebel cavalry. She thanked God he had been ordered out of Atlanta and hoped he would not come back. Her life was infinitely less complicated without him. The danger she'd read flashing in his storm dark eyes that night had frightened her—but not nearly as much as the joy she'd felt so briefly in his arms. One only threatened her life—the other her sanity and her soul.

It was the thirteenth of October now. She stood at the window, shivering in the chill breeze of the overcast day, and watched Atlanta belch forth Yankee soldiers like an overstuffed pig. Over two thirds of the army was ordered to Resaca in pursuit of Hood's infantry and Forrest's cavalry. Only a single corps was left to hold the city, and from her second-story window, Atlanta gave the feel of a ghost town.

Only a few days before, it had been filled to overflowing with one hundred thousand soldiers in a city of only eight thousand five hundred normal population. Now, with two-thirds of the civilians evacuated and only one corps of soldiers left behind, it was eerie, over-quiet, cloud-darkened, and lifeless. In the distance, Yankee troops crawled over the abandoned Confederate defense works from back to front, scaling logs piled with dirt and sandbags, ducking through the crisscrossed, sharp stakes of the *cheveaux-de-frise*, jumping over the holes where cannon had lain, separating like flowing waters on either side of high-built ramparts, finally disappearing into the scrubby tall pines northeast of the city. It was their earlier march in reverse. Atlanta, Ezra Church, Peachtree Creek, the Chattahoochee River, Marietta, Kenesaw Mountain—a brief clash there once again; Pine and Stone Mountains, Acworth, Allatoona Pass—a sharp skirmish; the Etowah River, Kingston, Calhoun, the Oostanoula, finally back to Resaca.

She knew Chase was still alive and unhurt only because of a scrawled note she'd received earlier today.

'Stay inside—allow no strangers in!' It was signed only by an initial. It was sheer foolishness to do anything else, she reflected bitterly. Sherman's declared intention—"to destroy Georgia's will and capacity for war"—had filtered down into the enlisted ranks in ugly form, a virtual mandate for looting, rape, burning, stealing, assault, and general mayhem. The days of the gentleman's war, army versus army, conducted according to rules almost as rigid as social protocol, had faded into memory. Like everything else from that finer, distant prewar way of life, she thought. Like believing in justice, in honor, in love, or in a future. How right Doc Lacey had been to warn her last winter. How foolish she'd been to disregard that warning.

Outside the day darkened, threatening rain. Leanna shut the window, but continued to stand in place. The hardware shop at the corner closed shutters over its glass windows. Faint music drifted from a saloon blocks away. An empty candy bag from Hagan & Co. Confectioners hopped and skipped in the wind down the wide deserted street. Leanna watched it, her violet eyes dark. Would the city ever recover from the shock of the Yankee seizure? Or would it look like this for decades until it finally, slowly, fell into ruin, cobwebbed and abandoned?

Suddenly, she leaned forward with a sharp motion, staring down at the street below. Where were Drake's soldiers who usually stood guarding the rooming house entrance? Had Chase somehow finally managed to convince the adjutant officer of her innocence? Or had Drake himself abandoned the vigil? Had he, perhaps, decided that there was nowhere for the girl to go, anyway, so he could afford to assume she would simply stay put? If so, it had been a poor decision. There *was* somewhere to go—for Leanna there was always somewhere to go. A place distant in miles, perhaps, but closely held in her heart—Blytheswood. Just thinking the name released a surge of longing. Blytheswood—her beautiful mountains, her rolling hillsides, the elegant, airy rooms of the white-columned main house, the ivy-covered ancient stone of the original cottage. The cottage where the fire had broken out and almost claimed little Miranda's life, the cottage where she'd first lay with her once-beloved Yankee.

That memory struck a painful chord in her heart, and Leanna turned slowly away from the window, fighting a familiar sense of anguish. Whether she loved Chase Courtland or not, though—what difference would either answer make? All they could offer each other was guilt and pain. The other night had proven that. All they'd *ever* had to offer each other was anguish. Better for him, too, then if she left his world. Better for him to forget her entirely, to go home to his soft-looking, pretty Susan, and build a future with her there in Philadelphia. And Stewart? If she were truly free now to go, shouldn't she try to rejoin her husband outside the city instead of to start a long, desperate journey back to Virginia?

No, she answered herself. No, she couldn't join Stewart. Maybe she didn't love Chase Courtland anymore, but she once had—that she would admit. And for the sake of that love, she would not condone the kind of viciousness and brutality that characterized her husband's brand of warfare.

It was bittersweet in a way, like leaving behind the pampered security of childhood, but it was time for her to do the very thing that had once seemed so inconceivable to her—to stand alone, to take the responsibility for her own life without requiring a man's approval or aid. For all that the war had taken away, it had given her something, too, then. Her freedom. And it was time to take it. Time to reclaim what she still could of her life from the devastation of war, time to be out of tragic Atlanta, to go home to her beloved Blytheswood. Alone, perhaps, at least for now. But at Blytheswood she could never be lonely. The spirit of the place was sweet and soft as any lover.

She lingered a last moment near the window, then turned for the bedroom to pack her few things. And a deep, strange sense of peace began to spread within her. For this Rebel, at least, the war was over; she'd found the limit to the price she was willing to pay. All the war's questions had finally found their answers.

It was lovely in Washington, D.C. Clear, cool, and crisp. The autumn colors were etched against deep blue, apples were turning red, and lawns were still green. The dust and bugs of summer were gone, and the mud holes of winter streets not yet here. With the war going so well at last, the Federal capitol was a fine place to be. Nothing could ever rival the sheer splendid beauty of autumn in Virginia, in the Shenandoah especially, but on a day like this, Washington came close. The broad silver Potomac gleamed, the marble fronted banks and government buildings were a brilliant white. The city exuded a new air of confidence, of quiet anticipation and more raucous relief. Carriages moved smartly, people walked briskly. It was an invigorating place and the future lay stamped all over it.

Inside the Federal military hospital at Massachusetts and "I" Streets, Doc Lacey was taking a rare moment of rest in the staff sitting room, reading a story on the paper's third page. The Homestead Act, passed in 1862, had gone virtually unnoticed here in the East—the war was a media obsession. But its promise of one hundred sixty free acres of public land tempted some uninvolved in the crisis and, even while the armies marched and bloodied eastern cities, western towns were growing bigger, stronger, and better.

Doc Lacey was reading about one called Denver, nestled in the foothills of mountains described in the newspaper as "splendid beyond description." Writers, he'd found, were rarely at a loss for superlatives, and that simple statement intrigued him as more grandiose terms wouldn't have. His dark eyes were thoughtful as he laid the paper aside to look out the window, and he nodded once finally. Then he picked up the pen to write 'Denver' down on the transfer application.

Behind him, Susan stepped quietly into the room, taking a moment to simply look at him before she spoke. Not nearly as handsome as Chase, she told herself.

370

Not as tall, not as dashing, not as charming. Inexplicable then, that she should love him as she did. "Am I interrupting you, Doctor?"

He glanced up, startled, and managed a smile no less artificial than hers. He held up the paper briefly. "No, I'm done."

"What is that?" She didn't walk closer. She went to the window instead, keeping several yards of space between them. Some days were easier than others. When weakness threatened, she stayed a greater distance away from him.

He was quiet a moment, hesitating. Then he shrugged. "Transfer papers," he replied finally, with a faint smile. "For Denver." He saw the sharp, sudden tension in her slender body, but she didn't turn.

"Isn't that a little premature?" She studied the empty street outside with intense concentration, willing herself not to react. "The war isn't over yet. If President Lincoln should lose the election—"

"I don't think he will. I don't think it matters much if he does. The war's over, essentially. The hospital's almost empty."

"Compared to this spring at least, yes." She sighed very softly. "Compared to the thousands of wounded from the Wilderness and Cold Harbor campaigns. City Point Hospital handles most of the load now by itself." She paused a moment, trying not to let herself ask the question. But she did. "Why Denver, Roger? And why now? Why not wait until spring, at least, in case the war turns around again or—"

"You know why." Silence followed the simple, quiet statement and he watched Susan's nervous little gesture of moving the ruffled edge of the eyelet curtain aside. He sighed and stood up slowly, watching her back. "Why ask when you know the answer, my love?"

She shook her head sharply and shrugged again. "Please, Roger, don't!"

A long silence followed this time, no more comfortable for him than for her. Why do this? he asked himself. It's senseless. It never changes. Aren't we in more control of our fate than this? Should we be swept along so helplessly, unable to make any real change in anything? Yes, he answered himself. You made your choice when you decided not to tell her of Leanna Leighton. "Have you heard anymore from Chase, yet? When he'll be coming home again next?"

Susan studied the street. "I understand the fighting's still going on in Georgia. The campaign isn't finished yet."

"Oh."

"You haven't answered my question, anyway." She made an attempt to sound lighthearted and finally dared turn from the window to face him. There was a cobweb on the gas-fed chandelier. She noted it absently and gestured for him to knock it down. The bugs were bad this time of year in the hospital. The colder weather was driving them indoors. Rats too, and mice, were worse. Once spring came, it would be better again. "Why Denver?"

"Why not?" He managed a smile, stepping on the sofa to reach the web.

"I think I can guess." She forced a soft laugh. "It was that old Doctor Anders from the territories—that story about how the Cheyenne Indians taught him to use tree moss poultices to reduce infection."

"I tried it and it worked. Maybe the medicine men out there know what they're doing."

"You'd go to the Eskimos for whale blubber remedies if you thought they had any."

"Probably would," he agreed with a more genuine smile. But the smile was short-lived. "Maybe the Confederates should be the ones sending doctors out to the Indians. They're the ones out of medicines at this point."

Her smile faded, too. "Yes, I know."

"Quinine's a hundred dollars an ounce in Louisiana, when it's available at all. They substitute berries of dogwood or some damn useless thing. The army in Virginia's out of morphine and chloroform both, I understand. Field surgery is done with whiskey as both anesthetic and antiseptic."

She nodded, silent. There seemed little she could say. She thought of Chase—if he were wounded, captured by the Rebels and subject to such ghastly privations. She guessed Roger read her thoughts, because the silence was suddenly strained. Strained and sad. It seemed oddly final and, in that, there was a kind of peace at last.

"Well, I have work in the wards to do."

Doc Lacey did not manage a smile as he left, and she only nodded, watching him go. While he was roaming the savage Indian territories in the years to come, she would be in a sedate, formal Philadelphia mansion, overseeing servants and bearing children with the last name of Courtland. Chase would cease to be a portrait framed in gilt filigree, a distant memory in a Federal uniform, and would be alive once more, part of her life—her husband. Every morning when she woke, it would be to him. He would be a banker then. He would be good to her and she to him. The war, and Roger, would fade into memory. It was the destiny she'd been raised from birth to fulfill. A promise made to her brother, now dead. And a good life, she thought with a faint smile. A fair enough future to have. She had, after all, survived the destruction of war.

"Lady Bennington." Jonathon glanced up from Joshua Courtland's rosewood-topped desk at the click of the door opening. He rose to his feet in habitual courtesy and nodded once. She smiled in return, somewhat wryly, and her eyes flickered around him to assess changes in the familiar room.

"Well, you've made yourself right at home, Major, haven't you?"

"At your father's suggestion."

"Of course." Elinor finished her examination of the room before looking back at Jonathon. As she did, she raised one brow almost lazily. "You've made a lot of changes, haven't you?"

Jonathon gave himself a moment of silence, a moment to smile before he replied. Lord, he thought. How good

373

it felt. "You mean the new rules regarding who goes into the bank vault?"

"Do I?"

"Do you not?"

"Thinking of changing the name to 'Penley' Bank and Trust, Major?" She smiled but not sweetly. "Pity, but that won't happen. You might remember I hold stock in the bank personally. So does my brother, Chase." Her smile was suddenly wicked, her green eyes flashed dark amusement. "You do remember Chase, don't you? He's the one presently 'protecting' your sister down in Georgia."

Jonathon flushed and then paled, anger replacing complacency. "What do you want, Lady Bennington?"

"I want you to remember your place, Major." Elinor's smile had faded also. Her eyes held his as she spoke, very softly. "I could have been a friend. You seem determined to make me an enemy, instead. I'm giving you a last warning before we open our own private war. A last chance to consider what's at stake.

"Your wife's pregnant again—she needs our hospital. Your homes are leveled in Virginia. Your money's trapped in CSA coffers and as good as lost to your forever. Your sister is in a very tenuous position, I understand, in Georgia, under suspicion of partisan activities. You need my brother's protection for her, Major, and my father's intercession on her behalf with the War Department." She paused as if to let him consider it a moment, then continued in a milder voice. "My father's an old man already. My brother's a thousand miles away. Let me put it this way. By the end of the war, if you decided to behave reasonably, I could assure you would return to Virginia a wealthy man again."

He considered it a moment, not really tempted. He'd said it once to her father, once not very long ago to Whitney. Honor was still important to him. He had already resigned himself to the notion it might be all that was left for him after the war. And as for the other things. . . .

"Sorry, Lady Bennington, but 'no deal,' as I've learned

374

to say here in Yankee country. You don't have control over most of those things, anyway. You're only running a bluff—and a last ditch one at that. The bank vaults stay closed." He hesitated, and then decided to gamble. "Go to your friend Roland Hodges if you need a little credit. He's wealthy enough to afford you."

She had begun to turn. She froze instantly, glancing back at Jonathan. For a moment, no one moved. He saw something close to murder flash in her eyes and kept silent to conceal his own shock at the violence of her reaction. Roland Hodges. Too old to be a lover. But, obviously, he was *something*. And something she'd thought a secret up to now.

"I see, Major." Elinor nodded once, a gracious, mystifying gesture of sudden surrender. The 'fine line,' she was thinking—how dangerously close she must have come to crossing it.

Jonathon watched her, astounded.

"Do you play chess, Major?"

"On occasion."

"You are familiar, then, with the term 'check.' "

"Check, and checkmate."

"Don't flatter yourself unduly."

"I'm not. You've been outflanked, to use a term from another military game. Your position is no longer tenable, Lady. You have no choice but to retreat."

"Those who live and run away, live to fight another day." She tried, but it sounded flat, even to her ears and she shrugged dismissal. Well, she'd known it was the plan's one real flaw—for someone to connect the missing bank money and Roland Hodges's guns. She hadn't counted on its being a fatal flaw, obviously, but pressing it any further at this point was sheer insanity. It would only risk everything they'd already gained, plus all the future income of inheritance from her ailing father.

"Forgive my lack of concern." Jonathon was puzzled still, but not to the point of missing the slow relief that grew as he watched her. There were pieces of the puzzle still missing, yes, but insignificant ones. The instinct of victory was unmistakeable. I beat you, you unconscienceless whore. I achieved something worthwhile here, and paid my debt. So it wasn't Yankee charity after all. That thought lifted a weight off his soul that Jonathon hadn't even realized was still there. The Penleys could hold their heads high again, free from shame.

Elinor only nodded once more, and stood silent a moment, glancing a last time around the room. Then she walked back through the double walnut doors, stately and unhurried, beautiful even in defeat.

In a rare moment of unrestrained emotion, Jonathon smiled broadly up at the gilt-framed portrait of Sumner Courtland, the bank founder, Joshua's grandfather. The picture had faintly irritated him up to now, giving the impression that suspicious Yankee eyes were always watching, waiting for that one slip, that one fatal mistake. Now, he felt an odd kinship with it instead.

"Yes, I accept your thanks, you leather-necked, grim old Yankee." He laughed softly, nodding once, and walked to the imported Irish cut-glass brandy decanter to pour himself a generous drink. As he raised the glass, he had the strangest feeling Sumner Courtland was seconding the toast.

It occurred to him suddenly that Whitney was right—that he owed his sister, Leanna, a letter. Not his approval, maybe, of anything she might or might not have done, but a reaffirmation, at least, of family ties. The war might have taken everything else, but the families—Penleys and Courtlands both— had survived. At least this way, they could all begin the rebuilding. Maybe they'd even gained something these past few years. Maybe. In comparison to how it could have ended, Jonathon was grateful even for that.

The Windhaven Saga
by Marie de Jourlet

Patricia Matthews

America's leading lady of historical romance.
Over 20,000,000 copies in print!
